MONSTROUS

MONSTROUS

A **SAVAGE** NOVEL

THOMAS E. SNIEGOSKI

SIMON PULSE
New York London Toronto Sydney New Delhi

SIMON PULSE

An imprint of Simon & Schuster Children's Publishing Division
1230 Avenue of the Americas, New York, New York 10020
First Simon Pulse hardcover edition May 2017
Text copyright © 2017 by Thomas E. Sniegoski
Jacket photo-illustration by David Field, based on a concept by Sammy Yuen Jr.
Jacket photograph of girl copyright © 2017 by Steve Gardner/PixelWorks Studios
All other photographs copyright © 2017 by Thinkstock
All rights reserved, including the right of reproduction in whole or in part in any form.
SIMON PULSE and colophon are registered trademarks of Simon & Schuster, Inc.
For information about special discounts for bulk purchases, please contact
Simon & Schuster Special Sales at 1-866-506-1949 or business@simonandschuster.com.
The Simon & Schuster Speakers Bureau can bring authors to your live event.
For more information or to book an event contact the Simon & Schuster
Speakers Bureau at 1-866-248-3049 or visit our website at www.simonspeakers.com.
Jacket designed by Karina Granda and Jessica Handelman
Interior designed by Karina Granda
The text of this book was set in Adobe Garamond Pro.
Manufactured in the United States of America
2 4 6 8 10 9 7 5 3 1
This book has been cataloged with the Library of Congress.
ISBN 978-1-4814-7718-5 (hc)
ISBN 978-1-4814-7720-8 (eBook)

This one is for Tyler McWeeney.

His enthusiasm for Savage was so infectious it made me

push myself all the more for the sequel.

Hopefully I don't disappoint.

MONSTROUS

PROLOGUE

The Calm Before the Storm

Delilah Simpson dreaded the sound, that low buzzing of her phone that grew in intensity, dragging her up by the ear out of the deepest of sleeps and back into reality.

It was time to get up for work.

Unngh, she thought as she reached out to the nightstand for the phone. Part of her was tempted to turn it off and roll over for just a little bit longer, but she knew that would only lead to trouble.

The old Delilah would have done just that and been late for work, or not shown up at all, but the old Delilah wasn't here anymore.

She hated to think of her old self as dead. That just seemed so morbid, although it wasn't too far from the truth. The old Delilah had had to go away permanently, as her life took a new path . . .

With her son.

Delilah sat up and squinted at her phone, yawning loudly. The temperature outside was still warm at sixty-five degrees, but it looked like there was a chance for showers.

Good to know. She stood up and stretched, then shuffled in early morning darkness to the playpen where Isaiah lay fast asleep. She leaned in to watch him, curled up on his side in his BB-8 pajamas. Delilah swore the four-year-old could have slept through a hurricane.

She reached down and gently rubbed her son's back, the love that she felt for him almost overwhelming, bringing her close to tears. He was why she'd had to change, why she had gone back to nursing school, and why she was up at the crack of dawn to work a co-op job at the Elysium Hospital in Boston.

Isaiah stretched at his mother's touch, and she again felt a wave of guilt over the fact that her son didn't have a proper bed and was forced to sleep in a hand-me-down playpen given to her by one of her mother's friends.

"Momma's gonna buy you a big-boy bed," she whispered softly, watching the cutest of smiles spread across his gorgeous face as he continued to sleep on. But first she needed to get herself ready and get to work so that she could get paid.

After her shower she quickly got dressed, deciding on the pink scrubs that day. It felt like a pink day for some reason. As she came out of her bedroom, the smell of strong coffee hit her like a physical blow, and she found that her mother was up and about.

"What are you doing up?" Delilah asked the woman, who looked much larger than she was in the heavy blue bathrobe.

"Tom and Jerry needed to eat," she said, referring to the two black cats that prowled around her slippered feet. She was preparing two bowls of cat food for the hungry felines.

"Those two are a pain," Delilah said, pouring herself a quick mug of the strong, black coffee. "That's why you've got to remember to close your door."

"I like the company," her mother said, putting the bowls down on a plastic place mat beside the refrigerator.

"Izzy still asleep?" her mother then asked.

"Out like a light," Delilah answered between sips of the scalding brew.

"Good. When he's up bright and early, I never get anything done around here."

Delilah took a few larger sips, not wanting to be late. She still needed to catch the Orange Line to Haymarket, and then a short walk to Elysium was required, and she wanted to be sure to leave herself enough time.

"When you coming home tonight?" her mother asked.

"Usual," Delilah said, throwing her purse over her shoulder and leaning in to give her mom a kiss on the cheek. "But if they ask me to stay late . . ."

"That's all right," her mother said, waving her away. "What's a few more hours with the tiny terror."

They both laughed at that, knowing that Izzy could be quite the wild man sometime.

"You be careful," her mother said as Delilah went to the door, undoing the locks to leave. "You might want to take your umbrella," she added. "Think it might be fixin' to rain."

Going back in to find the umbrella could throw off her timing, and she decided against it.

"I'm good," she told the woman. "I'll see you tonight."

Delilah closed the door and remembered something that she hadn't done. "Shoot," she said, standing there, hand still holding the doorknob.

Every morning when she left, she told her mother to kiss Isaiah for her and to tell him that his mommy loves him.

She actually considered searching for her keys and going back in but decided against it. She didn't want to risk being late.

And besides, she'd be home before she knew it and could tell him herself.

Outside the apartment on Columbus Avenue she could suddenly feel the change in the air. Yeah, it did feel like rain, she thought as she hurried across the street to make the trolley.

But it also felt like something more.

What that was she could not say.

CHAPTER ONE

Benediction Island, Massachusetts

It was as if all sound had been sucked from the tent as the realization of what Borrows had just relayed from his tablet began to sink in.

Another storm was forming. Not over tiny, peaceful Benediction Island, like yesterday, but over the city of Boston.

Sidney sat numbly on the cot, watching the expressions of the others there with her. The scientist who had been asking her questions about the previous night looked as though he might be sick. *What did he say his name was? Sayid? Dr. Sayid?*

The woman standing next to him, Langridge, immediately placed her hand on the butt of the gun that was holstered at her side.

Cody, Sidney's ex-boyfriend, and her friend Rich both looked like they wanted to run. Her new friend, Isaac, glanced around the tent as if bored. She had no idea what he might be thinking. And poor Snowy, her white German shepherd, whined pathetically and nuzzled Sidney's hand as if reading their vibes.

She didn't blame any of them in the least for their reactions now, not after what they had experienced last night—what they had lost to the . . .

Invasion.

The word was sharp, cutting, brutal in its revelation.

What had happened yesterday—what had come in the storm—it wasn't anything natural at all. It had been planned—directed.

She remembered the mental connection she'd made with something not of this world and shuddered so hard she thought her back might break. "I know what it is," she said. "It's an invasion."

They were all looking at her now.

"How do you know what—" Langridge started to ask, moving toward her.

"This is just the beginning," Sidney continued, ignoring the security officer, wanting, needing them all to know how bad it truly was—how bad it was likely to get. "They come in the storm."

She saw, clear as day, the thing in the cave, its quivering, gelatinous mass, the thick black tendrils that covered it, broadcasting its signals throughout the island—urging everything that crawled, slithered, and flew to attack and kill if they could.

No mercy.

There was no mercy in an invasion like this.

"The storm hides the arrival of the aliens. . . . It keeps us inside, isolated . . . and then they can—"

"Sidney, where are you getting this from?" Dr. Sayid asked.

She remembered the feel of the alien's slippery, rubbery flesh beneath her and the sucking sounds as she'd stabbed her makeshift spear into its body over and over again. She remembered the sudden rush of energy through her body as she'd somehow connected with it, the images of an alternate reality that had filled her mind, and the others. The others, who had not at all liked her presence in their realm, had tried to destroy her mind.

She could still feel something inside her head, something wrong—like a splinter just below the skin—imbedded, festering.

Poisoning.

"I . . . I somehow connected with it."

Langridge and Sayid looked at each other. Was that skepticism or fear on their faces?

"Okay," the scientist said, taking a deep breath and turning his eyes back to Sidney. "You're saying that you somehow connected with the organism in the cave?"

Sidney nodded, nervously petting Snowy's fur.

"Then maybe you can give us some insight into what we're dealing with here."

"We need to notify the NSA immediately," Langridge stated, hand still on her gun.

"Is that who you guys are working for?" a familiar voice asked. They all looked to see Doc Martin, Benediction's veterinarian, coming into the tent. "The National Security Agency?"

"We're a science division of the NSA," Langridge explained. "We need to let the authorities in Boston know immediately that a threat is imminent and—"

"Why? What's wrong now?" Doc Martin asked, pulling a pack of cigarettes from the pocket of her bloodstained smock.

"Another storm," Cody said grimly. "This time over Boston."

"Another . . . Shit," she said, putting the smoke into the corner of her mouth and fishing for a light. "We gotta do something."

"That's exactly what I'm going to do," Langridge said, turning quickly and rushing from the tent.

"If you'll excuse me," Sayid said politely, and then followed the security officer out toward a larger tent, where there appeared to be much hustle and bustle.

Cody and Rich were looking at Sidney now. There was something strange in their attention.

"What?" she asked them.

"Are you all right, Sid?" Rich asked. "This stuff about connecting with that . . . that monster . . ." He paused, and the look on his face told her that he was remembering the horror of the creature in the cave.

"She's fine," Cody answered for her.

"What are you guys talking about?" Doc Martin wanted to know. "Who connected with what?"

"I did," Sidney said, and told Doc Martin what she had already explained to Langridge and Sayid.

"But she's fine," Cody said again when she had finished.

"I don't know if that's true, Cody," Sidney said, struggling to keep her voice from cracking. "I guess I got inside their heads . . ." She paused, her stomach roiling. "But they got inside mine, too."

Doc Martin sat on the cot beside her and carefully looked her over. Sidney's hands were still bandaged from the insect bites, as were many areas of her body, but what she was feeling as a result of the connection, it was more than physical.

"*Are* you all right?" Doc Martin asked, the concern clear in her tone and her gaze.

Sidney didn't answer right away, not wanting to lie to someone who was as close to her as family. Something was still there, inside her head. Maybe it would go away over time, but as for right now . . .

"I really don't know," she finally admitted, hot tears beginning to roll down her face.

And Doc Martin pulled her close and hugged her.

CHAPTER **TWO**

The train was late.

"C'mon, c'mon," Delilah muttered, checking the time on her phone as she stood before the subway car's doors waiting for them to open.

They'd been stuck mid-tunnel since State Street, and she was tempted to pry apart the doors and walk the rest of the way through the dark tunnel to her stop at Haymarket. Although as she peered through the window in the door, she caught sight of something that might have been a rat moving from one patch of shadow to the next and thought better of it.

Thankfully, the train began to move, ever so slowly, and she finally reached her stop. The doors opened with a hiss, and she was the first one out, a wave of passengers spilling out to either side of her. She wasn't late yet—

Yet.

Usually she stopped at Dunkin' Donuts for a coffee, but if she didn't today, she just might make it in time. She dashed past the donut kiosk and up the escalator, pushing through the doors onto Congress Street. Now she had at least a seven-minute walk up to Cambridge Street and then down to Elysium.

Delilah checked the time again on her phone, just as a huge drop of water splashed upon the screen.

Please, just five more minutes, she thought as she gazed up at the weirdness of the sky. While she'd been underground, it had become incredibly dark, the clouds—which seemed so close to the ground—swirling and churning like smoke. Once again she regretted not listening to her mother and quickened her pace, practically running to beat the oncoming storm.

But the wind picked up, blowing the increasing raindrops sideways, and it was only a matter of seconds before she was soaked.

At Blossom Street she passed the construction site that would eventually be a grand subway station, connecting all of the various lines and exiting practically in front of Elysium. She'd heard it would be finished sometime in the early spring of next year—perfect for her commute, if Elysium hired her full-time after her graduation from nursing school.

The rain was coming down in drenching sheets now, as if someone had turned on a fire hose. She tried to quicken her pace even more as she turned up the drive to Elysium's front entrance, fighting the wind and rain but losing miserably.

She climbed the old stone steps and was reaching out to grasp the door when the wind seemed to decide that she wasn't going inside. It felt like a huge hand was pushing her back down the stairs, the pelting rain stinging her face and obscuring her vision.

But suddenly a strong hand took her arm, and she heard a familiar voice over the howling wind. "Come in, come in!" shouted Sam, the security guard, as he pulled her through the glass door and yanked it closed behind them.

"Thanks, Sam," Delilah said breathlessly, laughing as she tried to wipe away the water that cascaded down her face. "I wasn't sure I was gonna make it."

"I saw you coming up the drive and thought you might need a hand." The older man smiled warmly at her; his was the first kind face she'd seen when she'd started her job at Elysium. "Looks like you're gonna need a towel."

"Maybe two," she added, looking down at the way her scrubs were plastered to her body.

"I'm surprised you even came in today," Sam said, moving back to his desk.

"Little rain ain't gonna keep me away," she told him with a smile.

"Little rain?" he said. "Governor's declared a state of emergency. This thing's turned into a full-blown hurricane."

"Seriously?" she asked.

The old man nodded. "Yeah. They're calling it an atmospheric anomaly, came outta nowhere and it's gonna be big. You should get upstairs and see if they've got something dry for you to put on. You'll catch your death with these air conditioners blowing on you all day," Sam added as he returned to his seat behind the desk.

Delilah felt a sudden chill and had to agree with the old security guard. "True, and I don't want to be later than I already am!" she said, moving toward the elevators, where a few others waiting gave her wet clothing a look, probably glad it wasn't them.

Delilah's manager, Mallory, was so relieved that the co-op student had actually made it in to work when so many others hadn't that she ignored the fact that Delilah was late. She even managed to find a set of dry scrubs for the young woman.

The new scrubs were blue, and as Delilah peeled off her wet clothing, she realized that it did feel more like a blue day after all. She left the bathroom, carrying her own pink scrubs in a dripping ball, and caught sight of a housekeeping cart parked against the opposite wall outside the men's room. She walked over to it to grab a plastic bag for her clothes.

"What are you looking for, beautiful?" she heard a pleasant voice ask from behind her and turned to see Mason exiting the bathroom, carrying his mop.

"Hey, Mason," Delilah said. "How's the family?"

The man smiled as he approached her. "They're good," he said. "Thanks for asking. The baby is getting so big—six months now, hard to believe. You need something there?"

"Just grabbing a plastic bag for my clothes," she said, holding up the wet ball of pink. "I got caught in the storm coming in."

"Let me help you with that." Mason grabbed a roll of small plastic trash bags and tore one off, handing it to her.

"Perfect, thanks," she said, taking it from him and slipping the pink scrubs inside.

"Don't be showing that around," he warned with a wink. "Deacon sees it, he'll make you pay for it."

Deacon was the head of custodial services and had a reputation for nickel-and-diming his staff. Everyone seemed to be a little afraid of him.

"I'll be careful," she promised as she headed back in the direction of her unit for morning report.

She turned the corner and almost collided with a dog. Immediately she froze, her heart pounding and her breath catching in her chest as her eyes locked with the big dog's chocolate-brown orbs.

Nothing scared Delilah more than dogs.

She couldn't have been any older than six, playing with her friends at the playground when the rottweiler got loose. She remembered having seen it earlier, fascinated by its black-and-brown coloring and how powerful it looked.

She'd all but forgotten about the animal as she'd climbed on the monkey bars with her friends—until she heard the screams. Even at six years old she knew that those screams were not children having fun, but screams of sheer terror. She'd turned around to see the rottweiler on top of a little girl from the neighborhood, biting her, shaking her as she cried out for help. Blood was all over the little girl's face and clothing—and on the dog's face.

Delilah saw that face often in her nightmares, dark eyes wild, muzzle stained a deep, bloody red.

She remembered people trying to stop the dog, but the dog just went after them. Overwhelmed with fear and panic, Delilah had jumped down from the monkey bars and started to run. She knew now that it was the worst thing she could ever have done, like calling to the animal to come take a bite.

And it did, charging across the playground, chasing after her. She remembered screaming so loudly that it felt like her voice would break. She could hear the dog behind her, growing closer . . . closer . . . and closer still.

And just as it was about to get her—

Delilah suddenly realized that the dog in the hallway was simply sitting in front of her, staring at her with a tilted head and quizzical gaze.

But it didn't change a thing. She was still so very, very afraid.

"Bella!" Delilah heard a woman calling and looked up to see the pet therapist step into the corridor from the activity room two doors down.

Immediately the dog reacted, turning toward the woman with a furiously wagging tail.

"What are you doing, bad girl? Sorry about that," the woman said to Delilah. "I was setting up for pet therapy, and she wandered away."

Delilah tried to speak, but fear clogged her throat.

"Hey, are you all right?" the woman asked, concern creeping into her voice as she studied Delilah more closely.

"I'm okay," Delilah managed, the words tumbling out in a gasp. "Just really . . . really afraid . . ."

"Afraid of Bella?" the woman asked with surprise. "She's perfectly harmless. There's no reason to be afraid of her."

That's what everyone says, Delilah thought. *But I do have a reason.*

She had seen what a dog had done to a little girl on a playground, to those who tried to help . . .

To her.

The scar on her ankle suddenly ached and throbbed. She felt the dog's teeth as they ripped her skin, scraping across the bone.

"I—I'm just really afraid of dogs," Delilah stammered, not even wanting to look at the woman whose dog now stood beside her, nuzzling her hand.

"I'm so sorry," the woman said. "I understand."

But did she? Delilah wondered. Did the woman really get the level of fear that she experienced when encountering a dog, no matter how friendly they were supposed to be?

It was a bystander who had saved her. He'd jumped over the fence and used a bicycle pump to beat the dog over the head, finally driving it away.

Delilah had never gone back to that park and never looked at a dog—any dog—any way other than through fear-filled eyes since.

The woman gave her one last look before she and the dog went back into the activity room. Delilah waited a moment to be sure they wouldn't come back out, then practically ran past the doorway and into the nursing office.

"Jesus Christ, you look like you've seen a ghost," Mallory exclaimed as she walked in.

Worse, Delilah thought.

Much worse than a ghost.

This was real.

CHAPTER **THREE**

Sidney's friends were all sitting or standing around her cot. They weren't saying much, but she could read their concern for her in their watchful eyes. She wanted so much to tell them to cut the crap, that she was fine.

But then she could feel it—whatever *it* was—inside her skull, inside her brain—and she was so very glad that they were with her.

"They're upset," Isaac blurted out. He stood alone near the wall of the tent, staring out through the plastic window at the makeshift camp on the high school soccer field.

"What's that, Isaac? Who's upset?" Sidney asked, climbing off the cot to join him, grateful for the distraction.

Isaac turned as she approached, Snowy right behind her. Nervously he stepped back, still horribly awkward and shy around her even though they'd been through so much together in the last twenty-four hours.

"The scientist people," he said, gesturing toward the window.

Sidney stepped past him and glanced outside. "You're right," she said.

"What's goin' on, Sid?" Cody questioned as he and Rich headed toward her.

"I don't know, but they don't look all that happy."

Sayid and Langridge were talking, the scientist pacing. Other members of their team were milling about, all wearing the same stern looks.

"I'm sure it's about Boston," Rich said.

"Yeah, but what about it?" Sidney asked.

And suddenly she felt as if someone had stabbed the blade of a scalpel into her skull, twisting it in the soft mushy meat of her brain. She let out a shrill scream, her hands grabbing at the sides of her head as the world dropped away from beneath her.

Backward she fell, first into darkness . . .

And then into hell.

Sidney didn't understand the images that bombarded her with such painful fury.

At first she found herself in total darkness—a black so intense that it consumed all light, feeling, and sound.

Life. It consumed life.

Then there was a flash, tearing the darkness away like a curtain, revealing . . .

Somewhere deep beneath the ground, somewhere wet and muddy and hard with rock . . .

A city . . . a jungle of steel, stone, and glass . . . pummeled by a storm. So many live there . . . so many lives . . .

Eyes . . . she is looking out through hundreds—thousands—of eyes. It is ready . . . something . . . alien. The time for attack is now.

ELYSIUM.

The sign is before her, the rain pouring over its raised letters. She thinks she sees a building behind the sign, but . . .

The curtain falls, and it is darkness again.

"Sidney."

The sound of someone calling her name seemed to be reverberating through the length of a very long tunnel.

"Sid? Sidney? Are you okay? Sidney?"

She opened her eyes and realized she was lying on the floor of the tent, her friends and Dr. Sayid leaning over her.

"Hey," he said, that look of concern on his face. "Are you all right, Ms. Moore?"

"I saw a city," she blurted out, attempting to sit up but blocked by an excited Snowy licking her face. "I think . . . I think it was Boston."

"What do you mean you saw Boston?" Langridge pushed her way between Cody and Rich and squatted beside Sidney.

"Brenda, perhaps you should—" Sayid began.

But the security officer immediately cut him off. "Never mind that. What do you mean you saw Boston?" she demanded.

Sidney thought for a moment about what she was going to say, not completely understanding it herself. "I really don't understand, but it's like I told you already. When I connected with that thing in the cave, it . . . they . . . the ones who sent it . . . got into my head too. I think there's another one of those things in Boston . . . at least that's what I saw."

Langridge looked at Sayid and then back to Sidney.

"You realize that sounds like crazy talk," she said.

Sidney nodded. "Can you help me up?" she asked. Cody stepped in front of Sayid and reached down to grasp her hand, pulling her to her feet. She swayed ever so slightly.

"You good?" he asked, holding her arm to steady her.

"Yeah, thanks," she said. "Just a little dizzy."

"So what makes you think there's another one of those creatures and that you're somehow linked to it? Maybe it's just stress or something," Cody suggested.

"No," Sidney said, shaking her head. "It's hard to describe, but the feelings, I guess, were the same. And it was definitely Boston I could see."

"But you've been to Boston," Langridge said, clearly trying to debunk Sidney's story. "It could just be with all the talk of another storm . . ."

"Not during a hurricane," Sidney countered. "It's almost as if I'm somehow part of this thing . . . this alien organism . . . seeing what it sees . . . feeling what it feels . . ." Her voice trailed off as she remembered the painful, terrible sensations.

"Okay, so tell me then," Langridge said. "Is what happened here in Benediction going to happen in Boston?"

Sidney knew the answer but didn't want to face the truth. She felt suddenly cold and wrapped her arms around herself, avoiding the uncomfortably stern gaze of the woman questioning her.

"Sidney?" Langridge insisted.

She was sure they all knew the answer anyway.

"Yes."

CHAPTER FOUR

Sayid wasn't sure how much he should share; these people were civilians after all.

"We haven't been able to contact authorities in Boston, or anywhere else," he said carefully, feeling Langridge's eyes burning into the side of his face.

"Greg," she said. "Maybe we should—"

"It's all right, Brenda," Sayid interrupted. "I think that after what they've been through, they have a right to know." He paused, weighing what he would say next, before focusing his attention on Sidney and her friends. "Something is interfering with our communications."

"So Boston doesn't know," Rich said.

Sayid shook his head. "We're working on it, but . . ."

"It's them," Sidney said suddenly. "*They're* doing this . . .

blocking the signals, just like they did during the storm on the island."

"Perhaps, but we just don't know if . . ."

"No." The young woman was adamant. "Trust me . . . I know it's them."

"You're talking about aliens again," Langridge commented, her tone indicating her doubt. "Or whatever the hell they are."

Sidney nodded her head slowly.

"Then what can you tell us specifically? Do you have any idea of the number of alien creatures we're talking about here? One, or two or two hundred?"

"I—I don't—" Sidney stammered.

Sayid was fascinated. The young lady truly seemed to believe what she was saying. "How can you be so certain?" he asked her. "Is this actual knowledge, or a guess?"

"Look," Sidney began, and Sayid could hear the anger creeping into her tone. "I've already told you I don't know what's happening, and I'm getting a little tired of all these questions. Something happened in that cave, and now I seem to know what these things are trying to do and where they're headed. You can believe me or not, but either way, there are a lot of people in Boston who are gonna need help."

"So if that's true, does it work the other way?" Langridge piped in. "Do they know that you're aware of what they're planning?"

The young woman offered a sad, small smile before answering. "They do." She paused, then chuckled softly, although there was no humor in it. "And I don't think they like that one bit."

CHAPTER **FIVE**

The staff had just wrapped up report and taken their assignments when there was a horrendous boom. At first Delilah thought it was an explosion, and she had to admit that she let out a little scream when the thunder clap sounded and the lights went out. It seemed to shake the whole building and cause the very air to vibrate.

"It's all right," Mallory called out. "Give it a second."

And like magic, most of the lights came back on.

"There, emergency generators have kicked in," Mallory continued. "We should be good."

The storm continued to rage outside, the wind driving the rain so hard that it sounded like little rocks hitting the windows.

"Listen to it out there," Phil commented. "Don't think I'll be going out for lunch today."

"Has anybody heard anything more about the storm?" Annalise asked.

Cherrie looked at her phone. "Says it's gonna rain," she said in all seriousness.

"Really? I wouldn't have known," Delilah commented drily, and they all shared a nervous laugh.

It felt good to laugh after the scare. Delilah knew it was ridiculous, but she just couldn't shake the terror of her earlier confrontation with Bella. *Maybe it's the storm,* she thought. For a second she actually considered heading down the hall to find the therapist and the dog and trying to pet the animal. But then her heart started racing, and she began to sweat.

On second thought, maybe she'd just get to work.

As a co-op, she didn't have an assignment of her own; instead she was paired up with one of the nurses, meant to maximize her learning experience, and, if truth be told, she really was learning a lot. Today she was working with Cherrie, who was waiting by the doorway, still looking at her phone with a concerned expression.

"What's wrong?" Delilah asked as she joined the nurse.

"I'm not getting anything on this," she said, obviously annoyed. "The storm must be screwing everything up."

Delilah pulled her own phone from the pocket of her scrub pants and looked at it. "Yeah, I'm not getting anything either."

Someone cleared their throat loudly, and they saw Mallory glaring from the back of the room.

"Don't make me take those away from you," she said, reminding them that cell phones were not allowed on patient units.

"Sorry," Delilah said, quickly putting the phone back into her pocket.

Cherrie did the same. "Not like we can do much with it anyway," she grumbled as she and Delilah headed out on their first rounds.

Elysium was a long-term-care hospital that specialized in the treatment and rehab of people with traumatic brain injuries. Delilah's unit was a chronic-care unit, the patients not expected to ever really recover. It was a difficult job, but Delilah loved it. There wasn't much she found more rewarding than the occasional slight response she received from her mostly unresponsive patients.

She was feeding Lonnie Jorgenson, a thirty-five-year-old former music teacher who had suffered severe brain trauma in a car accident a little more than five years earlier. Her prognosis was poor, but Delilah could have sworn that every once in a while she caught a glimpse of the woman that Lonnie used to be.

She raised the spoonful of pureed peaches up to Lonnie's mouth, then gently wiped away the excess that dribbled from her lips.

"It's really awful out there today, Lonnie," Delilah said, making conversation even though it was completely one-sided. "In fact, a state of emergency has been declared." She brought another spoonful of the fruit to Lonnie's mouth. "But don't you worry, we've got it all under control here," she continued. "Everything is going to be just fine."

Delilah listened to the howling wind and driving spray against the windows, trying to believe her own reassurances. She wished that she could take a quick break and check in with her mother and Izzy, but the cell signals were still down.

She finished feeding Lonnie and carefully wiped the woman's mouth and face. "We good?" she asked the woman softly, but Lonnie just stared with that sad, vacant expression.

"Let's get you comfortable, and we'll put on your music. How's that?" Delilah asked her.

Lonnie did not answer, but Delilah felt she would be happy with that. She lowered the woman's bed, fixed her pillow and arranged her covers, then crossed the room to a shelf where a CD player sat, a stack of disc cases beside it.

Cherrie appeared in the doorway. "Hey, Lonnie," she said softly, touching the woman's hand before turning to Delilah. "You about done?"

"Almost. I just want to put some music on for her."

Delilah picked *Mozart's Greatest Hits* and placed the disc in the player. She hit play, adjusting the volume as the first soothing notes sounded, then turned to see that Cherrie was checking her work. She smiled to herself. She knew the nurses had to double-check her care, and, believe it or not, she was fine with that. She was pretty confident in the care she gave.

"How's that, Lonnie?" Delilah asked as she approached the bed where the woman lay still, eyes fixed on the ceiling above her.

"We'll leave you to your music, hon," Cherrie said, again touching the woman's hand and giving it a squeeze.

"Nice job in there," Cherrie said to her as the two left the room and headed down the corridor. "But now comes a real challenge," she added as they stopped at another room.

"Okay," Delilah said with trepidation as she realized they were at Winston's door.

Winston had managed to survive a massive stroke, but it had left him in a near-vegetative state. The poor man was mostly non-responsive but would occasionally have sudden, violent physical outbursts. There was really no way to predict when they would happen—add to that the fact that he weighed nearly three hundred pounds—making caring for him difficult, to say the least.

"Winston needs his bath," Cherrie said.

"Oh no," Delilah said. "Didn't he just have one?"

Cherrie nodded with a smile. "And now it's time for another."

Delilah peered into the semidarkened room at the large mound of humanity lying upon the bed.

"Do you accept the challenge?" Cherrie asked.

Delilah steeled herself. "Let's do this," she said, taking a deep breath and entering the room first.

CHAPTER SIX

"What do you think they're talking about?" Rich asked, staring through the plastic window.

Langridge and Sayid had quickly left and were talking outside, stepping far enough away from the fabric sides of the tent that those inside couldn't hear their words.

Sidney had returned to the cot and sat next to Doc Martin, stroking Snowy's fur in an attempt to keep both herself and the dog calm. There was an energy in the air now, and she felt like she wanted to scream. The shepherd was sitting on top of Sidney's feet and panting, clearly feeling that same crackling vibe.

Doc Martin pulled a cigarette from the pack in her pocket, placed it in her mouth, and lit up. "Obviously it's about Boston," she said as she took her first puff, "and what they're going to do."

"What can they do?" Cody asked from the corner of the tent

where he stood with his arms folded defensively. "You heard them—communications are out. There's no way to reach anybody."

"So that's it?" Rich said. "Boston is toast? My parents are in Newton, in case you've forgotten."

"I didn't say that," Cody explained. "I was just saying that the team *here* wouldn't be able to help anyone *there*. I'm sure there's somebody in Boston who could—"

"Deal with killer animals by the thousands—maybe millions?" Sidney asked, feeling a sudden touch of panic take hold. "Think of what happened here, on this tiny island, and then multiply it."

She could see by the expressions on their faces that they were doing precisely what she'd asked.

"Could be bad," Doc Martin nodded, puffing thoughtfully on her smoke. "Could be really bad."

"But they've got a major police force, SWAT, National Guard, and everything else, right?" Rich said. "I'm sure they can handle some psycho pets and a few bugs. . . ."

His words trailed off, the reality of the situation clearly sinking in. Sidney thought of all they'd encountered during the storm. She remembered the ground literally moving with life—things she never even knew lived on Benediction, the living wave of crazed animals, their right eyes covered with that silvery sheen.

"Shit," Rich groaned, and slumped down on the other side of Doc Martin.

"Can I have one of those?" he asked the veterinarian, gesturing to her cigarette.

"You don't smoke."

"Nah, but I need something to calm me down."

"Take a coupla deep breaths and have a drink of water," the older woman said. "These things'll kill ya."

Rich looked even more dejected, his shoulders slumping. "The whole time we were running around for our lives last night, I never gave my folks a thought. . . . They were safe back home." He paused, his eyes filling with tears. "But now . . ."

Sidney started to get up, to go to her friend, but stopped when Cody crossed the tent to stand before him.

"You can't think of the bad shit," he said. "You've got to be strong . . . at least until you know otherwise."

Rich looked at him, his face filled with annoyance.

"Thanks for that, asshole."

"Hey, man, Sidney and I already lost our fathers, and Isaac his mother," Cody snapped. "I just meant there's no reason to get yourself all worked up until you know something for sure."

Rich leaned forward, putting his head in his hands.

"Not worked up? How is that even friggin' possible—not get worked up." He had started to rock back and forth. "My mother is terrified of bugs—any bugs. She once had my father come home from a business trip to kill a spider that had made a web near the living room window."

"That's a little extreme," Doc Martin said.

"Ya think?" Rich offered, lifting his head from his hands. "He was in freakin' Michigan."

Isaac had been standing silently by the open tent flap, staring out at the activity of the encampment, survivors of the night wandering around like zombies while scientists and military types rushed about. Sidney saw him raise a hand toward his bad ear—his Steve ear, as he'd called it—and then lower it again.

"You okay, Isaac?" she asked him, moving to stand next to him, Snowy tight to her side.

"Yeah," he said, without looking at her. "Yeah, I'm good."

The conversation between Sayid and Langridge was becoming louder.

"I don't like it," Sidney heard the woman say. "Not one little bit."

"But it's a chance we have to take," Sayid responded. "We cannot risk the possibility of . . ."

Langridge looked like she was going to hit him but instead spun on her heels and stalked off. Sayid watched her go for a moment, thoughtfully stroking the scruff on his chin, then turned back to the tent.

"Everything all right?" Sidney asked, stepping back as he entered, not realizing until the words left her mouth how absolutely stupid her question was. No, things weren't all right. Things were very, very bad, and likely to get worse.

"Your connection to the invaders," Sayid began, catching her off guard.

"Yeah . . . ," she prompted cautiously.

"You say you know things."

Sidney nodded, feeling that awful, squirming sensation in her brain.

"Could it . . . could *you* tell us things?"

She thought about the question and the things that she had

seen inside her mind, things that only the invaders would know, and knew that there had to be more that she could see.

Even though the thought terrified her.

"Yeah," she admitted finally. "I think I could."

"You're a civilian," he began, his hand again going to his chin, "and I know that I shouldn't even be considering this, but . . ."

"This is what's got Langridge upset, isn't it?" Sidney said.

He nodded quickly. "And I completely understand why, but if there's even the slightest chance that we can prevent what happened here from happening in Boston . . ."

"What are you asking?"

"Sid, maybe you shouldn't," Cody warned, but she ignored him.

"What, Dr. Sayid—tell me."

"We're going to attempt to fly into Boston."

"And do what?" Cody asked incredulously.

Sayid shook his head. "We've been investigating incidents like what happened here in Benediction all over the world. This is the first chance at a breakthrough we've had, and if we can use it to our advantage . . . if we can get to Boston, and take Sidney with us, we might be able to—"

"No," Cody interrupted, nearly shouting. "Sidney is not going with you."

"Cody," Sidney said quietly.

"No, Sid, this is crazy!" His voice continued to rise. "I've already lost you as my girlfriend, but I'm not about to let you go off with these clowns and end up like our fathers."

Sidney closed her eyes at the mention of their fathers. Both men had sacrificed their lives to save their children and their friends. She knew what she had to do. There was no other choice. Taking a deep breath, she opened her eyes and faced Cody. "I have to do this," she said firmly, then turned to Dr. Sayid. "What do you need?"

Sayid was about to answer as Langridge came into the tent. It looked like she was going to say something, but a look from the doctor silenced her.

"We need whatever information you can give us about these things and what they're doing," Sayid said to Sidney. "I know it's a lot to ask and I know it's risky, but right now it's all we have. There's a chance that you can help save a lot of lives and stop these things. If that happens, it will be completely worth the risk."

"What about *her* life?" Cody interjected.

"Cody, please," Sidney said.

"He's right, Sid," Rich piped up.

"Come on, not you, too!"

Rich stood up from the cot. "After what we've been through together . . ." He shook his head. "I can't stand the thought of losing you."

Sidney looked at Doc Martin, who continued to sit silently on the cot. "Everybody else is offering their two cents. What do you think?"

The veterinarian looked her square in the eyes, and Sidney braced herself for what was to come.

"If I had an opportunity to potentially save thousands of lives, I know what I would do," she said. "But that's just me." She pulled the pack of cigarettes from her pocket again and got up from the cot with a grunt. "If you'll excuse me, I'm gonna have a smoke outside."

They all watched Doc Martin leave, the tension so thick in the tent that Sidney felt she could cut it with a knife.

"I'll go," she said after a moment.

"If you're going, then I'm going," Cody said.

"Not a chance," Langridge said. "We're already risking the life of one civilian, I won't take responsibility for—"

"Three," Rich interrupted, and finished her sentence.

Langridge glared at Rich as he held up three fingers.

"This is ridiculous," she said. "None of you are going. Tell them," she ordered Sayid.

"They did pretty well here last night," he said. "Look at what they survived together."

"I can't believe I'm hearing this," she said, and Sidney noticed that Langridge's hand was on her gun again.

"Well I guess that's the deal." Sidney shrugged. "If you want me, you have to take my team."

"We're a team?" Rich asked her.

"Would you rather 'posse'?"

Cody shook his head and rolled his eyes.

"Posse is good," Rich agreed.

"Okay," Sidney said, looking back to Sayid and Langridge. "We're all going . . . me and my posse."

Snowy whined pitifully, rubbing her large head up against Sidney's leg.

Langridge looked at the shepherd with distaste. "I suppose the dog is part of your posse as well," she said.

Sidney looked down, scratching the powerful animal behind the ears.

"We've been through a lot, she and I. I wouldn't dream of being separated from her."

CHAPTER SEVEN

The big man hung limply in the sling above the bed.

"You ready?" Cherrie asked Delilah. The nurse was standing on one side of the bed, holding the remote control for the Hoyer lift.

Delilah was opposite her, pulling on the sides of the sling to keep Winston's body in position over his bed. She nodded, and Cherrie hit the button on the remote control, slowly lowering the hydraulic arm.

Winston's mass settled upon the bed, with not a sound from him. "He's good," Delilah said proudly. Today's shower had been relatively easy, but moving Winston was a tiring chore, with or without the bad behavior.

Together, Delilah and Cherrie unhooked the sling from the metal bar of the hydraulic arm, and Cherrie slid the lift back into the corner of the room. "Let's get that sling-pad out from underneath him, and we'll be good," she said as she returned to her side of the bed.

They turned him onto his side facing Cherrie, and Delilah rolled the sling, pushing it as far underneath him as she could. "All set," she said, reaching out to pull him back toward her.

"Got it," Cherrie said, as she pulled the green canvas-and-foam sling out from under Winston and hung it on a hook behind the door.

They positioned him on his back and raised the head of the bed; then Cherrie leaned over to fix Winston's pillow as Delilah reached down to pull up his sheet and blanket.

Winston's arm suddenly shot out to the side and connected with Cherrie's midsection. The young woman let out a horrible-sounding grunt as she stumbled backward and fell to the floor, narrowly avoiding hitting her head on the wall under the windows.

"Oh my God," Delilah said as she threw herself on top of Winston, holding his flailing arm down so that he did not hurt himself. She could hear Cherrie moaning on the floor.

Winston immediately went still, and Delilah waited just a second to see if he would remain that way before cautiously backing away and rushing around the bed to her friend.

Cherrie was curled in a tight ball, clutching her side and gasping.

"Hey, are you all right?" Delilah asked as she knelt down beside her.

"I think he might've cracked a rib," Cherrie said between gasps.

"I'll get Mallory," Delilah said, standing up.

"No," Cherrie said. "Just help me up." She struggled to sit up and then reached out for Delilah. "On the count of three."

Delilah braced herself and hooked her arms under Cherrie's.

"One," they said in unison. "Two." They began to rock back and forth. "Three," they yelled, and Delilah rocked back, standing and pulling Cherrie to her feet.

Cherrie cried out, bending forward and clutching her side.

"Oh God, he really hurt me," she gasped.

"Let me help you to the chair, and then I'm definitely going to get Mallory," Delilah said, trying to turn the nurse in the direction of the chair by the door. Cherrie didn't move, and Delilah realized the nurse seemed to be staring at something behind her. She turned and froze.

Winston's bed was empty.

All three hundred pounds of the man who had, until this point, been completely helpless, was standing at the foot of the bed, blocking their way to the door.

"That's impossible," Cherrie said in a fearful whisper.

"Somebody should tell Winston that," Delilah said as the wall of a man lumbered toward them.

CHAPTER **EIGHT**

"So you're going?" Doc Martin asked her.

"We all are," Sidney replied, nodding toward Cody and Rich who stood near them.

"Taking Snowy girl too?" Doc asked, reaching down to pet the dog, who stood with her side pressed against Sidney's leg.

"Yeah," Sidney said, as she ran her fingertips over the dog's head. "Can't bear to be without her since . . ."

She felt it inside her skull again, writhing around, a foreign presence gradually coming alive.

But for what purpose exactly?

She was determined to find out.

"Are you sure about this?" Doc Martin reached over and affectionately rubbed her arm. The veterinarian was the closest thing to a mother that Sidney had had since her own mom had walked out on her and her dad when she was little.

"If I can help some people . . ." Sidney responded, although she was more than a little frightened.

Doc Martin looked carefully at her for a moment as if debating what to say next. Finally, she simply nodded.

"We'll fly into Logan, let the proper authorities know what's going on, and they can take it from there. Easy peasy." Sidney tried to sound confident but was pretty sure she wasn't fooling the doc.

"Easy peasy," Doc Martin repeated, and smiled weakly.

"I'll be fine," Sidney said, feeling a lump starting to form in her throat. Damn those pesky emotions.

"I know," the older woman said. "You're a tough cookie—always have been."

Suddenly Sidney couldn't help herself and threw her arms around the woman in a powerful hug, squeezing her as hard as she could, just in case she didn't get another chance.

Doc Martin hesitated, probably surprised by the unusual show of emotion, but quickly cracked, wrapping her own arms around the girl.

"You'll be home before you know it, and Isaac and I will make sure that everything stays fine for you here."

"Where is Isaac?" Sidney asked, realizing that he wasn't with the others as she released her friend.

Doc Martin looked around. "He said he wasn't feeling well; maybe he went to lie down."

Sidney scanned the camp. "Yeah, maybe he did."

"Looks like they're ready for you," Doc Martin said, pointing behind her.

A military-style Humvee had pulled up near Cody and Rich. Langridge had opened the back door and was motioning for them to get in. Sayid was already sitting in the front.

"Okay then," Sidney said, starting to back away from Doc Martin. Snowy was right by her side.

"Be safe," Doc Martin said, fumbling in her filthy lab coat pocket and producing her rumpled pack of cigarettes.

"When I get back we're gonna work on that nasty habit," Sidney said, smiling at her friend, and turned toward the Humvee.

"It's a deal," she heard Doc Martin call to her, making her smile and giving her something to look forward to when this business was over and done with.

Isaac was scared.

The bad radio—it was back.

He lay on his cot and pulled his knees up tight against his chest, trying to concentrate, to push the awful signal out of his head and back to where it came from.

Go away, bad radio. Go away.

His whole body still hurt from what it had gone through the previous night. His body hurt, and so did his heart.

He missed his mother and the cats—even though they would often mess up his room. What was it Mother used to always say? *You only miss something once it's gone.*

Yeah, he understood that now.

Sidney was about to be gone too, and that made him sad as well.

He'd thought about going with them . . . Cody, Snowy, and Rich, but they were going on a plane.

Isaac had never been on a plane, and he thought that it might be quite scary, so he'd decided to stay right here in the camp where he could maybe help Doc Martin and the other people.

The bad radio had gone away after Sidney had killed that thing in the cave, and at first Isaac was ecstatic, thinking it was gone for good . . .

But now it was back.

It was softer than it had been . . . like a station that wasn't quite tuned in. But it was definitely there. He'd even tried turning his hearing aids down, remembering his mother yelling at him whenever he touched them. But he could still hear it, and he wished so hard that it would go away. He hated how it made him feel—the way it made him angry, telling him to hurt people.

No, he told the bad radio. *I won't do that.*

And he tried to be strong as he lay on his side, perfectly still so the bad radio would think he was asleep.

But it knew he wasn't.

And it continued to buzz inside his head, telling him things that he did not want to hear.

Telling him that there was nothing he could do . . . nothing that anybody could do.

The bad radio had won.

The bad radio was here to stay.

CHAPTER **NINE**

"Be careful," Cherrie gasped from where Delilah had left her supporting herself against the wall.

Delilah was cautiously approaching the man who continued to shuffle closer on thick legs. "Winston?" she said gently.

He turned his head stiffly toward her, and she noticed something very strange—something that she'd never seen before, although she'd been taking care of this man for the past month and a half. There seemed to be something wrong with his right eye—a kind of reflective coating, like a thick, silvery cataract.

"It's okay. Let's go back to bed," she continued as she took his hand in hers and began to guide him toward the bed.

Winston immediately yanked his hand away as if she was burning him.

Delilah jumped back, but he was faster, grasping her throat

tightly with his large hand. She gasped, unable to breathe, struggling to pry his fingers away. Strangely beautiful explosions of color erupted before her eyes, although they couldn't hide the horrifying lack of expression on the man's face.

And that eye. That strange, silvery eye.

She couldn't stop looking at it. It was like she was slowly being sucked into its shiny center as everything faded to black.

"Drop her!" Delilah heard from somewhere far off, and suddenly the murderous pressure on her throat was gone, and she was falling to the floor.

Through bleary eyes she saw that Cherrie had thrown herself at Winston, pushing him backward where he stumbled on atrophied legs. The two were struggling on the floor beyond the foot of the bed, but it was clear that Cherrie was in terrible pain, and she was barely holding her own against the large man.

"Cherrie . . . no!" Delilah choked, struggling to gather her strength. Something was seriously wrong. Winston's outbursts had never been this violent, never mind that the man hadn't stood on his own two feet for years.

"Help!" she finally managed to scream. "We need help down here."

Without another thought, she pushed herself to her feet and dove toward the fray, only to be rewarded with a vicious slap that sent her flying to the floor again, her mouth filling with the taste of copper.

Crazy colors danced before her eyes, and her ears were filled with a sound like the rush of the ocean, but the cold of the floor on her face partially revived her. She managed to sit up, but dizziness spun her perceptions round and round, and she knew she would only fall if she tried to stand.

Cherrie was screaming now. Winston had her around the waist in a savage bear hug and was lifting her off the floor. The nurse thrashed in his clutches, wildly kicking him as he shook her from side to side. Her cries were gut wrenching.

"Help!" Delilah screamed. *Why hasn't anyone come?* She climbed to her feet and surged toward Cherrie, trying to pull Winton's arms from around the woman's waist. "Help us, please!" she cried again as Cherrie went eerily silent.

Delilah continued to scream and claw at the man's arms and the back of his hands, even as blood poured from Cherrie's mouth, staining the front of her mint-green scrubs. Her body was limp, her arms and legs flopping loosely, her head lolling to the side like a rag doll's. Finally Winston tossed her away, and she crashed to the floor in a lifeless heap.

He turned his attentions once more to Delilah, his large hands open and reaching for her. She backed away from him but stumbled against the bed. Winston lunged. She threw herself onto the bed and rolled across its surface and off the other side, landing on the floor with a thud.

Where is everyone? she thought in a panic as the large man shambled around the bed, his face completely emotionless, his right eye glinting in the soft lighting of the room. Frantically she scuttled backward, away from the giant, until she slammed into something with a clatter, metal jabbing the flesh of her back. At first she had no idea what she had collided with but then realized it was the Hoyer lift. She reached up and grabbed hold of the arm of the lift, using it to haul herself to her feet, all the while keeping her eyes upon the approaching Winston.

She managed to maneuver the Hoyer between herself and Winston, although she wasn't at all sure how long she could hold him off with just the heavy metal lift. Desperately she looked for anything that she could use as a weapon, and her eyes settled on the metal lever used to open and close the legs of the device. Quickly she reached down and pulled on the pin that held it in place. For a moment, she was afraid the pin would stick, but with a surge of adrenaline she gave it a vicious yank and it popped free. She grasped the top of the two-foot-long lever and pulled it from its housing. It felt heavy—the perfect weapon.

Delilah looked up at Winston. She took a deep breath and pushed the machine hard at him. The arm of the lift hit him squarely in the belly, and she heard a satisfying grunt as she turned away and raced for the door, weapon in hand.

He was suddenly behind her. She could feel his fingernails scrape along the back of her neck as they curled around the collar of her scrub top. And then she was viciously pulled backward, the V-neck of her top nearly choking her.

Without even thinking, Delilah twisted and slammed the Hoyer lever into Winston's side with a loud thwack. Again she was rewarded with the sound of a soft grunt as the large man released his grip and stumbled to the right.

But it was only a momentary reprieve. Almost immediately

Winston was shaking off the strike as if it were nothing at all and coming at her again.

She drew back and swung her metal bar again, this time striking him in the meat of his neck. She watched as his eyes went wide, the silver-coated right eye bulging as though it might pop from the socket.

Delilah backed toward the door, holding her weapon like a baseball bat, ready to swing. "Don't make me hit you again," she said, sure that Winston didn't understand but feeling the need to warn him anyway.

The big man hurled himself toward her, and she swung the metal lever, striking the side of his round head with a muffled crack. Winston stumbled to one side, stood for a moment, and then came at her again.

"C'mon!" she screamed, hitting him over the top of the head.

The man dropped to his knees, swaying, but he still managed to lunge across the floor at her. Delilah let out a scream and swung with all her might, the metal bar hitting the man just above the eye—his right eye, to be precise.

Finally, it seemed to have some effect on him, the large man's head moving about strangely as if he was suddenly blind.

Delilah didn't waste any time. She dove through the doorway and slammed the door to the room closed behind her.

"Help me!" she screamed as ran down the corridor strangely void of life.

She saw Mrs. Denahy's door open ahead of her and stuck her head into the room. The sixty-eight-year-old woman had suffered a massive brain aneurism and was bedridden—

Except that her bed was empty.

Delilah felt a cold finger of dread, a spider running down her neck, and stopped just inside the doorway to peer into the darkness. The storm still raged outside, the wind sounding like the wails of some mournful ghost.

Maybe they've moved her, Delilah thought as she stepped farther into the room. Maybe something happened while she and Cherrie were in with Winston.

The sudden image of Cherrie, blood streaming from her mouth, nearly made her sick, but she forced herself to concentrate on the dusky room around her. The sheets on the bed were rumpled, and she considered the fact that the poor old woman may have somehow fallen from her bed. Cautiously she made her way around the bed to the other side.

There was indeed a body crumpled on the floor, but it wasn't Mrs. Denahy.

Delilah quickly knelt beside the still figure. "Are you all right?" she asked, grasping the figure's shoulder and gently turning the body over.

She recognized Rose, one of the unit's nursing assistants. Rose's skin was cool to the touch; her eyes protruding from their sockets, her swollen tongue sticking from her mouth, heavy bruising around her throat.

Delilah immediately thought of Winston and quickly looked over her shoulder. Could he have done this before she and Cherrie had seen to his shower? But that still didn't explain the whereabouts of Mrs. Denahy.

Delilah wanted to scream, but instead she took yet another deep breath as the words of her last clinical instructor ran through her mind. *It's the responsibility of the nurse to maintain calm and control— no matter the situation.*

Yeah, easier said than done.

Delilah rose to her feet and quickly bolted from the room.

The hallway was still strangely—eerily—silent, and as she glanced quickly into every room she passed, she found each empty.

Her mind raced. Had there been some kind of emergency that caused the evacuation of the floor, and she and Cherrie had been somehow forgotten? Had they not heard the announcements as they'd fought with Winston?

She reached the nurses' station desperate for a sign—anything— that would tell her what had happened. But again all she found was the chilling absence of any life. She grabbed the receiver of one of the desk phones and placed it to her ear. Instead of a dial tone she heard an odd buzzing. The sound was like an angry nest of wasps ready to attack, and she found it strangely annoying.

So annoying that she had the urge to hurl the phone at the nearest wall.

She slammed the receiver down hard, attempting to pull herself together while her eyes scanned the corridor.

The stairs—she'd take the stairs down to the lobby and get Sam. Sam would know what to do.

Quickly Delilah moved around the nurses' station and over to the stairwell door. She was about to turn the knob when she heard a sound. She froze and cocked an ear to listen.

Yes, there was something—something just below the spattering of hard rain on the windows and the ghostly cries of the heavy winds.

It sounded like the moan of someone in pain.

She released the door handle and cautiously walked a bit farther down the hall, her feet suddenly growing heavy as she realized the sounds were coming from the activity room.

She hesitated and was seriously considering turning back when she heard the sound—the moan—again.

What if somebody needed her? What if she could help? Delilah's brain raced, overriding her fear and sending her down the corridor toward the activity area.

She rushed into the room, ready for anything—or so she thought.

In the center of the room was a small circle of four wheelchairs, each occupied by a patient from her unit. They sat awkwardly, all leaning precariously one way or the other. Jagged wounds had been torn in the delicate flesh of their throats, and their clothing was stained red with blood.

But on the floor in the center of the small circle, the nightmare vision became even worse. The body of the pet therapist lay there, the large dog, Bella, beside her.

Again Delilah's brain attempted to process the scenario in the most logical way—but it just wasn't happening.

The body of the therapist twitched and flopped as the dog did to her what it had done to the poor patients in their chairs, the only sounds in the room now the dog's licking and the tearing of flesh.

Hot bile shot up into her throat, and Delilah gagged.

The dog turned toward her, its muzzle covered in blood, bits of its owner's throat dangling from the corners of its mouth.

It stared at her silently, and that was when she noticed it.

A silvery glint in the dog's right eye.

Delilah barely had time to ponder that mystery before the dog stood and bounded silently toward her.

CHAPTER TEN

The ride to the airport from the encampment on the high school soccer field stirred up all kinds of emotions within Sidney—fear, sadness, anger—all vying for her attention as the Humvee drove through the debris-strewn streets of Benediction.

The things she saw . . . what had been done to her island home and its residents . . . it just wasn't right.

Houses burned, bodies—people that she had known her entire life—dead in the streets or on their lawns near the bodies of the animals that had savaged them.

Survivors wandered aimlessly about, many of them still holding the weapons they had used to survive the night. Some of them managed a tentative wave as the vehicle passed.

Snowy whined, her nose tilted into the air, sniffing the terrible odor of the storm's aftermath.

"Jesus," Rich muttered.

Sidney reached over and grabbed his knee, giving it a quick squeeze.

"I thought I understood how bad it was," he said, his voice cracking sadly. "But it's so much worse."

Cody remained silent. He too was looking out the window, his expression stoic, as if daring the nightmares they were seeing to affect him.

"We'll get people here as soon as possible to help with the cleanup and recovery," Sayid offered.

"Why bother," Cody replied, not taking his eyes from the scenes outside the Humvee. "You should just burn it. It'll never be the same."

"That's a little harsh, don't you think?" Sidney commented, although she would have been lying if she said she hadn't had the same thoughts.

"Yeah," he agreed, without looking at her. "Very harsh."

They'd all lost so much to the horrors of the previous night, but Sidney had to believe that there was still too much to live for—to fight for. They had each other; she still had Snowy and Doc Martin.

And besides, if they gave up, wouldn't they be doing exactly what those things wanted?

She, for one, wouldn't give them that satisfaction—no matter how hard it was, she owed that much to her father, who had sacrificed himself to save her.

Something momentarily wriggled around inside her skull, and she forced it back, concentrating on the other members of their little team. Sayid sat in the front, but Langridge and two others sat across from

Sidney and her friends—a young, athletic-looking woman named Karol, and a heavyset, bearded older man that she'd heard Langridge call Fitzy.

"What if the storm's too bad to fly into Logan?" Sidney asked no one in particular.

Langridge answered. "The plane's military transport; it handled the storm getting here, should be able to get us to Boston."

"Anything?" Sayid asked, turning around to speak to Fitzy, who was busily typing on a tiny laptop.

"Nothing." Fitzy shook his head. "Something's still blocking the signal."

Sayid sighed, then caught Sidney's gaze and forced a smile. "Don't worry," he said. "We're working out the bugs."

She made a face; she'd had more than enough bugs after last night.

"Sorry, poor choice of words," Sayid apologized. "Problems . . . we're working out the problems."

"What do we do once we get to Boston?" Rich asked. "What happens then?"

Again Langridge answered the query. "We'll head for the city's emergency operations center and take control of the situation."

"Sounds easy enough," Cody said, at last looking away from the hellish view of their island town.

"It could be," Langridge said. "As long as there aren't too many surprises."

Cody laughed, but there wasn't any humor in the sound. "No surprises? Have you forgotten what the last twenty-four hours brought to this island? It's nothing but surprises," he said with a shake of his head as he turned back to the passing ghost of Benediction.

CHAPTER ELEVEN

Tyler Payton could barely contain his excitement.

Yeah, sure, it was terrible what had happened to this tiny New England island, but hey, an actual alien species had been discovered.

The burned mass that had been the life-form lay upon the floor of the cave, and all Tyler could do was stare, his imagination running amok. Where had it come from? How did it get here? Had it been intelligent? The questions were like a line of dominos knocked down one after the other.

"Should I do this, or do you want to?" Doug Charmers asked, his voice reaching Tyler through the speaker in his headgear, shaking him from his reverie.

The two scientists were wearing special decontamination suits, though it didn't appear that there was any chance of foreign contamination, and had been assigned to get samples of the life-form for a preliminary workup back at the camp.

"I got it," Tyler said, squatting down in his white plastic suit and riffling through his kit for a container to hold the fragment. "Why don't you bag up one of those," he suggested, gesturing toward the back of the cave, where the floor was littered with dead animals—twisted and deformed, barely resembling the earthly species they had once been.

"Seriously?" Doug asked. "You want me to touch one of those?"

"And you call yourself a scientist," Tyler said with a laugh.

"Molecular biologist," Doug corrected, moving cautiously across the rocky floor toward the largest pile of dead animals. Supposedly they'd all died once the main organism—the transmitter, as it was being called—was killed.

"You're still a scientist, and dead animals shouldn't make you squeamish."

"Have you looked at these things?" Doug asked. "They're like something out of Stephen King's worst nightmare."

Tyler laughed again as he raised his scalpel to an area of charred alien flesh, then paused a moment. It could have been a reflection caused by one of the spotlights that had been placed around the cave for illumination, but Tyler could have sworn that he saw something move.

"Doug," he began.

A tentacle shot out from beneath the blackened mass, pink and dripping, its needle-sharp tip penetrating the plastic face mask of Tyler's decontamination suit as if it was paper and continuing on through the bone of his skull.

Tyler never even had the opportunity to scream.

Doug absolutely did not want to be in the cave.

At first it had been an honor to have been picked for Gregory Sayid's team and exciting to think of the missions he would be a part of. But the reality had proven to be terrifying, and far riskier than he had expected.

He was about to pick up something that looked like a cross between a cat and a hermit crab when his partner's voice came through the speaker in his helmet.

"Doug."

"What?" he asked, annoyed. He wanted nothing more than to leave this place and get back to the comfort of the lab and his electron microscope.

He turned when his question was met with silence. Tyler knelt before the burned mass of the organism, his back to Doug.

"What is it?" Doug asked again, and again his partner remained silent.

Annoyance turned to anger as Doug headed toward Tyler. The man was a jerk, fancying himself a practical joker. But there was a time and a place for things like that, and this was certainly not one of them.

"What the hell do you want?" Doug asked, reaching out and grabbing Tyler's shoulder with his yellow-gloved hand.

Tyler fell backward, allowing Doug to see a thick, vein-covered tentacle reaching through his partner's faceplate.

"Oh shit" was all Doug could manage as he pulled his hand back.

The tentacle violently retracted, and Tyler's body slumped limply to the cave floor. For a moment Doug watched in fascinated terror as the tendril reared up, cobralike, a thin, needlelike tip made of something like bone extending . . . retracting.

Slowly Doug backed up, but the cumbersome decontamination suit made it difficult for him to move, the rustle of the heavy vinyl fabric sounding exceedingly loud in the silence of the cave.

The tendril stopped swaying, and its sharp tip seemed to be pointed directly at him.

He continued to step away, his hand fumbling through the pouch at his side for the short-bladed knife he knew was in there somewhere. *Damn these vinyl gloves.*

Suddenly the appendage shot out at him, and Doug dove to the side as its tip missed him by merely an inch. The muscular tendril twisted and shot toward him again, but Doug had found his knife and slashed at it.

There came a horrible, ear-rending keening from somewhere close by as the tentacle retracted, spewing a dark liquid. The scientist glanced at the ground to see the tentacle's severed tip, the needlelike protrusion still pulsing in and out of its fleshy housing. Then he turned his gaze back to the burned mass of the alien creature. The blackened flesh twitched and cracked as something moved beneath it.

Doug forced himself to his feet and lumbered toward the ladder that had been placed against the wall to allow them to come down, desperate to get out, not even remotely curious as to what was moving beneath the burned flesh of the alien organism.

He was halfway up the ladder when something wrapped around his ankle. "Yaaaahh!" he screamed, almost losing his hold on the rungs as he twisted around. Another, smaller alien had emerged from beneath the ashes of the first, its skin moist and translucent, shimmering in the beams of the spotlights. Frantically Doug sank his knife into the rubbery flesh of the tendril around his ankle and began to saw. Again the monster wailed, before the tentacle whipped back and away.

Doug scrambled to the top of the ladder and over the ledge, breathlessly crawling into the tunnel passage. The cries of the nightmare creature increased, and he chanced a quick look over his shoulder, only to glimpse multiple, flailing tentacles. He got to his feet and ran, cursing the bulky bio-protection suit as he struggled through the passage leading up to the surface.

He was breathing heavily, growing light-headed within the confines of the helmet, even as the heat of his struggle clouded the faceplate. He stumbled, falling to his knees, and, feeling as though he just might suffocate, he threw protocol to the wind and removed the headgear, greedily sucking in the musty salt air wafting down from the cave's entrance.

He listened for the sounds of pursuit behind him but heard nothing. Taking a deep breath, he pushed himself to his feet, using the jagged stone wall for support as he forced himself to continue his climb toward freedom.

The passage angled toward the left, and he quickened his pace, the muscles in his legs painfully burning as the smell of the ocean grew stronger. He rounded the bend to find the entrance no more than twenty feet away.

And froze.

His eyes moved over the gathering that blocked the opening—dogs, raccoons, cats, and a fox or two. Even the ground around their feet writhed with insect life.

He watched them as they watched him. The right eye of every single animal he could see was obscured by a strange, silver coating.

Doug took a tentative step toward them, hoping, praying that it would frighten them and give him his chance to escape.

But they just watched him, their silvery eyes strangely mesmerizing.

He knew it would be foolhardy to try to get past them, even with his knife. But what choice did he have? He didn't dare return to the cave and the thing that awaited him there.

Doug clenched the knife in his gloved hand and, taking a deep breath, was ready to rush the pack keeping him from his freedom when he sensed something behind him.

Turning quickly, he cried out, startled by the sight of his colleague, his slack, pale face peering out through the broken faceplate of his helmet.

"Tyler," Doug exclaimed, feeling a rush of relief. "I thought you were dead!"

But relief quickly turned to horror as Tyler's hands shot out, wrapping tightly about Doug's throat, cutting him off from that sweet, salty air and forcing him violently backward to the floor.

The last thing he saw was Tyler's right eye, glinting silvery in the weak light from the mouth of the cave.

CHAPTER **TWELVE**

The military transport plane was huge.

"We'll get this show on the road as soon as you're all buckled in," Langridge said, watching as they each took their seats.

"Is there a movie on this flight?" Rich asked, wiggling his butt, trying to find a comfortable position. "They're really scrimping in first class these days," he said, reaching for his seat belt.

Cody just shook his head, barely able to crack a smile at his friend's attempt to lighten the mood. He took an empty seat away from the rest of the group.

Sidney watched him as he buckled himself in and turned to look out at Benediction Airport.

"The airfield isn't used to stuff this big," Cody said. "Remember a few years back when *Air Force One* landed for the president's vacation? They had to repair the runway after it left."

"I remember that," Sidney said, feeling a certain lightness at the memory of a time before things had gone to hell. She wished briefly that she was back there, when her father had been healthy—when he had still been alive.

When the island had not tried to kill them.

"She's gonna need to be strapped in," said a voice, breaking Sidney's reverie.

Sidney looked up to see Langridge standing before her, pointing at the dog nearly sitting on her feet.

"Sure," Sidney said, catching Snowy's attention and patting the seat next to her.

The German shepherd hopped up and sat awkwardly in the seat.

"There ya go," Sidney said, kissing her head as she reached around her for the buckle and snapped the belt in place. Snowy looked at her questioningly.

"It's all right," Sidney told her, patting her chest. "It's for your safety."

The shepherd began to pant but didn't move.

"That's a good girl," Sidney said, strapping herself in.

Karol and Fitzy silently took seats off to the right, and Sidney caught the grim looks on their faces.

She wondered how many times they'd done this already, how many times they'd had to witness something like the devastation that Benediction had experienced last night.

Sayid returned from the cockpit, where he had been speaking with the pilot, Bob.

"Ready?" Langridge asked him.

"Just about," Sayid said, taking his own seat. "Everything okay back here?"

Everyone glanced in his general direction, although no one said a word.

"Bob said we shouldn't be in the air for much more than forty minutes," he continued. "Maybe an hour depending on how bad the storm screws with our approach to Logan." He took a deep breath and looked around at everybody. "Okay then," he said. "Let's get this done."

As if on cue the engines whined to life, filling the compartment with the loud hum of the four propellers, two on either side, spinning so fast that they became nearly invisible.

"Here goes," Rich said, gripping the arms of his seat.

Sidney found herself doing the same, looking to see if Snowy was okay. She seemed nervous, so Sidney reached over and placed a comforting hand upon her broad chest, scratching her thick, white fur.

"That's a good girl," she said, her words nearly drowned out by the deafening din of the plane's engines, but it didn't matter to her Snowy girl, her world was silent anyway.

The transport shuddered and began to move.

This is it, Sidney thought, feeling her heart begin to race. And then it was there in her head again—that wriggling sensation just inside the front of her skull. A wave of nausea flowed over her, and she bent forward in her seat.

"Sid?" she heard Cody yell.

"Stay in your seat," Langridge commanded.

"I'm good," Sidney said. "Little headache is all."

She managed to sit up and offer a reassuring smile to the group.

I'm fine, she mouthed toward Cody and Rich, who stared hard at her, concern on their faces.

The transport rolled slowly toward the runway.

Sidney tried to keep a good face, or at least one that didn't look as though she was about to throw up. But something was wrong; something had riled up whatever was inside her head, and she wished that it would stop.

She could feel Sayid's eyes on her and ignored them. Instead, she reached out to Snowy, hoping that petting her would be enough to distract her from the nauseating sensation, as she imagined a fistful of maggots squirming around at the front of her skull.

The engines became even louder as the transport picked up speed, rolling down the runway toward the sea.

Sidney leaned her head back against the seat and closed her eyes, feeling the vibrations of the plane through the headrest. And suddenly it was as if someone had stabbed her in the center of her forehead. She let out a pained squeak and sat up with a gasp.

"Jesus," she heard Langridge say, just as the plane left the ground—

And the attack began.

The plane started to tremble and shake as it climbed.

It sounded as if the craft was being pelted by rocks.

Langridge looked to Sayid.

"What now?" she bellowed over the engines that had started to sound strained.

Rich had just angled himself in his seat to look out the window when something smashed against it, leaving a bloody smear. "Oh shit," he exclaimed.

Cody had unbuckled himself and was standing up to get a better look out the window.

"Return to your seat!" Langridge screamed, even though she and Sayid had both freed themselves.

"Birds," Sidney heard Cody say. He looked away from the window to stare at them. "We're being attacked by birds."

The plane lurched and fell. Sidney let out a scream as her stomach shot up into her throat. She watched as Cody was thrown up into the air, and then fell awkwardly back into his seat.

"They're going after the propellers," Rich screamed.

Sayid, who had fallen to the floor, was struggling to make his way up the aisle toward the cockpit.

The plane was making a horrible sound now.

Sidney glanced over at Karol and Fitzy, who remained belted into their seats, and saw that they were holding hands. She leaned over and wrapped her arms around Snowy, trying to calm the panicked animal, as well as herself. They were going down—she knew it.

The sound of birds pummeling the aircraft was unlike anything she had ever heard before. She was expecting their feathered bodies to fill the cabin as they punched through the sides of the plane.

Langridge had managed to get back into her seat, but Sayid was still trying to get to the cockpit. "Hold on!" he screamed as he was suddenly flung up toward the ceiling of the craft as if by a great invisible hand, before dropping back down to the floor.

Then the engines quit; the smell of something burning filled the suddenly silent cabin.

And they began to fall.

CHAPTER THIRTEEN

There wasn't much Doc Martin could do at the camp; all of Benediction's animals had gone missing when the storm—and whatever had come with it—took control.

As she walked through the camp, she saw familiar faces among the survivors: the Hennesseys, who had two cats, a Pomeranian, and a cockatiel named Pretty . . . Bob McDowell, who had to put his chocolate Labrador, Sugar, down last June . . . Veronica Preston and her daughter, Lizzy, who had gotten a kitten less than two weeks before.

She acknowledged them as she passed, the looks in their eyes and the injuries to their bodies telling her everything she needed to know.

Doc Martin was tempted to go to them, to say that she was sorry—to explain that it wasn't their pets' fault at all, that something *inhuman* had been controlling the animals.

But she doubted they would want to hear it. The fear was still there, the anger and the physical hurt.

She was down to her last two smokes but fished one out of the crumpled pack anyway. As she lit up, she realized that she was angry too, although she really didn't understand at what.

Something had affected the brains of the animals on Benediction. After listening to all the talk from the scientists who had saved them, she knew it had happened in other places and that it wasn't any kind of accident, no environmental disaster.

No, it was much worse than that. This had been intentional; something not of this world had turned pets into weapons.

There was the source of her rage. That somebody—some . . . *thing*—could take a poor, innocent creature and twist it into something that could commit the most murderous of acts was enough to make *her* want to commit murder herself.

Or at least deliver a substantial beat down.

She puffed on her smoke, gazing about the encampment and wondering how many more casualties there were from yesterday's event. She was sure there had to be more folks holed up in their homes, afraid that it wasn't yet over, afraid to venture back outside.

She remembered the things she'd experienced back at her clinic and shuddered, just as she noticed a little boy approaching her. She didn't remember his name but knew that his family had a greyhound/shepherd mix named Seamus.

"Hey," she said, putting her cigarette down by her side so as not to get smoke in his face. She noticed that he was filthy, and one of his hands was bandaged.

He stood before her and stared with large, brown eyes.

"You doing okay?" she asked him, gesturing to his injured hand.

He looked at the dirty bandage as if noticing it for the first time. "Seamus bit me," he said, looking it over carefully. "He's . . ." The boy hesitated. "He was my dog."

"Yeah, I remember him," Doc Martin said, bringing her cigarette up and taking a quick puff.

The boy tried to bend his bandaged hand and made a pained face. "My dad killed him."

Doc Martin wasn't quite sure how to respond, but the boy went on.

"After he bit me, he was gonna bite me some more so my dad . . ."

Tears started streaming down the boy's face, cutting clean tracks through the dirt that covered his cheeks.

"Yeah," Doc Martin said. "I get it. I think a lot of people here had to do the same thing."

"Why did Seamus hate us?" the little boy asked her, his lips quivering as the tears continued to run from his eyes. "We didn't do nuthin' to him. . . . We loved him."

And Doc Martin felt the anger again, anger at the alien force that had been responsible for the horrors that had befallen her island home and could very well be turning its attention to Boston and God knew where else. She wasn't generally an emotional person, but she just couldn't help herself. She reached out and took the boy into her arms, hugging him close.

"Yeah, he knew you loved him," she told the child, whose

body was now racked with sobs. "But something really bad got into him . . . and it changed him."

"But . . . but we killed him," the boy cried, now holding her as well.

"Yeah, I know," she told him. "And it was terrible, but you guys did what had to be done . . . He wasn't Seamus anymore. And if you hadn't stopped him the way you did, he might've hurt some other people too."

The boy slowly pulled away from her.

"Did the bad thing . . . the thing that changed Seamus," he asked her, "did it get into the other animals too?"

She nodded slowly. "It did."

The boy seemed to think about that for a moment, and then examined his hand once more. "Is it gone now?"

Doc Martin thought of Sidney and the government scientists on their way to Boston. "I hope so," she said, trying to be reassuring as she reached out to give the boy's shoulder a gentle squeeze. She looked up over his head and saw his parents looking at them. They waved at her, and she waved back.

"Think your folks are looking for you," she said, pointing them out.

"Yeah, they probably are," he said, starting in their direction. "Thanks for talking with me and stuff," he said as he walked away.

"Yeah, nice to talk with you, too."

She watched him go, suddenly feeling more concerned for Sidney's safety, and the safety of the world, but there was nothing she could do.

The sound of screaming drifted on the air, stopping people as they walked and turning them in the direction of the horrible sound. Almost immediately Doc Martin recognized it as coming from Isaac, the boy with a developmental disability.

"Isaac?" she called out, starting toward the tent where he had been resting. "Hey, Isaac, you okay in there?"

She passed through the entryway and at first believed the tent to be empty, but then she heard the pathetic moans coming from somewhere in the area of the cot—

Under the cot.

She found Isaac curled tightly into a trembling ball, wedged beneath his sleeping place.

"Hey, Isaac," she said as calmly as she was able, not wanting to startle him. "What's wrong, buddy?"

He shook even more, and he tried to push himself farther under the cot. He was moaning now, a horribly sad and disturbing sound.

"Isaac, what's wrong?" Doc Martin asked more firmly.

"The bad radio," he gasped between pained moans and groans. "The bad radio is still here!"

Doc Martin felt a sudden jolt of fear. The bad radio is what Isaac had called the transmission that had turned the animals into killers. He seemed to be able to somehow pick it up.

"Naw, buddy," she said, approaching the cot and lowering herself carefully to her knees beside it. She knew she would regret it later, but she had to reach the boy. "The bad radio is gone," she said. "The army guys burned it up in the cave, remember?"

She leaned forward to peer under the cot.

"Burned it up in the cave?" he repeated.

"Yeah, you remember that. Why don't you come out from there, and we'll talk about it, okay?"

"The bad radio was burned up in the cave," he said again.

"C'mon," she said, reaching a hand toward him.

Tentatively he took it, and she helped him the best she could to squirm out from his hiding place.

"There ya go, buddy," she said, watching him as he climbed easily to his feet.

"The bad radio was burned up in the cave," he said as if reviewing the information again.

"Yep, it was." She tried to stand but found herself in an awkward situation, her knees having locked. "Hey, Isaac, think you could give me a hand getting up?" She reached up to him.

Isaac just stared at first, but the idea eventually permeated, and he took her hands, helping the older woman to struggle up from the floor of the tent.

"Thanks," she said, grunting as she stood, her knees making muffled popping sounds. "Oh, man . . . getting old."

"Yes," Isaac said to her. "You're very old."

She resisted the urge to crack him one, telling herself that he had issues. And besides, he was right. She was getting old.

"The bad radio was burned up in the cave," he told her again.

"That's right," she assured him. "The army guys went into the caves and found you, Sidney, and the others, and then they burned it to a crisp."

"Sidney went to Boston," he told her. "With Cody, Rich, Snowy,

Dr. Sayid, and Brenda Langridge." He waited for her response, rocking from side to side.

"Yes she did," Doc Martin said. "She had special business there." She reached over and took his arm. "Why don't we go outside and get some fresh air, and maybe a bottle of water."

Isaac resisted, pulling back his arm.

"There's a bad radio in Boston, too," he told her.

"Yeah, there probably is," she agreed. "But Sidney and the others are going to try to stop that one too."

He seemed to think about that for a moment, his hand hovering around his left ear. "The bad radio is in Boston, too," he said.

"Yeah," she told him again. "Let's go get a bottle of water."

"It's here, too," he said firmly, not moving.

"No," she said. "We talked about it, the one here—"

"There's more," he told her, rocking more quickly from side to side. "There's more . . . there's more . . . there's more . . ."

Doc Martin was moving to comfort him when she heard the first gunshot and then the people outside the tent began screaming.

The organism was able to control the two higher life-forms after neutralizing their neural functions.

The first one had been simple—piercing the subject's skull and shutting down most of the brain's higher capabilities. The second had required some effort, and the organism had had to use the first as a vessel to chase the other down and render him . . .

Less complicated.

It was proving a little more difficult to control these two than it had been to control the many lower life-forms during the training exercise; however, the organism managed to move the pair down from the caves, through the woods, and toward the open area where the interlopers had set up a makeshift camp.

The two vessels entered the encampment side by side.

"Hey, where the hell have you two been?" came a sudden, harsh voice.

The organism turned the two toward the sound. A human male stood there.

"Where's the jeep?" he asked. "Don't tell me it broke down."

The vessels did not respond.

"And what the hell is wrong with your eye?" the human asked, pointing with one of his appendages.

The organism allowed one of the vessels to drive its fist into the face of the man, knocking him to the ground.

"Hey! What the hell'd you do that for?" the human screamed, lying in the dirt. The blow had drawn blood.

The second vessel stepped forward and kicked the downed human in the chin, then fell upon the stunned man, wrapping its hands about the man's throat and squeezing.

"What's going on over here?" the organism heard from behind and turned the first vessel to see another human quickly approaching. This one was clothed differently, and in his arms he carried something that the organism recognized from the information it had pulled from the folds of the vessels' gray matter.

An automatic weapon.

The organism propelled the first vessel toward the man.

"Explain yourself, Tyler," the human ordered.

The words were nonsense—inconsequential to the mission—and the vessel struck with absolute fury, hitting the man savagely, stunning him, and ripping the gun from his grasp.

The organism in its inhumanity felt something akin to excitement as it raised the weapon and took aim.

Doc Martin rushed from Isaac's tent as the thunder of the gunshot receded in the air, a roar of disturbing noise before a return to eerie silence.

The events of the previous night had left nothing to make any noise—no birds chirping, no insects buzzing, no dogs barking off in the distance. The island was silent now.

One of the soldiers, a heavily built guy with a buzz cut had fired his weapon, bringing another from Sayid's team to his knees. This one was wearing one of those heavy decontamination suits, its stark white now stained red with blood.

A crowd had gathered and was watching fearfully as Buzz Cut approached the figure on the ground. Doc Martin pushed through the bystanders for a closer look and caught sight of a rifle on the ground beside the man from Sayid's team. Another man in a decontamination suit struggled to break free as more soldiers held him down on the ground.

What the hell is going on around here?

She wasn't sure if the guy on the ground was alive or dead until she saw him twitch on the grass. And wasn't it awfully strange that no one seemed to be getting him any medical attention?

She wanted a cigarette, but she only had one left. Instead she strode forward. "What the hell is going on here?" she asked.

Buzz Cut didn't even turn around, continuing to stand over the man he had shot. "Ma'am, if you would be so kind as to step back—"

"I'll do no such thing," Doc Martin interrupted as she continued forward.

Two more security officers appeared to either side of her and took her arms.

"Are you shitting me?" she exclaimed. "Since when did this become a police state?"

Buzz Cut finally looked at her, and she didn't like what she saw in his face. The guy was clearly worried.

No, afraid.

"You're the vet, right?" he asked, recognizing her. She remembered him now, one of the guys who had saved her in the parking lot of the animal hospital.

"Yeah, what the hell is going on?" she asked again.

Buzz Cut nodded at the two soldiers who held her arms, and they quickly let her go, receding toward the crowd.

"Look at his eye," Buzz Cut said. "Look at his right eye."

The words turned her insides to ice. She didn't want to look, but what choice did she have?

The man was still wearing the headgear of his suit, but she could see that the faceplate had been shattered. His forehead was stained with blood. And then she saw it.

"Shit," the old veterinarian muttered. Just as it had been on the eyes of the dogs and cats that had gone murderously insane at the animal hospital, shiny and metallic and encompassing the entire eye.

"Yeah," Buzz Cut said. "That one too." He pointed to the other member of the science team being held down by four soldiers.

"But I thought it had been taken care of," Doc Martin said aloud, the worry filling her voice.

There was a murmuring commotion behind her, and she saw Buzz Cut begin to raise his weapon. She turned to see Isaac forcing his way toward them, wild-eyed. Quickly she stepped between the young man and the soldier, holding her hands out to slow his approach.

"Slow it down, buddy," she told him, placing her hands flat against his chest as he reached her.

"Is he all right?" Buzz Cut asked, the paranoia already starting to seep into his tone.

"Yeah, he's fine," she said, although she wasn't at all sure that he was. Isaac had stopped and was looking past her, toward the figure lying prone and bleeding upon the ground.

"The bad radio," he said, and lifted a hand to point. "The bad radio was here."

She followed the young man's finger and saw the body on the ground go suddenly rigid, twitch slightly, and then become completely still.

"What happened?" she asked, following Buzz Cut for a closer look.

He didn't answer, but as they leaned down toward the body, Doc Martin noticed that the silvery coating over the man's eye seemed to be decomposing, melting away and running down his face.

"Mr. Burwell?" Another soldier called out to Buzz Cut, and Doc Martin looked up to see that the other man in the decontamination suit had also gone still. She brusquely hipped Burwell aside and knelt beside the body, feeling that cracking sensation in both knees as she did so. She reached down and removed his helmet.

"Careful with that!" Burwell ordered, moving to stop her, but she shrugged him off.

She placed her fingertips on the man's neck, looking for a pulse. There wasn't any.

"He's dead," she said.

"Crap," Burwell said.

"He was probably close to being that way before all this," she said as she moved her finger up to touch the silvery slime running down his cheek. "I'm guessing the other one is dead too."

Burwell turned around. "Is he alive?" he called to his men.

Tentatively the soldiers felt for a pulse. "No pulse," confirmed one.

"What do you think?" Burwell asked Doc Martin as he turned his attention back to her.

"I think that whatever was in control of them has gone," she answered. "Where were these two before here?"

"Velazquez?" Burwell called out.

A short woman with thick horn-rimmed glasses appeared, pushing through the crowd. "Yes, sir?" she said.

"Where were these two supposed to be?"

She pulled a small tablet from the waist of her pants and tapped it. "They were supposed to be collecting specimens from the cave."

"So there you have it," Burwell said. He reached down to grab Doc Martin's elbow as she struggled to her feet.

"Thanks," she said.

"So I guess that thing we burned to a crisp in the cave isn't really dead," he said to her.

"I'm guessing you're probably right, unless there's another one, of course. What are you gonna do now?"

The security officer thought for a moment. "Shit," he said. "Looks like I'm gonna get my flamethrower and head back up into that cave."

Someone laughed behind them, and they turned to find Isaac still standing there, rocking back and forth, one hand up near his bad ear, fingers twitching.

"Isaac, what's wrong?" Doc Martin asked him.

"The bad radio . . . ," he began in a creepy, singsong voice. "The bad radio isn't there anymore. . . ."

"What's he saying?" Burwell asked.

"What do you mean, Isaac? The bad radio isn't there anymore?"

He nodded as he rocked, staring out across the field in the direction of the cliff, as well as the cave.

"No reason to go. It isn't there . . . it left."

Isaac looked at them, and there were tears in his eyes.

"The bad radio isn't in the caves anymore."

CHAPTER **FOURTEEN**

Delilah was six years old again, and the demon dog was gonna get her.

She raced down the corridor, the sounds of the dog's nails clicking on the floor behind her.

Getting closer.

She wanted to turn around, to see how close the horror actually was, but she fought off the need, putting the energy into speeding up, finding someplace safe.

She caught the strains of classical music and realized that Lonnie Jorgenson's room was just up ahead. She pushed herself even faster.

It was just like before, the monster nipping at her heels. She could feel it—the hot breath, the scrape of claws, the nip of teeth as it attempted to grab hold of her.

Delilah was crying now, gasping for air as the music grew

louder. The doorway was before her, welcoming her, telling her to get the hell into the room before the dog bit her . . . tore her, slashed and ripped her. She dove through, grabbing the edge of the door and swinging around to slam it closed.

The beast was indeed closer than she had thought. The heavy door swung shut, hitting the dog's side and pinning it against the doorframe.

Temporarily stunned, it was motionless, gazing at her with lifeless eyes. She found herself staring at its right eye, that strange silvery globe, and thinking about the moon.

Then it started thrashing. Delilah wasn't all that big of a woman, no more than 120 pounds soaking wet, but she knew how to use that weight. She turned herself around and slammed her back against the door, crushing the animal between it and the doorframe.

How odd that she was the one making all the noise over the strains of Mozart. The dog remained silent, even as its body thrashed and its jaws snapped.

From the corner of her right eye, Delilah caught a hint of movement, and too late it dawned on her that Lonnie's bed was empty.

And Lonnie Jorgenson was coming toward her.

Lonnie Jorgenson, whose brain was so damaged that she was unable to take care of herself, to speak, and to wash and feed herself.

To walk.

"Lonnie," Delilah croaked as the woman rushed her, her hands reaching for Delilah's throat.

Survival was all that Delilah could think about, her own animal instincts kicking in to keep her alive. She reached out, swatting

Lonnie's clutching hands away and grabbing her by the front of her pretty, flowered pajamas. She spun the woman around, slamming her back against the door.

"What is happening?" Delilah screamed in frustration, looking into the slack face of the woman who had grown to be her favorite.

And seeing her eye—her silver-coated right eye.

Delilah had to do something, and quickly. As she struggled with Lonnie, the door was moving, and the dog was coming in. Her muscles burned and were beginning to feel more like rubber. She couldn't hold out for much longer.

Suddenly her little boy's face flashed in her mind. He was at home waiting for her, and she had promised him a big-boy bed.

A surge of strength rushed through her. Delilah slammed her forehead into Lonnie's face, stunning her, then pulled the patient toward her, allowing the door to open and the dog to enter.

The dog's claws scrabbled for purchase as it lunged into the room, its mouth wide open, ready to bite.

Forcing herself not to think about what she was doing, Delilah pushed Lonnie backward, where she landed hard on the dog's back. Both collapsed in a heap on the floor.

But they won't be there long, Delilah thought, already on the move.

She leaped over the thrashing bodies of patient and dog as the two struggled to recover enough to resume their attack upon her.

She was running again—so much like the nightmares she'd had for most of her life, running to get away from the monster that was chasing her. For a brief moment she wondered if maybe it was a dream. Maybe she should just allow herself to be caught, and then she'd finally wake up and everything would be fine.

Thunder roared outside, and she could have sworn that the building shook with the onslaught of the storm.

No, this wasn't a dream; this was all too horribly real.

She ran, the dog again in pursuit, this time with Lonnie close behind it. Ahead of her, at the other end of the corridor, she could see patients slowly leaving their rooms—patients who had not walked for weeks, months, and even years.

She took a sharp left, back toward the elevators and some administrative offices, and ran full tilt into Mason's cleaning cart, tipping it over and knocking the wind from her body. For a moment she lay among the rolls of toilet paper and sheets of paper towels strewn across the floor, unable to move—until the dog's blood-covered snout appeared from around the corner.

She scrambled to her feet, only to lose her balance and pitch forward hard onto her hands and knees. *Get up! Get up!* she screamed in her mind as hot tears flowed from her eyes.

A closed office door suddenly opened, and she saw somebody standing there. Delilah let out a scream as the figure reached for her.

"Get in here," the man she recognized as Mr. Deacon, the head of janitorial services, said as he pulled her inside the office and slammed the door shut.

Just as the monster—*monsters*—reached the other side.

CHAPTER FIFTEEN

Sidney didn't know how she'd gotten there—she just was.

Her father was sitting in the center of a circle of explosives, old dynamite that he'd used to use on his job as a contractor to remove stubborn old tree stumps and boulders from properties he was hired to build on.

"Dad?" she said, her voice sounding funky in the garage of their home, a garage that had stored everything but a car for as long as she could remember.

He was playing with the wires of a detonator.

She knew what it was for—and how it would be used—and felt an icy hand reach into her chest and squeeze her heart so very tightly.

He looked up and smiled, and she felt the tightness slip away. She missed that smile.

She missed him.

"What's going on, Dad?" she asked. She herself was sitting on a flipped-over bucket of spackle. She remembered whacking the tops of these with paint stirrers, believing that someday she would be in a rock band.

"Just getting some work done," he said, going back to his wires.

She could hear sounds outside the garage. Scurrying, scratching sounds as something—*lots of somethings*—tried to get in.

"You need to put that down," she ordered him, feeling a surge of panic within her. "You need to put that down and come with me." Sidney stood up and extended her hand.

"Can't, Sid," Dad said, sadness in his tone. "I'm dead."

Sidney remembered how he'd always said that after his stroke. It used to make her so angry.

But something told her—reminded her—that this was different. That maybe he was right this time.

"No," she yelled, pushing those thoughts from her confused mind. "You need to come with me before—"

The sounds on the other side of the garage door grew louder and even more insistent.

Her father continued to ignore her, playing with the wires that ran from his arms to the detonator positioned precariously on his lap.

"I need you," she told him, meaning it to the core of her being.

He looked up and smiled.

"I know that, kid," he assured her, going back to wires. "But you're far more capable than you think."

He'd always told her that with a little hard work she could do whatever she wanted in life. And work hard she did. It was how she'd prepared herself for college and for veterinary school.

Her dad gave that to her . . . the level of confidence that had gotten her so far.

"And I think they know it too," he added.

"They?" she asked, suddenly confused. He was looking up at her again, even though his fingers still worked on the wires of the detonator. "Who's they?"

The sounds of the things outside continued to scratch upon the door, but there was something else now.

"They're afraid of you, Sid," he said, his gaze slowly scanning the crowded garage. "You weren't supposed to happen."

She didn't know what he was talking about, but a nagging sensation, a strange, uncomfortable tickle told her that she should.

A tickle that was gradually becoming something more.

"Ow," she said, reaching up to touch her head.

"They don't know what to do about you," her father continued.

His hands worked all the faster on his task, and Sidney suddenly realized how well the hand affected by the stroke was doing. She felt a surge of hope then; maybe things *would* get better for her father. . . .

"You've got to do something about them before—"

"Who, Dad?" she demanded.

The boxes of tools and discarded furniture rattled as the scratching and pounding on the other side of the garage door intensified.

"Show them how strong you are," he said, looking suddenly fearful.

And then the stuff in the cluttered garage fell away, sucked into the black of nothingness that seemed to exist behind them.

And from within the darkness something watched them.

Something watched *her*.

She couldn't see them, but she knew they were there . . . *felt* that they were there.

Inside her head.

The room continued to shake, more and more of it breaking away to reveal the sucking void of blackness.

She was being assaulted from all sides, and she was on the verge of panic. She wanted to run to her father, take the detonator and wires from him, and pull him from the room.

But again that nagging sensation told her that this had already happened, and an overwhelming sadness spread through her. She had failed.

The garage was disappearing, replaced by nothing—and the things that hid within it.

She knew that these were the *they* her father was talking about, the *they* that were responsible for all this madness and pain.

"You gotta go now," her father said. He was done with the wiring, his finger hovering over the detonator switch.

"But, Dad, I—"

"We've already done this," he interrupted her. "You gotta go out there and do your thing. . . ."

The darkness had eaten up most of the garage, and she could feel their eyes on her.

Did they even have eyes?

"You've got to show them that they're right. . . ."

"I don't understand what—"

"You've got to show them that they're right to fear us . . . to fear *you*."

"Dad," she said, reaching out to touch him one last time.

"Don't," he said, and she saw that bugs were swarming over his body, crawling into his mouth, pulling back the skin to burrow beneath his eyes.

"Dad . . ."

Her father smiled. It was a smile that told her he would be fine . . . a smile that told her that she had things to do and she'd better get going.

"I already know," he said, and pressed the switch on the detonator.

The fiery explosion that followed pushed upon the darkness, driving it back from whence it had come.

But she knew that it would return.

And when it did, she would be waiting.

The darkness had come back, and this time it stank of burning rubber and jet fuel.

Sidney slowly fought through the inky black, pulling herself up toward the light.

"Is everybody . . . is everybody all right?" somebody asked as she fought to open her eyes.

Something sticky was keeping them closed, and when she moved her hand to rub it away, she sensed that something was very wrong. It took her a moment to figure it out, but finally she realized that she was hanging upside down.

The smell of spilled fuel made her gag, and she coughed as she struggled with reality. She could hear Snowy's cries from somewhere close by, followed by her bark.

At last she managed to focus, and her eyes fell on Snowy staring up from what used to be the ceiling of the aircraft but was now the floor. She fiddled with the buckle on the seat belt until it came undone, and she dropped like a stone to the new floor.

Snowy was there at once, claws clicking upon the rounded metal, as she crazily kissed and nuzzled Sidney.

"It's okay, girl," Sidney said, still trying to pull it all together.

Their plane had crashed. The cabin was filled with smoke that seemed to be getting thicker.

"Hello?" she cried out.

"Sid?" It sounded like Rich.

"Hey! You okay?"

"Freakin' great." Yep, it was Rich.

"I can't see much in this smoke. Make some noise, and I'll try to follow it to you."

"Ms. Moore?"

Sidney recognized Sayid's voice right away, and he appeared before her out of the thick, noxious fumes, a handkerchief pressed to his mouth and nose.

"Everybody all right?" Langridge bellowed.

"I've got Sidney!" Sayid called, reaching out to lead Sidney and Snowy toward Langridge's voice. "We're heading to you!"

Carefully they navigated through the smoke and equipment strewn across the ceiling of the craft and met up with Langridge. She was kneeling beside someone lying at a weird angle, and Sidney realized it was Fitzy.

"Oh my God," she said, fearing the worst. "Is he all right?"

"No," Langridge replied in her usual matter-of-fact way. "He's not. Looks like his neck is broken."

"C'mon! Everybody up front!" someone called out from somewhere farther forward.

Sayid moved to get Fitzy's body, but Langridge reached out and pulled him back.

"There's no time for that," she said. "The whole plane could blow any minute."

Sayid hesitated, then pushed forward. They didn't have to go far before they could feel a rush of air and the smoke seemed to thin. They found themselves at a huge break in the craft's fuselage, Rich, Cody, Karol, and Bob standing just outside.

"Hurry up!" Bob urged, motioning with his hands, the smell of jet fuel suddenly very strong.

"Where's Fitzy?" Karol asked. She was cradling her left arm with her right.

"Didn't make it," Langridge said with little circumstance. It was just how it was, and that was that.

Sidney watched Karol's expression go slack; then she slowly turned and walked away from the group, beyond the break in the plane, farther out onto the tarmac.

"What the hell happened?" Langridge asked as they reached the pilot.

"Birds," the man said. "I've never seen so many . . . and so many kinds. They threw themselves into the props and stalled the engines. I tried to bring us in as gently as I could but . . ."

The scream was short, but bloodcurdling.

Sidney was already looking straight ahead as the others turned toward the sound of terror.

The birds that had brought the plane down had descended upon the injured Karol in a silent, voracious cloud. They swarmed around her, a vortex of talons, feathers, and beaks.

She tried to run back toward the cover of the downed plane, but the attack was too quick.

Too relentless.

The poor woman was reduced to a tattered and bloody mass that crumpled to the ground, already dead by the looks of her.

"Get in here, now!" Langridge screamed, pulling Bob in first, as Rich and Cody joined them inside the smoke-filled fuselage.

"We can't stay in here," Bob said. "It's only a matter of time before that spilled fuel ignites and—"

"Yeah, I get it," Langridge interrupted. "How far down the runway do you think we are?" she asked Bob.

"I was turning around when I lost everything, I'd say about a quarter of the way down, so three quarters to any cover."

Snowy was whining, her eyes riveted to the break in the plane and what might be lurking beyond.

Rich remained closest to the break, trying to see more outside. "I thought it was over," he said as clusters of smaller birds darted past. "I thought when we killed that thing . . ."

"Maybe there was more than one," Sayid said. "I don't know."

Sidney felt that presence in her head again, a dirty feeling she would have given anything to be free of.

"There's something still here," she said, holding Snowy tightly. "And it doesn't want anybody to leave."

They all looked at her, and she just shrugged.

"All right," Langridge said. "We don't have much time before one of two things happens—one, the plane explodes, or two, those birds find their way past the smoke and say hi." She paused. "We've got to get to the hangar. We should be safe there, and then we can figure out what we're going to do."

"The only way we can get there is to run," Sayid said. "We'll need some kind of cover to protect us." He crawled back through the wreckage of the fuselage and disappeared in the smoke.

It was as if the birds outside had heard him thinking aloud; they dove down at the plane, slamming their fragile forms against it.

"I think they've figured out that the crash didn't kill all of us," Langridge said. "What have you got, Doc?" she yelled. "The clock is ticking."

"What about the others?" Sidney suddenly blurted out.

Langridge looked at her, and by the expression on her face Sidney could tell that she'd already thought of the very same thing.

"Can't worry about that right now," the head of security said. "Sayid, c'mon!" she yelled, just as the scientist emerged from the smoke, coughing, eyes fiercely watering, his arms filled with . . .

"Rain ponchos?" Langridge said. "Sorry, Doc, but this storm has razor-sharp beaks and talons."

"If we keep moving and watch each others' backs, these should do a pretty good job at protecting us. The surface is slick," he explained. "It'll be harder for their talons to take hold. I've got these too—to protect our faces." He held out plastic visors used by surgeons to protect from spatter.

Langridge ran her fingers over the slick, green surface of the poncho. "This is the best you got?"

"At least it's something," Bob said, grabbing a poncho and visor.

Everybody followed suit, slipping the ponchos over their heads and slapping the visors on their faces. Sidney grabbed the last one and wrapped it around Snowy, adjusting it so as not to interfere with the dog's movement.

"Okay," Langridge said, smoothing the front of her poncho down as she slid the visor on over her hooded head. "We stay together, help each other when you can."

"You have no idea what it's like," Cody said suddenly.

Sidney could see the haunted look in his eyes and knew he was thinking of his father.

Killed by birds.

"You had your guns and your flamethrowers," he said. "But you don't have any of that now."

"Which is why we play this smart," Langridge said. "We move fast, and we look out for one another."

Cody nodded, but Sidney could see that he was unconvinced.

"It'll be okay, Cody," she said, gently touching his arm through the thick plastic.

Rich came up on Cody's other side, nodding in agreement, but his face said something very different.

"I'll take point," Langridge said, moving past them to the break in the plane.

One after the other they followed her, the sounds of birds' bodies crashing into the skin of the fuselage like a rain of rocks.

CHAPTER SIXTEEN

The encampment was being moved inside the high school. After the incident with the two scientists and hearing Isaac's chilling words, Burwell and his team had decided it would be safer to move the operation into the main building rather than remain outside on the soccer field.

Doc Martin did what she could to help, all the while keeping an eye on Isaac. This new bad radio was clearly taking its toll upon him.

The little boy whom she'd hugged earlier walked by with his folks and gave her a friendly wave. She could see the look of concern on the parents' faces and mouthed, *It'll be okay*, as they passed. But as the survivors filed past her into the school, she found herself also watching other areas around them—the shadowy corners, the sky. She'd believed that most of the animal and insect life on the island had died when the alien life-form was destroyed.

But now there was a new wrinkle, and she wondered if any had actually survived, only to be under the influence of this new force.

This new bad radio.

"I'm stationing men around the perimeter," somebody said, and she looked to see Burwell standing near her at the bottom of the school steps. He was looking out over the property as well, as survivors continued to straggle up from the soccer field. "So another one of those things," he said, sounding as though he was trying to convince himself that it was true.

"According to Isaac, yeah," Doc Martin said.

"Do you think he's right? Can we trust him?" he asked. "He doesn't seem all that right in the head."

Doc Martin glared at the man. "Can you trust what you saw with those two men?"

Burwell made a face. "If there's another one of those things on the island, we can't just stand around with our thumbs up our butts waiting to see what it does."

Doc Martin continued to search for signs that something might be amiss. She even found herself watching the residents for symptoms of anything . . . abnormal.

"What are you suggesting?" she asked Burwell.

"I'm thinking we put a small team together and head out there to find it."

"Easier said than done," Doc Martin said. "Isaac said it left the cave. You have no idea where to even begin. Benediction may be a small island, but we've got lots of nooks and crannies where things can easily hide."

Burwell remained silent, continuing to scan the horizon.

Doc Martin wanted a cigarette very badly, then remembered she only had the one. Better to save it for an emergency.

"He seems to have some kind of connection to it," the security officer said finally.

"Yeah," she said, turning to face Burwell directly. "Not sure how or why . . . could be something to do with an injury he had as a child, but I really don't have a clue."

Burwell looked at her. "But he does hear it somehow?"

"Yeah, he does," she said slowly, wanting that cigarette all the more.

"I'm thinking of taking him with me," Burwell said.

"Not on your life," Doc Martin growled. "The kid has already been through enough and managed to survive. I'm not about to let you risk him getting hurt."

"That's not your decision. It's his," Burwell said, turning to head into the school.

Without a word Doc Martin followed, her eyes shooting death beams into the back of the man's head.

Isaac sat alone in a corner of the gymnasium listening to the distant call of the bad radio.

He wanted to be as far away as he could from the people of Benediction, afraid that the bad radio would make him try to hurt them.

As if on cue, the bad radio was suddenly stronger, blaring inside his head, filling both his ears—not just the Steve ear—with a buzzing static like a thousand bees trapped between a screen and a window. The sound made his legs and arms twitch.

He let out a little cry as he flopped upon his cot and had to wonder if people were looking at him. It didn't really matter. He was used to people watching him. His mother said it was because he was different.

His mother, lost to the events of the previous night, that thought filled him with incredible sadness. So much had changed in such a short period of time. Isaac wished it could be back to the way it was, only cleaner and less cluttered, recalling the condition of the home that he'd lived in, the only oasis of order being his ultra-neat room.

He missed his room the most—and his mother. She was a good person.

Was a good person.

He remembered what the cats had done to her, and the bad radio became even louder.

More insistent.

It made him angry . . . made him want to lash out. To hurt.

That was what the bad radio did.

But suddenly he realized there was something else . . . a different sound . . . a different signal. Not just trying to fill him with anger so that he would hurt someone. This sound . . . this signal was different. This was trying to speak to him.

Reaching out to him—

And him alone.

As if trying to say hello.

———

"Isaac," Doc Martin called as she and Burwell approached the young man sitting on a cot in the far corner of the gymnasium, away from the other survivors.

Isaac did not look up. His hands covered his ears, and he was rocking back and forth.

"Hey, Isaac?" she said, standing directly in front of him.

He still didn't answer, continuing to rock.

"Isaac, are you hearing it now?" Burwell asked, coming forward as well. "Are you hearing the alien receiver?"

"The bad radio," Doc Martin corrected.

"What?"

"He calls the signal the bad radio," she explained.

Isaac was rocking faster now and had started to hum.

"What the hell is wrong with him?" Burwell asked. "Is this because of the bad radio business, or is he just crazy?"

Doc Martin spun on the man. "Don't you dare," she said with a ferocious snarl. "After what the poor kid's been through I'm surprised he's doing this well."

Burwell ignored her outburst and continued to stare at the young man. "I need to know if he can help . . . if he'll help."

"I'd say the answer to that is . . . ," Doc Martin began, but didn't get the chance to finish.

"You want help?" Isaac suddenly asked. He was still rocking, hands still over his ears.

Burwell glared at Doc Martin, then pushed past her to squat in front of Isaac.

"Yes, Isaac," he said. "We have to find the bad radio." He paused, waiting for a response, but Isaac just continued to rock.

"We can't let another bad radio do what the first one did here on the island," Burwell continued. "Do you see all these people here?" He gestured toward the others in the gymnasium, although Isaac didn't look up.

"All these people are going to be in real danger if we don't do something to stop the new bad radio."

"It's not where it was anymore," Isaac said.

"So that means that I need to find it," Burwell said. "And I think you might be able to help me."

Doc Martin jumped in. "Isaac, you don't have to do anything that you—"

"Can you find it, Isaac?" Burwell spoke over her. "Can you help me find the bad radio so I can destroy it, and keep everyone on the island safe?"

"Isaac, don't listen to him," Doc Martin said. "You can stay right here and—"

"Yes," Isaac said. He stopped rocking and lowered his right hand. His left continued to hover around his ear, as if considering adjusting the hearing aid there.

"Yes, I think I could help you find the bad radio."

CHAPTER **SEVENTEEN**

Delilah's legs were shaking so badly that she couldn't stand and simply dropped to her knees in the office.

"You okay?" Deacon asked.

It was the first time she'd ever actually spoken to him, and she was surprised by how low and deep his voice was.

"Yeah, I'm good."

She looked around the office. Phil, Mallory, and Mason were there, as were two other women that she didn't recognize.

"What the hell is going on?" she asked as she climbed to her feet.

"Everything's gone crazy," Mason said nervously. "The patients got out of bed and . . ." His voice trailed off, and he turned away to stare out of windows noisily pattered by rain.

Delilah looked to Mallory. The woman appeared haggard, her hair wild, her hands and arms covered in deep scratches.

She shook her head slowly, her gaze not focused on anything in particular. "It shouldn't be possible," she said. "But they . . . they just started getting up."

"Where's everybody else?" Delilah asked before thinking about what the answer might be.

Phil looked to Mallory, and then shrugged. "It got crazy so fast . . ."

His eyes filled up, and he waved his hands in front of his face as if to calm down.

"Does anybody else see how insane this all is?" asked one of the women whom Delilah didn't recognize. She wasn't wearing scrubs or a housekeeping uniform, so Delilah assumed she was a secretary of some kind. There was panic in her voice.

"Let's everybody just stay calm," Deacon said, his low voice strangely calming. "Somebody is bound to realize that we're not around and—"

"They could all be dead," Mallory said.

Deacon glared at her.

"You saw them," Mallory went on. "There was only one thing on their brain-damaged minds, and that was throttling the life out of us."

Deacon rubbed his neck, and Delilah wasn't sure, but she thought there might be some bruising on his throat.

The other woman went to the desk and picked up the phone, holding the receiver to her ear. "Still nothing," she said, randomly pushing buttons on the body of the phone.

"Storm's knocked everything out," Deacon said.

Something heavy bumped against the door, making them all jump.

Deacon brought a thick finger to his lips, staring at the door. There were a few more thumps, and then nothing. They remained quiet for a few moments, the sounds of the storm outside seeming to grow louder in the silence.

"Do you think it's the storm?" Delilah finally asked no one in particular.

"What are you talking about?" Mallory questioned.

"The reason why this is happening . . . with the patients . . . Could the storm somehow . . . ?"

"Hey, there's a police car out there!" Mason exclaimed. He was still standing by the window but had moved closer, practically pushing his face against the glass.

They all ran to the window, jamming into the space so they could see too. Delilah was smaller and managed to find an area right beside Mason, who had his hands pressed to the glass. The window looked out on the front of the hospital, and, sure enough, a cruiser had just turned the corner and was heading toward the entrance.

Delilah squinted through the rain-spattered window. Something seemed to be wrong—the car seemed to be moving erratically. "Why are they driving that way?"

"What way?" Mason asked. "There's nothing . . ."

The police cruiser suddenly veered off the road and struck a light post, sending the metal pole crashing down on top of it.

There was a collective gasp from the small group as everyone tried to squeeze closer to the window for a better view.

The front doors of the cruiser opened, and two officers tumbled out, the driver falling to the ground. The second officer, holding his arm as if injured, ran to the driver, pulling him up from the rain-swept street.

"What the hell is that?" Phil said, tapping the glass with a fingernail.

At first Delilah couldn't see it, and then her mind mistook it for a piece of wind driven debris. But as she pressed her forehead harder against the cold glass, she realized that she was looking at a small black dog.

"What the hell?" Deacon grumbled, as more animals appeared, all coming from the same direction as the cruiser had.

Delilah felt her heart begin to race. Even this far away they terrified her.

The police must have heard them and turned toward the pack.

That was what they were—a pack of dogs of every conceivable size, shape, and color. Delilah had never seen anything like it. It was as if they were moving as one entity—as if the pack were one giant, running animal with many legs.

Converging on the police officers.

The two tried to run, but they were clearly hurt, the officer with the injured arm having a hard time moving the driver along. After a short distance they stopped and drew their guns, firing on the pack of dogs, each shot sounding like a mini clap of thunder. They seemed to have hit several of the animals, but it wasn't enough.

Delilah wanted to look away as the officers began to run again, but the fear held her tightly and whispered in her ear, *This is why you're afraid.*

The pack swarmed upon them. There were two or three more pops of gunfire, but then it was over.

The police officers were done.

Finally Delilah was able to push herself away from the window.

Something was very, very wrong. Not just here at Elysium, but in the city itself.

The others slowly drifted away from the rain-spattered glass, expressions of shock on their pale faces.

"I've never seen dogs move like that," Deacon said, shaking his head, clearly trying to wrap his brain around what he'd just observed.

"You just seen them," Mason exclaimed. "You just seen dogs move exactly like that."

"Yeah," Deacon said. "But it isn't right."

"They should never have left their car," one of the secretaries said on the verge of tears. She found her way to the chair behind the desk and carefully sat down. "If they'd stayed in the car . . ."

"What the hell is going on out there?" Phil asked. He was looking at his phone, searching for some answers. "Piece of shit phone," he grumbled, but still held on to the device like a lifeline.

They were all quiet again, the tension within the confined space growing by the second.

"What are we going to do?" the other secretary asked. "We can't just stay here like this; we have to . . ."

"We have to get out of here," Delilah said firmly, turning herself toward the door, thinking of her mother and her son back at the apartment. Whatever was happening here was very likely happening there, and she needed to be with them.

CHAPTER **EIGHTEEN**

It was like some heavy-metal-video version of hell—the sky filled with billowing black smoke and birds.

"All right, people, let's move!" Langridge yelled, leading the way out of the relative safety of the cracked fuselage.

Once outside Sidney chanced a quick look back at the twisted wreckage of the plane and gasped. She couldn't believe that any of them had survived, feeling a momentary pang of guilt at the thought of Fitzy and Karol.

"Move! Move!" Langridge ordered, and Sidney turned her focus to the airport hangars near the end of the runway.

"Stay together!" the security officer continued as they moved quickly in a group away from the plane.

Things were actually going well, and they seemed to be making progress, the smoke from the burning fuel providing some semblance of cover from the swirling mass of death above them.

Until the plane exploded.

The blast was deafening, the shock wave so strong that it threw the group to the tarmac. Snowy was the first to her feet, running to Sidney, licking her face to be sure she was fine, then trotting to the others, sniffing and nudging each as if to say *Get moving*.

Sidney managed to push herself to her knees, then slowly stood, swaying dizzily, waiting for the high-pitched whine in her head to fade as she faced the burning wreckage.

And that was when she knew they were in trouble.

"Run," she said . . . and then screamed, turning toward the others and waving her arms. They didn't seem to understand at first, but then Sidney saw the expressions of terror spread across their faces as they all started to run.

The air was filled with burning birds, set afire by the blast. And although their wings were aflame, they were heading directly for the small group on the tarmac.

Snowy was faster than all of them, running ahead and then stopping to watch them reach her before setting off again. To Sidney it felt like a weird dream, one where she was running and running but never seeming to get any closer to her destination.

And then Langridge went down in front of them. Sidney wasn't sure what had happened, but they all stopped to help, which was the worst thing they could have done.

"Keep going!" Langridge screamed, frantically waving her arms as Cody tried to help her up.

But it was too late.

The birds were upon them.

The cloud of living, fluttering, flying things descended on them, the only sounds being the flapping of their wings. Fewer were burning, but all were trying to kill them.

Sayid's idea of the rain ponchos and face masks had been a good one, but the protection was short-lived as razor-sharp talons sliced through the thick plastic.

Langridge was up, limping forward, and they were once again fighting their way through the cyclone of beaks and feathers. Their progress was slow, with Sayid, Langridge, and Snowy in the lead, Cody and Rich close behind them, and Sidney and Bob bringing up the rear. Snowy was barking crazily, darting back and forth, snapping at the birds, literally pulling them from the air. She gave them a violent shake before dropping them on the tarmac and going after the next.

Suddenly Sidney realized that Bob was no longer beside her.

"We've lost Bob!" she screamed over the pounding wings, stopping to look back, flailing her arms and swatting aside sparrows and robins that dove to attack her.

She caught sight of Bob, not too far back, and surged toward him. So many birds swirled around her that it was nearly impossible to see. Sharp beaks pecked at the flesh of her hands, but she fought them, not about to let them have the satisfaction of slowing her down.

There was a brief break in the maelstrom, and she could see Bob standing just ahead of her, his arms hanging at his side, his back to her. "Bob!" she screamed, but he didn't move. Birds fell upon him, and as she drew closer, she could see the blood running over the dark plastic of his poncho.

"Bob, we gotta move," Sidney cried, reaching for the man's shoulder even as a blue jay picked mercilessly at her outstretched hand. She spun him around, promising to be his guide through the storm. . . .

A gull was perched on his chest. It had managed to get underneath the face mask and was savagely dismantling Bob's face. His eyes were gone, nothing more than dark, sucking holes into which the gore-covered bird plunged its needle-sharp beak.

"Oh God," Sidney gasped as his body finally fell to the pavement. She leaped back, nearly tripping over Snowy, who had come to her side. "C'mon, girl, go!" she screamed, waving her arms, but the dog would not leave without her, and she was having a hard time moving forward.

Her visor was covered with a mixture of blood and bird droppings. Birds continued to peck at her hands and arms as she frantically tried to wave them off. Then something hit her from behind, like a basketball thrown as hard as possible, and she went down, the wind knocked from her lungs. Kneeling upon the tarmac, trying to catch her breath again, she turned to see an owl sitting near her, its wing broken, its huge, silver-covered right eye watching her.

"Yeah, screw you, too!" she said with a snarl as the owl hobbled toward her.

And that was when Bob fell upon her, driving her to her stomach. She struggled beneath him, managing to turn herself over.

His right eye had been replaced with a wet, silvery copy that pulsed with a life all its own, zeroing in on her as she pried at his bloody hands, now closed around her throat.

Faithful Snowy was suddenly there again, plowing into Bob and knocking him from atop her. The dog was enraged, wildly biting at Bob's (*can he even be called Bob anymore*) neck and arms.

The flock of birds was growing heavier, choking in their numbers, and Sidney knew they had to move or die. She climbed to her feet, swatting birds aside as they continued to swarm her, then reached out and yanked on Snowy's tail. The shepherd spun, the white fur around her mouth stained red with blood. Sidney felt a momentary twinge of fear then quickly gestured for the dog to follow her.

Together they fought their way through the storm of wings, their ponchos nearly in tatters. Sidney hoped they were going in the right direction but couldn't be sure—even Snowy seemed confused. She couldn't help but wonder what had happened to the others and why only Snowy had come to her rescue, and then she heard the sound, just below the flapping of wings.

It was a growling sound and getting louder. Sidney moved toward it, holding on to Snowy's poncho and steering the dog along beside her. There was no mistaking the sound of a revving motor and the blare of a horn.

It was as if the birds knew she might be saved and were making one last-ditch effort to get her. They hit her from all sides, trying to fly up under her poncho, through her mask, but she fought them until she felt herself begin to falter.

"Sidney!" screamed a voice that she recognized at once as Cody's.

She tried to cry out, but a gull came down at her visor, smashing into it full force and knocking her backward to the ground. She looked up into a sky filled with swirling bodies that seemed to grow thicker by the moment.

So thick that soon there was nothing but the pounding of wings around her, inside her head.

And then—nothing.

CHAPTER NINETEEN

The coffee was bad and made her want a cigarette even more.

Doc Martin's hand shot to the pocket of her smock and stopped. She still only had the one left. Was this enough of an emergency to smoke it? Part of her said yes, while the rest of her said not yet.

She'd been sitting in the school cafeteria, watching the activity outside through the windows. The soldiers were still on alert, patrolling the area with their big bad guns.

Doc Martin scoffed at that. Fat lot of good an M16 would do against a swarm of wasps controlled by an alien intelligence. But she didn't want to tell them that—why spoil their day?

She got up and walked to the door and out into the afternoon sunshine. There was a freshness in the air, something that could only be experienced after a really bad storm. It was like a rebirth of some kind. Not good or bad, just something new.

Burwell was loading the back of an SUV with the equipment they'd need for their little quest. Velazquez was helping him.

Doc Martin looked around for Isaac but didn't see him anywhere. Maybe the kid had gotten cold feet, she hoped, but knew it wasn't likely.

Maybe *she* would get cold feet.

She grunted in response to her thoughts as she approached the soldiers. That wasn't likely to happen either.

Burwell placed a metal box in the back of the vehicle.

"Doc." He acknowledged her approach.

"Hey," she responded.

"Can I help you with . . . ?"

"I'm going with you," she said, already regretting the words as they spilled from her mouth.

"I don't think that would be wise," Burwell said, continuing to pack. "I'm already babysitting one civilian, we add another and it becomes even more complicated."

"I see your point, but I think I could be helpful," she said, looking out across the school grounds.

Burwell said nothing.

"Isaac is a little . . . different," she continued. "I think I can help you understand his quirks. I've also lived on this island for my whole life, and I know it like the back of my hand."

Burwell paused in his packing. "It's still a bad idea," he said.

Doc Martin nodded slowly. "Truthfully? I agree, but somebody needs to keep an eye on Isaac, and that job seems to have fallen to me with Sidney gone."

Burwell finished loading the back and closed the hatch with loud finality.

"Can you shoot a gun?" he then asked.

"It's been a while, but I'm sure it's like riding a bike."

Images of the insects swarming into her car, biting and stinging her, filled her head. The only reason she could think that a gun would be useful in a situation like that would be if she decided to use it on herself.

"We're leaving now. Are you ready?"

"As ready as I'm gonna be," she said.

Burwell looked around. "Now we just need the man of the hour. Any idea where . . ."

Doc Martin looked around as well. "I'll go get him, and we can get this shindig on the road."

In the darkness of the closet, Isaac listened.

The bad radio was there, fading in and out, but there was something else, too.

It was like trying to hear a soft piece of music over the roar of the ocean. It was most definitely there, but so very faint.

Isaac knelt among the mops and cleaning supplies, rocking back and forth, thinking about what he had agreed to do, and wondering if he should.

He could feel the bad radio all around him, feel its pull as it tried to get inside his skull and make him do the unthinkable.

For now, he was stronger and could resist its call, but if he was to let his guard down, the bad radio would pull him toward it.

He had let it happen before when he'd gone to the cave in the cliff.

The memory made him rock all the faster. It was Sidney who had saved him.

The thought of his neighbor brought a fleeting smile to his face. He very much liked the blond-haired girl who always seemed to know what to do. The smile left him then, and he let out a sad moan as he thought of the girl going off with the others.

Boston, he thought. They were going to Boston, where another bad radio was up to no good.

Isaac felt the fingers of the island's new bad radio tickle the inside of his skull.

Something moved in the faint strip of light coming under the door, and he gasped.

Ants. A line of ants marching directly toward him.

He was about to jump to his feet and run from his quiet place when he realized they had stopped moving toward him and were instead walking round and round in a circle.

And then they stopped—and then they were watching him.

Something that might have been a greeting—a hello—came from very far away beneath the roar of the bad radio.

"Isaac?" a voice called softly, followed by multiple raps upon the wooden closet door. "Are you in there?"

The animal doctor, Isaac thought, startled by the noise. He remembered how she used to go to the house to give the cats their shots. She had been very kind to his mother, and to the cats.

And to him. She was kind to him now.

"Yes," he said, looking back at the ants but finding they had gone, scurrying back into the dark.

Doc Martin opened the door and stuck her head in. "Are you okay?"

"Yes," he answered as he climbed to his feet, trying not to knock anything over.

"What are you doing?"

"Thinking," he said.

"Are you having second thoughts about going out there with Burwell, because if you are, we can tell him right now that you're not interested and—"

"No," Isaac told her. "I'm still going."

The bad radio seemed to get even louder then, and that other sound . . . the voice that he could barely make out . . .

He could have sworn it said . . . *Come.*

CHAPTER **TWENTY**

Delilah looked at the pictures of her son on her phone.

She wanted to hold him, to hug him tightly and kiss his usually filthy face, telling him over and over that she loved him with all her heart and soul.

And if she couldn't have that, to at least be able to speak to him over the phone, but that had been denied her as well.

"Dr. Majib is going to be furious about this," one of the Nancys said, shaking her head in disapproval. They'd found out that both the secretaries were named Nancy.

Deacon had removed a center drawer from the heavy wooden desk and was breaking it up into pieces to make weapons, something that Dr. Majib's secretary did not approve of in the least.

"Dr. Majib will understand," Deacon said as he snapped the sides of the drawer and held the piece of wood tightly in his hand

and gave it shake. "We need to protect ourselves. And if that means we have to damage some of the doctor's property, well, then that's just the way it's got to be."

Nancy did not look in the least bit pleased, glaring at Deacon, but she kept her mouth closed.

They'd decided to make an attempt to leave the office and head for the parking garage, where they would retrieve their cars and escape.

Delilah looked at the pictures of her son again, telling him that she would see him soon and that she loved him, before slipping the phone back into her pocket.

Mason was going through the other desk drawers looking for things that might help them. Phil had found a letter opener and held it out before him, staring at the silver blade.

"I guess I'll take this," the nurse said.

Mallory walked over to him. "You're going to actually stab somebody with that?" she asked. "One of our patients comes at you and you're going to stab them, is that what you're saying, Phil?"

"I don't know," Phil admitted. "But I need *some* protection."

Mason laughed out loud. "He'll use it if he has to," he said, picking up a pair of scissors and staring at the twin blades. "If it comes down to me or somebody else? I know who I'm picking."

Delilah felt a sudden chill run down her spine as the realization of what they were doing truly sank in. They were planning a defense against . . . *what exactly*?

It was all so crazy, and she was having a difficult time wrapping her brain around it. She glanced out the window at the view of a frightening world. It wasn't just inside here—inside the hospital—that things were different. Out there the world looked different as well. Smoke seemed to be rising up from several nearby buildings, but she heard no sirens, no wails from fire engines.

And there wasn't any traffic.

Even in the worst of weather conditions, there was always traffic in Boston.

Delilah moved away from the window, ready to act.

Deacon had broken up the drawer and used some Scotch tape from the desk to fasten a stapler to the end of the wood. The head of maintenance swung his makeshift club. "It needed some weight," he said, catching Delilah's inquisitive look. "It'll do more damage now."

"May I?" she asked him, pointing to the remaining pieces of the drawer.

"Sure."

She hefted the wood, and her eyes fell on Dr. Majib's metal nameplate.

"Can I have the tape?" she asked Deacon as she reached for the nameplate. She began to tape it to the flat piece of wood as Dr. Majib's secretary silently shook her head.

"So what's the plan?" Delilah asked, making sure that the tape was tight.

Deacon looked at the door. "Well, it ain't much, but it's all we have. Basically, we open the door, head out into the hall, and hope that nothing tries to kill us."

"And if something does?" Mallory asked.

"Then we defend ourselves," Deacon said firmly.

The unit manager folded her arms defiantly. "They're my patients. I can't even begin to think about hurting them," she said.

"Not even when they're trying to hurt you?" Deacon asked.

"There's something wrong with them," she argued.

"Yes," Deacon agreed, nodding fiercely. "Something wrong that makes them want to kill us." He pulled his shirt collar down to show off the bruising on the dark skin of his neck. "And I have no intention of letting them do that to me."

"We could lose our licenses, or worse!"

"A license will do you no good if you're dead," Deacon said with a disgusted shake of his head, muttering beneath his breath as he approached the closed office door.

Delilah realized that she was holding her breath, gripping her weapon tightly while she watched him lean his ear toward the door and listen. "Do you hear anything?" she asked, forcing herself to breathe again.

He held up a finger, cocked his head for a moment. "I think it's clear," he said as softly as his deep voice would allow. "Are we ready?"

Delilah turned to look at the others. They appeared tense but ready to move. She looked back to Deacon, locking eyes with the man and nodding slightly.

"We'll head out into the hallway as quietly as we can," he started, turning the knob. "Take a right, and we'll—"

He pulled open the door to reveal the dog standing there.

"Shit!" Deacon yelled, and Delilah let out a little scream as the man attempted to close the door again.

But the dog moved in a flash, slamming its muscular body into the door, causing Deacon to stumble back, tripping over his own feet and falling to the floor.

The dog was on him, its open jaws snapping for his throat, but the man managed to jam his forearm into the animal's mouth, crying out as its jaws clamped down on his arm.

Delilah resisted the urge to run, forcing back her panic as Deacon's scream echoed through the office. The crazy part of her that she'd tried to keep under control since her teenage years surged forward, and she found herself running toward the conflict instead of away, raising her homemade club and bringing it down with all the force she could muster upon the dog's blocky, orange-furred head.

The weighted end connected with a sickening *thunk*, sliding off the furred skull, leaving a nasty bleeding gash in its wake. The dog did not make a sound; instead it released Deacon's arm and turned its horrible gaze on her.

The dog tensed, and she could see that it was ready to spring, the others behind her screaming for her to watch out. She was raising her weapon again when Deacon sprang up from the floor and wrapped his powerful arms around the animal's neck, dragging it back.

The dog struggled in the maintenance man's grasp, and he was having a hard time holding on to the animal. One of the Nancys had started to scream, while everybody else had retreated as far behind the desk as they could. Delilah was tempted to join them, fear like a living thing attempting to take possession of her limbs.

But she fought it down, struggling to push it aside, so she could help the man who had saved her.

Once again she swung her club with all her might and felt the satisfying thud as it connected with the dog's side.

The animal didn't make a sound—no growling, no yelping in pain. Silent.

It was wrong on so many levels.

"Delilah, get back with the others!" Deacon screamed as he tried to force the animal onto its side on the carpeted floor, but it continued to thrash, its clawed paws raking the man's exposed skin.

There was blood, quite a bit of it, but she couldn't be sure who or what it belonged to. Delilah didn't listen to the man as he continued to struggle, moving closer to smash the club down again and again upon the animal's body.

"Delilah!"

She turned at the sound of her name and saw Phil stepping out from behind the desk. He held up the letter opener he had claimed as a weapon earlier, then tossed it toward her. It landed at her feet as he dove back behind the cover of the desk.

Delilah snatched up the silver opener, and, holding it like a dagger, moved closer to the struggle. Deacon was tiring, losing his hold on the dog as it twisted its body for the kill.

She couldn't let that happen. She stomped down her fear and acted, plunging the point of the letter opener deep into the dog's neck.

The dog reared back, turning its attention from Deacon to her. It threw its full weight at Delilah, and she cried out in panic as she fell backward, the animal atop her. The stink of its breath was awful, and suddenly she was back at the park again—only this time the dog had caught her.

The monster had her.

But she wasn't a scared little girl anymore. People depended on her now; Izzy depended on her. The sudden thought of her son spurred her to action, and she lashed out with the letter opener, plunging the blade into the dog's neck again. The force behind her strike was powerful, driven by her fear, and the blade sank in deep.

Delilah held on to the gore-covered blade, trying to pull herself out from beneath the animal. She focused upon the silvery white orb in its head, somehow sensing that it was the true problem, and jammed the blade into its offending center with a terrible popping sound. She was so repulsed by the act that she let out a scream but resisted the urge to remove the blade and instead pushed with all her might until . . .

The dog went suddenly rigid, dropping its full dead weight onto her body. Thick, milky liquid tainted pink from blood oozed from its right eye socket onto her pants, and she wanted nothing more than to be far away from the weighty corpse.

Delilah frantically struggled to push the dead dog from her body, suddenly on the verge of total panic as she realized what she'd actually done. And then she felt a strong hand on her shoulder as the weight of the dog lifted. She hadn't realized she'd closed her eyes until she opened them to see Deacon standing above her, the animal's corpse lying on the floor beside him

"Thank you," she said, feeling herself breaking down, her resolve cracking, ready to tumble.

But then she saw his bloody arm, bitten in two places, and she pulled herself together.

"Let's take a look at that arm," she said, climbing to her feet. She could be afraid another time.

When somebody didn't need her help.

CHAPTER **TWENTY-ONE**

Sidney was experiencing memories that were not her own.

First there was darkness . . . thick, tactile, fluidlike ink, and then a sudden painful sense of movement.

Movement from the black oblivion of there . . .

To here.

Riding the storm . . . hiding in the fury of the elements . . . coming to rest somewhere . . .

Dark. Cold. Wet.

Hidden.

Beneath the thriving metropolis, it nested, growing. Soon it pulsed with purpose, reaching out, powerful emanations touching the primitive brains of the city's vast animal ecosystem . . .

And more.

Sidney watched as the letters flashed before her.

Ely . . .

At first she had no idea what they meant . . .

Elysi . . .

Then suddenly she understood what it was she saw.

Elysiu . . .

Raised letters. Raised letters on a sign in front of a building.

ELYSIUM.

The sign says "Elysium," she thought, just as a steel spike came down into her skull.

At least that's what it felt like.

Sidney awoke with a scream, sitting bolt upright with the urge to run away as fast as she could.

Snowy was in her face, warm, wet tongue lapping eagerly at her nostrils. She gently pushed the dog's white head away and felt beneath her nose.

Blood.

She felt as though the inside of her skull had been scraped with a metal brush. Quickly she looked around and realized that she was lying in the back of a van. The rear doors were open, and she cautiously slid out through them.

"Hey, you're up!" Rich said, walking over to her. "Your nose is bleeding," he said, touching beneath his own as if she didn't know where her nose was.

"Yeah," she said, wiping her face with the sleeve of her shirt. "Where are we?"

"Airport hangar," Langridge said, as she joined them. "You all right, Moore?"

Sidney nodded, trying to remember how they had gotten there.

"We were just about to the hangar when we realized that we'd lost you, Bob, and the dog," Langridge explained. "Cody found the van parked outside, managed to hotwire it, and drove back to get you."

She remembered the fury of the birds, and Bob.

"Bob . . . ," she began.

"Yeah, what happened?" Sayid asked.

"The birds . . . he got hurt," Sidney said, the images of his empty eye sockets making her stomach feel all the more queasy. "Hurt so bad that the thing . . . that the thing doing this took control."

"Yeah, what's up with that?" Rich asked. "I thought we killed it."

"Obviously there was more than one," Cody said from where he stood beside a table covered in greasy tools.

"Well that just sucks," Rich muttered. As if sensing his distress, Snowy went over and leaned against his legs. He reached down to pet her.

"Or the one that we thought was destroyed wasn't." Sayid offered another explanation. "We know nothing about these things and . . ."

"Almost nothing, but we do know something," Sidney offered, fingertips feeling beneath her nose for any more leakage.

"What are you talking about?" Langridge demanded.

Sidney thought for a moment, trying to make sense of her

visions, or dreams—whatever they were—as she listened to the birds outside slamming their bodies against the unrelenting structure of the metal hangar.

"I saw some things," she said finally.

"What did you see?" Sayid asked eagerly.

"I'm pretty sure it was Boston again. At least one of those things is there . . . it came with the storm from . . ." She remembered the liquid darkness and felt her stomach churn with dread. "From wherever the hell they're from."

"Do you have any idea where in Boston?" Langridge pressed.

Sidney shook her head. "Someplace dark, rocky, and kinda wet. Underground, I would think. But there was also a sign, on a building. It said 'Elysium.'"

"Elysium?" Langridge repeated, then looked to Sayid. The doctor shook his head.

"I have no idea."

Cody returned to the group, holding a long screwdriver in his hand like a weapon. "If there's another one of those things here, we have to get back to the high school," he said. "Who knows what they could be dealing with."

"No," Sidney said emphatically. "No, we have to get to Boston." She didn't know why, nor did she understand why she felt such urgency. All she knew was going to Boston was what they were supposed to do.

What they had to do.

Cody gave her a disgusted glare. "Boston is a long ways away, and we don't have a way of getting there now."

"Boston is important," Sidney said.

Langridge watched her carefully, as did Sayid.

"Why is that?" Sayid asked.

Sidney shook her head. "I really don't know. I just have this gut feeling that it's what we have to do."

"Do you think it might have something to do with . . . ?" Rich asked, tapping the side of his head as if he didn't want to voice her connection with the alien.

"Maybe." Sidney shrugged. "All I know is something is telling me that Boston is very important, and we have to get there as quickly as we can."

"Well, even if we had a plane, we've lost our pilot," Langridge said.

"Maybe someone back at the camp can fly," Cody suggested. "That would at least give us a chance to check on them and . . ."

Sidney felt a sudden wave of panic shoot through her, making her whole body vibrate with its intensity. "We can't go all the way back there," she practically shouted. "We have to get to Boston. I don't think there's a lot of time left."

"The survivors at the camp should be fine," Langridge stated. "Our best men are there. If something happens, they'll know what to do. Sidney's right—it's Boston we should be worrying about."

"So how do we get there?" Rich asked.

It was Cody who had the answer.

"Boat," the son of Benediction's harbormaster said as they all looked at him. "We go by boat."

CHAPTER **TWENTY-TWO**

Everything looks normal, Doc Martin thought as she sat in the back of the SUV with Isaac, looking out the window as they passed through Benediction. Well, everything other than the fact that the streets were mostly empty of life and were strewn with animal corpses.

"So they all died when the original organism was killed?" Burwell asked from the driver's seat.

"That seems to be the case," Doc Martin said, eyes fixed on an enormous pile of what looked to be squirrels rotting in the weak sunlight.

"So we're looking for another organism . . . bad radio."

"That's entirely possible," Doc Martin agreed. "No one mentioned seeing another organism in the cave, but that doesn't mean it wasn't there."

Velazquez turned in the front seat to look at her.

"What do you think, Isaac?" Burwell asked, his eyes focused on the young man in the rearview mirror.

Isaac said nothing, silently staring out the SUV's window. For a moment Doc Martin didn't think he was going to answer, but . . .

"Our cats had babies once," he said abruptly, still staring out the window, his eyes unblinking. "We didn't even know she was pregnant."

Everybody waited for something more, but Isaac offered nothing else.

"Well, that's interesting, Isaac," Burwell said after several moments. "But what about this bad radio? Do you think it's the same or—"

"The kittens were very cute," Isaac continued as if he'd never stopped, the hint of a smile playing at the corners of his mouth. "There were seven of them . . . no, six," he corrected himself. "One died."

Doc Martin saw a shroud of sadness pass over his face.

"Okay, okay, enough about cats," Burwell said, obviously annoyed. "Is this another bad radio we're dealing with?"

Isaac turned his head, his eyes meeting Burwell's in the mirror. "It had a baby," he said, his voice lacking all inflection.

"Shit," Burwell said. "Seriously?" He looked over at Velazquez. "Do you think that's possible?"

The woman shrugged. "We really didn't get a chance to do any workup on the corpse, so who knows what's possible and what isn't. Doug and Tyler were supposed to be getting tissue samples for study, but we saw how that turned out."

"Maybe they had a run-in with the offspring," Doc Martin offered.

Burwell slowly stopped the SUV by the side of the road and turned around to look directly at Isaac. "What do you say, Isaac?" he asked the young man, who had already turned back to the window. "Picking up anything? Is the bad radio sending out any—"

Isaac interrupted with a scream. A bloodcurdling sound that Doc Martin couldn't quite understand.

Until she leaned over, following his gaze through the window.

And then she wanted to scream too.

Isaac had never believed in monsters.

His mother had told him that they didn't exist.

Now, Isaac, we all know that there's no such thing, right? she would say when something on the television scared him, or he heard a noise that he could not immediately identify.

But since his mother had died, things had changed.

Isaac had seen with his own eyes that monsters did indeed exist.

And that was what he saw, surging around the side of the house, racing across the lawn—like an enormous snake, slithering in a crazy zigzagging pattern toward them. It wasn't one thing, one single giant animal, but many animals having all come together to form—

A monster.

Isaac was still screaming when the creature hit the side of the SUV full force, flipping the vehicle onto its side.

They were all screaming then as glass from the shattered

windows fell around them like rain. Isaac landed on Doc Martin, his flailing arms smacking the older woman in the face, leaving her stunned.

After a few moments Burwell sprang into action.

Isaac did not really like the man. There was something about him—maybe his gruffness—that made Isaac very anxious. But Burwell did want to stop the bad radio, and that was all right with Isaac.

"Out the back!" the man shouted as he climbed over them, Velazquez right behind him.

"Move, people!" Burwell screamed, his voice very loud in the confines of the car. He was forcing supplies aside to get to the rear window, and once there he knocked it out with a vicious kick. He climbed through the window, dragging a metal case behind him.

"Isaac, we have to go," Doc Martin said, giving the young man a push as Velazquez followed Burwell out the window.

Isaac glanced behind her, over the front seat, and saw that the snake of many animals was slithering in through one of the broken windows.

Doc Martin must have seen it too, because she was grabbing at him, practically hitting him to get him to move. Isaac finally crawled over the backseat and then the supplies toward the open window.

The buzzing inside his head was back and grew steadily louder—more painful.

Angrier.

He got to the window and glanced back to see Doc Martin

following close behind him, her fearful, yet determined expression urging him on.

Behind her, the snake was fully inside the SUV, watching them with multiple silver-covered eyes.

Doc Martin could feel it through the soles of her sneakers, an increasing vibration that told her that something was close.

Very. Very. Close.

Isaac had just made it through the back window and out onto the road with the others when she felt them.

Hundreds of tiny teeth biting into her legs, thousands of claws on her skin as they crawled up her pants leg.

She screamed, screamed with the effort of moving her old body through the detritus in the back of the SUV, screamed in pain as she was bitten, clawed, and scratched. She kicked wildly, trying to fling away anything that wanted to make a meal of her. But it was a losing battle. They were everywhere, covering her body in a blanket of writhing fury. There were warm-blooded vermin, as well as insects with carapaces practically clear, indicating they were recently hatched.

"Grab her arms!" she heard Burwell yell, just as she decided she wasn't going to make it after all.

She felt strong hands grab hold of her, and then she was roughly pulled through the window of the SUV and dumped unceremoniously on the road. Immediately she rolled on the ground, slapping at herself, trying to knock the clinging pests away, then practically leaped to her feet, jumping up and down to dislodge the more stubborn of the attackers.

The swarm of warm- and cold-blooded things surged out from inside the truck.

"Get back!" Burwell yelled.

Doc Martin continued to swat at her body as Velazquez grabbed her and pulled her away from the SUV.

Burwell stood his ground. The metal case he had dragged from the SUV contained the flamethrower, which he had ignited. Flames spewed from the nozzle, and the advancing swarm went up in a silent rush of fire. He continued to spray flame across the vehicle and around it, leaving no patch of ground or shadow untouched.

"Everybody good?" Burwell asked when he finally turned from the burning wreckage.

Doc Martin took a quick inventory of her injuries, mostly superficial scrapes and scratches, then looked around her.

"Where's Isaac?"

CHAPTER TWENTY-THREE

The bites on Deacon's arm were nasty.

Mallory and Phil cleaned them up as best they could with what was left of a bottle of water that Phil had with him. Delilah had found a white lab coat hanging on a coatrack in the corner and cut some strips of cloth that Mallory used to wrap Deacon's arm, tying the ends so it wouldn't come loose.

"Thanks," Deacon said to them when they were finished, his gaze lingering a bit longer on Delilah.

She knew his thanks were for more than the bandages. "You're welcome," she acknowledged, then quickly looked away.

Her eyes fell upon the corpse of the dog, and she felt her entire body go rigid, that frightened-little-girl part of her expecting the animal to spring up from the floor and resume its attack upon them.

"Did you notice that it didn't make a sound?" she asked no one in particular, not taking her eyes from the dog. "No growling or barking or even crying out when we hurt it. It isn't right," she said, finally tearing her eyes away and turning to the others. "Nothing . . . normal acts like that."

"There's nothing about any of this that's normal," Deacon said. He'd slipped his green work shirt back on and was slowly flexing his arm, testing it.

"Did you see its eye?" Delilah asked. "Its right eye?"

"Sorry, I was too busy worrying about its teeth," Deacon said. He came around the desk to join her near the dog. "What's wrong with its eye?"

"There's a shiny film covering it," she said, moving her fingers around her own eye. "It almost looked like it was covered in metal."

Deacon carefully knelt down and angled the dog's head so they could look at the right eye. Even though Delilah had stabbed it there, a thick, silvery ooze was still noticeable.

Phil, Mallory, and one of the Nancys stepped cautiously closer, curiosity seeming to get the better of them.

"Why do you think that is?" Phil asked.

Delilah shook her head. "I don't know, but Winston and Lonnie had the same thing."

"Winston and Lonnie?" Mallory asked. "What was wrong with them?"

"Winston killed Cherrie," Delilah blurted out with a shudder. "Lonnie nearly killed me, and both of them had that same silvery covering over their eyes."

"What do you think it means?" Phil asked.

No one seemed to have an answer.

"You don't think it's some kind of disease, do you?" Nancy asked, as she slowly backed away from the dog's body, a hint of panic in her voice.

"I don't know what it is," Mallory replied. "I didn't notice it on any of the patients I saw up and about, but then again, I was pretty busy trying not to get killed."

"I can't imagine there isn't something to this," Delilah said, looking at the dog's oozing right eye.

"And you may well be right," Mallory said. "It's something to tell the authorities, or the CDC, or whoever the hell we finally meet up with once we get out of here."

"So are we gonna try this again?" Deacon asked.

Mason went to the door this time. "Ready?" he asked anxiously.

Delilah could see the concern for his wife and new baby practically written on his face. She wondered if hers was just as obvious.

It took a few moments for everyone to retrieve their weapons, but finally they were ready and gathered at the door behind Mason.

"Do it," Deacon said, his club raised and ready to bludgeon.

Mason squeezed the knob, taking a deep breath, then opened the door to an empty corridor. Cautiously he stuck his head out, looking right then left, as if getting ready to cross a busy street.

"It's clear," he said, carefully stepping out.

The others followed, one at a time, each checking from right to left before leaving the safety of the office. It was strange to hear the hospital so quiet, the only sounds from the raging storm outside.

Deacon took the lead again. "We'll head to the stairs," he

whispered, waving his hand for them to follow. "We go up two flights, cut across the skywalk and head down into the garage."

They all nodded in agreement, eyes wide with fear. Clumped together in a tight little group, they cautiously, quietly began to make their way past several offices toward the stairwell at the end of the corridor.

Suddenly one of the Nancys broke away and headed for a nearby office. "I've got to get my purse!" she said as she pushed open the door and disappeared inside.

"For God's sake," Deacon grumbled, but the group stopped anyway, frightened eyes glancing up and down the corridor looking for signs of trouble.

It seemed to take forever, but Delilah knew they had only been waiting for a few minutes.

"What the hell's taking her so long?" Deacon whispered harshly.

Still there was nothing.

Finally Delilah couldn't stand it anymore. She felt as though she would jump out of her skin if they had to stand in the hallway any longer. She moved to the darkened office and placed her fingers upon the partially closed door.

"C'mon, Nancy," she began as the door swung open. "We really need to . . ."

Mr. Armstrong had the honor of being the longest-living resident of Elysium, having been at the facility since it opened in 2005. Delilah knew that because the staff had had a little party for him during her first week on the job. She'd thought that odd at the time, but as she'd grown into her new job, she'd begun to understand the connections staff made with the patients.

What didn't make sense was that Mr. Armstrong was standing in the center of the office, strangling Nancy.

"Shit!" Delilah exclaimed, instinctively charging into the space. She raised her club and swung it at the man's side, forcing him to lose his grip on Nancy and sending him stumbling into a desk.

The woman fell limply to the floor, and as Delilah leaned toward her, she could see that her neck was already swollen and a horrible shade of blue.

She reached down to check for a pulse, just as Mr. Armstrong fell upon her back, his scrawny arms draping around her shoulders as his hands sought out her throat. The two tumbled forward over Nancy's body and into the desk.

Mason was suddenly there, grabbing at Mr. Armstrong, trying to pull him off her.

"Help me with this guy!" he shouted as Phil and Deacon appeared.

The three of them managed to haul Mr. Armstrong away from Delilah, slamming him back onto the desk and holding him there, even as he continued to struggle.

Delilah scrambled out of the way, pushing herself into a corner as she tried to catch her breath. She looked around the room, trying to take it all in. Mallory was kneeling beside Nancy's body, sadly shaking her head, while the other Nancy stood over her, her hand to her mouth. Deacon, Mason, and Phil were still fighting to hold the struggling Mr. Armstrong down on top of the desk.

And then she caught sight of the office computer. It was on the floor in the opposite corner, where it would have been hidden to anyone first entering the office. It had been partially taken apart, its pieces neatly stacked in piles nearby.

Curious, Delilah pushed herself to her feet and approached the disassembled technology, noticing wet smears of red on the inside of the hard-drive casing. She looked back at Mr. Armstrong, flailing on the desk. Mason reached out to grab his arm and pin it to the desk—

But not before Delilah saw that the man's fingertips were raw, ripped, and ragged.

Bloody.

CHAPTER TWENTY-FOUR

Cody's idea was a good one—sail to Boston.

But first they had to get to the marina, and then they had to find a boat that was still in the water and ready to sail.

Realizing that their time was running short, they all clambered into the panel truck, all except for Langridge, who waited outside, ready to slide open the hangar doors. Cody was behind the wheel; Sidney and the others sat on the floor behind him. Waiting.

"So, we're going to the marina and we're going to steal a boat?" Rich asked.

"That's the plan," Cody said. His eyes were fixed on Langridge, who held up one hand, fingers closing one at a time as she counted down.

"Just wanted to make sure that I understand how I'm going to die," Rich said.

"That's no way to talk," Sidney said, although she did understand where her friend was coming from.

"Sorry," Rich apologized. "Just can't think of anything good coming out of being on open water, sailing into the hurricane."

"Can't think like that," Sidney said, watching as Langridge folded her fifth finger into the fist and pulled the metal door open wide enough for the van to drive through.

Cody immediately stepped on the gas, and the van lurched forward as birds flew through the opening.

Langridge covered her head with her arms and ran toward the van as the robins and sparrows swarmed her. Cody barely slowed down as Langridge grabbed the passenger door and threw herself into the front seat—bringing a robin with her.

"Shit," Cody said as the angry bird came at them.

From one to the other it attacked, avoiding their hands with its evil swiftness as they cursed and flailed. It was Snowy who finally dispatched the bird, snatching the assassin from the air and crushing it in her mouth.

"Good girl," Sidney praised, prying the dead bird from the dog's clenched jaws. She could see that the dog was disappointed at having her prize taken away, but Sidney didn't want to risk anything happening to her best friend. Who knew what would happen if Snowy were to eat the thing?

Sidney took the bird, glancing at its lolling head just long enough to see that its tiny right eye was covered in that nasty silver covering. It made her stomach squirm, as well as something inside her head. She tossed the robin corpse into the back of the truck, signaling to Snowy to leave it there.

The birds did not want them to go, dive bombing the truck with intense ferocity. The larger birds thumped and bumped off the hood and windshield, leaving bloody smears and hairline cracks that they all hoped wouldn't get any larger.

Cody squirted the windshield with wiper fluid and turned the wipers full on. Langridge shot him a look, and he just shrugged as he sped through the airport parking lot, trying to avoid the plummeting fowl.

"I thought most of the animals died when the original life-form was destroyed?" Langridge questioned.

"Maybe there were animals that weren't initially affected," Sayid said. "That the life-form could only control a specific number of—"

"They were held in reserve," Sidney suddenly said, causing them all to look at her. "Just in case," she added. "They were held in reserve just in case they were needed by the other."

"The 'other'? Sid, how . . . ?" Rich began to ask.

Sidney stared straight head, eyes blinking with each new bird hit.

"I just know," she added, really not wanting to talk about it anymore.

"How far to the marina again?" Sayid asked, filling the sudden silence with something other than the sound of birds pummeling the van.

"Not long," Cody said. "Shortcut down Herbert Road, and then we'll cut over to . . ."

Sidney saw it up ahead but wasn't quite sure what it was. It looked like someone had tied lengths of string across the road, from one tree to another. "Cody, you might want to . . . ," she began.

But it was too late. The white strands sliced through the top of the windshield, shaving off part of the roof with a shriek of rending metal as they drove into it.

They all cried out, ducking down beneath the strands that remained unbroken as Cody slammed on the brakes. The van spun wildly, its movement finally stopped by the taut, white strands that stretched across the road.

Slowly, cautiously, they lifted their heads.

"What the hell just happened?" Sidney was the first to ask.

Langridge was doing the same, only she was reaching out through the missing part of the windshield to touch the strange white strands of—

"Don't touch that!" Sidney yelled.

But Langridge had already touched the filament. She hissed with pain, pulling her hand back quickly, beads of blood on the tips of her fingers.

"That shit's razor wire," she said, sticking her fingers in her mouth to suck away the blood.

"Who the hell would put razor wire . . . ," Rich started to question.

"It's not razor wire," Sidney said, sensing and finally seeing what had started to descend from the foliage in the trees. "We have to get out of here quickly," she said, already sliding through the van to the back doors.

"Sidney, what . . . ?" Sayid began.

"It's webbing," she said, reaching out to throw open the doors to the center of Herbert Road.

"Webbing?" Sayid repeated, the meaning slowly sinking in.

"Oh shit," said Rich.

Oh shit, exactly, Sidney thought as she climbed from the back of the van with the others following close behind.

Before the spiders showed up.

CHAPTER TWENTY-FIVE

The new voice was speaking to him.

This wasn't like the first bad radio—the one that hurt his head and tried to make him do terrible, terrible things.

No, this was something else . . . something was speaking directly to him and telling him to come.

Alone.

And somehow Isaac knew that if he did as the new voice asked, Doc Martin and the others wouldn't be hurt. He waited just long enough to be sure that the doc got out of the SUV safely, but as Burwell's weapon spit its liquid fire, the voice became quite insistent, and he felt a sharp pain inside his head.

Isaac wasn't sure how to feel about this mysterious new presence in his mind. But the voice was quite persuasive, and as he slowly backed away from his companions, the pain in his head began to subside.

Come, said the voice.

But where? Isaac thought.

It was as if someone . . . or was it some*thing* . . . was directing his movements. He would feel the sharp pain in his head when he strayed in the wrong direction, relief when he headed in the direction the voice desired.

Isaac paused for a moment, feeling a pang of guilt over leaving his friends and then the sting of his indecision. The new signal wanted him so very desperately and wasn't about to let him go.

He crossed through a backyard loaded with toys and hundreds of dead animals, swollen in the heat of the day. The nasty smell made his stomach churn, but the new signal in his head—sensing his distress—fixed the problem.

And Isaac could no longer smell the stink of decay.

That was its way of showing him that it meant him no harm, that it wanted only to show him something.

To share something so incredibly important.

Come.

CHAPTER TWENTY-SIX

Delilah watched as Phil and Mason held the thrashing old man in place.

Deacon must have seen her look, because he stepped away from them. "What is it?" he asked her.

"The tips," she said, using her own fingers to show him. "They're all cut up."

"Yeah," Deacon agreed. "So . . ."

"He did that to his fingers by taking that apart," she said, pointing at the disassembled computer.

The surviving Nancy and Mallory were looking over there now.

"Why would he be taking a computer apart?" Mallory asked.

"Yeah, why?" Delilah said. "So somebody who's been in a vegetative state for close to twenty years wakes up and starts to take apart a computer."

"As well as strangling somebody to death," Phil added, trying to hold the man's wild, flailing arms down.

Mallory moved to stand beside Mr. Armstrong.

"Don't get too close," the surviving Nancy said, taking some steps back.

"What this is, is impossible," Mallory said, studying the man who was struggling to be free.

"Well, it seems very possible now," Mason said.

"Look at his eye," Mallory gasped.

The right eye bulged strangely outward, moving independently of the left, turning its silvery murkiness to the nurse.

Fixing upon her.

The inhuman presence controlling the human vessel fixed its view upon the female looming over it.

These humans, it thought, making a calculated determination, *are a threat.*

It reached out to the near limitless forms of simple life that thrived within its reach.

So many vessels . . . so many tools.

To use.

Mallory moved to touch the strange coating over Mr. Armstrong's eye.

"Mallory, I wouldn't," Delilah warned again, but the supervisor ignored her, the tip of her fingernail touching the shroud—

With dramatic results.

A tendril of electrical energy leaped from the curve of the eye, striking the tip of Mallory's finger. She stumbled backward and fell to the floor.

"Jesus Christ!" Mason screamed, letting go of Mr. Armstrong and jumping back.

"Hey, man! A little help here!" Phil yelled as Mr. Armstrong broke free, pushing Phil away and climbing unsteadily to his feet.

Delilah ducked past them to Mallory. "Hey," she said, helping her to sit up. Mallory looked stunned.

"Guess I shouldn't have touched that," she said.

"Told ya," Delilah said as her supervisor climbed to her feet.

Mr. Armstrong was attempting to throttle anybody he could get his hands on. Deacon was finally able to grab him about the waist, lift him up off the ground, and slam him to the floor savagely.

"Anything we can restrain this guy with?" Deacon asked, struggling to hold the man in place.

Mason bolted from the office.

"Where the hell are you going?" Deacon yelled after him.

But it was only a few moments before Mason returned, holding up a roll of silver duct tape.

"Had this on my cart," he said, kneeling beside Deacon and the thrashing Mr. Armstrong. "For temporary fixes," he continued, pulling up a strip and breaking it off with his teeth. He and Deacon managed to wrap the old man's wrists and ankles together.

Deacon got up off the floor with a grunt, looking down on the scrawny old man that flopped like a fish. "So are we just gonna leave him here?" he asked.

"What else should we do with him?" Mason said with a shrug.

"All right, then," Deacon said. "Let's get this show on the road again. No detours this time."

They filed out of the office, Delilah bringing up the rear when she stopped. There was one more thing she had to do. Quickly she grabbed a black jacket that had been hanging on the chair behind the desk and gently placed it over Nancy's face. Beneath her breath she said a little prayer, asking God to look after Nancy, as well as apologizing for not being able to save her.

"Delilah?" Deacon called.

She took one last look at the covered corpse of the woman whom she barely knew, but who had become part of this whole bizarre experience.

"Yeah," she said, leaving the office. "I'm coming."

CHAPTER TWENTY-SEVEN

Large, spiderlike things dropped out of the trees on razor-sharp strands.

They weren't like any spiders that Sidney had ever seen before.

"I don't even know what to say," Dr. Sayid said, coming to stand beside her.

"We saw things like these back in the cave," Sidney said. "Part spider and part whatever else the alien thing decided to mix with it."

"These are pretty big though," Rich said, peering around the van.

"You're saying that the alien organism makes these things?" Sayid asked.

Sidney nodded. "Yeah, in those fleshy sacks that hung from the roof of the cave."

The scientist looked both fascinated and horrified. "So I'd say this confirms that another alien presence is on the island."

"And it wants us to stay here," Sidney blurted out.

They looked at her.

"It knows we're heading for the marina," she said. "To get to Boston and try to stop their plans. It doesn't want us getting there."

Snowy could sense the spider-things crawling toward them and began to whine. They were skittering along what remained of the van's roof, entering the vehicle through the broken windshield, and moving along the ground.

"So I'm guessing that this road is still the quickest way to the marina," Langridge said, pulling her gun from its holster.

"Yeah, it is," Cody confirmed.

"So we move forward, then," Langridge said, as the first of the spider-things came around the back of the van, tensing its eight, hairy legs, preparing to spring.

She blew it into a million slimy pieces with one shot from her gun.

"Got another one of those?" Cody asked.

"Sorry," Langridge said. "Most of the weapons blew up in the plane or are back at camp."

Sayid had a small pistol as well.

"Looks like we're gonna have to go MacGyver again," Rich said, turning toward the back of the van.

The spider-things were inside, but Langridge took care of them.

Sidney had to admit the woman was an incredible shot.

Cody and Rich jumped inside the back of the vehicle and rummaged around for anything that might be used as a weapon. Whoever had had the van must have been doing some kind of plumbing or electrical work, as there were rows of thin metal pipes—excellent for swiping and smashing.

"Here," Cody said, handing Sidney a blue canister that she recognized right off as a welding torch.

"Nice," she said, checking to make sure that the tank was full. "Got a light for this?" she asked. Cody went through a tool bag and pulled out an old striker.

Sayid was firing his weapon as Sidney turned the knob to release the gas from the canister, brought the striker up, gave it a quick few squeezes to produce the spark, and—

The torch came to life with a whoosh, the flame burning an icy shade of blue, just in time for use on the long, segmented legs that crawled from beneath the van.

"Get back, Snowy," Sidney ordered, pushing the dog behind her as she bent to touch the flame to a hairy appendage. It pulled back, blackened and smoldering.

"Man, these things are awful," Rich said, jumping from the van. Cody was right behind him. They each held long pieces of metal piping, with various tools sticking out from the pockets of their jeans.

Sidney started toward the front of the van, where Sayid and Langridge were already waiting to take their shots. But the spider-things weren't the only things they had to worry about—the webbing was dangerous as well.

"We won't be going anywhere fast if we have to maneuver our way through that," Sidney said, pointing out the crisscrossing patterns stretched across the width of the road.

Rich and Cody had joined them.

"Rich and I can go up ahead and break it down with these," Cody suggested, hefting a pipe.

"Or I could do this," Sidney said. "Watch Snowy for me," she told Cody as she strode toward the first line of webbing.

"Sidney, what the hell are you—"

She touched the flame to the webbing and watched as it disintegrated with a snap and crackle. "Used to burn webs with my father's torch in the garage," she said, holding the torch to more of the thin strands.

The spider-things didn't care for her efforts and turned their full attention on Sidney. More floated down from the trees on strands of webbing trailing from their egg-shaped abdomens.

"Something tells me you never played with dolls," Langridge muttered as she fired at a cluster of spiders. The bullets struck their targets, raining guts onto Sidney's head.

A spider darted toward the girl from the side of the road, and she quickly responded, warding it off with the hissing flame. The abomination stopped, throwing up its front legs to block the fire, and Sidney used the opportunity to lunge at the thing and stomp on it, crushing its body with a disgusting crunching sound.

"Watch your back!" Cody yelled, coming up quickly behind her and swinging his pipe into a fat, shelled body that was about to land on her back.

"Thanks," she said.

Their eyes touched briefly, and she felt a sudden connection with him that went far beyond what they'd once had. It was a connection she doubted could ever be broken, probably arising from the fact that they'd survived—up until then anyway—something so enormously catastrophic.

"Hey! More web burning!" Rich yelled, breaking into Sidney's thoughts. He was swinging his pipe and crushing anything that survived his blows.

Sidney quickly brought her torch to where the webbing was thicker up ahead. Through the hazy gossamer she could see two spiders weaving furiously ahead of them, attempting to halt their progress.

"Could use some exterminators over here," she called as she pushed forward to the last of the webbing that blocked their way.

Rich reached her, Snowy by his side.

"What's the haps?" he asked. She looked at him, experiencing that same feeling she'd had with Cody. They'd all been through so much together.

"See those two nasties?" she asked, burning a hole that made the two weaving insects all the more obvious. "They need to go, and then I think we'll be good."

Rich took a deep breath and strode closer, planting his feet and jabbing through the webbing. "Stand still, you son of a bitch," he grunted, the gore-stained end of the makeshift weapon tearing through the web but missing the spiders entirely. He tried again, with similar results, and even with Sidney burning the webbing, the insects eluded him, continuing to build a wall of silky evil.

"Maybe bullets'll work," he finally said, turning away to call to Langridge and Sayid.

His pole was still stuck through the webbing, and as he called out to Langridge, who was closer, one of the spiders began crawling the length of it toward him.

Langridge saw it before Rich realized the danger he was in.

"Watch it!" she cried out, raising her gun as Sidney reached to set the spider afire with her torch.

But they were both too late. The spider sprang onto Rich's arm and sank its horribly sharp pincers into his flesh.

"Ahhhhh! Son of a bitch!" Rich screamed, releasing the pole and shaking his arm frantically. His weapon clattered to the ground. Snowy jumped back with a bark.

The spider fell, and Langridge dispatched it with a single shot. The remaining spider appeared, but Sidney was there to scorch its limbs, sending it skittering back up into the trees.

Rich had dropped to his knees and was sucking on the red, angry wound, then spitting on the ground.

Sayid rushed forward and knelt beside him.

"Is he all right?" Sidney asked, keeping an eye on the webbing, burning away sections now with no interference from the weavers.

"I don't know," Sayid answered, gazing at the wound. "That's a nasty-looking bite."

"It's all right," Rich said. "Think I sucked most of the poison out." He continued to spit on the ground.

"How we doing there, Sidney?" Langridge asked as she ejected the empty clip from her gun and pulled another from her pants pocket, slipping it in place.

"We can get through now," she said.

Cody was crushing some last-minute spider stragglers coming from the side of the road as Langridge headed toward Sidney, picking up Rich's pipe on her way.

"Good job, Sid," Rich said, waving Sayid away and standing to retrieve his pipe from Langridge, who looked as though she really didn't want to give it up.

"You've got a gun," Rich told her, and she handed it to him with a disgusted look.

"Let's move," she said, motioning them through the opening burned in the wall of webbing. "Don't want to give whatever it is that's tracking us a chance to come up with something else."

Sidney took a look at what they were leaving behind. The ground was covered with the obliterated remains of countless spider-things.

Maybe the alien presence inside her head would get the idea that they weren't to be messed with, she thought, making sure to take it all in just in case the presence could see. She would have liked that.

But doubted it would happen.

CHAPTER **TWENTY-EIGHT**

As they stood, wondering where Isaac had gotten off to, the gas tank on the SUV exploded with a sound like a clap of thunder, tossing them violently to the street.

"Shit," Doc Martin heard Burwell exclaim above the painful ringing in her ears. She was on her hands and knees, attempting to focus. She shook her head to eliminate the annoying buzz, her vision focusing on Velazquez, who had been thrown onto a nearby lawn. The woman looked stunned, rolling around as if attempting to build the momentum to stand.

Burwell let out another expletive, and Doc Martin looked in his direction to see that he had risen to his feet and was looking at a deep, bleeding gash in his leg.

"Shit," she muttered, shaking off the muddiness. She forced

herself to her feet, almost losing her balance again but catching herself as she started toward the injured man.

Just as the screams ripped through the air.

Doc Martin spun toward the sound and saw that it was coming from Velazquez. The poor woman was covered in bugs—carpenter ants from the looks—and was struggling to stand.

Doc Martin changed direction and rushed toward the woman, trying to slap the ants from her body. But it wasn't long before they were climbing onto her, their pincers biting into her own exposed flesh and sending stinging pain through her body. Velazquez seemed to be growing weaker as more and more ants swarmed over her. Frantically Doc Martin tried to rub them off her, ignoring her own pain, but it was soon clear that there was nothing she could do to help Velazquez.

Burwell had hobbled closer, holding on to his bleeding leg. "Velazquez!" he screamed.

"Get back!" Doc Martin warned, swatting at the bugs that attempted to crawl upon her own body. "Keep away or you'll end up the same."

The veterinarian moved quickly away from Velazquez's remains, away from the seemingly limitless insects that were surging up out of the earth.

"We've got to get away," she said to Burwell as she rubbed at her face where some ants had crawled down from her hairline. She grabbed his arm, trying to move him, but he cried out, tripping over a leg that seemed not to work.

"You've got to get up," Doc Martin urged, watching the writhing black carpet that had engulfed Velazquez move from what little remained of the woman's body and head directly for them.

Burwell tried to get up, but the bleeding from his leg was fierce, and he was weakening fast. He fell back to the ground, nearly unconscious.

Doc Martin couldn't leave him, too. Neither did she want to die like Velazquez, with the skin eaten from her body. That thought seemed to fill her with a surge of strength the likes of which she hadn't felt since her forties.

And that had been a long time ago.

She reached down and practically picked Burwell up from the ground. "You've got to help me," she grunted.

Burwell moaned but did little to help her as she dragged him down the middle of the road. The shadow on the ground that flowed toward them gave her the inspiration she needed to keep going.

She felt as though a million volts of electricity were coursing through her body, and everywhere she looked, Doc Martin thought she saw movement.

Animal life converging upon them.

She steered them toward a house on the right side of the street, and that's when Burwell went completely limp, his body becoming so much deadweight that she could no longer hold him up. She stumbled, and they both fell to the pavement.

"C'mon, you've got to get up," Doc Martin begged. She didn't want to turn around . . . didn't want to see the moving shadow of life crawling toward them.

Burwell just moaned. She could see the blood continuing to

pour from his leg wound, and deep down she knew that he wasn't likely to get up anytime soon.

She was about to make the terrible decision, and one that she was sure would haunt her for the remainder of her years, when she heard it. The creak of a rusty door, followed by a voice almost as rusty sounding.

"Hey, you."

Doc Martin looked up at a tiny cottage nestled in a patch of shadows thrown by two enormous oak trees. An old woman stood on the front steps, holding a double-barreled shotgun that looked as if it weighed probably as much as she did.

"I need some help," Doc Martin said, straining to get up from where she and Burwell had fallen.

"Well I certainly can't help you," the old woman said. "I'm eighty-seven years old, for Pete's sake, but if you get him and yourself inside . . ." She gestured toward the door behind her, then slowly maneuvered her ancient body around and headed back into the house.

The ants were close. Doc Martin could practically hear them as their mass flowed across the street like water.

Using the last of what she had, Doc Martin hoisted the man up, throwing one of his arms across her neck, and dragged Burwell onto the sidewalk and up the crumbling brick steps that led to the front door of the old woman's house.

And then inside.

CHAPTER TWENTY-NINE

They passed through a set of heavy double doors into a part of Elysium that felt like the frozen food section of Stop & Shop.

Delilah had heard this area referred to as the server center but had never been inside. It housed the servers that made up the hospital's state-of-the-art computer systems, systems that were considered almost as important as the nurses and doctors in the care of their patients—particularly those on the top floor.

The eighth floor housed the neediest of Elysium's patients, those whose neuro systems were so damaged that they required constant care and monitoring. The patients in the Vegetable Patch, as the floor was insensitively called, were kept alive entirely by mechanical means—complex computer programs that fed them, breathed for them, administered their medicines, and monitored their vital signs and bodily functions. Without the machines, and the computers that ran them, the poor souls who resided on the eighth floor would die.

Delilah had to wonder if that might have been a blessing.

There were offices just on the other side of the double doors, and signs of violence were immediately obvious. Whatever had happened here had happened quickly.

"Where are the stairs?" Delilah asked, feeling her heart begin to race.

"Just at the end of the hallway here," Deacon replied as the group approached the main server room, whose walls were made entirely of glass.

And that was when they saw them—the revived patients inside the room.

"Shit," Deacon muttered as he quickly pushed the group back into a small alcove that led to a conference room.

"Did they see us?" Mason asked.

"No," Deacon answered. "Looks like they're too busy."

"Busy doing what?" Mallory wanted to know, sticking her head out from the alcove to see.

Delilah looked as well, at first confused, and then it made a kind of sense. "They're taking apart the servers," she said.

Mallory looked at her. "Like what Mr. Armstrong was doing back in the office?"

She nodded. Many of the servers had gone dark, their blinking lights extinguished as they were gutted. "Just like it, only this is worse," Delilah said.

"How so?" Deacon asked.

"The Vegetable Patch," Phil said.

"Yeah," Delilah agreed, although she didn't like the nickname at all. "Without those systems running, the patients up there will die."

"Not much we can do about that now," Mason said. "I just want to get home to my family. Can we get to the stairs without them seeing us?"

"They seem totally preoccupied," Deacon said. "If we stay close to the far wall and creep low enough, we might be able to get by without them even noticing."

Delilah watched the patients in the server room, recognizing some from her own unit. They seemed to be working quickly, with little thought to their actions. Their hospital gowns were covered with blood, and their fingers were ragged from the work they were performing without tools.

"Are we going to try this or . . . ," Nancy finally asked, but her voice trailed off as she turned to look in the opposite direction. Had she heard something?

"Yeah, we don't have a choice," Deacon said. "They don't seem to be paying attention to anything but the computers anyway."

Then he explained where they'd be headed—through the door at the end of the corridor and up two flights of stairs to the skyway that would take them to the garage.

But before they started on their way, it was Delilah's turn to hear something. She looked back in the direction they'd come from, toward the double doors at the end of the hallway.

There were more noises, and this time they all stared for a moment.

"Let's go," Deacon ordered, drawing the group's attention back to him as he led them out of the alcove and down the hallway past the server room where the patients worked feverishly to take apart the machinery inside.

The sounds were suddenly louder and seemed to be coming from the ceiling above them now. Delilah was bringing up the rear and stopped for a moment, her eyes on the patients in the server room. Their movements slowed, and several looked up toward the hallway, but almost immediately they returned to their work, adding to the growing stack of computer components in the center of the room.

What are they doing, and why? Delilah wondered as she turned away and headed for the others who had reached the door at the end of the corridor.

She was almost to them when a loud noise sounded behind her, as if a piece of the sky itself had fallen. She turned to see the ceiling behind her had caved in. It took her a few moments to realize that what poured from the damaged ceiling was not water from the heavy rain outside but plump rats and cockroaches.

"Oh God" was all Delilah could manage as the flood of vermin flowed silently toward her.

"Delilah!"

She heard somebody calling her name, but she couldn't move.

The wave was closer now, flowing up against the glass windows of the server room. The patients inside barely looked up; nothing would keep them from their task.

"Delilah, come on!"

Again she heard her name, and again she remained frozen in place, watching the ocean of life flow up to her sensible nursing shoes, the rats—almost as big as her mother's cats, Tom and Jerry—swimming through the shiny brown sea of cockroaches.

A roach the size of her thumb crawled atop her shoe, and that spurred her to action. She let out a scream as she kicked, flinging the bug back into the ocean of filth. And then powerful arms wrapped tightly around her waist, yanking her up and off the floor so fast that the air was squeezed out of her lungs.

It was Mason who had her, dragging her the rest of the way to the stairwell door through which the others had already disappeared. He shoved her forward, but as she stumbled into the stairwell, she heard him cry out behind her.

Delilah spun around to see that the wave had started to take him. He was going to be swept past the door, swallowed up by the—

She reached out, grabbing the front of his work shirt, holding tight, ignoring the roaches that skittered over her hand. Mason took hold of her arm, struggling against the flow that threatened to take them both now.

Delilah screamed, and then Mallory was beside her. The two of them managed to pull Mason into the stairwell, where they collapsed on the cold concrete floor, kicking the door closed against the onslaught of vermin.

The three of them lay there, gasping, Mason's gaze silently thanking them as the sound of thousands of claws scraping on the metal door filled the air.

CHAPTER **THIRTY**

From the top of the road Sidney could see the marina parking lot and knew they would have trouble.

But what else would I expect?

The air above the marina swirled with life, mostly gulls from the looks of it.

"We're not going to make it," she told the others as they caught their breath. She looked closely at Cody. He had watched similar birds kill his father in that very place. *Was it really only twenty-four hours ago?*

As if sensing her thoughts, he looked at her. There was a coldness in his eyes that hadn't been there before. Something was missing—something taken by this whole series of insane events.

She wondered if that certain something was gone from her as well.

"My father kept extra keys for the boats in the office," Cody said.

Sayid and Langridge looked down the road at the marina.

"They'll tear us apart," Sayid said.

"Too many for our guns, and ammunition is getting low," the security chief said.

"We can't stand around here much longer," Sidney said, noticing how twitchy Snowy was becoming as the dog glanced from one side of the road to the other. No doubt there were all kinds of things crawling through the woods in hot pursuit of them.

"Hey," Rich called out.

Sidney looked behind them in the direction of his voice and saw him turning up a hidden dirt driveway. She headed toward him, the others following, and saw that the drive led to a rickety old garage. Rich was standing beside an old bread delivery truck, backed halfway up the dirt drive.

"We could use this to get down to the office," he said rather breathlessly, and Sidney noticed how pale he looked—his skin almost gray.

"Do you think it'll run?" Langridge asked, grabbing a chrome handle and sliding the side door open with a grunt. "Oh," she said, looking inside, her lip curled with distaste.

"But we only have to get as far as the office," Rich said.

His forehead looked damp and he kept slowly blinking his eyes.

"Yeah, but it doesn't look like this thing has run in years," Langridge said, hands on her hips.

"Doesn't have to," Rich commented. "Bet in neutral it would roll quite nicely."

The security officer looked back to the truck, and then to him.

Rich walked down the driveway to the street and gestured toward the marina below. "We're on a hill," he said. "We'll just roll down into the parking lot."

Langridge smiled and slowly nodded. "Not bad," she said. "Not bad at all." She hopped into the driver's seat and put the truck in neutral. There was a little resistance, but eventually it moved . . . and stopped.

Sayid quickly opened the front door and began to push, while Rich and Cody went to the rear doors and did the same. Sidney moved to join them but was distracted by Snowy. The dog was seriously freaking out, but she couldn't see what was causing it. And she wasn't about to discount it, for if Snowy was upset, there was a reason.

"Hey, guys, we might want to speed this up a bit," she said as she scanned the road behind them and the woods on either side.

She caught sight of the underbrush moving. At first she thought it was a soft breeze . . .

And then a wave of forest animals appeared, flowing out from both sides of the road to become one writhing mass of angry life.

"Time to go!" Sidney shouted, ushering a crazily barking Snowy into the front of the truck beside Langridge.

They had all seen what was approaching, and the guys pushed the van even harder, grunting with exertion. Sidney added her own strength to theirs.

"It's moving!" she cried. "We almost got it!"

"Don't stop—let's do this!" Cody urged, and they screamed

and groaned and strained muscles that had already been strained to the max.

Snowy barked, and Sidney didn't know if it was to encourage them or warn them of the horror that was still on the move toward them.

"Go! Go! Go! Go!" Sidney screamed, using every bit of strength she had left and hoping that everybody else was too.

She glanced over at Rich and saw that his skin looked even more gray than before, and she thought that he might pass out—but then the vehicle began to roll faster, and Langridge cheered from the driver's seat.

One by one they all jumped into the van, Sayid into the seat next to Snowy and Langridge, Rich into the back, followed by Sidney, who chanced a quick look over shoulder and felt an icy chill run up her spine.

The mass of life was slithering in a serpentine motion down the road toward them. It moved like a single organism, multiple forms of life under the command of a single, malicious intelligence.

The more she stared at it the more she seemed to get inside the malevolent force that powered it, understanding its purpose and how nothing must stand in the way of its plans for this world.

Sidney shook her head violently, somehow breaking the connection; a spike of pain jabbed into the center of her brain as a wave of nausea rolled over her.

"We really need to get out of here," she gasped, and then she realized that Cody wasn't in the truck. "Cody?" she cried.

"Where is he?" Langridge asked. "Should I put on the brakes or . . ."

"No." The word left her mouth, and she felt the grip of terror on her heart. She knew that to slow down would be the end of them. She turned around and saw Cody still running behind the van, just beyond the reach of the door. The living mass was close behind, the sound of thousands of claws scratching the pavement nearly overpowering.

"Cody!" Sidney screamed as she realized he was trying to dislodge something from his back. Their eyes connected, and she saw something that she didn't want to see. He was going to give up . . . he was going to stop.

"Don't you dare," she screamed at him. "Don't you dare give up!"

He moved in such a way that she saw what clung to him. It looked like it might have been a gopher at one time, but now it was filthy, crusted with blood and writhing insects.

For a moment Sidney thought that she had failed, that her demands were about to be ignored and he was going to give in to the darkness that had been present since he'd watched his father die. She was going to scream at him again, but he surprised her, grabbing his shirt and pulling it up over his head. The gopher went with the shirt, and so did most of the bugs.

"Hurry it up!" She screamed at him, hanging from the doorway and extending her hand.

She could see the look slowly start to fade, replaced by a fire to live, and she leaned out even farther, afraid that she might tumble out, when she felt strong hands grip her, holding her in place— Rich, and Sayid had hold of him from over the front seat.

Cody grabbed her hand, and she pulled, the muscles and

tendons in her arm threatening to snap like rubber bands, and suddenly he was in the vehicle, where the two collapsed backward, he on top of her.

She couldn't breathe, gasping for air as he lay upon her. "We've got to stop meeting like this," she said, before breaking into giggles.

It felt good.

CHAPTER **THIRTY-ONE**

Doc Martin barely got Burwell through the door before the old lady was pushing them out of the way, kicking what looked to be some kind of draft preventer in the shape of a wiener dog beneath the door.

"You'll let the goddamn bugs in," she cursed, making sure that the stuffed roll was pressed tightly against the bottom.

The old woman stared at it for a minute, leaning against her shotgun. "That looks good," she muttered. "Can't leave 'em an inch or they come squeezin' in."

Doc Martin couldn't hold Burwell up any longer and let the man drop to the floor; she wasn't too far behind him.

The old lady turned and looked at them. "For Christ's sake, he's bleedin' all over everything!" she yelled, walking across the room, using the shotgun as a cane. She grabbed a small stack of newspapers from the top of a bench beneath an old piano and tossed them to Doc Martin. "Here, put him on top of these so he don't stain my carpet!"

The newspapers hit the floor in front of Doc Martin, and she quickly knelt to stuff them beneath Burwell's legs. She could see that blood had already stained the rug, but the old woman seemed a little crazy, so she did not draw attention to it.

Burwell was barely conscious, muttering and shivering as he lay on the floor.

"He ain't going to die, is he?" the old woman asked.

"He's lost a lot of blood," Doc Martin said as she leaned painfully forward to examine the man's injuries. "But I think I can keep him alive if you can help me with a few things."

The old lady offered a loud sigh and rolled her eyes. "What do ya need?"

"He has a piece of metal in his leg that I need to get out," Doc Martin explained. "I'll need some tweezers, something to clean the wound out with, a needle and thread to close it up, and some bandages."

When she didn't get a response, she looked up to see if the old woman was listening.

"Is that it?"

Doc Martin nodded. "Yeah, that should be good."

The old lady turned toward the kitchen. "If I'd known I was gonna be playing nurse, I would have left you out there to the critters," she said with a grunt.

Doc Martin could hear her banging around in the kitchen, and then she returned, dropping a pin cushion, some thread, a pair of scissors, and a bottle of alcohol on the floor beside Burwell. "Gotta go to the bathroom to get the rest," she said as she headed out of the living room and down the short hallway.

Doc Martin leaned over Burwell, undid his belt, and tugged his pants down and over his boots. "Don't worry about a thing," she said as she tossed his pants to the side. "No interest whatsoever in your naughty bits."

"What the hell are you doin'?" the old woman asked, returning from the bathroom.

"What does it look like?"

"Don't think you want me answerin' that question," the woman said. "Here's the bandages and the tweezers. Brought you an old towel, too, just in case."

"Thanks." Doc Martin grabbed the tweezers before they hit the floor and poured some alcohol over them, remembering to use the newspapers to "protect" the rug. She leaned toward Burwell again and, using the tweezers, gently pulled a jagged piece of metal from the wound in his leg, praying it wouldn't hit an artery on the way out.

"That from the explosion I heard out there?" the old woman asked. She was sitting in a wingback chair in the corner.

"Yeah," Doc Martin answered. "Nasty thing," she said as she placed the metal on the newspaper by her side. The wound was bleeding, and she wiped the flow away while dribbling alcohol on it. Finally satisfied that it was as clean as it was going to get, she began to stitch the two sides of sliced flesh back together.

"So what are you, a doctor or something?" the old woman asked around a piece of hard candy she'd taken from a dish on the table next to her chair.

"Veterinarian."

"Huh. No wonder I've never seen you before. Didn't go to the vet."

"No pets?" Doc Martin asked.

"Oh yeah, plenty of pets," the old lady said. "Just never needed to take them to the vet."

"Didn't you bring them in for their shots?" she asked.

The old lady laughed. "They didn't need any shots."

"If you say so," Doc Martin muttered with a shake of her head, continuing to pull the sides of wounded flesh together.

They were silent, the only sounds coming from outside as the wildlife tried to get in.

"Clara," the old woman said suddenly.

The veterinarian lifted her head. "Excuse me?"

"My name's Clara . . . just in case you were wondering."

"Oh," the doc said. "I'm Patricia, but everybody just calls me Doc Martin."

"You all right with just Doc?"

"Perfectly fine, Clara."

"So, is he gonna live?" Clara asked.

"Probably," Doc Martin said as she tied a knot in the last stitch and clipped the extra thread. "It ain't pretty, but it looks like I've pretty much got the bleeding to stop."

"What more could you ask for?" Clara commented. "What's his name?"

"Burwell. I don't know his first."

"Burwell?" Clara repeated. "What the hell kinda name is that? Burwell. Huh."

Doc Martin dressed the wound, then pushed herself backward off her knees as a wave of exhaustion threatened to overcome her.

"Tough day at the office, Doc?"

She looked at the old lady and chuckled. "You might say that," she said. "You seem to have done all right last night."

The old lady seemed to think a bit before answering. "Wasn't easy," she finally said. She leaned forward in her chair and pulled down the high white sock on her left leg, revealing several nasty bite marks.

"Want me to take a look at those?"

"I cleaned them good," the old lady said. "Hurt like hell, but not as much as . . ." Her voice trailed off as her eyes welled up.

"You okay, Clara?"

Clara nodded. "She was old, probably close to her time anyway."

Doc Martin listened, already having a pretty good idea as to where this was going.

"Most of my other dogs passed when I wasn't looking. Figured Allie would go the same way. Here one minute, gone the next." Clara sniffed and rubbed at her nose and eyes.

"Did Allie hurt you?" Doc Martin asked quietly.

The old woman nodded.

"That's what happened everywhere on the island."

"What caused it?" Clara managed to ask. "What made my poor old girl lose her marbles and attack me?"

"I hear that it was some outside influence," Doc Martin said, not wanting to get into too much detail.

"The Russians?" Clara asked, with a squint and a sneer. "I saw on Fox News that—"

"Not the Russians," Doc Martin interrupted. "Something maybe beyond this earth."

Clara leaned back in her chair. "You don't say."

Doc Martin nodded. "Do you mind if I get off the floor and sit on your couch?"

"What, my floor ain't good enough?" Clara asked disgustedly, and then laughed. "Go on, I don't care."

With a groan, and the popping of many joints, Doc Martin left Burwell lying on the floor and hobbled over to collapse on the coach with a loud moan.

"That better?" Clara asked.

"Oh yeah. These old bones aren't getting any younger."

"Wait till you get to be my age," Clara said. "I'll be eighty-seven in December, if I make it that long."

"Well, you've come this far," Doc Martin said. "A few more months won't matter."

"Allie would have been thirteen," Clara said, again her eyes filling up.

"Ripe old age for a dog," Doc Martin said as Clara nodded in agreement.

"She had a good run." Clara's voice was trembling. "Really wish I didn't have to kill her though."

"Lots of people are saying the same thing," Doc Martin said.

"So lots of people survived?" Clara asked.

"Yeah," Doc Martin said. "We did all right."

"The phone still don't work, and I can't get nothing on the TV."

"Those outside forces again," Doc Martin said.

"Figures."

The noises from outside the house, the thumps and the crashes, grew a little more hectic.

"We good, or should we . . ."

"Naw, we're good," Clara said. "My husband—God rest his soul—made this place practically airtight. Just in case the Russians tried germ warfare."

"You two had a thing for the Russians?"

"Can't trust those borscht-eating bastards," Clara said with a sneer.

Doc Martin couldn't help but laugh.

"So how long you think it'll go on for?" Clara asked her.

"I thought it was over early this morning," Doc Martin explained. "But then it started up again. I hear it might even be spreading to Boston."

"Boston?" Clara questioned as Doc Martin nodded. "Shit, that could be bad."

"Very," Doc Martin agreed.

"Was that other kid with you?" Clara then asked.

Doc Martin perked up. "Other kid?"

Clara nodded. "Yeah, odd-looking kid. Might've been simple. I saw him through the kitchen window, going through the back into the woods. It was the weirdest thing . . . ," she added, her voice trailing off as she remembered.

"What made it weird?" Doc Martin urged.

"Well here's every kind of animal and bug outside out for blood," the old lady explained. "And then this kid was walking right in the middle of it."

Clara looked directly at Doc Martin.

"Nothing was showing any interest in him at all."

CHAPTER **THIRTY-TWO**

"What the hell was that?" Delilah asked, her eyes going to the cream-colored metal door that separated them from . . .

"I don't know," Deacon said. "I really don't know."

Deacon and the rest of the group had already climbed the first flight of stairs before they'd realized that Delilah, Mallory, and Mason weren't right behind them. They'd come back down to help the three.

"It wasn't normal," Phil said.

"Ya think, Phil?" Mallory asked sarcastically, moving her hands across her body as if feeling for bugs.

Delilah stared at the surface of the door. It was vibrating slightly, the sounds from the other side growing more intense. Deacon reached a hand out toward it.

"Don't," Delilah warned, her voice nothing more than a

scared whisper barely audible over the horrible scratching sounds.

He didn't listen and lay his hand flat upon the cool metal surface. "It's the rats," he said. "They're trying to chew through the metal."

Phil laughed nervously. "Good luck with that," he said. "They'll never—"

"I've seen a rat eat through a steel sewer grate," Deacon interrupted. "And that was just a regular, ordinary, everyday rat." He looked back to the door. "This is something completely different."

"Something worse," Delilah added as the first piece of metal in the bottom of the door was pulled away, and a grayish pink snout pushed through.

"Oh shit," Mason said.

"Oh shit for sure," Deacon agreed. "We gotta move! Let's go, folks! Up the stairs to the skyway." He was waving everyone up as the first of the insects streamed through the holes made by the rats.

Delilah was the last to the stairs, stomping on bugs as she went, but there were so many, and the bottoms of her shoes were soon slick with their guts. She had just grabbed hold of the rail and begun to climb, eyes on Deacon waiting on the landing above her, when there came a horrifying sound from behind her. She couldn't help herself, stopping and turning back to see what was happening.

The door was shifting in its frame, the metal around it disintegrating as if it had been exposed to some highly corrosive acid. Then down it went, and a torrent of vermin flowed through. Delilah spun around and raced up the stairs toward Deacon, but as she neared him, the slick soles of her shoes slid and she pitched forward, whacking her shins on the edge of the steps.

"Oh God," she cried, floundering upon the steps. Her legs from the knees down had gone practically numb, and what little she could feel was nothing but excruciating pain.

She struggled to find purchase, frantically pulling herself up with the metal handrail. Deacon was reaching for her, trying to yank her up, just as she felt the first bites of razor-sharp teeth sink through the leather of her shoe. Delilah screamed, kicking back with her foot and losing her shoe in the process. But it was that sock-covered foot that allowed her to step firmly on the stair again, giving Deacon the help he needed to draw her up to the landing.

"Don't turn around," he ordered as they raced up the second flight. At the next level he pulled open another metal door and unceremoniously shoved her through. He quickly followed, slamming the door closed, leaning his back against it.

Delilah had fallen to the floor. She looked up to see that the others were already on the move, heading down the corridor toward the skywalk exit. She looked behind her at Deacon, who still leaned against the door. She could hear the intensifying sounds from the other side, and she knew there wasn't much time before that door also came down.

"Go! Go!" Deacon screamed as bugs filed through tiny openings beneath the door.

Delilah got up as the others reached the skywalk exit and rushed through it into the passage. She was moving to follow them until she realized that Deacon wasn't with her. She looked over her shoulder and froze.

Bugs were pouring underneath the door as the metal was torn away by thousands of eager, yellow-toothed mouths. She knew that Deacon couldn't hold the door for much longer and as soon as he stepped aside, it would fall.

She knew he'd never make it.

Frantically Delilah looked around, and her eyes fell on the door marked 8TH FLOOR almost directly across from her.

The Vegetable Patch.

Without a thought, she made her move, darting toward Deacon and grabbing his wrist, pulling him away from the door. Almost immediately it started to collapse inward, but Delilah was already hauling the startled head of custodial services along, the sounds of hundreds of thousands of claws scratching upon concrete only inspiring her to move all the faster. She thought of her mother and her son and made a silent pledge that she would get home to them.

That she would see them again.

She was moving so quickly that she slammed into the door, Deacon crashing into her back. Both fumbled for the handle, but she won out, slamming it down, and pulling the door toward her. She rushed through, Deacon stumbling in behind her. In unison they spun and pulled the door closed.

But it wouldn't shut.

"Look!" Delilah screamed, pointing to the door's edge. Rats were attempting to wedge themselves through as cockroaches flowed around them.

"No more," Deacon bellowed, giving the door an almost inhuman yank, slamming it shut.

And three severed rat heads dropped to the floor.

Their horrible mouths still working, biting at the air.

Delilah and Deacon stood in the dimly lit, powder-blue corridor leading to the Vegetable Patch, soaking in the silence, their eyes darting about, searching for signs of danger, but at the moment . . .

Her eyes met Deacon's, and something passed between them, something that said it's all right—for now.

And Delilah immediately began to cry.

It wasn't the sad cry of loss, or anything connected to emotion. This was a cry of utter relief, as if her body had absorbed so much from her harrowing experiences that it had to release some before it could function normally again.

Finally, she was able to wipe away her tears and immediately felt a flush of embarrassment. She gave Deacon a sideways glance from the corner of her eye and saw that he too had tears streaming down his face as he bent forward, breathing heavily, hands clutching his knees.

His gaze shifted from the darker blue carpet to her, and he saw that she was looking at him. Delilah could not control it—she smiled.

And Deacon began to laugh.

Within moments they were both laughing, crying, and barely holding it together.

"What the hell is going on?" she asked in between gulps of air as she tried to get control of herself.

Deacon was wiping at his eyes and shaking his head. "I don't know, I don't know," he repeated as he took in deep lungfuls of air. "But I'm guessing that it's big . . . that this . . ." He looked around at their surroundings, and she understood that he meant the entire hospital. "That this is just part of something bigger going on out there."

"I have a little boy." The words tumbled out of her mouth.

He nodded. "I've got three grandbabies," he said proudly. "Live with their parents in Roslindale."

"Do you think they're safe?" she found herself asking.

He thought for a moment, his expression growing dim. "You good?" he asked her instead.

She could only nod.

"We still need to get to the parking garage," he said, looking back in the direction they'd come. "But I can't imagine we can use the skywalk now."

"Do you think the others made it?" Delilah asked.

Deacon's face took on that grim look again, and she thought he would once more change the subject. "I can't say," he said instead. "We might've bought them enough time to get to their cars, but . . ." He stopped.

"I think they did," Delilah said firmly. "And maybe they're sending help." She studied Deacon, looking for just a glimmer of hope but seeing nothing but doubt.

"It would be something," he said, turning away from her.

CHAPTER **THIRTY-THREE**

Sidney was on her knees in the back of the van with Cody and Rich, holding on to the front seat and staring through the dusty windshield as the bread truck picked up speed.

Sayid and Snowy still sat in the front beside Langridge, who struggled with the ancient steering wheel to keep the bread truck on course.

They careened into the marina parking lot at thirty miles an hour, narrowly avoiding several cars that were still parked there. The sky above them was filled with writhing darkness, a storm of birds sent to prevent them from reaching their goal.

The marina office was coming closer, closer, and then the front tires of the van hit the concrete curb. The van bucked and tilted to the side, its momentum carrying them through the air and into the side of the building with a horrendous crash, followed by the shattering of glass and the sounds of splintering wood.

Everyone in the truck had become airborne, but then gravity reclaimed them as the van settled on its side, and they slammed back to earth in a heap.

There was a peaceful silence that seemed to go on forever, and Sidney wondered what was happening. She tried to open her eyes, but there was only darkness.

A darkness so very deep and all encompassing.

But then she saw . . .

It was dizzying and nauseating, and it took her a few moments to realize that she was looking through eyes not her own, and not through just a single set of eyes but . . .

Hundreds . . . thousands.

And the things she saw: people hunted, attacked . . . murdered.

As her brain attempted to understand, she felt nothing but the alien presence, so very cold in its efficiency. It had one purpose—to take as many lives as it could to create terror and confusion.

While the next phase of the attack was assembled.

The next phase?

The taste of blood filled his mouth.

Cody lay on his back, feeling his body scream in protest over the beating it had endured throughout the past thirty-six hours or so. He opened his eyes and looked around. He, Rich, and Sidney were practically on top of each other, but he managed to push himself away and cautiously sit up.

As always, Snowy sat obediently by Sidney's side. Sidney seemed to be stirring, and although Rich looked very pale and sweaty, his eyes were already open. The van was resting on its side, the windshield shattered but intact. He could just see Sayid and Langridge over the front seat, pressed together against the passenger door.

Keys, he thought. *I've gotta get the keys for the boats.*

He crawled over to the back doors of the truck and gave them a kick with both feet. It took two tries before one popped, falling open.

Cody peered out into the lot. The sky above the truck was filled with birds, and he knew they'd be on him in an instant. It wasn't far around the van to the office door, but he'd have to be quick before . . .

He saw the body lying in the lot. There was no question in his mind whose body it was.

He saw it again, replaying inside his head. They were running for the SUV, the birds nearly upon them. His father had practically thrown him into the backseat, sacrificing his own life so that his son could live.

Cody remembered the nightmarish sight of the birds as they descended on his father, tearing him apart. He had wanted to go to him, had tried to save him, but . . .

The guilt was like a weight around his heart, a weight made all the more heavy by the sight of his father's body, alone and unprotected, lying in the middle of the parking lot.

Sidney returned to consciousness with a nearly overpowering sense of dread.

The next phase.

She had no idea what that was, but she understood enough to know that they had to get to Boston.

She pushed herself over onto her side. Snowy was there to lick her face, and she reached out to give her best friend a loving pet.

"That's my Snowy girl," she said, eyes focusing on the inside of the tipped-over bread truck. Langridge was coming awake and had a nasty gash over her eye. Sayid seemed to be underneath her somehow, but he too was beginning to awaken. Rich was beside her, simply lying there, eyes gazing blankly at the other side of the truck that was now the roof. He still didn't look so good.

"Hey, you okay?" she asked, crawling over to him. She touched his arm, and his skin was burning hot.

"Not sure," he said, his voice sounding raspy and weak.

She pulled up his sleeve to look at the wound on his arm. The arm was swollen, the skin a dusky shade of red.

"Hey, Dr. Sayid," she called. "I think you'd better take a look at this." As the words left her mouth, she realized that Cody wasn't in the van. "Where is Cody?" she suddenly asked, eyes darting about.

"Where's who?" Langridge asked groggily.

"Cody," Sidney clarified, and then she saw the open rear door. She crawled over and peered out.

In the distance, near the middle of the parking lot, she saw him, swinging a pipe at a flock of birds that swirled silently around him.

Not too far from him, a body was lying on the ground.

And then she felt a whole new world of sick descend upon her.

"We have to get out there," she yelled, looking for a weapon.

She found another of the pipes they'd used to fight the spider creatures and grabbed it. She jumped from the back of the truck and was immediately set upon. Enormous gulls dropped at her, beaks ready to peck and tear, but she swung the pipe with crude efficiency, knocking them out of the sky and stomping on their heads when they hit the pavement.

She could see that Cody had made it to his father's body, still swinging his pipe against the onslaught of birds, but she knew that neither one of them could keep this up for long.

"Cody!" she called out to him.

"I'm not going to leave him here like this," he shouted, and as she drew closer, she could see the intense despair filling his eyes.

Gun shots suddenly rang out, and then Sidney was hit by a stream of water. She chanced a look behind her and saw that Langridge and Sayid were shooting at the birds, while Rich had found the fire hose left by Cody's father. With renewed hope, Sidney raced to Cody's side.

"Pick him up," she said, lashing out with the pipe and taking a gull to the ground.

He looked at her for a moment as if not understanding, then leaped into action, bending down and picking up his father's ravaged body. Together they raced for the safety of the marina office. Rich continued to spray the hose, giving them a somewhat clearer path back, while Langridge and Sayid shot any birds strong enough to resist the torrent of water.

They burst through the office door. Cody continued on into a small back room and laid the body down on a cot his father had kept there for the busiest times of the summer. Sidney held the door open for Langridge and Sayid, who were followed closely by

Rich and Snowy, then slammed it closed the best she could.

The door frame was bent, probably thanks to the bread truck's impact with the side of the building, but the door seemed to be staying closed for now. She pressed on it again to be sure, then turned around to see that Rich had collapsed.

Sayid was already kneeling beside him. "He's in tough shape," the man said. "He's burning up, and this arm is definitely infected. He really needs antibiotics, but it might help if I can at least get the wound cleaned."

"Maybe there's a first aid kit around here," Sidney offered as she started going through file cabinets and drawers.

Langridge pulled open the desk drawers and rummaged around. Neither of them found anything.

Cody was still sitting beside his father's body in the back room. Sidney hated to disturb him, but Rich needed help. Slowly she approached, tentatively clearing her throat.

"Yeah?" Cody asked, without looking at her.

"Rich is pretty bad," she said quietly. "Is there a first aid kit or something around here that Dr. Sayid could use to help him?"

Silently Cody stood and walked to a small closet in the far corner of the room.

With him gone, Sidney could look directly upon the body lying there. It was horrible—made worse by the fact that it had once belonged to a person—a living, breathing man who had loved his son very much.

"Not really sure what's in here," Cody said, turning from the closet and holding out a small white plastic box.

"Thanks," she said as she took it from him. "Why don't you spend a little more time with your dad while we look after Rich, but then we've got to get going, okay?"

Cody nodded, quickly turning away and returning to his seat beside his father's body.

Without another word, she stepped out of the room, pulling the door partially closed behind her.

"That's his father?" Sayid asked as she handed him the first aid kit.

"Yeah," she answered. "We came here to get him out, but he ended up . . ." She stopped. She didn't have to say it. It was clear how he had ended up. Instead she concentrated on Sayid as he opened up the kit and riffled through its contents. "Will that help?"

"Better than nothing," the doctor said, already getting to work. "I'll see if I can't clean out the wound and bandage it up. We'll just have to hope for the best at this point."

"Found some aspirin in the bathroom," Langridge said as she approached, holding up a small white bottle.

"Good," Sayid answered. "That'll help bring his fever down."

Sidney stood silently and watched as the man cared for her friend, but her mind had already begun to wander . . .

Whatever this next phase in the invaders' plan was, it had to be stopped.

CHAPTER **THIRTY-FOUR**

Doc Martin quietly poured herself some water from a jug on the counter. Clara had fallen asleep in her chair, and she wanted to keep her that way for as long as possible—she'd heard more than enough about the Russians and their coconspirators, the Chinese.

The actual truth really didn't matter to Clara; she had her own, which was just fine with her.

There was blood on the kitchen floor and something in a little bed in the corner, covered up with a sheet. Doc Martin guessed it was what was left of the old woman's dog.

She leaned against the counter and stared out the window at Clara's backyard, where the woman had said she'd seen Isaac. *Nothing was showing any interest in him at all.* Doc Martin sipped on her lukewarm drink and thought about those words. She had wondered about the young man's strange connection with the alien presence and considered that perhaps that connection was getting stronger. She thought of Sidney and what she was going through. *Might Isaac be going through something similar?*

"See anything good?" an old voice asked from behind her.

Doc Martin turned to see Clara standing in the doorway. "Oh, you're awake."

"Yeah, I ain't croaked yet," the old lady said, her gaze drifting over to the corner of the room. "I guess you seen that," she said.

"Yeah," Doc Martin answered.

"Didn't have the heart to put her outside. She loved that bed."

They stared at the little mound under the sheet for a few moments, and then Doc Martin decided a distraction might be in order. "So where does that path go?" she asked, pointing through the window at the backyard.

"That heads out to the marsh and the south cliffs," Clara said. "My husband used that path for fifty years to go fishing, but then the cell phone company came and bought up a lot of the land and put up their goddamn towers." Clara waved her hand in disgust. "Actually had my husband arrested for trespassing once. Like he gave two craps about their cell towers!"

Doc Martin found herself staring at the path and thinking of the young man out there alone. She'd made a promise to Sidney and the others to look out for him. *Not good,* she thought, sipping her water. *Not good at all.*

"I think your buddy is starting to come to," Clara said, hooking a crooked thumb over her shoulder toward the living room.

Doc Martin took a final look out the window, at the path that disappeared into darkness, before heading back into the living room.

Burwell was awake. "Things are a little bit fuzzy," he said. "How about filling me in."

Doc Martin held her water out for him. "Drink?"

He nodded, reaching out with a trembling hand.

"Might want to sit up first," she said, pulling the glass away and practically falling to her knees beside him. She helped him maneuver into a sitting position, then pulled a chair over for him to lean against before giving him the water.

Burwell grunted, wincing in obvious pain.

"Where are we?" he asked, bringing the glass up to his mouth.

"Clara was nice enough to take us in," Doc Martin said, looking over to the old woman, who stood in the doorway to the kitchen.

"Yeah, I'm a regular saint," Clara grumbled. "Anyone want a sandwich?" she asked, turning around and heading into the kitchen. "Might as well use up the bologna before it goes rotten."

"She seems quite pleasant," Burwell said as he finished the water with one last gulp.

"Quite," Doc Martin ruefully agreed.

"Where'd my pants go?" he asked, looking at his naked legs and underwear.

"Off."

"You?"

Doc Martin shook her head. "Clara."

Burwell laughed, and then winced.

"He's still out there," Doc Martin said.

"Who? The kid—Isaac?"

She nodded.

"I doubt it."

"Clara said she saw him walking through her backyard."

"So."

"Nothing was bothering him," Doc Martin said, watching as Burwell's expression went from one of confusion to gradual realization before she continued. "She said that he walked right onto the path, and nothing tried to harm him."

"Why do you think that is?" Burwell asked.

Doc Martin thought some before giving an answer. "I can't be sure," she said slowly. "But maybe it's got something to do with whatever is going on inside his skull. Something to do with the bad radio."

Burwell moved and hissed in pain. "Jesus, this hurts," he said.

"Nasty wound," she replied.

"So you think he's still out there—alive," Burwell said.

"I do."

"And you think that he has a connection to whatever it is that's here and trying to kill us. . . ."

"Maybe," she answered.

"Any idea as to where Isaac might've been going?"

"We brought him out here to find the new transmitter," Doc Martin said. "I think that's what he's doing."

Clara appeared in the doorway holding two paper plates with a sandwich on each. "I didn't know what you want on them," she said. "And then remembered I'm not a freakin' restaurant, so I didn't put anything on them."

Doc Martin took both plates and handed one to Burwell. "Thanks, Clara."

"Right," the old woman grumbled, heading back into the kitchen for her own sandwich.

"So what now?" Burwell asked, chewing his first bite of sandwich.

"We eat our sandwiches and tell our gracious host how much we love them."

"I can hear you, ya know!" Clara yelled from the kitchen. "I might not be able to run the Boston Marathon, but I can still hear."

Doc Martin smiled as she bit into her own sandwich.

"And then?" Burwell prodded.

"Well, you're not going anywhere," Doc Martin said, using her sandwich as a pointer and directing his attention to his wound.

"Yeah, I figured," he grumbled. The bandage was stained a lovely shade of maroon. "So that leaves you."

Doc Martin slowly nodded.

"So that leaves me," she agreed, and took another bite of her sandwich.

CHAPTER THIRTY-FIVE

Cody left the back room a few minutes later, slipping a Benediction Boat T-shirt on over his head as he came. She could see that he had placed a winter coat over his father's damaged face. Snowy went over to him, tail wagging, and he scratched her affectionately.

"Are we ready?" he asked, Snowy now sitting on one of his feet, tongue lolling as she panted.

"Is there a boat we can use?" Langridge asked.

Cody chuckled humorlessly. "Yeah, I can think of one that we can borrow," he said. He went to the desk and fished around, pulling out a key, and then went to a wooden case hanging on a wall near the file cabinet.

"Most of the bigger boats were taken out of the water for the season ahead of the storm," he said, opening the cabinet door to reveal multiple sets of keys hanging on hooks. "But there is one. The owner had planned to sail her to Key West but got sick at the last minute."

Cody found the key and removed it from the hook.

"We prepped it for the storm, and it's sitting in its berth." He gave the key ring a shake, making it jingle. "Let's go to Boston."

They gathered at the exit at the rear of the office.

Cody stood, hand on the knob.

"It's berth twenty-four," he said. "The *Spanish Lady*. Like I said, it's been fueled up and ready to go since before the storm. We just need to cast off the mooring lines, and we should be good to go."

The tension was thick, and Sidney's eyes kept going to the covered body lying on the cot. Snowy had been sniffing at it with great interest, but Sidney quickly pulled her back. She looked from Cody's dad's body to Rich and saw her friend barely able to keep his eyes open.

"Hey, you good?" she asked, slapping his arm with the back of her hand. They were all listening now.

"Yeah," he said with a quick nod. "Just a little frazzled. Hopefully I'll be able to rest some on the boat ride."

Sidney stared, not sure if she truly believed her friend, but what choice did she have at the moment? She was suddenly struck with an overwhelming urge to tell him, to tell them both, Rich and Cody, how much they meant to her, but chose to keep it to herself.

"Ready?" Cody then asked. "Slip twenty-four," he repeated. "On the right-hand side, about halfway down."

Langridge and Sayid had their weapons out again. Sidney held tightly to the metal pipe, which she'd grown quite attached to.

"Go!" Cody said, pulling open the door and rushing out onto the dock. He waved them on in front of him. "C'mon, c'mon!"

Langridge and Sayid ran past; Rich, as quick as he was able, behind them. Sidney and Snowy after that.

Sidney was running, her dog faithfully at her side, when she looked for Cody. He wasn't there. This was starting to become a habit. Though she knew that she shouldn't, she stopped, turning to see where he was.

He had lagged behind, watching as the birds that had been circling the marina office figured out that their prey was escaping. And there was something else now, something dark and flowing across the parking lot, between and over the cars still parked there.

"Cody, c'mon!" Sidney called.

The birds were coming—the smaller ones first, the little sparrows and wrens that zipped through the air like fighter pilots. One came at her face, and she batted it away.

"Cody!"

"Go!" He waved her on. He was at the fuel pumping station on the dock, fiddling with the levers. He removed a key from his pocket, opening up all the locks.

She went to him, taking his arm. Snowy had begun to bark, warning them of the approaching threat.

"Get to the boat, Sid," Cody ordered.

She saw that determined look in his eyes, a look that she'd grown to both despise and admire when they were dating, the look that told her there wasn't a chance she could change his mind.

He pulled the nozzle from the pump and pointed it away from her. "Go on," he said. "I've got this."

The larger birds circled above their heads, as if checking things out before launching a full-scale attack. The living wave had made it to the top of the docks and was slithering toward them.

She wanted to know what he was going to do, but there wasn't enough time for explanations.

"Don't do anything stupid," she said instead, then turned and ran with Snowy toward the boat.

His dad was once a smoker.

Cody hadn't really paid attention to it, but he remembered how his mother used to nag him to quit. Dad had always ignored her, but when she got sick, he'd stopped. There was no weaning, no tense moments of craving, he'd just stopped. One day he smoked, and the next day he didn't.

But he'd still continued to carry that silver Zippo lighter, and now Cody had it, taken from his father's pocket where he'd known it would be.

The birds swarmed above his head, growing thicker and bolder, testing his resolve by dropping down suddenly to attack. Cody was quick, using the metal of the pump nozzle to swat a few of the larger birds aside. He knew what he had to do to buy them the time they needed to get the *Spanish Lady* out into open water.

And he also knew how he was feeling about Benediction since the nightmare of the previous day. His island had been tainted, and he thought it might be best if the diseased version of what he loved went away. Maybe something that wasn't blighted would rise up to replace it.

It was something to think about, he mused as he ducked beneath the beak of a swooping gull. Cody pointed the nozzle and squeezed the lever, spewing gasoline at the attacking birds. Those that were hit immediately reacted, dropping to the wharf to flap spastically as they were choked by the fumes.

He could see the wave of life now and was even able to distinguish the specific animals that made up the loathsome abomination spreading toward him. There were insects of every conceivable kind, as well as rats, squirrels, cats, dogs, and even chipmunks all mashed together into one, enormous nightmare thing.

Yeah, he thought as he aimed the nozzle and squeezed, spraying a steady stream of gasoline down onto the dock. *Maybe it would be best if it all* was *burned away.*

He flicked open the lid of the Zippo and lit the flame, carefully bringing it to the stream of gasoline. The fumes ignited first and then the liquid. Cody continued to spray the burning gasoline into the air, igniting the attacking birds, as well as the dock.

Soon there was only fire, ravenously eating up all that it touched.

And Cody smiled into the searing flames and choking black smoke, whispering to his father that this was for him.

Sidney and Snowy had reached berth twenty-four when the gasoline ignited.

There was a rush of air followed by a blast of heat, which spun them both around on the dock to look back where they'd come from.

"Oh my God, Cody," she found herself whispering as she watched the flames leap into the sky, setting the attacking flock on fire and sending up billowing plumes of smoke that obscured the end of the dock from view. She was tempted to go back but . . .

"Sidney!" Sayid called from the bridge of the yacht.

She looked to him as he beckoned her to board and then back to the end of the dock, where the fire had begun to spread, and the smoke grew blacker and thicker.

Had he actually done it, she was forced to wonder. Had he taken his own life over the sorrow that he felt for the death of his dad? She felt her resolve begin to crumble, her legs beginning to tremble. Sidney made a few stumbling steps toward the fire and smoke and stopped, her mind suddenly filled with flashes of memories of their times together. She remembered the first time that they'd talked, how he'd asked her out as his friends looked on and she'd said no, their first kiss after the Thanksgiving football game, his mouth tasting like beer, the night they broke up, the yelling and the tears . . .

Sidney moved closer to the fire, her cheeks seared by the heat. She needed to know for sure if he was gone.

Snowy whined beside her.

"I know, girl," Sidney said, turning from the fire and smoke. She had to get on board the *Spanish Lady* and head to Boston. There were too many lives at stake.

But something caught her eye and she paused.

She thought she saw something moving within the smoke, something that could have been . . .

She stared for a minute longer, and just as she was convinced that it was merely a trick of the fire or shifting smoke, he appeared.

His clothes and skin were filthy as he emerged, coughing crazily and falling to his knees in a gagging, coughing jag.

Her heart leaped in her chest so hard she thought it might explode from her rib cage as she ran to him.

"Did anybody ever tell you that you're a stupid ass?" she asked, helping him to stand and practically dragging the choking young man down the dock to the waiting boat.

"Yeah, you," he gasped in between coughs. "All the time."

"Well that hasn't changed," she said, bringing him to the boat, where Sayid helped him to climb aboard.

"Nice to know something hasn't."

CHAPTER **THIRTY-SIX**

Isaac continued to walk through the overgrown path.

The bugs and the animals under the control of the bad radio did not try to harm him.

But the other signal, the one that sounded more and more like a voice, told him to go on.

To continue.

To come.

He heard screams from somewhere nearby and stopped in the center of the path. Looking through the trees, he could see a house, its backyard filled with old automobiles, and he was reminded of his own home and how his mother used to like to collect things.

Isaac smiled at the memory of his mother and her odd ways.

Collect things . . . His sister had said it was a disease. What had she called it? *Hoarding.* Yes, yes, the word was "hoarding."

The screams intensified, and then Isaac gasped as the glass doors leading to the deck of the house shattered. A man tumbled out and over the deck rail, landing in a heap on the ground. Isaac squinted for a better look as the man rolled and flailed on the grass, flinging furry little animals away.

Cats. Kittens really.

Isaac felt a combination of sadness and fear, remembering his own feline companions, but also remembering what they had done to his mother when the bad radio had gotten into their heads.

A woman stumbled through the broken doorway holding a tiny bundle in her arms. A baby. She was screaming, and as she ran from the deck, Isaac could see that her back was covered with small cats that ripped and dug and scratched.

He had to help them.

But as he stepped off the path toward the house through the trees, the voice echoing inside his head told him no.

Isaac tried to fight it, to push it down, but it grew so loud, and it made his head hurt so bad that he thought he would be sick.

He stumbled back onto the path, and the pain went away as the voice urged him on.

Come, it said to him.

Isaac looked back to the house, silent now.

Come, said the voice, louder and more firm.

He turned, his gaze on the path before him.

Come.

CHAPTER **THIRTY-SEVEN**

"I can make it," Burwell said from the floor.

"You won't," Doc Martin scoffed. "You'll be nothing but a hindrance."

"You wound me," the security officer said.

Doc Martin chuckled as she sat down on the couch.

"So, you two an item?" Clara asked.

Burwell looked shocked.

"Are you crazy?" Doc Martin said. "Business associates at best, and even that's a bit of a stretch. The only reason I came along was to keep an eye on the boy."

"That turned out well," Burwell muttered.

"Yeah, and you didn't do much better. How the hell was I to know he'd take off?"

"Is the kid really worth the risk?" Clara asked from her

wingback in the corner. "It ain't no party out there."

Doc Martin nodded. "I think he is," she said. "He's a good kid, and I promised someone special I'd look after him. Besides, if he has some kind of connection to whatever's causing the problems on this island, that could prove very useful. So, long answer short, yeah, he's worth the risk."

The old woman nodded. "Okay, how're you gonna pull it off?"

Doc Martin sighed and shrugged. "I have to find a vehicle to borrow, and once I do, I'll have to find Isaac."

Clara glared at her. "That's it?" she asked with a tinge of disgust. "That's your plan?"

"It's what I've got right now," Doc Martin said.

Clara made clucking sounds as she shook her head.

"What?" Doc Martin asked. "You have anything better to contribute?"

"The plan does suck," Burwell agreed with the old lady.

Doc Martin shook her head with exasperation. "Well I can't just stay here," she said. "I have to go and find him . . . I can't leave him out there."

Clara pushed herself up from her chair with a grunt. "I've heard enough," she grumbled as she hobbled through the living room and disappeared down the hallway, only to return a few minutes later with a shoe box in her hand.

"Here," she said, holding the box out to Doc Martin.

"What?" Doc Martin asked. "Are you giving me a pair of comfortable shoes to wear?"

"You're pretty funny," Clara said as the vet took the box from her. "Surprised you didn't go into comedy."

Doc Martin lifted the lid from the box and gazed inside at several clips of ammunition and a gun. "Okay," she said, hefting the weapon.

"Nice," Burwell said with a smile and nod. "Colt .45, old school, but effective."

"If you're going out there, you're gonna need to protect yourself," Clara said. "Belonged to my husband. He brought it home with him after the war."

"Thanks" was all Doc Martin could say.

"That's quite all right," Clara said. She dug into a deep pocket on her powder-blue slacks and produced a chain with a single key hanging from it. "This should help you too." She tossed the key at Doc Martin.

"Okay," Doc Martin said as she caught it. "And this is for?"

"Car in the garage. I don't drive it anymore on accounta my age, but I still start it up every other day or so . . . should be workin' just fine."

Doc Martin didn't know what to say. Clara had begrudgingly brought them in, allowed them a place to stay, and fed them, but this level of generosity was surprising. Finally, she just repeated, "Thanks."

"Wasn't usin' either," Clara said with a shrug as she returned to her chair. "And besides," she added, lowering herself down with a loud groan. "The sooner you get out of here, the sooner I can be alone with handsome boy over there." She made her gray eyebrows waggle as she cackled insanely.

Doc Martin looked over to a nervous Burwell.

"Might as well use that forty-five on me right now," he said, and the veterinarian's laughter joined with that of the crazy old woman.

CHAPTER **THIRTY-EIGHT**

Phil Ramos thought he had forgotten how to pray.

As a little boy in the Philippines, he would attend church with his family in Manila, pray to God and all the saints to take care of his family and all the people he loved and his country. But as he'd grown older, his thoughts had turned to other things besides prayer.

He'd dreamed of going to the United States, getting a good education, and becoming a nurse. Praying to God became less and less of a priority, replaced by hard work to put him on the road to making his dreams become a reality.

And did they ever. He finally had the life he'd always wanted, and prayer no longer seemed quite so important.

Until now.

He had made it to the garage . . . *they* had made it to the garage.

They'd waited as long as they could for Deacon and Delilah, but something was coming.

He tried to picture what it was and found that he couldn't. It was like looking at everything in the world that terrified him all rolled into one horrible thing that was chasing him.

Chasing all of them.

They had managed to put a door between them and the . . . something, although it was what he had seen of the city outside, through the windows of the skywalk as he'd raced into the parking garage with the others, that had made Phil even more afraid.

The storm still raged, and the sky was filled with heavy dark clouds and also thick black smoke from the fires that burned uncontrolled in buildings not far from Elysium.

Father Jon had always warned of God's dissatisfaction with the world and that the end of all things was closer than anyone knew. Phil had scoffed at such superstitious nonsense, but now . . .

Is that what's happening? he considered. Was God so tired of human-kind's disrespect that this day was the day He'd chosen to end it all?

He saw Father Jon on the pulpit in his memories, warning them to always be prepared . . . for their souls to be clean.

And that was when he remembered.

"Our Father, who art in heaven . . . ," Phil prayed, as he raced toward his car.

"Hallowed be Thy name . . ." He could see it at the far end of the garage, squeezed in the last space before the wall.

"Thy kingdom come, Thy will be done . . ." He reached the Subaru, grabbed the door handle, and pulled. Locked.

"On earth as it is in heaven . . . ," he gasped as he dug in his pocket for his keys.

"Give us this day, our daily bread . . ." The key ring was jammed with keys of all sizes and shapes, and he fumbled to find the right one. "And forgive us our trespasses . . ."

He found the key and shoved it in the lock, turning it—unlocking the door.

"As we forgive those who trespass against us . . ."

Phil pulled open the door and was about to climb inside when he felt it, a strange tingling sensation on the back of his neck.

As if he was being watched.

He couldn't help himself. Slowly he turned to face the garage behind him. All he could see were the cars that remained unclaimed and wondered briefly if those who had driven them that morning were even still alive to retrieve them.

"And lead us not into temptation . . ."

Dirt, or maybe rust, dropped from the ceiling, striking the back of his car with a metallic *ting*. Immediately Phil's eyes turned to the ceiling.

It was lined with pipes going this way and that, sprinkler pipes, pipes housing the wiring for lights and alarms—pipes on which perched rows and rows of black, furry bodies, hairless tails dangling down beneath them.

Rats.

And each and every one of them was looking directly at him, their plump, hairy bodies vibrating with repressed energy as they readied themselves to pounce.

"But deliver us from evil."

He finished the prayer, the Lord's Prayer, wondering if his soul would be clean enough for heaven, even as the flesh was torn from his body.

"This way!" Mason screamed to the two women who were running off in the opposite direction.

He knew their time would be limited, that the strange mass of insects and animals was probably not done with them.

Nancy and Mallory seemed to have their own plan . . . and where did Phil go?

Never mind. He thought of his wife and baby girl at home alone and spun around, racing away toward his truck parked on the other side of the garage. In his mind he saw them safe, not knowing what he was dealing with here, but that idea was quickly derailed as he recalled what he'd seen outside the office window. A city in the grip of a storm, but also something else.

Something that he did not understand, something that terrified him.

Mason rounded a corner, spotting his truck not too far from a stairway exit. Quickening his pace, he dug into his pocket for his keys, then glanced down quickly to find the right key before looking up.

Into the eyes of the dog standing silently in his path.

It was quite possibly the hairiest and filthiest dog that he had ever seen, its eyes barely visible through long strands of matted fur.

Slowly, never taking his eyes from the dog, he withdrew the pair of scissors he still had in his back pocket. "I'm just going to my car," he told the animal, holding the scissors before him.

But the dog just stood, staring at him menacingly. Silently.

He moved to go around the dog, and it moved in kind, again blocking his path.

"You don't want to play that game with me," he warned, lifting his weapon higher as he made another move for his truck.

And once again the dog was right there, but this time closer. Mason reacted at once, bringing the scissors down, cutting a vicious furrow the length of the dog's snout.

The dog made no sound as its head lolled forward and a steady stream of blood puddled on the concrete floor.

"There's more where that came from, you ugly son of a—"

The dog charged, nails scrabbling across the concrete as it lunged. Mason managed to stumble back, swinging the scissors again and catching the animal on the side of its head. The force of the blow sent the dog veering to the left, giving Mason time to catch his balance and ready for another attack. His heart beat crazily, and his blood felt like liquid fire coursing through his veins, but he gripped the scissors tightly, forcing himself to wait for the dog's next move instead of lunging recklessly forward.

The dog swayed for a moment as blood continued to drip from its damaged snout, and Mason noticed that part of a floppy ear was missing as well. Then it started toward him again. He gripped the scissors all the tighter, wishing every ounce of strength he had into his arm, ready to channel it into the force of his next blow.

But the dog did not attack. Instead it slowly dropped to the floor of the garage, sitting Sphinx-like, staring at Mason as if it was waiting for something.

Slowly, cautiously, Mason lowered his arm. The beast began to pant—the first sound the dog had made, and Mason found it chilling as it grew in intensity, like a locomotive preparing to roll down the track.

"Stay there," he ordered with a snarl, holding his weapon in front of him as he carefully backed away and moved toward his truck.

The dog suddenly stopped its rough breathing, and its body went rigid as if electrified. Mason was ready, again raising his weapon to ward off an attack.

But it wasn't the dog that he needed to worry about.

The dog's fur had started to move. At first he thought there was something wrong with his eyes, but then he realized that he wasn't seeing things at all. The dog's fur *was* moving; there were things coming out from beneath the thick, filthy coating of hair, things black and shiny that dropped to the ground at an alarming rate. The dog had opened its mouth, showing off its nasty yellow teeth, and the pink cavern of its maw.

And living things were flowing from there as well.

How many bugs can be inside one dog? Mason wondered as he tried to make it to his truck.

Hopefully not enough to kill a man was the answer.

"Where did you park?" Mallory asked Nancy. She pushed the button on her key, and a large, bronze-colored vehicle beeped and flashed its lights.

"I didn't drive today," Nancy replied as if just realizing this bit of information. "I came in with a friend!" she added, her voice rising.

"Don't worry," Mallory said. "I'll take you with me."

"Get in," she ordered.

Nancy raced for the passenger door as Mallory climbed into the driver's seat, slamming the door closed. Quickly she looked around, checking all the mirrors for signs of anything coming after them.

"Do you think the others made it?" Nancy asked, reaching for her seat belt.

Mallory did the same, eyes going to the rearview for another look. "I don't know. I certainly hope that—"

Something moved rapidly across the lot, disappearing from view as it neared the car. Quickly Mallory turned the key in the ignition, feeling a sudden, nearly overwhelming sense of panic.

Just as the SUV was struck from below.

Mallory and Nancy screamed in unison as something pounded the underside of the vehicle, making it rock from side to side.

"What is it?" Nancy cried, frantically looking out the windows.

"I don't know!" Mallory shouted, slamming the car into drive and lurching forward, smashing into the Chrysler minivan parked in front of her. "Shit," she hissed, putting the car in reverse and stomping on the gas again. The SUV lurched back, but then the tires began spinning as if stuck on ice.

"Why aren't we moving?" Nancy cried, her voice rising with panic.

"I don't know!" Mallory yelled again, that answer seeming to be perfect for everything that day. She stepped harder on the gas pedal but only succeeded in making the engine rev all the louder. She looked again into the rearview mirror and felt the grip of terror as she watched the floor of the parking garage move with insect life, a living wave flowing beneath the car.

Having lived through many New England winters, she found herself suddenly thinking of her brother Denny's advice on how to get through snow.

You have to rock it.

And she did just that, putting the car in drive, surging forward into the van, before reversing and attempting to back up again. She was actually having some success. The car's tires caught, and Mallory managed to drive about six feet away when they were once more struck from beneath. This time the blow was so powerful that it lifted the front of the car, and as it crashed back onto the floor, the air bags deployed, filling the interior of the vehicle with white powder.

Mallory was stunned, the taste of blood in her mouth.

"What?" she found herself saying aloud. She tried to focus and looked over to see Nancy leaning forward, her bleeding face pressed to the rubbery pillow as it slowly deflated.

"Hey," Mallory said, reaching over and giving Nancy's shoulder a shove.

The yellow jacket just *appeared*, sinking its stinger into the flesh below Mallory's thumb.

She screamed, pulling her hand back as Nancy moaned. There were more yellow jackets inside the car, and she reached for the knob to close the air vents. But her hand fell upon a clump of wasps that stung her palm and between her fingers, clinging to her hand. The pain was excruciating, and she waved her hands and arms about, attempting to protect herself, hysterical with pain and fear. Nancy had begun to twitch, but her face was covered with the black and yellow insects. Mallory screamed and thrashed, her hands so swollen that she could no longer bend her fingers. The cloud of insects grew thicker, a steady stream of the wasps flowing through the air vents into the space.

It was too late for Nancy, but Mallory knew she couldn't die that way too. Frantically she jammed her swollen fingers into the button to release the seat belt, then managed to get the door to the SUV open, stumbling awkwardly from the vehicle.

The floor beneath her feet was moving, as if the cement had somehow gained a life of its own. Immediately the insects surged upward, covering her legs. She began to run, screaming for somebody . . . anybody to help her, but knowing there was no one.

"Oh God," Mallory wailed as her numbed legs finally gave out, and she pitched forward into the writhing mass of insect life on the floor of the parking garage.

It's like falling into the sea, she thought briefly, before oblivion mercifully claimed her.

CHAPTER **THIRTY-NINE**

The marina burned as they sailed away, clouds of billowing black smoke reaching into the sky, small clapping explosions echoing across the water.

Sidney wondered if there would even be a marina anymore when she got back.

If she got back.

She watched the sky for birds, but the fire and smoke seemed to be keeping them away . . . or maybe something else was.

"Maybe the signal only reaches so far," Sayid said from beside her, startling her.

She hadn't heard him approach, but she watched him now as he gazed out over the bluish-gray water.

"The alien presence," he continued, without looking at her. "Maybe that's why the birds aren't chasing us . . . its influence can only reach so far, and the further we get from the island the better."

Sidney shrugged. "I don't know," she said. "Maybe." The awful sensation in her brain was quiet. *Resting?* She didn't know.

"How does the connection work?" Sayid asked.

She turned her attention toward the water seething in the large boat's wake.

"Sometimes it's there, and sometimes it isn't." She shrugged again.

"So you're not aware of it all the time?"

"Oh, I'm aware, all right," she said, feeling a sudden flash of anger at the questions. "I know it's there, but sometimes I just don't know where."

He was looking at her as if she were some kind of bug under a microscope. She knew he was a scientist, and the information she had in her head was important, but the questions still made her uncomfortable.

"It's like being in one of those big houses on the island, those McMansions?" she continued, not sure he would understand the analogy, but it was the only way she could explain what was happening to her. "I'm in one room and that . . . thing is somewhere else in the house."

He nodded slowly, then returned his gaze to the ocean.

"I'm sorry," he said after a few moments. "Sorry that you and your friends . . . the island . . . had to go through—this."

"It sucks," she agreed, unable to think of any other response.

"We should have moved faster," Sayid said. "We should have known."

"How could you have known?" Sidney asked. "It's not like this stuff happens every day."

The way he moved his head then, it was almost as if he didn't want to look at her. "No, not every day," Sayid said slowly, reluctance in his tone. "But it has happened a few times. Sporadically over the past three years or so. We just hadn't been able to figure out what we were dealing with . . . until now. Honestly, I think we didn't want to believe what we were seeing."

"Shit," Sidney muttered, not really knowing how to react.

"We'd never encountered anything like this before," Sayid said. "The world never encountered anything like this . . . there's no precedent."

She thought of the island and what had happened there, her thoughts drifting to Boston and what was likely going to happen there, and beyond. "Let's hope it isn't too late to create one," she said.

She could see by the grim look on his face that he agreed.

Let's hope.

Cody wasn't sure he'd ever been so tired, but at the same time he felt strangely alive.

He was piloting the yacht toward Boston, watching the gathering storm clouds and thinking about the future.

He'd thought his life was over—the breakup with Sidney, the insaneness on the island, the gruesome death of his father. It had been hard imagining life beyond that very dark place in time.

But now . . .

He had somehow found the strength to act. He had done what

he had to do, burning the evil with fire—chasing the darkness away with light.

It was all kinda corny, he realized, but it had helped.

Cody gazed ahead, hands clasped upon the wheel, steering the boat into the storm with a confidence he had been missing for quite some time.

Steering himself toward a future that he didn't believe he had—until now.

Rich didn't know he was dreaming. It felt so real.

He was back home with his parents in Newton, Massachusetts. They were sitting in the dining room about to have dinner. The amount of food on the table was outrageous, and Rich couldn't remember if it was Thanksgiving or not. He didn't think it was, but he wasn't about to tell his mother; besides, he was starving.

His father stood at the head of the table, the enormous turkey laid out before him, carving knife and fork in hand. Rich watched with hungry eyes, his gaze traveling across the crowded tabletop as he thought of what he would have for his first helpings.

Something skittered across the table, hiding behind the bowl of mashed potatoes. He waited to see if whatever it was would emerge again but instead caught sight of something else that had crawled onto the turkey plate and disappeared inside the bird.

His father plunged the twin metal tines of the fork into the meat of the bird.

"Dad," Rich said suddenly. "You might not want to—"

But his father didn't listen, cutting into the juicy meat of the turkey breast, revealing a living core.

"Oh God," Rich said, recoiling as spiders, worms, and beetles spilled from the turkey.

His father continued to slice, as if not noticing the insect life swarming over the plate and onto the table.

Rich couldn't move, frozen in his chair, watching in horror as the bugs crawled up his father's arms. He glanced toward his mother, hoping she would do something, but he saw that she didn't seem to notice either, carefully arranging the bowls of potatoes, squash, thick homemade gravy, and stuffing.

"Mom!" he cried out, but she just smiled, leaning across the table to light the candles at its center.

The insects were everywhere now, flowing across the table, onto the food, and onto his mother.

Rich tried to move again, but his body remained frozen. "I can't move!" he cried out. "Mom . . . Dad, I can't . . ."

The insects had covered his parents, marring their features with their shiny shelled bodies. But Dad continued to fuss with the carcass of the bird, while Mom moved a few more things and stood back, hands on her hips to take it all in.

Rich was crying, the horror of what he was seeing almost more than his brain could stand. He managed to move himself sideways in the chair, hitting against the side of the table, causing things to tumble.

The lit candle landed upon the table with a hiss and a whoosh of air as the tablecloth caught fire.

"No, no, no!" Rich screamed, watching as the flames grew

higher and more bold. He tried to squirm and push himself away as the heat of the fire singed his skin.

It wasn't long before the flames caught his parents, as unaware of the fire that ate at them as they were of the thousands of insects that crawled upon their bodies.

The wallpaper was peeling away in fiery strips that floated through the air like fish swimming beneath the sea. Burning embers dropped upon Rich's paralyzed body, setting his clothes afire. He could feel his skin blistering.

The pain was excruciating, but all he could do was scream helplessly as his parents continued to prepare their Thanksgiving feast.

Even though they were nothing more than burning skeletons.

Dr. Sayid pressed down on Rich's shoulders, attempting to keep the thrashing young man in place on the narrow bunk in the boat's cabin. His skin felt hot with infection.

"It's all right," Sayid said, attempting to soothe the moaning Rich. He wasn't sure if it was his words or something else, but the young man calmed, his body falling back limply on the bunk.

Sayid waited a moment to be sure Rich slept, then checked the bandages and the wound. It still looked infected, but there was little more he could do, other than keep it clean.

He crossed the cabin, drawn by an old CB radio sitting in a place of honor upon a shelf. It looked as though it was still operational, and the doctor turned it on. The dials glowed as it came to life with a loud, crackling static. He glanced at his patient to be sure the noise hadn't disturbed him, but Rich was still fast asleep, muttering incoherently. Turning his attention back to the CB, Sayid turned the dials, hoping for an open channel, only to hear that angry hissing sound dominating the airwaves.

He wondered about the beings that were responsible for what was happening. Why would creatures so advanced travel from wherever it was they came from only to commit such violent acts upon another intelligent species? It perplexed him, but then he reminded himself that he was human. For these otherworldly beings, what they were doing might just be how they functioned, what they did to survive. It angered him to think that humanity's first real contact with an alien species would result in violence, but very little opportunity was left now for peaceful discourse.

Being without any form of communication with the outside world chilled him to the core. What was going on in Boston . . . as well as the rest of the world? He pushed those thoughts down and focused on the current objective—get to Boston, then contact the authorities.

Suddenly he realized he was no longer alone and looked up to see Sidney standing in the cabin.

Sayid gasped. He must have been far more tired than he realized, for at first he didn't see Sidney—he saw his own daughter standing there.

And felt the panic immediately set in.

He thought of her back in Chicago, and then found himself thinking about the weather.

They come in the storm, he heard a child's voice say. The little girl who had managed to be the sole survivor of another isolated-island attack.

"Thought I'd come down and check on Rich," Sidney said. "Are you all right, Doc?" she asked.

Sayid sighed, squeezing his eyes shut. "Yes, Sidney, I'm fine. I'm just a little fatigued."

"If you want to rest . . . ," she said, making a move to climb the stairs back up to the deck.

"No, that's quite all right," he said quickly. "I think some fresh air will do me good." He smiled as he walked past her. "Stay here with your friend; he might need reassurance that things will be fine." He had started up the stairs when he heard her from behind him.

"Will they?"

Sayid stopped and turned, leaning down so he could see her below the deck. "Sorry?"

"Will things be fine?" she asked him point-blank.

There was an awkward silence between them that said more than any words could.

"There's some Tylenol on the table if he should wake up," Sayid said finally, and turned to the deck above.

Sidney watched the scientist go, feeling her mood plummet even lower than it had been.

What the hell are we doing? she asked herself. Sailing into a storm to get to a city in the midst of . . .

Invasion?

It was crazy, but that's exactly what it was, and it was even crazier to think that they might be able to do something about it. Who the hell were they?

She felt the presence inside her mind flutter just enough to remind her that it was still there. It hurt, and she considered the Tylenol on the table for herself.

But then Rich moaned, and she found herself going quickly to his side. Her friend looked terrible, his skin pale, yet hot to the touch. Sidney looked around the cabin and went to a small wet bar in the corner, where she soaked a strip of paper towel in some cool tap water, then returned to Rich and laid it upon his burning brow. He shivered as she leaned forward to stroke the side of his face.

"You're gonna be okay," she told him. "We're gonna get to Boston and find you a hospital, and get some antibiotics into you."

He seemed to calm a little bit, so she continued to stroke his dampened hair.

She knew how Rich felt about her; she would have to have been stupid not to understand the meaning of the years of sidelong glances and smirks when he thought she wasn't looking. And she did actually love him . . . but not in that way. He'd been like a brother to her for so very long that she couldn't imagine him any other way. It would crush her to lose him from that special place he filled for her. She imagined they would be having a talk in the not too distant future.

If there was a future to have.

"How are you going to take it?" she found herself asking her unconscious friend. "If I tell you that I don't like you in that way? It's not that I don't love you. . . ." She found it hard to say the words, but now just seemed like the right time.

"I do love you," she told him. "So very much, just not in the way that you'd like. And I'm sorry for that." Sidney stroked his cheek.

"Hopefully, when you get better, we can have a good talk and work this crap out."

Sidney looked at him, lying there so frail and sick, and thought how terrible it would be to lose him.

"You rest and get better, okay?" She half expected him to answer in some wiseass fashion, but he remained quiet and sleeping in the grip of infection.

A bluish light on the other side of the cabin caught her eye, and she went over to it. It was an old CB radio that had been left on, hissing softly to itself. *This must be what Sayid was looking at,* she thought. She moved closer, reaching out to turn the silver dial.

Her entire body seemed to grow numb except for a strangely cold sensation in her hand on the CB dial. She felt as though she was falling, everything around her stretching and distorting, as that cold, horrible presence grew inside her mind, writhing in the dark places that had begun to expand, swallowing up reality and bringing her . . .

Someplace else.

The imagery was fast and furious. A city engulfed in storm, towers of metal perched on hills and rooftops, reaching up to the heavens, entwined with thick, pulsating tendrils of red and lined with buzzing circuitry. Thinner veins branched out from the larger, webbing the entire structure, making it into something more than it was.

But what?

Sidney reached for the information, trying to draw it closer so that she might understand, but someone . . . *something* . . . didn't want her to know.

And that just made her angry. In her mind she surged forward, wrapping her fingers within the vision, pulling it away like a sheet covering a piece of furniture.

The pain she felt was excruciating, needles of intensity jabbing into her brain; they did not want her to see, but for the briefest of instances—

She did.

Then it was if she'd been ripped from her body, only to be shoved back in like dirty clothes into an overstuffed laundry bag.

Sidney actually screamed as she rushed back, snapping forward on the curved bench below the radio, where she'd fallen, gasping for air as she attempted to reacclimate herself.

She realized that she wasn't alone and looked into the disturbed face of Brenda Langridge. The woman's eyes were wide, shocked, and Sidney had to wonder exactly what she'd seen.

"I'm okay," Sidney gasped.

Langridge slowly shook her head. "No," she said. "You're not—look at your hands."

Sidney's hands were covered in blood, and for the briefest of moments she wondered who it belonged to, but that was just before the pain kicked in, the nasty feeling of thousands of tiny lacerations on the tips of her fingers.

"How?" she managed to get out, staring at her still bleeding fingertips.

When Langridge didn't reply, Sidney glanced up to see her looking at the table and suddenly understood where her injuries had come from.

The CB radio had been completely dismantled, every single piece of the device taken apart and separated into neat piles.

"Jesus," Langridge said as she grabbed some paper towels from the sink and stuffed them into Sidney's hands. "Why?" she asked.

Sidney looked as surprised as she was, almost as if the girl had no idea that she'd done it. "I don't know," she answered, squeezing the gradually staining paper towels. "I was trying to find a signal on the radio," she began. "And then . . ."

Langridge moved back to the table, reaching down to examine the circuitry that had been set aside. "Why were you taking the high-tech stuff out and discarding the rest?"

"I said I don't know," Sidney snapped.

"What was it like?" Langridge persisted. "Was it like a blackout? Were there visions this time or . . ."

"Yeah, visions," Sidney said.

Langridge looked at her and noticed a trickle of blood beneath one nostril. "Anything useful?" she asked, motioning with her finger beneath her nose.

Sidney wiped her nose with the paper towels. "Thanks," she said. "I really don't know. . . . I saw the city again . . . felt what it was doing . . ." A vague look appeared in her eyes. "I saw towers," she continued softly, and Langridge had no doubt that Sidney was seeing them again.

"What kind of towers?"

Sidney didn't answer right away, keeping that weird vagueness to her expression.

"Sid? What kind of towers?" Langridge repeated.

The girl was back, her eyes focusing on the here and now. "Cell towers?" she asked, as if not quite sure. "But there was something different about them. . . . They . . . they were changed."

"Changed," Langridge repeated. "How?"

"They were changed to hurt us," Sidney said.

Langridge was about to pursue that when the boat shuddered as if it had struck something.

"Did you feel that?" she asked Sidney, looking around. Had they hit something in the water?

It happened again, and then again.

And then Langridge realized that the yacht hadn't hit anything at all. Something was hitting the yacht.

CHAPTER **FORTY**

Delilah had been on the eighth floor—the Vegetable Patch—only one other time. It had been during the first week of her orientation when Mallory had given her a tour of the special unit, even though as a student, she would never work up there.

The unit was fascinating. She remembered how eerily quiet it had been, only the soothing hum of the life-support beds and the beeping of the computers that monitored them. There had been one nurse on the unit that day, Betty, and Delilah found herself wondering about Betty's fate this day.

She reached out and pulled open the doors to the unit, Deacon following close behind her. The lighting was soft, muted, and Delilah realized she was holding her breath as she searched the shadows for signs of attack.

"I've always hated the quiet up here," Deacon said. "It's like a funeral home."

"But the folks here are still alive."

He made a noise of disapproval as they walked down the soft-blue corridor. "You call what's up here alive?" he asked her.

"They're alive," Delilah retorted. "Just not able to move around is all."

"The only reason they are alive is these damn machines."

"Yeah," Delilah agreed. "That's right—but they're still alive."

"That isn't living," Deacon scoffed. "It's a form of cruelty is what I say."

"Some people believe that life is sacred, no matter what."

"Yeah, and I ain't one of them."

The emotion in Deacon's words made Delilah wonder if there was something more behind them, but they had reached the nursing office. The door was closed, and the vertical glass windows on either side showed that the lights were off.

"Doesn't look like anybody's home," Deacon said, leaning in close, trying to see into the darkened office. "Shouldn't there be a nurse up here?"

"Yeah," Delilah said. "I met one, named Betty." She reached for the knob and turned it. The door wasn't locked, and she cautiously pushed it open.

It swung halfway in before something stopped it.

"Something's in the way," she said, wedging herself into the opening to see that a chair had been placed beneath the door. She grabbed the wooden arms of the chair and was attempting to push it aside when—

Something jumped up from behind the desk, something large and screaming like a wild animal. Delilah tried to pull back but wasn't quick enough. Something smashed over her head, making her grunt as stars danced before her eyes.

Deacon grabbed her by the waist, pulling her out. Through bleary eyes Delilah saw her attacker—Betty—once a kind, caring woman, now wild-eyed and full of rage. She was coming at them, using an umbrella as a club, preparing to strike again.

"Betty," Delilah cried out. "It's okay! Remember me? You told me I reminded you of your granddaughter."

The large woman stumbled back, bringing the umbrella down.

"Delilah, right?" the woman said.

"Yes, ma'am," Delilah said.

"Who's that with you?" she asked, raising the umbrella again.

"It's Mr. Deacon," Delilah said.

"Deacon," she said. "Yeah, I know him, but I usually deal with Mason." She moved the chair out of the way and opened the door wide. "Get in here before they notice," she ordered, her eyes darting up and down the hallway.

She slammed the door behind them and wedged the chair underneath the knob.

"They?" Delilah asked.

The woman stared at her for a moment, as if deciding if she should answer or not. "The patients," she finally said, her voice a whisper.

Delilah felt the cold finger of dread run down her sweating

back, and it made her shudder. "What's been going on up here?" she asked.

Betty stared off into space, absently reaching up to rub at her neck, where multiple scratches and bruises were evident. Delilah could see that she was holding back the tears.

"Everything was fine," Betty finally began to explain. "Just as it always was . . . my babies were in their beds, and I was at the nurses' station finishing up my paperwork. Then the power went out, and the alarms started to go off. I got up to check on the babies."

She paused, staring at the door for a moment before continuing. "I can't begin to tell you how insane it was," she said, tears rolling down her cheeks. "Here were these people, most of them I've been taking care of for years, and they've never moved, never changed . . . and yet they were all up and out of their beds." Betty shook her head. "At first I didn't believe it . . . my brain was telling me there was no way I could be seeing what was right before my eyes."

She stopped and looked at them.

"And then I saw the pieces on the floor, and I realized that they were taking apart their beds."

"Just like the computer room," Deacon said, nodding toward Delilah.

"Their fingers," Betty continued as if not hearing him. "They were all bloody. I tried to help them." The look on her face went from sadness to fear, and she rubbed at her neck again. "But then they tried to kill me. They rushed me all together. I barely got in here with my skin intact. I don't think I would have if it wasn't for their years of immobility—even our technology can't prevent the muscle wasting from lack of weight bearing.

Betty's face grew very still as she looked toward the door. "I've got to get out of here," she said quietly. "I've got to get home."

Delilah nodded in agreement, reaching out to touch the woman's arm. "We all need to get home."

Deacon had moved to the door and was listening for sounds in the corridor. "We just have to figure out how to do that without getting killed."

They all heard it at the same time.

"Did you hear . . . ?" Betty began, pushing off from the desk.

"I thought . . . ," Delilah said, moving toward Deacon.

Deacon pressed his ear to the door and raised his hand for quiet. "I think it came from out there."

And then they heard it again. *"Help."*

Deacon nodded excitedly. "I heard that."

Delilah and Betty looked at each other uncertainly.

"I don't want to open the door," Betty said fearfully, clutching her umbrella all the tighter.

"Help."

"But we can't . . . ," Delilah began, understanding the fear. But how could they possibly ignore cries for help?

Deacon carefully opened the door, just enough to cautiously peer up, then down the corridor.

"Help," came the voice again.

"Holy shit," Deacon cried, and ran out into the hallway.

"Deacon, wait!" Delilah called out, racing after the maintenance director.

"Shut the door!" Betty screamed, and Delilah heard it slam behind her as she caught sight of Deacon farther down the hall, dragging a lifeless body back toward her.

"Phil," Delilah gasped, immediately recognizing her friend.

"He's bit up pretty badly," Deacon said, and as he neared her, Delilah could see the bloodstains and rips in Phil's scrubs.

She turned to the office door, grabbed the knob, and pushed, but it didn't budge. "Betty?" she called through the door. "It's okay! It's another nurse from my floor, and he's hurt!"

Deacon had reached her and they waited, nervously watching the hallway for signs of danger.

"Betty!" Delilah called again, more forcefully this time. "Please!"

Another few moments passed, and Delilah wondered if Betty would allow them back into the office, but then she heard the scraping of a chair on the floor and the door opened.

Deacon dragged Phil into the office and laid him gently on the floor as Betty rushed around behind the desk, her umbrella poised for action. Delilah slammed the door closed and replaced the chair under the knob before turning to kneel beside Phil.

He was lying on his side, curled into the fetal position.

"Hey, Phil. It's me, Delilah. You're going to be okay now," she said as she gently touched his arm. He was trembling but didn't respond. "He's pretty bad," Delilah said, looking to Betty. "Is there anything in here we can use to clean up these bites?"

Betty just stared, gripping her umbrella.

"Betty," Delilah nearly shouted. "Is there anything to clean his wounds?"

Finally, Betty seemed to focus. "Yeah," she said. "Yeah, right here." She walked to a file cabinet in the corner and pulled open a drawer.

As Betty rummaged through the drawer, Delilah rolled Phil over onto his back. At first he fought the movement, but then he seemed to relax, his eyes still tightly shut. Delilah looked him up and down, her gaze pausing on his bloodstained scrubs pulled tightly over a bloated belly. That was odd. Phil was very thin, and she was sure she would have noticed a potbelly before.

"Here's some alcohol and cotton balls," Betty said, approaching them, her hands full. "I've got some bandages . . ."

Alarm bells went off inside Delilah's head, and a wave of panic washed over her. "Get away from him," she cried out, scuttling backward across the floor.

"Delilah, what's wrong?" Deacon and Betty asked, almost in unison, sudden fear evident in their tones.

Delilah's gaze was locked on Phil's face. His eyes snapped open—his right eye covered with a silvery sheen.

And then he opened his mouth—they all thought it was to scream in pain.

But it was to let the wasps out.

The swarm of yellow and black insects flowed out onto his body, fluttering their wings, drying them as they readied to take to the air. Deacon and Betty looked as though they might pass out, so Delilah knew it was up to her to do something.

She reached out, grabbed the alcohol from Betty's hand, and ripped off the cap. She stood over Phil's trembling body—and poured the full bottle over the largest concentration of wasps.

As if sensing danger, Phil's body arched violently; his head threw back and his mouth opened wider, and wider still. Delilah blanched at the terrible sound of his jaw dislocating as more insects emerged in a mound of writhing panic.

"A match," she said, looking at Deacon and Betty.

"A match!" she repeated, nearly screaming when they didn't move.

Deacon tapped his pockets. "I don't . . ."

"A match!" Delilah shouted at Betty, swatting at wasps that had finally taken to the air.

"I'm trying to quit," Betty said, her voice soft, almost dreamy. Her eyes, wide with shock, were riveted to the insects pouring out of Phil's open mouth.

"I don't care! Give me a match!"

Finally Betty jumped to action, moving left, then right, as if not sure where she was. She went to the small desk, yanked open the bottom drawer, and pulled out a tattered matchbook.

"There's only one left," she said pathetically.

Delilah ripped the book from the woman's hand and lit the lone match, silently relieved when its head flared. Then she dropped the burning match on top of Phil and watched as the alcohol ignited, setting wasps and Phil afire.

Delilah gasped in horror as Phil rolled onto his side and began to climb to his feet. "We have to get out of here," she cried, taking a step back as Deacon rushed forward with a chair.

The maintenance director rammed into Phil, sending the nurse stumbling backward into the window, igniting curtains that hid a view of the back of the building.

Papers on the desk had begun to burn as flaming wasps fell on them. Smoke and the stench of burning flesh filled the small room, and then the sprinklers kicked in, creating an artificial rain to douse the spreading fires. It slowed the wasps somewhat, but Delilah knew it wouldn't last. "Betty, c'mon," she urged from the door.

The woman still stood near the desk. "They're out there," she said, terror in her voice.

"And the wasps are in here," Delilah retorted. "I'd rather take my chances out there. Let's go!"

"But where are we going?" Betty asked, near panic.

"We're going to get the hell out of here," Deacon said, taking a step forward and holding out his hand to her. "We'll go together."

Delilah stood with her hand on the doorknob, watching, waiting.

"I need to see my grandkids," Betty said finally, moving toward Deacon and reaching to take his hand.

But she never got there.

From out of the smoke, Phil emerged. Before anyone could move or make a sound, he'd wrapped his hands around the woman's throat and savagely twisted.

Snap!

The sound was horrible in its finality, and all Deacon and Delilah could do was watch helplessly while Betty's limp body fell to the ground in a twitching heap as the life left her.

Something inside Delilah let go then, a wave of overwhelming anger washing over her like the flames that had burned Phil's body, and she rushed the nurse, pushing him back with all her might.

Phil tripped over Betty's outstretched arm and fell awkwardly against a high wooden bookcase. The force of the collision made the bookcase fall forward atop Delilah's former friend, driving him to the floor and pinning him there.

Delilah knelt beside Betty's still form, hoping that maybe . . .

She felt for a pulse and found nothing, Betty's skin already beginning to cool.

"C'mon, Delilah," Deacon said, putting a hand firmly on her shoulder. "We can't stay here anymore."

She knew that he was right, the smoke getting thicker by the minute.

"You ready for this?" he asked her as she started toward him.

"Yeah," she said, thinking of Betty's grandchildren and then her own son.

"You should take her shoes," Deacon said softly. "You've only got one now—I think two would be better."

She was horrified by the idea but knew that he was right. Betty's feet didn't appear much bigger than hers, and she found herself apologizing as she slipped the woman's white loafers onto her own feet.

"We just have to get across this unit to the stairs on the other side," Deacon explained. "Those'll take us to the roof. I parked my truck up there this morning. I was gonna lay some tarp down around the roof vents for leaks on Six South."

"Okay," Delilah said, swatting at the remaining wasps that were flying drunkenly out from the smoke and artificial rain. She could feel her heart rate begin to quicken as she watched Deacon's hand grip the doorknob.

"Go," he ordered, opening the door, sending a gust of thick black smoke wafting into the hall with them.

CHAPTER **FORTY-ONE**

Doc Martin bundled herself up like it was the middle of January.

Heavy winter jacket, hood up over her head, scarf across her face, thick gloves, pants tucked into boots tied tight to keep things from crawling inside; she was ready for the swarm of insect and animal life that would most certainly try to prevent her from getting to Clara's car.

"Turn around and let me take a look," Clara ordered from her chair.

Doc Martin was already sweating bullets, but she turned for the old lady.

"Can't be too careful," Clara said. "Those buggies can find their way into the smallest cracks."

"Don't talk about my cracks," Doc Martin joked, catching Burrell's exasperated eye roll from across the room. "Feeling any better?" she asked.

"What if I said yes?" Burwell countered. He'd moved to the sofa, and the trash bag Clara had made him lie on crinkled as he carefully shifted his weight.

"Then I'd be taking this getup off, and *you'd* be going to find Isaac."

"You better get goin' before you pass out," Clara said, interrupting their banter. She grabbed hold of the arms of her chair and slowly pushed herself to her feet. "I'll help you to the door." She staggered to one side, caught herself, and then continued on to the kitchen. "Got the gun?"

Doc Martin felt the hard lump in the pocket of her coat through gloved hands. "Yes I do."

"Good," Clara said, entering the kitchen.

Doc Martin saw her glance briefly at the dog bed before heading over to the kitchen door covered by a heavy tarp that had been nailed to the frame. Clara grabbed a hammer from the nearby counter and began to remove the nails that held the tarp in place.

"Let me help with that," Doc Martin said as she tried to take the hammer from the old woman.

"I can do it," Clara said, pulling the hammer away from the veterinarian.

"I was just going to help," Doc Martin said, throwing up her hands and backing off.

"You help by getting out there, finding your friend, and stopping this bullshit from getting any worse," Clara said, pulling the nails from the wood with a squeaking groan.

The tarp came down. "It's a straight shot to the garage from the steps," the old woman said as she struggled to pull the tarp away from the door. "Don't slow down for nothing."

"I won't," Doc Martin said, feeling her heart rate begin to quicken and the blood rush through her veins. She would have loved a cigarette right then.

"And it would be great if you could bring the car back in one piece," Clara continued as she carefully pulled back the multiple dead bolts locking the door. "Good luck," she said, finally pulling open the door.

Doc Martin recognized Benny immediately. He was once a beautiful, gunmetal-gray Great Dane with a gentle and loving disposition. Now she wasn't sure what he was, but he stood at the bottom of the concrete steps, staring, and it stopped her cold, filling her heart with a sickening dread.

Large patches of the dog's fur were missing; appendages that looked like the limbs of some large and frightening insect protruded from the mottled flesh. And its right eye . . . its terrible, silver-coated right eye.

"Close the door!" Doc Martin barked as Benny silently lunged forward.

But Clara wasn't fast enough or strong enough. "Shit!" she screamed as the dog wedged its horselike head between the door and the jamb, knocking her backward to the floor.

Doc Martin rushed forward and slammed her full weight against the door, pinning the dog before it could get completely in. Silently the beast struggled to wriggle its muscular, misshapen body into the room.

"Son of a bitch," Clara growled, rolling onto her hands and knees and crawling toward the counter.

The dog-thing thrashed, its mottled skin tearing and dripping on the linoleum floor. It pushed one of its insectlike limbs through the narrow opening, digging deeply into the floor in an attempt to drag itself into the kitchen.

Doc Martin managed to turn and braced her back against the door, putting her full weight into it, but she knew it wouldn't be enough to keep the twisted animal-thing out.

"What the hell is going on out there?" she heard Burwell yell from the living room.

"Could use some help!" Doc Martin screamed. Her words were punctuated by a crash from the other room, and she knew Burwell was likely trying to make his way to the kitchen. She also knew he wouldn't be in time.

The thing that used to be Benny was slowly, steadily pulling itself through the doorway. Doc Martin could feel her feet moving forward even as she tried to press her back harder against the door. Clara had managed to haul herself to her feet and was leaning against the counter, muttering and swearing, but she wouldn't be much help against this monster.

And then Doc Martin remembered the gun in her pocket. She ripped the thick glove off and jammed her hand into her coat pocket, closing it around the gun. She yanked it out, the dog far enough inside that it could turn its head directly toward her. She looked into its eyes, focusing on the silvery orb, almost mesmerized by its pulsating lens.

She raised the gun, aimed at that horrible, metallic eye, and was about to pull the trigger when—

A serpentine tongue erupted from the dog's open mouth. It wrapped around her wrist, squeezing with incredible force. Doc Martin tried to twist her arm. Her finger tightened upon the trigger and she fired, but the shot went wild, burying itself in a nearby wall.

She was losing her fight with the door. The dog was almost completely in the room, only its hind legs pinned against the jamb. Another insect limb clawed at the air, snagging the shoulder of her winter coat, pulling tufts of white insulation from the tear.

"Gah!" Doc Martin cried, trying to pull away, but the muscular tongue just squeezed her hand and wrist all the tighter, slowly drawing her closer.

Suddenly Clara was beside her, raising a silver meat cleaver high over her head. "Watch it!" the old woman roared, bringing the blade down and severing the thick tongue in one swift move.

The dog silently reared back, retracting the bleeding stump of its tongue and giving Doc Martin the opportunity to aim her weapon and fire. The first shot struck the dog-thing in the lower chest, but the second went exactly where she wanted it to, blowing out the silvery eye and the back of the poor dog's head. Finally, it collapsed to the kitchen floor in a lifeless heap.

"What the hell?" Burwell exclaimed, and Doc Martin turned to see him leaning against the doorway to the kitchen, the bandage on his leg once again saturated with blood.

"Couldn't have said it better," Clara muttered as she held up the creature's severed tongue and stared at it. "Never saw anything like this before."

"It's the thing on the island," Doc Martin explained. "From what I understand, it can alter animals. . . . It puts them in a kind of cocoon and mixes various characteristics together."

Clara just stared in disbelief, as Doc Martin moved to help Burwell back to the sofa in the living room. She settled him once again on the trash bag and quickly rewrapped his leg before heading back into the kitchen.

She retrieved her glove and her gun, then grabbed Benny's twisted corpse and dragged it outside the back door, pushing it off the top of the concrete steps. When she turned back to the door, Clara was standing there, hammer in one hand, tarp in the other.

"Hopefully, I'll be back," Doc Martin said.

"What if you're not?" Clara asked.

"Don't even want to think that far in advance," Doc Martin said. She pulled the door closed and could already hear the sound of Clara's hammer as she took a deep breath and began her journey across the backyard toward the garage.

As a multitude of insects and vermin converged upon her.

CHAPTER **FORTY-TWO**

Something was attacking the boat.

Sidney couldn't make out what it was as she stood at the port rail, holding on tightly. Cody, at the wheel, tried to outrun the submerged threat, piloting the cabin cruiser in a zigzag pattern across the choppy water.

"What is it?" Langridge demanded. She had her gun out and was peering over the side.

"Don't know," Sayid replied. He too had his gun out, eyes searching the water, waiting. "Looks like my theory about the signal only reaching so far is wrong."

The boat lurched suddenly, its twin outboard engines whining as it rolled to starboard. Snowy was going wild, too close to the edge, barking insanely at something below the waves. Sidney stumbled across the deck, wrapping her still-stinging fingers around the shepherd's collar—

Just as something enormous and gray erupted from the water.

It snapped at the boat but missed as Cody expertly spun the wheel and turned the cruiser just out of reach. With an explosive splash, the great white shark dropped back into the water, the ocean once again concealing its terrible presence.

Sidney held tightly to the whining, barking Snowy as the ocean spray chilled her flesh, and the water churned and frothed around the boat.

And suddenly it was as if someone had fired a confetti cannon across the deck. Only it wasn't raining confetti; it was raining fish—hundreds and hundreds of fish of every conceivable size. Langridge was struck by what looked like a flounder and stumbled backward, almost going over the side.

"Look at this," Sayid said, snatching one of the fish out of the air as it leaped at him. He held the wildly thrashing animal in two hands. There was no way anyone could miss the wide, silver-coated eye.

"As if there was any doubt," Langridge said wryly.

The boat's engines suddenly made a strange screeching sound. Sidney could feel a shudder through the hull, and they were definitely slowing down.

"Shit," Langridge said as she made her way aft.

Sidney followed, dragging Snowy with her. She motioned for Snowy to stay near the door to the cabin, then joined Langridge. They peered cautiously over the side of the boat, and Sidney gasped at the sight of the water, stained crimson with blood. Chunks of fish torn apart by the sputtering propellers floated on the surface, as more schools of fish rushed the spinning blades.

"The fish are jamming up the props!" she screamed over her shoulder to Cody just as the propellers stopped moving.

She could see him on the flybridge, struggling with the throttle, trying to get the propellers moving again, but she knew if they weren't cleared, he would only succeed in burning out the motors. Without thinking, she leaned over to pull the flesh and internal workings of the fish away from the propellers.

Langridge grabbed her and pulled her back. "What the hell are you thinking?" she shouted.

But Sidney wasn't thinking; she'd panicked. The idea of being still out there . . .

They had to come up with another way to free the propellers. Frantically Sidney looked around the small aft deck, her eyes falling on a gaff lying half under a deck seat. She grabbed it and leaned over the side, stabbing it into the bodies of fish that jammed the propellers.

But it was no use—for every fish she tugged away, a hundred more surged forward to take its place.

"It's not working," she cried, dropping the gaff to the deck. "We need something else." She and Langridge began pulling the deck apart, trying to find something, anything that might help.

"That!" Sidney yelled, catching sight of a red gas canister strapped into a corner of the deck.

Langridge grabbed the canister and brought it to Sidney, who took the heavy plastic container and unscrewed the cap.

"Can I ask what you're doing?" Langridge asked.

"Poison the water, kill the fish," Sidney responded as she

dumped the gasoline into the water, nearly choking on the thick fumes that filled the air.

"Okay," Langridge said with uncertainty.

An oily rainbow sheen immediately appeared upon the surface of the water, and a few moments later the bodies of barely twitching fish began to float to the surface.

"I think it's working," Langridge then said excitedly.

Sayid appeared next to them at the edge of the deck with the gaff in his hand. "The gasoline is choking their gills," he said as he poked at the dying fish around the propellers.

Sidney looked up at the flybridge to see Cody watching them. "Try it now!" she yelled up to him.

He gave her a thumbs-up, then ran back to the controls. A strained whine sounded from the motors, but then the propellers began to turn, slowly at first but picking up speed until the boat began to move once again.

"Gun it!" Sidney screamed.

And Cody did, opening the throttle wide, sending the craft lurching forward with a roar.

From the corner of her eye, Sidney saw Sayid fall against the side of the craft, dropping the long wooden gaff. At the same time an almost painful electric tingle ran from the base of her brain down her spine. Something was going to happen; she knew it— could feel it.

"Watch out!" she cried, not really understanding why.

The enormous shark surged out of the water, straight up into the air. The massive fish angled its body as it started to fall, flopping heavily onto the deck, its weighty mass knocking Dr. Sayid to the deck, where he lay, dazed.

Langridge pulled her gun, aiming at the creature's pointed face, at the silver right eye that resembled a large ball bearing stuck in its rubbery head. It spun with incredible speed, lashing out with its tail and swatting the woman and her weapon away.

Snowy ran toward the great white's snapping jaws, barking crazily.

"Sid!" Sidney heard Cody scream. "Sid, what's happening!"

"Just keep going!" she yelled back.

Sayid's legs were now pinned beneath the thrashing behemoth. Its jaws were wide, eager to snap, to take something into its mouth, and Sidney knew it was only a matter of time before it found it. She dove across the slick deck and grabbed the gaff that Sayid had dropped. The shark caught her movement and directed its attention to her as she stood and stepped toward it. The shark opened its mouth wide, ready to claim her, but instead Sidney drove the gaff up behind its razor-sharp teeth, wedging its mouth open.

The great white thrashed wildly from side to side, its powerful tail catching Snowy and sweeping her four legs out from beneath her. The shepherd yelped as she went down hard on her side. The cry froze Sidney's blood, but Snowy was already scrambling to her feet on the water-covered deck, darting away.

The angry shark's silvery eye appeared to grow larger, bulging from its rubbery socket. Sidney saw an opportunity and went for it, sliding across the deck on her knees, reaching out to Dr. Sayid.

"Grab my hands!" she screamed.

The man was terrified, his eyes wide as he tried to squirm out from beneath the sea beast.

"Do it!" she screamed, leaning in closer. She seemed to get through this time, and she saw his eyes focus with realization. He raised his arms toward her.

Sidney grabbed him at the elbows and pulled, using all her strength. The shark's movements were frantic now, shaking its head from side to side in an attempt to dislodge the piece of wood jammed vertically in its jaws.

Sayid had just slid free when Sidney heard the snap.

It was like the crack of a whip, and she saw the gaff had broken and the shark's mouth was free. She watched as it turned its gaze to Sayid's legs, swiftly angling its head in such a way to scoop both of the dangling appendages into its yawning mouth.

There was nothing that she could do.

Nothing at all but watch the horrible event occur.

For a moment time was frozen, the event locked solid as if to say, *Here it is—get a good look.*

But then it happened. It was like something broke inside her brain. She felt something pulled so very, very taut . . . give way.

And then the rush of . . . *what exactly*? It felt like fluid . . . *blood?* No, she didn't think so. *Brian fluid, then?* Maybe. *Was there such a thing?*

But then she realized that this fluid . . . it was so much more than that.

For in this strange, watery substance . . . there were images . . . memory . . .

Consciousness.

Sidney was no longer in her body. Her awareness had transferred to the alien organism growing inside the shark's skull, an organism that allowed an unearthly force from beyond to take control of so many primitive life-forms and turn them into instruments of violence.

And at that moment *she* was the force controlling this organism.

She was the shark—

About to bite into the two flailing appendages of the human lying on the deck in front of her.

Or not.

Sidney suspected then that she had the power, the ability, to counter the commands of the alien intelligence that had been controlling the shark through the organism that had grown inside its simple brain.

She could feel the power of the animal she now inhabited, experiencing that it was unable to breathe, drowning in the oxygen-rich air, knowing that the bite it was about to inflict would likely kill its prey.

This was what the organism wanted. What the organism was created for.

But it wasn't what she wanted.

Looking out through the single, modified eye of the shark, she saw as the jaws were about to close—

Stopping them before they did.

She could see the human through the organism's right eye, watching as he reacted, realizing that there had been some kind of reprieve.

That his legs weren't going to be eaten—at that time.

She could feel the struggle as the alien organism attempted to regain control, but she fought back, denying the growth within the sea animal's brain its true, murderous purpose.

She fought but found herself weakening by the second. She could not hold the control of the shark for much longer. The human was safe, for now, but that did not mean that he—or the others on board the boat—would remain that way.

The threat would need to be removed.

She moved the great white, its powerful muscles flexing and thrashing its mass, sliding the beast across the deck of the boat until . . .

Sidney came back to her body in time to see the shark flip over the side, taking a piece of the railing with it as it fell back into the sea.

Dr. Sayid was staring out over the ocean, as if waiting—expecting—the next wave of attack.

But she knew that it would not come and that she was somehow responsible.

Langridge retrieved her weapon, moving across the rocking boat toward them.

Sayid looked back at her, and she saw his expression change.

"What's wrong with her?" Langridge asked him.

"I don't know," the doctor said. "Sidney? Are you all right?"

She wanted to tell him that she was fine, but the words would not come, and then she felt the warm stream running down from her nose and brought her hand up to wipe the snot away.

But it wasn't snot.

Her hand came away spotted with blood.

And something in her brain twitched and writhed, and she thought she heard it laughing at her.

Just before the lights went out.

CHAPTER **FORTY-THREE**

Isaac remembered the Terrible Day.

That was what his mother had called it, the day that he'd almost been taken from her.

It had been raining, but he'd wanted to go outside to play. He remembered demanding that his mother take him, remembered her angrily hushing him—she hated to be interrupted when she was watching her shows.

Isaac had stood at the screen door, looking out at the soaking wet world. It had practically called to him, hollering for him to c'mon out—it wasn't raining all that hard.

But his mother had forbidden him to go outside alone. He wasn't big enough yet, she'd said. He needed to be at least six years old she had told him.

And he was only five.

He was still one birthday away.

But even so the outside had called to him. As he'd looked out through the screen door, he'd thought of all the things he could do, the trucks he could play with, the ball he could bounce. There was even a swing set in the backyard.

And his bicycle.

He could see it leaning against the tree in the front yard where he had left it the last time his mother had taken him out to ride. He'd tried to remember when that had been, but to his young mind it had seemed like a hundred years had passed.

He really wanted to ride his bike.

He had turned away from the door, considering bothering his mother again, but he hadn't wanted to make her mad—she wasn't very nice when she was mad. He could still hear the noise of her shows, the ringing of bells and the clapping of hands as people won fabulous prizes. She loved it when they won prizes.

Isaac remembered looking out the door again and wished he could freeze the flow of his memories there. It would be a good place to wake up, to pull himself from the dream state he seemed to find himself in.

But the dream . . . no, it was a nightmare . . . the nightmare of the Terrible Day continued to play out. It felt different this time, more real than his past nightmares.

And he felt as though he was being watched—his memories scrutinized.

The five-year-old Isaac had convinced himself it would be okay to go out onto the porch. He could still be a good boy if he went no farther than that . . . just to be out of the house for a while after days of rain.

How could his mother be mad at that?

He'd pushed open the screen door and stepped out onto the porch. The outside felt wonderful, the air fresh and damp and clean. And for a few minutes he'd been happy to be on the porch.

Until he'd caught sight of his bike again, leaning against the tree. Waiting for him.

As he had many times before, Isaac tried to stop his nightmare there, and as he had every time before, he failed. The memory of the Terrible Day was strong and was not to be altered in any way . . . or forgotten.

Isaac saw his young self carefully descending the four steps from the porch to the front yard. He'd looked back, half expecting his mother to appear at the screen door and scream his name.

But her programs had been on, and she had told him to stay inside.

He remembered briefly considering going back. That's what a good boy would have done.

But that day, Isaac hadn't been a good boy.

Just one ride around the house, he'd told himself, then he'd go right back inside, and his mother would never know how bad he'd been.

It was a good plan, for a five-year-old.

Isaac could still feel the bike pedals through the soles of his Keds, the muscles in his young legs straining to pedal the bike across the grass to the sidewalk in front of his house.

His mother had always warned him about the street and the cars that went too fast. But he wasn't going to go into the street. He was only going to follow the sidewalk to the driveway, then ride once around the house and back to the tree where he'd left his bike before.

He'd hit the sidewalk, and the bike had picked up speed. He remembered how wonderful it had felt—the greatest sensation in the world to be riding his bike after being cooped up inside for so long.

Isaac had never been exactly sure what had happened—maybe he'd hit a patch of dirt at the end of the driveway, maybe it had been a crack in the sidewalk. But the whys really didn't matter because the end result would always be the same.

He'd lost control of the bicycle. It tipped over on its side, spilling him into the street—

And into the path of an oncoming car.

And that was when his own memories stopped. The rest of the nightmare came from his mother's stories about the Terrible Day.

She'd heard the screeching of brakes, and it must have been during a commercial, because she came to the door.

She liked to tell him that she'd thought he was dead . . . how she couldn't have imagined how anyone hurt that badly could survive.

But he had.

He had been in a coma for nearly a month, and when he finally woke up, he was different. A metal plate had replaced part of his damaged skull. His hearing was bad, and his thoughts just didn't come together the way they used to.

His mother told him over and over again that he was lucky to be alive.

Isaac had always imagined there was some sort of truth to that.

And the voice inside his head, speaking over the hum and crackle of the bad radio, agreed.

Isaac awoke on the path in the woods where he had fallen, exhausted by his journey and the struggle inside his head.

The bad radio was so very loud, but the other sound—the voice—was slowly growing louder, more forceful.

It was that voice that commanded him, that was bringing him through the woods, that had made him rest.

It was that voice that had forced him to remember the Terrible Day and what had made him the way he was.

Showing him why he could hear the bad radio.

Showing him why he was so special.

The voice was pleased, and Isaac could feel it buzzing around inside his brain, near the metal plates. He wasn't sure he liked that . . . first it had been the bad radio trying to get him to do terrible things, and now . . .

Somehow the voice calmed him, turning off his escalating emotion as if throwing a switch. He was on the verge of something great . . . of something truly wondrous. No longer would he be locked away, hidden from the world because of his mental infirmities or his mother's fear that he might be hurt again.

The voice said, *No more* . . . he was destined for greatness.

Isaac stood and brushed the dirt and leaves from his clothing. They were wet, but he felt no discomfort.

The voice had seen to that.

At first it had scared him, echoing strangely inside his head, fighting to be heard over the static of the bad radio, but now . . .

Isaac began walking, a certain spring in his step, an excitement that hadn't been there before. He was reminded of the feeling he'd had when he'd looked out that screen door at the bicycle leaning against the tree, and he was eager to see what was in store for him.

Where the voice might take him.

CHAPTER **FORTY-FOUR**

Sidney could hear them calling to her.

Trying to bring her back from . . .

Where am I exactly?

The sky was gray, filled with storm clouds. She could see dark buildings—skyscrapers, some burning.

Is this Boston? New York? Tokyo?

Perhaps it was all of them.

Perhaps she was seeing what was happening all across the planet—

Or would be happening?

And that terrified her.

She wanted to break the connection but feared that there might be something there that she could use—that *they* could use—and continued to allow the images to pound her relentlessly. She saw swarms of insects, packs of animals patrolling the body-strewn streets seeking out humans.

To kill.

Homes and businesses under siege . . . people falling beneath the onslaught of claws, fangs, beaks, and pincers.

Again she tried to look away . . .

And found something else.

Visions of a world before the animal attacks. Before the storms. Scenes of daily life . . . people going about their lives, their business.

There were millions of images. She felt as though she was drowning in those simple scenes of life.

She knew that she was seeing through alien eyes.

But there was something more to those seemingly simple observations. Something that she couldn't quite grasp—yet.

Something that tied them all together.

Something she should have sensed but—

The images were suddenly, violently yanked away, replaced by a sucking void of darkness that screamed inside her brain.

And in the darkness she felt the invaders trying to draw her closer . . . trying to end her life . . .

Before she could understand what it was that they were doing.

Sidney opened her eyes with a gasp.

"Your nose is bleeding again," she heard someone say over the sound of running water. Rich came into her view. "Here," he said, holding out a damp paper towel.

She took the towel and put it beneath her seeping nostrils. "You're up," she said groggily.

"Yeah," he said, kneeling beside the bunk.

"Did I kick you out of your bed?" she asked.

"Yeah, but that's all right, I was getting bored," he said. She could see that he was still pale.

"You feeling better?" she said as she tried to sit up but was stopped by a wave of dizziness.

"I'm better—weak, but better. I think the fever's broken. . . . What about you?"

She shook her head, wet paper towel still beneath her nose. She then removed it. "Still bleeding?" she asked, sniffing and tilting her head back a bit.

"Looks like it might've stopped," Rich said.

She dabbed at her nose again, and then gave sitting up another try. This time she did it without the dizziness but caught Rich watching her.

"What?" she asked him.

"Nothing," he said, but his expression said so much more. "I'm just worried about you," he added, looking everywhere but at her.

"Nothing to concern yourself with," she said. "Just some nasty side effects from our island adventure." She smiled at him, but he didn't smile back.

"They think that there's something really wrong with you," he said.

"They?"

"Sayid, Langridge, and Cody."

Snowy was lying on the floor nearby, watching her with great intensity.

"Snowy wasn't in on this?" She gestured for the shepherd to come to her, and the dog bounded up from the floor. With two graceful movements she joined Sidney on the bunk, demanding affection.

"I have to agree with them," Rich said. He was looking intently at his bandaged arm, gently touching, probing the bandage.

"I'm fine," she said, patting her dog.

"What's that old saying?" Rich asked. "Don't bullshit a bull-shitter?"

Sidney smiled and shrugged. "It's nothing that I can't handle."

"Of that I have no doubt," Rich told her. "Don't think there's much that you can't handle . . . you've been like that since I first met you."

She smiled as she rubbed one of Snowy's pointy ears.

"I've always admired that about you," he said. He was scratching Snowy's broad chest with the tips of his fingers. "Doesn't seem like there's ever been anything to slow you down."

"You'd be surprised what slows me down," she said, her thoughts going to her father and her broken relationship with Cody.

"Bumps in the road." He chuckled. "You're relentless."

"Relentless," she repeated with a smile. "I kinda like that."

"Sid," he began, then stopped.

She held her breath. This wasn't the time or the place to have the conversation she dreaded, but how could she stop him cold once he began?

"I'm scared, Sid," he said finally.

She could see the fear in his eyes, even as she breathed a silent sigh of relief.

"Terrified, really."

"We all are," Sidney said, reaching out to take his hand. "But it's okay, we've got each other's backs. We'll be fine."

"It's all just so much to take in. And when I start to think about it, to try to understand what's going on . . ." He shook his head. "I don't even know if my folks are alive."

Sidney nodded, understanding exactly where he was coming from. "We just need to stay focused," she said. "One thing at a time . . . we'll be good."

He looked at her. "Promise?"

Sidney nodded again and smiled. "Remember who's relentless here," she said, hooking a thumb toward herself. "This gal."

They both laughed at that until the boat began to rock fiercely, and the sound of the wind outside became nearly a howl.

"We must be near the city," Sidney said, looking nervously about the cabin. "Closer to the storm."

"We were only an hour or so away when they brought you down here," Rich confirmed.

She and Snowy climbed from the bunk, heading toward the steps that would take them above deck.

"Relentless," he said to her as she passed him.

"Relentless," she agreed.

CHAPTER FORTY-FIVE

Deacon cautiously opened the door to the patient ward, Delilah close behind him.

"What the hell?" he asked, stopping short and looking around.

"Oh my God," Delilah managed as she slipped around him and farther into the room.

The ward was large, separated into twenty-five life-support units. But now it was in complete disarray. Bloody fingerprints were on nearly every surface. The walls had been ripped open; wiring dangled from the holes; pipes were bent. Pieces of the various machines used to keep the patients alive lay scattered upon the floor, opened and scavenged, only their outer shells remaining, like discarded fast food containers. Even the special beds had been torn open, dissected, the high technology within ravaged.

But why?

Delilah studied the scene around her, and a strange picture began to come together. She was about to try and explain her idea to Deacon when something clattered onto the floor in the tub room in the far corner of the ward.

Deacon flinched. "We should get out of here before . . ."

"What if it's somebody?" Delilah asked. She was already inching toward the back of the room.

"What if it's somebody . . . or some*thing* that wants to kill us?"

She knew he was right, but what if it was someone like Betty, someone they might be able to help this time.

She kept moving, trying not to step on random screws and attachments that had been discarded to the floor.

"Delilah," Deacon warned, although he was following her now.

There were noises coming from the tub room for sure. She peered carefully around the corner. She saw nothing and was about to venture farther into the room when a powerful hand grabbed her arm.

Deacon looked at her, wide-eyed. *Where?* he mouthed silently.

"At the back," she said as quietly as she was able. "Behind that curtain."

Deacon moved around to stand between Delilah and the curtain. He was about to reach for the curtain when he paused, looking around, then stepped over to an old plunger standing up in the corner. He pulled off the rubber end and glanced quickly over his shoulder at Delilah as he raised the wooden handle and grasped the curtain. He pulled it aside with a hiss.

A naked man stood there, eyes bulging.

She saw it immediately, the right eye, shrouded in a shiny metallic covering, but then she saw what was behind the man, wedged into the corner of the large, and quite open, shower stall.

It pulsated with life, expanding and contracting as it spread out across the damp tiles, what could only be described as tentacles writhing upon the floor, its pale flesh shifting colors from blue to green and then to an angry red.

Delilah saw, but she didn't understand.

And then the naked man attacked. He slipped as he lunged, grabbing hold of the front of Delilah's scrubs and dragging them both to the floor.

She went down hard on her back, the wind punched from her lungs. The man was atop her, his hands seeking out her throat as she struggled to slap them away.

"Get off her!" Deacon screamed, his voice echoing off the tiles. He swung his plunger handle, striking the man on the side of the head with little effect.

Delilah focused on the man's silver-coated right eye. It was as if it was taunting her as it glared at her. With a sudden surge of adrenaline she reached up, hooking her thumb into the corner of that eye and gouging the shiny silver orb with her thumbnail.

The man went rigid, but something else in the room screamed. The sound wasn't even remotely human, and then Delilah heard something wet and heavy begin to slide across the floor.

She rolled out from beneath her attacker as Deacon turned toward the dragging sound.

The thing that had been in the corner, whatever it was, moved toward them in a strange, undulating fashion. It was unlike anything that she had ever seen before, something out of her worst nightmares.

Deacon positioned himself between it and Delilah, and jabbed at it with the ragged end of his plunger handle.

Again it screamed, and she saw multiple holes—like wailing mouths—open on the surface of the thing. A whiplike appendage suddenly appeared from beneath its mass, rearing up like a snake, before striking at Deacon. He swung the plunger, batting the tentacle aside.

"Delilah, get out of here," he ordered without turning around.

"No," she immediately responded, moving closer.

The appendage sensed her movement, turning its attention to her, swaying mesmerizingly in the air.

"Go," Deacon cried out, moving forward suddenly.

The tentacle lashed out at him, wrapping around the wooden plunger handle and yanking it from Deacon's grasp. Before either of them had a chance to react, it dropped the club and wrapped itself around the man's throat, drawing him forward.

Delilah froze, stunned, and then her eyes fell on Deacon's makeshift weapon. She went for it but fell hard, her chin striking the tile floor and causing stars to appear before her eyes. It took her a moment to gather her wits, but then she snatched up the plunger shaft and jumped back to her feet. Deacon hung limply, his body held up by the single appendage wrapped about his throat. Other, thinner tentacles had appeared, entwining themselves about him as he was drawn toward the monstrous thing.

"No," she screamed, terrified that she could be alone now.

Holding the shaft of wood like a spear, she made her way across the room toward the monster. The thing's skin turned a scarlet red, and even more of the thinner, wriggling tentacles emerged. Delilah let out a primal scream as she jammed the rough end of the plunger shaft into its gelatinous form.

There was some resistance, the end of the handle stretching the rubbery skin of the monster before finally plunging into the meat of its body.

She had heard the thing scream before, but nothing like this. It was like somebody's nail running down the length of a blackboard, amplified by a million.

And not only did she hear it in her ears, she felt it inside her skull as well.

The thing bucked and writhed, its mass expanding toward her as more tentacle-like appendages appeared, lashing out at her as it attempted to pull itself away from her assault. One of the boneless limbs whipped out, sweeping her feet out from beneath her, sending her crashing to the floor. Delilah made sure that she held on firmly to her weapon, for she knew that without it she would surely be dead.

She saw that the thing had dropped Deacon, and he lay unmoving upon the shower room floor. Quickly she slid over to his side, keeping her eye on the pulsating creature as she gave his arm a shake.

"Deacon," she shouted. "Deacon, wake up!"

She heard the man moan and felt immediately better, or at least as better as she could feel given the current situation.

Glowing a bloody red, the monster came at her. She could still hear it inside her head, the screaming so loud that she thought her eardrums might burst. It moved so quickly that she barely had time to react, falling backward to the floor and raising the shaft straight up as the thing fell upon her.

Its full weight landed on her, and again she felt the end of the weapon puncture its rubbery hide. The thing wailed and writhed as it lay atop her, thousands of tiny, clawed limbs that it must have used to propel its gelatinous bulk ripped at her clothes and flesh. Delilah was screaming now, holding on to the shaft for dear life, pushing upward with all her might, piercing more and more of the creature's internal workings.

She wasn't sure how much longer she could bear the weight of the thing, it was becoming harder and harder to breathe, but then—suddenly—the weight was lifted, and she greedily sucked in fetid air as she scrambled to move away.

There was a ruckus and the clatter of falling supplies as the thing fled to the other side of the room, leaving a slimy black trail in its wake.

Delilah crawled over to Deacon again.

"Hey," she said, again tugging on his arm. "You gotta get up."

He moaned softly but did not move.

"Let's go," she said. She reached over and slapped one of his cheeks.

Deacon's eyes flew open as he instantly reacted, pulling in his legs and scrambling across the tile floor until his back hit the wall, stopping him.

"Where is it?" he asked, the terror clear in his tone.

"It took off to that last stall," Delilah told him. "Are you all right?" she asked. "Are you hurt?"

He started to look himself over. "Think I'm good," he said. His hands went to his throat, and he swallowed. "Thought I'd bought the farm there for a minute."

She moved in close, looking at his neck, the intense bruising, as well as strange, red circular impressions left by the weird, tentacle-like limb.

"Do those hurt?" she asked, touching one of the puffy rings of flesh. Deacon winced.

"Yeah," he said. "They burn."

"Bet they'll scar," she told him.

"Better than being dead," he retorted as he fought to stand.

There was a crashing sound, and the two of them instinctively grabbed hold of one another.

"Do you have any idea what the thing is?" Delilah asked, feeling a mortal terror begin to creep upon her.

"No idea," Deacon said, reaching out to take the plunger shaft from her.

"I've never seen anything like it," Delilah said, reluctantly releasing her weapon.

"Don't think anybody around here has." Deacon slowly moved in the direction of the racket.

"What are you saying?"

"I'm saying that I don't think it's from here."

"Then where's it from?"

They had reached the last shower stall that was clearly being used to store supplies. The area was in a complete shambles.

"I don't know," he answered tersely. "Space."

"Space?" she repeated. "Like some kind of alien?"

"Do you have a better explanation?"

The wall in the corner had been broken open, exposing the inner skeletal structure of the wall behind it.

"There was a grate here," he said, poking at the wall with the shaft of wood. The floor around it was covered in thick black slime. "It got away through here."

"If it's an alien, how did it get in here? Where's its spaceship?" Delilah demanded.

Deacon squatted down in front of the hole. Carefully he looked inside and then upward into the wall.

"This passage goes up to the roof," he said, and then looked at her hard. "Maybe it's parked up there." He wedged his body farther up into the space as more noise came from the hallway.

Delilah turned toward the front of the tub room and felt her heart begin to race as the door opened.

Patients that she recognized, and some that she didn't, had found their way into the room. They stopped inside the doorway and stood stiffly, their heads moving at strange angles as they scanned the room with their right eyes.

Searching.

Delilah turned back to find that Deacon had disappeared into the hole in the wall. "Deacon!" she hissed as softly as she could.

She heard the sound of movement within the wall, and then his head popped out.

"What's—" he began, but she didn't let him finish.

"The patients are here. We're trapped," she said, trying to keep the panic from her voice.

"Not necessarily. C'mon," he said, reaching through the hole for her hand. "This building is part of the old Elysium before the big renovation," Deacon continued. "When it was still called Boston Neurological."

"Where?" she asked, bending into the jagged opening.

"Maintenance shaft. My father worked at Boston Neurological when I was a little boy, knew the place like the back of my hand."

He drew her up into the dark, cramped space with him. There was a sharp odor, like rotten meat and something chemical. She guessed that it had something to do with the creature that had traveled inside the wall before them.

"Saw the new construction get built up around the old," Deacon went on. He grabbed her hand, leading it toward something.

Her fingers wrapped around something cold and metal. The rung of a ladder.

"Climb," he ordered.

The sounds of movement outside the room were getting louder, and she wasted no time.

The rusty rungs cold and damp beneath her fingers as she started to climb.

CHAPTER **FORTY-SIX**

The bug spray actually helped.

Doc Martin buttoned up tight against insect bites and whatever else was waiting for her as she found her way to the garage and the awaiting Ford inside.

The wasps were the main source of attack, and she took the can of bug spray from her pocket and sprayed a noxious cloud all around her as she made her way to the driver's-side door. The spray seemed to do its job, shutting down their systems even though an alien force was controlling them.

Inside the garage was an abundance of spiders. She could see them skittering across the ceiling, dropping down on their fine strands of webbing. She gave them a good spray of the poison as well, as she climbed into the Ford as quickly as she could, slamming the door closed.

Some bugs had made it inside. Quickly she closed all the vents, remembering her experience in the parking lot of the animal hospital, then held her breath and sprayed. She watched as the insects choked and died on the poison, falling to the seat and floor, before she put the key in the ignition and turned it. As Clara promised, the car turned right over, and she revved the engine just to make sure she wasn't going to stall out, before putting the car in drive and leaving the garage.

Doc Martin drove the car down the short driveway, giving the house a quick look before reaching the street. Clara was at the front door giving her a thumbs-up as she passed. At the end of the driveway she looked to the left and then to the right, trying to figure out the best way to get to the back roads behind Clara's house.

On the right she could see their van, still smoldering a little from the explosion that had consumed it. She didn't want to look but saw what little remained of Velazquez upon the sidewalk. Doc Martin glanced away quickly, sure the image would be branded into her brain for years to come.

She put her blinker on to go left and immediately laughed at the irony—as if there were any other cars on the road.

She was headed into a little-developed area of Benediction where the houses were spaced farther and farther apart. They were all quiet, dark, and her laughter died as she imagined what might have gone on inside them—what might still be going on.

Just beyond the last house on the street, Doc Martin caught sight of a dirt road through a break in the trees and slammed on her brakes to give it a better look.

It was deeply rutted and overgrown with weeds, but she figured it would bring her closer to Isaac. Cautiously she turned onto the road—path, really—and slowly drove forward, the Ford creaking and rocking back and forth as a growing swarm of insect life formed a living cloud around it.

She put her wipers on, crushing the flying vermin and smearing the windshield, temporarily blinding her. She gave it a few squirts of wiper fluid to clear it, just as a large animal appeared out of nowhere, slamming its bulk against her door, causing the side window to spiderweb and her to cry out in absolute terror. The car slid to one side as she stomped on the gas, trying to get the vehicle as far away from her attacker as possible. Gripping the steering wheel for dear life as the car bounced and banged against the uneven ground, she looked into the rearview mirror to see what had attacked her.

A horse was galloping in pursuit.

Who the hell has a horse on Benediction?

It was close—close enough that she could see its silver-coated right eye—and she knew that the animal would stop at nothing to get to her.

Doc Martin sped up, watching through the rearview as the alien-controlled horse did the same. When she had enough speed built up, she did what would have been unthinkable for her a mere thirty-six hours earlier.

She hit the brakes.

It was like she was hit from behind by a Mack truck. She pitched forward with the impact, her chest slamming into the steering wheel, causing the horn to beep. The horse's torso exploded through the glass of the rear window.

Peeling herself off the steering wheel, feeling as though her chest had collapsed, she watched in horror as the steed continued to flail, stuck half in and half out of the car. Its body was a twisted, bloody wreck, the metal and glass of the car having lacerated its taut flesh in hundreds of places.

Even after everything she'd been through, there was still a part of her that couldn't stand the sight of the animal's suffering. Making sure she was properly protected, she forced open the passenger door and climbed out of the Ford. Taking the gun from her pocket, she walked around to the back of the car.

The animal lay atop the crumpled back end, and as she approached, it lifted its head, craning the silver eye toward her.

Doc Martin felt an incredible anger then, something bubbling up inside her that she was unable to contain. She hated whatever the thing was that had invaded her island, tainting everything with its presence.

The horse had been beautiful until . . .

And so had the island of Benediction, but now she wasn't so sure anymore.

She raised the gun so that whatever was looking out through the horse's eye could see.

"This is for everything you've poisoned," she said, putting a single shot through the silver orb and into the horse's altered brain.

The animal went still, its head dropping limply to the roof of the car with a thud.

There was a noise behind her, and she saw that the alien force was not about to give up—forest rodents slowly emerged from hiding.

Keeping an eye on the encroaching wildlife, she stuck the gun back in her pocket and grabbed hold of the horse's back legs. It was heavy, but she managed to pull it just enough to allow the weight of the dead animal to help her slide the corpse to the ground.

She turned just as the first of the vermin sprang. She ripped it from the front of her heavy jacket and threw it to the ground as she raced for the driver's seat of the car. She jumped in and slammed the car into drive almost before the door was shut. The animals were after her in full force now, throwing themselves against the moving vehicle. Silently Doc Martin hoped—*prayed*—that nobody in the area had bought an elephant.

As she feared it would, the road was getting worse, and she had to slow the car even more. The ground was muddy from the previous night's storm, and she could feel the car's tires sinking into the muck and mire as the wheels spun for purchase.

"C'mon, c'mon," she muttered under her breath, hoping that she wouldn't get stuck.

So much for hope.

The car came to a lurching stop, the front wheels spinning crazily in a patch of mud far deeper than she would have thought possible.

Panic started to set in, but she knew those kinds of emotions were useless and forced herself to try freeing the car. She tried every trick that she had learned from driving in New England winters, but the mud was proving to be more difficult than snow, and she found herself digging deeper and deeper as the Ford's tires spun.

Insects formed a swarming cloud above the car, while the terrestrial life formed a living carpet around the vehicle, growing thicker with every passing second she remained stationary.

Doc Martin's mind raced. Staying inside the vehicle wasn't an option; the vicious life would be inside the car in a matter of seconds with that shattered rear window.

She felt the gun in her pocket and imagined placing it under her chin like she'd seen people do in the movies. But did she really have the courage to pull the trigger?

Courage.

No, it wasn't that at all, she thought. It was the easy way out.

Instead, she pulled the heavy hood up tight over her head, grabbed the can of bug spray from the seat beside her, and stepped out of the car—onto a carpet made up of every insect and vermin she could think of, just waiting for her to emerge.

She stomped her booted feet into the center of the squirming mass and laid down a cloud of poison from the can of bug spray both above and below her.

She had no idea where she was going, or what she would find beyond where she was, but it beat the alternative: to die, eaten alive by the animals that she'd loved and had dedicated her life to.

It was unbearably hot in her many layers, and she found herself sweating profusely as she chugged along the muddy path. Insects swarmed around her head, and she could hear the sounds of movement behind her but refused to turn around. If they were going to get her, she didn't want to see it coming.

Maybe I'll have a heart attack just as it's about to happen, she thought as her heart pounded inside her sweating chest. *That wouldn't be so bad.*

The sounds behind her were growing louder, more frantic, and she imagined a wave of vicious life building in size, flowing across the dirt and rocks, picking up speed until . . .

At the top of the inclining road, Isaac appeared.

"Isaac!" she found herself screaming, suddenly more concerned about the young man's safety than her own. "You gotta run," she cried breathlessly, finally turning around to gauge just how much time the young man might have and what she could do to buy him more.

The animal life was surging toward them with blinding speed.

"Dear God," she managed to get out, closing her eyes as she prepared for the inevitable.

An inevitable that did not come.

Doc Martin opened her eyes, gasping at the sight before her. The wave of life had stopped, hanging in the air mere feet from where she stood, swaying like some gigantic venomous snake preparing to strike. Cautiously she turned to see that Isaac was just standing there, perfectly still, staring straight ahead at the terrifying sight, and she was about to scream at him to get the hell out of there, but then she noticed something that chilled her more than the sight of the single organism.

"Oh, Isaac," she found herself saying aloud, his gaze zeroing in on her. "What . . . what's happened to you?"

She noticed his eyes, not just the right one, but both.

Both of them covered with a glistening silver sheen.

CHAPTER **FORTY-SEVEN**

The storm wanted to destroy them, the wind and waves trying to flip their craft and give them to the churning sea as a sacrifice.

Cody struggled to pilot the yacht, knowing how desperate the storm was to see them fail.

But he wasn't about to give it that satisfaction. He'd been sailing for most of his life and knew full well that the sea could be fickle, calm and gentle one moment, but able to turn in a heartbeat to prove how wild she truly was.

Visibility was poor, and all he could see before him were the surging waves and roiling clouds.

But then the view began to change. Through the storm, he saw it, like black fingers rising up from the churning ocean.

The city.

Boston.

He felt a flush of excitement as he held tightly to the wheel, trying to keep the boat on course. But as they grew closer, he saw how dark the city was, no lights in the buildings, no headlights on the roads, no flashing beacons from the airport across the harbor.

And the smoke. At first he thought it was part of the storm, darker clouds moving across the sky, but then he realized otherwise—some of the buildings were burning.

He and the others had survived the island and made it through the storm to the city.

But are we too late?

Langridge checked the number of bullets she had remaining in her gun and the extra clips in her pocket.

"Not really all that much, is it?" Dr. Sayid commented over the howling of the storm.

"Enough if used sparingly," she said, slipping the gun back into its holster.

Sayid shielded his eyes against the driving rain as he gazed out over the side of the yacht. "It shouldn't be long now. What then?"

"We see what's happening and figure out how to contact the Emergency Management Agency, just as we've planned," she said firmly.

"And when has anything in the last thirty-six hours gone according to plan?"

"That's why you learn to roll with it, or—"

"Get crushed beneath it," he said with a nod. "I know. If

Sidney could give us more pertinent information about the alien organisms," he began, then stopped when he caught the look on Langridge's face. "What is it?" he asked, reading the seriousness in her gaze.

She didn't answer, instead checking her weapon again.

"It's Sidney, isn't it?" he urged.

"I'm not sure how we should be handling her," she admitted.

"I'm sure she could be beneficial to us if . . ."

"And she could also be a danger," Langridge cautioned. "A threat."

"What are you talking about?" Sayid asked.

"You know exactly what I'm saying," she responded. She didn't care for it either, but it was something that had to be discussed.

"We don't have any understanding of her condition," Langridge continued. "For all we know . . ."

"Do you seriously believe that Sidney could mean us harm?"

"No, I don't believe *Sidney* could," she said, stressing the girl's name. "But there are other forces at play here."

"We don't fully understand what's happened with her," he attempted to explain.

"Exactly," she interrupted. "That's all I'm saying . . . we don't fully understand."

Sayid went quiet, looking out over the seething waters.

"What are you suggesting?"

"Absolutely nothing more than keeping an eye on things," she said. "Being observant."

"And if you see something that you don't agree with?" he asked.

"We'll deal with it if it happens," she said coldly, letting her hand drop down to the holster, where her gun rested, waiting.

Ready if needed.

Sidney came up on deck, her eyes immediately finding Sayid and Langridge sitting side by side. Likely discussing Mission: Impossible stuff, she thought as Rich and Snowy came up beside her.

She had sensed that they were close to Boston. There was an uncomfortable buzzing in her brain threatening to drive her just a bit more crazy.

Cody glanced over his shoulder at them, and she could see how tired he looked, the stress of sailing them through the storm obvious.

Rich approached their friend, placing a hand upon his back.

"Dude, let me take this for a bit," he said.

Cody looked as though he'd been slapped. "No," he said flatly with an abrupt shake of his head. "I'm fine. I got this."

"You're exhausted, Code," Rich persisted. "I can take us from here."

"Back off, Rich," Cody said angrily.

Sidney glanced from the swirling clouds over the city, like something out of a bad science fiction movie, to catch sight of Cody pushing Rich away from the wheel.

"Dude!" Rich exclaimed.

"Seriously, guys?" Sidney said, moving to stand between them. "I thought we were way past this."

Cody looked as though he might want to argue, and she was ready.

"You can barely keep your eyes open," she said. "Why can't you let Rich handle this for a little while?"

"It's going to be a bitch docking, and . . ."

"And when it comes time for that you can do it," she said. "Go below deck, have some coffee, close your eyes," she told him. "Rest up for what's to come."

They were both looking at her now.

"And what is to come?" Cody asked. "What if we get there and it's just too much for us to handle?"

She felt a wave of exhaustion start to creep over her as that weird static buzz continued to intensify inside her skull.

"We do what we can . . . whatever can do the most good."

The buzz was growing, and she wanted to grab each side of her skull to keep it from vibrating.

"Talk about *me*?" Cody said. "You look like you're going to drop."

"You try looking good with an alien in your brain," she said, and tried to laugh, but just a moan came out.

"Sid." Cody stepped closer and took her arm to keep her steady as Rich reached for the wheel. "You don't look so good—even worse than before."

Sidney looked at him. "Why did I ever break up with you?" she asked, feeling her legs turn to rubber. "You're such a sweet-talker."

She knew that the last words were slurred, and she was going to repeat them when she felt the warm, tickling sensation beneath her nose and knew it was bleeding again.

"Crap," she managed to say as her legs gave out, and her gaze fell upon the Boston skyline through the storm.

And then she heard it as clear as day, as if somebody was standing very close to her, whispering in her ear.

Come.

Sidney was getting pretty tired of the visions, or whatever the hell they were. They made her head ache awfully, and there didn't appear to be any rhyme or reason connected to what she was seeing, but she guessed that this was likely totally wrong. She could sense that they didn't want her to see these things, and she hadn't quite yet figured out their meaning.

But she was determined that she would.

Random images again—day-in-a-life kind of stuff. Moms pushing carriages while they happily chatted on their phones; kids watching cartoons, playing video games, wrestling with their siblings.

Towers.

The towers again. What was it about these things? She wanted desperately to know. There was something terrifying about them . . . the way they reached up into the sky, thick, fleshy veins of blood red wrapped around the metal skeleton like vines in a garden gone wild.

And then the voice was there again.

Come.

It wasn't a voice that she recognized, and it filled her with a sense of dread unlike anything she'd experienced before.

Whatever it was attempting to speak to her, she could sense that it was close.

And getting closer.

————————

She was awake again, looking up into the face of her white shepherd.

"Hey, Snowy girl," she said, and the dog bent forward to lick her cheek and the skin beneath her nose.

She reached up, quickly scratching Snowy behind the ear as she sat up. She was lying on one of the benches on deck and saw that all the others had gathered around Cody who was back behind the wheel.

Staring silently, intensely ahead.

"Sorry about that, guys," she said, rising to join them.

They didn't even turn around, transfixed by what was before them.

And then she too stared.

Boston.

The city was dark, no lights in the buildings that she could see along the waterfront. The sky was filled with clouds, but also smoke. There were buildings burning in the distance, and as they grew closer to Rowes Wharf, she could see cars and some delivery trucks haphazardly parked around the aquarium as if they had just stopped.

And there were bodies.

She didn't want to see them—to acknowledge them—but they were there, lying on the sidewalks as if struck suddenly by death.

But she knew otherwise.

What looked like pieces of trash in the street were actually birds, squirrels, and even some cats and dogs.

She felt that terrible tightness forming in her chest. She knew that what had happened on Benediction was happening here as well, but there was a part of her that had hoped it wasn't . . . that perhaps it hadn't started and they still had time to warn people before . . .

"We can dock at Rowes Wharf by the aquarium," Cody said.

"We could get into the aquarium today," Rich said. "Bet there's no line."

Nobody responded to Rich's attempt at black humor, most of all Rich. The expression on his still-pale features was one of intensifying fear.

Cody maneuvered the craft like an absolute pro, even though the heaving swells were doing their damnedest to smash their boat up against the docks. There weren't many others out there who could have steered through the storm the way he had.

They were as close as they were going to get, and Rich jumped into action. He stood at the side of the boat as it rocked wildly in its berth.

Seeing his opportunity, he sprang over the side of the craft, landing awkwardly and rolling across the dock.

Sidney ran to the side, holding her breath, to make sure that he was all right. But he got to his feet, reaching out as Sayid tossed him the ropes.

It didn't take long before the boat was as secure as it was going to be, and Sidney mentally prepared herself for what was to come.

She had always enjoyed her trips to Boston and had been looking forward to going to college and living in the city.

Wasn't it just her luck that an alien invasion had to come along to screw it all up.

CHAPTER **FORTY-EIGHT**

Delilah continued to climb the ancient metal ladder, ascending toward the light.

Deacon was close behind her, keeping her calm with stories of his childhood, although she suspected it was just as much for his benefit as for hers.

"Yeah, Dad used to bring me into work on Sundays," he was saying, a slight breathlessness to his voice as he climbed. "We'd stop for donuts first—coffee for him, hot chocolate for me. It'd be way before six and still dark."

She craned her neck, squinting her eyes to what waited above her. The light still wasn't great, and she could make out the confined shapes of the new, surrounding walls and what might have been ductwork.

"Sunday was the day that he got all his odds and ends done,"

Deacon said. "And I would help him, which is how I got to be so knowledgeable about the old building."

"There's something up above us," Delilah said, slowing down, attempting to discern specifics.

"Yeah, those are probably the new air-conditioning ducts that were put in before the new walls were put up," he explained.

Something down below them crashed and thrummed in the darkness. They felt a sudden vibration moving up the metal ladder, and it felt as though it was coming away from the brick wall.

"Just keep climbing," Deacon ordered before going on with his story. "Yeah, this ladder ran up the outside of the building then, to the old section of roof where the original air-conditioning unit was."

The ladder vibrated again.

"We're going to come to a skylight," he said. "That will be how we get out onto the roof."

"Is there a door?"

"No," he said. "They put a skylight in when they built the new walls."

"So it opens?"

"Not exactly," he said. "We'll cross that bridge when—"

Deacon's scream was chilling, freezing her in place upon the ladder.

"What is it?" she called, looping her arm around the rung of the ladder so she could look down into the darkness below her.

Deacon wasn't there.

———

They grabbed him from below, clawed hands wrapping around his ankles and pulling. His hands lost their grip, and he fell, his chin narrowly missing the iron rail.

He frantically tried to catch the rungs with his hands, feeling the tips of his fingers brushing against them as he fell. More hands wrapped around his legs to his knees.

Finally he managed to grab hold of a rung, and it took nearly all his strength to stop his downward momentum. He kicked at his attackers again and again, getting one foot back on the ladder.

"Deacon!" he heard Delilah yell from far above him.

"Keep going!" he shouted at her as he struggled. At last he was able to pull his other leg free and scrambled upward.

He had climbed only two or three rungs when something buzzed near his ear, and then he felt a sharp pain in his hand. Deacon cried out, almost losing his grip as his hand immediately began to swell.

"Deacon?" He could hear the panic in Delilah's voice as she called to him again.

He had to hold on.

Delilah needed him.

He tromped down the pain, ignoring the swelling, and quickened his ascent. She was still hanging from the ladder, waiting. He could just about make out the expression of fear on her face, the terror glistening in her eyes.

"Thought I told you to keep going," he said, urging her on.

She turned and began to climb again. "I wasn't going to leave you," she said.

But he wished she had, for he could feel the ladder shaking from below as more of the patients made their way up in pursuit.

"You keep going no matter what," he said, waiting for the sensation of hands upon his feet and lower legs. "Do you understand?"

"I don't . . ."

"Do you understand?" he repeated.

"How much farther?" she asked, ignoring him.

"Not much," he said. There was some illumination just above him, and he imagined that it was the light from the outside coming in through the skylight.

To the right of where they were climbing he saw the first of the new air-conditioning ductwork.

The patients grabbed him again from below, their arms and fingers wrapping around him. He yanked one of his legs from their grasp, and, holding on as tightly as he could with his stung hand, he reached up to grab the edge of the metal duct. With all his might he pulled and could feel the middle section loosen.

He gave it another yank as multiple sets of hands gripped him, pulling him from his perch.

The piece of ductwork pulled away with a deafening clatter, and he guided it the best he could toward the area beneath him as he desperately hugged the ladder.

He heard Delilah cry out at the sudden sound, and then felt the hands on his legs begin to pull away as the heavy piece of metal connected with those climbing up behind him, knocking them from the ladder.

He didn't know how much time they would have until the next

batch started up, so he gave it all that he could, increasing his speed and urging the woman above him to climb faster.

They were so very close now.

He was climbing so fast that he crashed into her.

"I can't go any further," she said.

He tried to look past her, at the more intricate ductwork that had been put in place.

"We're here—we just have to climb over the ducts," he told her.

"Over the ducts, I don't . . ."

"Over the ducts," he repeated, starting to climb onto and over her. "The ductwork is just below the skylight," he said as he managed to get above her on the ladder.

The lighting was slightly better here, the illumination from the roof coming in through the frosted and partially painted over glass in the skylight. He reached up, his fingers touching pebbled glass.

"We just need to break through, and we can climb out onto the roof."

Delilah didn't respond.

"Delilah?" he called.

"Deacon, they're coming!" she cried. He could feel her inching up the rungs, getting closer.

He felt around the frame, feeling the dry, weathered caulking crumbling beneath his fingers. "I'm working on the glass," he said, frantically digging his fingers into the material to free the first of the panels.

He could feel the vibration becoming more pronounced and knew that they were almost here. He tried to remove the pane, but it needed more work.

"Deacon!" Delilah screamed, and he knew that the first of the patients was there and that they had her.

He could feel her struggle, feel the shake of the ladder upon the wall.

Deacon lashed out with his swollen hand, punching the loosened pane of glass, shattering it. The sudden burning told him he'd been cut, but he managed to grab a piece of the glass, and, holding it like a knife, went to Delilah's aid.

"Move!" he cried out, clutching the glass and stabbing at the bodies below her. "Break the windows!"

The glass was digging into his palm, and he knew that he was bleeding, but it didn't stop him. He kept stabbing and slashing, listening for the sounds of glass breaking above him.

"Hit it harder!" he screamed, as he continued to try and drive their attackers back. "Hit it with everything you have!"

Delilah punched at the glass, hurting her knuckles. It was hard—pebbled and thick—but she had to break it.

She had to break through.

She felt something snap within her, and suddenly she was wild, ignoring the pain in her hands as she struck the glass over and over again, and when that wasn't enough, she angled herself in such a way that she was able to use her elbow. She heard the glass crack, and that was all she needed, the sound providing her with the strength to continue.

She did it again, and then again, listening to the sounds of the glass breaking and falling away from the skylight. There was a covering of wire behind the glass, and for a moment she believed that another obstacle had risen up to stop her, but the wire, very much like chicken wire, was easily pulled from the rotting framework.

"I'm through," she shouted to Deacon, feeling his weight shift on the ladder as he pulled himself up beside her.

She broke away all that remained of the glass and was greeted with a rush of cool, damp wind.

"Go," Deacon told her, motioning with his chin.

She tried to maneuver herself through the opening but couldn't quite get enough leverage. She felt her scrub pants rip as she struggled, and her phone fell from her pocket. There was a moment of panic over what she had lost, but it was quickly forgotten. Staying alive was far more valuable. She suddenly felt Deacon beneath her, gripping her legs, and she was pushed upward into the opening and over the edge.

The rain was still pouring down, and the air was filled with the heavy smell of the ocean. She crawled onto the roof, small pebbles and stones digging into her palms as she dragged herself up over the side. There wasn't any time for her to catch her breath, and she immediately returned to the edge and reached down for her friend.

He was there, but still fighting the patients attempting to take him.

"C'mon!" she yelled, and he looked up to meet her gaze.

There was moment where she wasn't sure what he was going to do, a look in his eyes that said, *I'm not sure I can do this.*

"Take my hands," she told him, trying to make that look leave his eyes. "Deacon, listen to me and take my hands!"

He looked away and her heart plummeted, but he'd only turned to deal with the latest attacker before turning toward her and jumping from the ladder to grab hold of the skylight edge.

As he struggled to climb up and over, Delilah tried to help by grabbing his clothes and arms and pulling with all her might until he was rolling onto his side on the wet rooftop, exhausted.

There were noises from below, and she looked down into the broken skylight at the sight of one of the patients, his right eye glistening metallically as he reached up for her.

Deacon was rising to his feet. He was still holding on to his piece of glass and slowly opened his bloody hand to let it fall to the ground.

"I'll look at that as soon as we get a chance," she told him.

"As soon as we get the chance," he repeated, and he reached out to take her hand in his.

Both of them ran across the rooftop.

CHAPTER FORTY-NINE

Isaac cocked his head strangely.

The action reminded Doc Martin of a curious puppy hearing a strange noise for the very first time.

"Isaac," she said again. "Isaac, are you still there?"

He remained silent, and Doc Martin couldn't help but turn around to check on the still-swaying mass of life behind her. She could swear that she felt every single right eye of the snakelike abomination staring at her.

Waiting—for some yet-to-be-given command.

Isaac was still staring at her with his two horrible eyes. The fact that he hadn't yet attacked her gave her some hope that maybe the young man that she knew was still in there somewhere.

"Isaac, can you tell me what happened?" she asked.

Again he cocked his head, and she watched as his mouth

started to move and his hands twitched at his sides.

Doc Martin imagined the inside of the young man's skull; the strange alien growth having formed alongside and connecting to the brain, tendrils flowing down to enshroud the eyes.

Change the eyes . . .

She remembered the right eyes of some of the animals she'd examined at the hospital. They were like the aperture of a lens—like looking into a camera.

Was that what Isaac's eyes had become, she wondered. Cameras looking at our world in service of the force that was trying to invade?

She found herself moving toward the youth.

Isaac went rigid at her approach, stepping quickly back. The mass of life looming behind her surged forward as if sensing a threat.

Her hands instinctively went up, and she stepped back a few inches.

The mass moved back as well.

Doc Martin could feel Isaac's altered gaze upon her, and, as much as it freaked her out to do so, she looked into the silvery orbs, imagining what might be looking back.

"What am I talking to?" she asked, the young man's head again moving oddly from side to side, his mouth moving like he was attempting to speak.

Learning to speak?

The thought chilled her to the core.

"I . . . I'm not talking to Isaac . . . am I?" she said, feeling both stupid and terrified.

Isaac—or whatever it was—studied her face, her mouth, her

lips, leaning in toward her, close enough that she could see the organic mechanism of the eyes moving as they attempted to focus.

Doc Martin had no idea what to do. She was completely at the mercy of the events unfolding in front of her and felt her anger begin to grow again, fed by a nearly overwhelming anxiety.

"What the hell is going on?" she blurted out, the words bubbling up and out of her like lava. "What do you want?"

Isaac's head snapped back, as if sensing her hostility. She quickly glanced at the snakelike organism that continued to stand guard behind her.

But it just swayed ever so gently. She looked back to Isaac, waiting for something . . . anything . . . to happen. It was excruciating.

Finally, without a word, Isaac simply turned away from her and walked swiftly up the road. She watched him, noticing his movements. There was no doubt he was being controlled by something, and it was growing accustomed to the body it was using.

Should I follow? Or should I just stand here like an idiot, terrified out of my freaking mind?

She glanced back at the snake of animal life still swaying behind her and took a step toward where Isaac had gone. The snake did not move. She took another step, and still there was no outward sign of aggression. Taking a deep breath, she followed Isaac up the road.

There was a slight incline to the dirt road, and she felt the muscles and tendons in her legs straining with exertion as she came over the rise, exiting from the path to a wide open area with a spectacular view of the Atlantic from the cliffs beyond it.

She'd never been to this part of the island, there really had never been a need, but she remembered a town meeting. She'd been there to do her yearly pitch for vaccinations and spaying and neutering, but recalled that there had been a proposal submitted by one of the larger telecommunication companies about putting a cell tower on one of the island's high points.

There had been some grumblings, she vaguely remembered, but not too long ago she heard that it had gone through. The tower was going to be built.

And from what she saw, it had been.

She watched Isaac's back as he walked across the open area to where a white metal maintenance shack, surrounded by a chain-link fence, had been erected, and beside that the cell tower itself.

But something didn't appear right. Something was odd.

Doc Martin stopped because she couldn't quite understand what she was seeing. Around the base of the tower, snuggled up close, were these . . . *things*.

Her brain attempted to define them in the most normal way possible: A tarp had blown in and gotten caught against the base of the cell tower.

No, it wasn't that.

She started to walk again, more cautiously, but the closer she got the more confused she became.

A parachute fluttering in the breeze coming in off the water? Some sort of sea foam brought up from the shore below the cliff by the wind?

Nonsense, not even close.

Isaac had reached the base of the tower and stood very close to the *things*. She wanted to call out to him, to tell him to get away from whatever the hell they were, but she doubted he would have listened.

No more than ten feet away now, she decided they looked like jellyfish. Pale fleshy sacks of skin with streaks of pulsating colors emanating from within.

She knew what they were likely to be now and was surprised that it took her brain that long to get there. It just went to show how one's mind would avoid the complexities of the impossible, just to find a more plausible answer.

These things lying at the base of the cell tower were somehow connected to Isaac's bad radio . . . they might have *been* the bad radio for all she knew.

They were awful-looking, and to see them this close, she instantly knew that they were not of this planet.

She saw that the tendrils of various sizes and thicknesses that originated from the strange organisms' bodies were wrapped about the cell tower, like creeping vines moving upward, spreading out to entwine the entire structure.

Becoming part of it. Transforming something so mundane and commonplace in this day and age into something . . .

Different.

She stopped a few feet from the organisms. Isaac—or whatever it was that was in control—was just standing there, his expression blank as he stared at the alien life-forms swelling and vibrating with disturbing life.

"Why?" Doc Martin asked, not expecting an answer but feeling the need to ask.

Isaac's head slowly swiveled to look in her direction.

She looked at him, the silvery eyes in his head still incredibly disturbing to look at. She then pointed to the things.

"Why?" she asked again. "What is this for . . . what's its purpose?"

Isaac's eyes just seemed to stare through her, the lenslike quality of the orbs moving in and out as if attempting to focus on her—on her question.

She didn't think that he understood, but she was wrong.

"The beginning . . . ," Isaac said, his voice sounding strange, a vibrating quality making it sound as though he were speaking through the blades of a spinning fan.

"The beginning," Doc Martin repeated. "The beginning of what?"

And he told her, the finality of the words chilling her blood to ice.

"Of the end."

CHAPTER FIFTY

The wind between the buildings was like an invisible giant's hand, reaching down to swat them around like toys, the torrential rain like tiny needles stinging their skin and eyes.

Langridge motioned toward one of the hotels near the water, and they all headed in that direction.

Sidney didn't want to see them, the bodies that littered the streets like broken umbrellas. She tried not to look at their faces. There were dead animals as well, mostly rats and birds, but also the occasional dog and cat, many still wearing their colorful collars and harnesses.

Snowy darted over to the bodies, giving each a brief sniff before moving to the next. At the body of an older woman, the German shepherd looked up to meet Sidney's eyes, the dog's gaze saying so much.

This is all so very sad.

Sidney signaled for the dog to come and gave her an affectionate pet as they reached the rounded, brick archway that led from the waterfront to the street and the front of the New Englander Hotel. The passage offered them some protection from the rain, and they stopped to catch their breath.

Cody was staring out at the street and moved his head for Sidney to look.

She turned and saw the swarm in the distance, a living carpet of rats and other vermin. The mass appeared to be searching for something as it flowed across the streets near the hotel.

"We should probably think about getting inside," Sidney said, and they all agreed.

Without a word, Langridge went back the way they had come and turned right through what would have been patio seating for the hotel's posh restaurant. She approached the door, stopping with her hand on the handle.

"Give me a hand here," she called to them.

As the group joined her, they could see through the glass windows the furniture piled high against the door. Cody and Sayid joined Langridge, and they managed to pull the door open and push the furniture aside just wide enough for each to slip through into the restaurant.

Sidney motioned for Snowy to come in, and the shepherd obeyed, zipping inside, her eager nose pressed to the ground, taking in a whole host of new smells.

"Anybody want a drink?" Rich asked, walking toward the bar.

"Don't tempt me," Cody said. "A cold beer and—"

The gunshot—and there was no doubt that's what it was—obliterated the silence, and they all froze.

"Snowy," Sidney cried suddenly as she realized the shepherd was missing. She was already on the move, weaving in and out between the tables, heading in the direction of the gunshot.

Snowy came bounding around the corner, crashing into Sidney's legs and knocking her down. It hurt like hell, but she was ecstatic to see her dog in one piece.

"Snowy, come," Sidney said, motioning for her dog to come near. "I want to make sure that you're . . ."

A fat man in a security guard uniform appeared in the doorway of the restaurant, still aiming his gun.

"Put that away!" Sidney screamed, pulling her dog tightly to her as she knelt. The security guard looked stunned, but he didn't lower his weapon.

"Don't do anything stupid," Langridge's voice boomed with authority. Sidney glanced over to see that the head of security and Sayid both had their weapons drawn. Cody and Rich looked ready to pounce as well.

"That dog could be dangerous," the fat man said. He'd lowered the gun, but not all the way.

"My dog is fine," Sidney told him. "She's not affected by the signal."

The man stared intensely as Snowy growled. It took everything Sidney had to hold the animal back.

"Please," Sidney said. "Put the gun down—we're okay."

A man and two women appeared behind the security guard. One woman was holding a butcher knife, while the younger one had a piece of metal that might have come from a coatrack.

"What's going on?" the younger woman asked.

"She says the dog is fine," the security guard said, lowering the weapon a little more.

"Good idea," Langridge said, walking between the tables. She had lowered her weapon as well, but still held it in her hand if needed.

"Who are these people?" the older woman with the knife asked.

The security guard was obviously the keeper of all knowledge, Sidney thought sarcastically.

"Who are you people?" he asked.

"I'm Brenda Langridge of the NSA, and this is Dr. Sayid." Langridge moved her head in the doctor's general direction. "These people and the dog are with us."

"I didn't know the dog was okay," the security guard said. "There've been others that have tried to get in . . . have attacked . . ."

"This dog is fine," Langridge told him. She put her gun away, confident, for now, that any problems had been averted.

"There's an auditory signal being broadcasted," Sidney said, "that makes the dogs and all the other animals go savage. Snowy here is deaf."

"Auditory signal?" the woman with the knife asked, coming farther into the restaurant. "What the hell does that mean? That there's a sound making the animals go crazy?"

"That's pretty much it," Langridge said.

"Where's it coming from?" the man standing with the younger woman asked.

"That's confidential, I'm afraid," Langridge said.

Sayid stepped forward to further calm their fears.

"Right now we're working on finding our way to the proper authorities so we can deal with this situation before it has a chance to escalate."

"We came in here to finalize a plan," Langridge said.

They had all come to stand with her now, their strange little group of unlikely heroes on a mission.

"Well come on in," the security guard said. "I'm Fred, one of the security guards here at the New Englander."

Fred walked from the restaurant, the others in his party moving along with him. Sidney and the rest followed.

They exited the restaurant, walking a short corridor out into the main lobby, where other survivors of the attacks had gathered. Some survivors eyed them suspiciously, while others looked at them with an anticipatory hope.

Sidney could not help but hear them muttering among themselves.

"Who are they?

"Maybe they can tell us what the hell is going on."

"What is that dog doing in here? Don't they know?"

There were more children than Sidney would have thought, and she felt for them. It must have been scary enough to be caught in the city in the midst of a hurricane, never mind having the animals go completely berserk.

But all things considered, they seemed to be doing well. There were a few sitting in their parents' laps or holding tightly to their hands. But there was another group, probably a little older than the others, a little more independent, off in the lobby seating area, playing with their electronic devices, seemingly unfazed.

"Were many people . . . ?" Rich began as he looked around the lobby at the survivors.

"We really don't know," Fred the security guard said. "Many of our guests were inside because of the storm and all, but there were some that had ventured out to look at the water."

"Most didn't make it back," said the woman with the knife, gazing off sadly. "We're hoping that . . ."

"Mary's two sons went out first thing this morning," the younger man that had accompanied the two women said. He put his arm around Mary and gave her a compassionate squeeze.

A front-desk employee with a name tag that read CHRIS approached them.

"Hi," he said to them with a warming smile. "I'm Chris, the assistant manager here."

"You're the manager now," said one of the hospitality workers.

Chris made a face. "I guess," he said.

"I'm guessing that something happened to the manager?" Langridge asked.

Chris and some of the other workers nearby all nodded.

"Dogs," Chris said, eyeing Snowy with a fearful look and loud swallow.

"She's good," Sidney said, hugging her dog close and patting her.

Chris smiled politely before looking back to Langridge and Sayid. "They say that you're from the authorities?" he asked. "Can you give me any information, anything at all, that might help calm my guests' frazzled nerves?"

Langridge immediately began her assessment of the situation, explaining that they would need to find the local MEMA satellite and eventually reach the governor.

Sidney found herself drifting, this moment's respite from the horror of what was going on sending her brain into a kind of fugue state. Wandering into the lobby seating area, she and Snowy plopped down in one of the chairs. It felt amazing, and it was taking everything she had to not close her eyes and drift off.

The kids looked up from their smart phones and tablets, and she waved. They acknowledged her presence with brief smiles, and then went back to doing whatever it was they were doing on their devices—probably playing games since there were no cell signals.

She found herself staring at the kids as she absently stroked Snowy's head. Watching them made her think of the visions she'd been getting from the alien source, those seemingly random images of life as it happened upon the planet.

But she realized then that they weren't random at all.

Sidney felt the tingle at the base of her spine with the realization and sat up quickly.

It was the same in the visions. Every one of the scenes that she saw involved somebody doing something with technology: on the phone, watching TV, playing with some sort of electronic device. It was such a commonplace thing.

It was why she hadn't seen it—until now.

She turned in her chair, about to call out to her friends when she felt it. It was as if a clawed hand had suddenly materialized inside her skull, taking hold of her brain and giving it a good squeeze.

"Unngh!" was all she could manage as she slumped in the chair, feeling herself starting to slip away.

She was being watched again, the level of hostility from the things on the other side of her vision filling her with a near-murderous rage.

They were trying to take her, to prevent her from continuing her mission to thwart their plans.

Sidney fought them with all her might, her eyes rolling back painfully in her head as her back arched in the chair. Snowy had begun to bark; she could hear her as if from the end of some mile-long corridor.

They would not have her. She'd made up her mind, mentally planting her feet and resisting the pull of obliteration.

They wanted her stopped in any way that they could. What had happened with her was an unfortunate accident that put their plans in jeopardy.

The invaders did not care for accidents.

Sidney continued to fight back, sensing a commotion all around her.

"Sid!" She heard Cody call her name from down the length of the same long corridor. "What's wrong, Sid? Sid?"

He was gripping her shoulders, attempting to shake her awake, and she focused on this contact, using it like a tether back to the real world, pulling herself along its line.

Back to where she belonged.

She felt that she had escaped them, that she was almost back when she sensed it. Thousands of simple brains touched by one.

Controlled by one.

For a brief moment she saw through multiple sets of eyes, eyes fighting the winds and rain of the storm descending upon the city.

Descending upon this very hotel.

Sidney opened her own eyes. There was blood on her face, but there wasn't time for that. She scrambled from her seat, eyes wide.

"Everybody needs to get to safety," she screamed to the terrified onlookers.

"Sidney, what's wrong?" Langridge asked in her no-nonsense style.

"They're coming," Sidney said.

Her words were followed by the sounds of multiple somethings violently hitting the windows and skylights.

And the sounds of breaking glass.

CHAPTER **FIFTY-ONE**

Deacon held Delilah's hand so tightly as they ran across the hospital rooftop that she swore her fingers were about to break.

But she didn't mind the pain, it made her realize that she was still alive, that she had—up until this point anyway—managed to survive.

The wind and rain whipped at them, as if trying to drive them back, but they surged ahead, heads dipped to keep the stinging raindrops out of their eyes.

"Where?" she yelled above the howling wind, hand up to block the pelting rain.

"Next skylight!" he yelled back.

They were temporarily shielded by the air-conditioning and heating unit, and Delilah took a moment to swipe at her eyes and gaze back.

The patients were swarming up from the broken skylight, their progress slowed only slightly as they all tried to fit through the opening at once.

Delilah quickened her step, getting ahead of Deacon as they came around the large heating-and-cooling unit to see his truck parked against the short concrete barrier that separated the roof of Elysium from the roof of the parking garage

Her heart fluttered at the sight, and her thoughts skipped ahead to getting home and holding her little boy in her arms again.

She should never have done that.

The gray metal ventilation units had also blocked their view of the remainder of the garage roof and as they reached Deacon's truck, they saw what the fans had been keeping from them.

A cell tower had been built on the far corner of the roof of the parking garage not all that long ago. The only reason that Delilah was even aware of it was because of protests about safety issues and whether or not it would interfere with the various medical equipment in the hospital directly below.

The protests had eventually died down, and the tower was installed without any problems whatsoever.

Delilah and Deacon came to a sudden stop before his truck, attempting to understand what it was that they were seeing.

There were more of that thing they'd found down in the shower room spread out along the base of the cell tower, their thick tentacle-like limbs entwined around the metal structure, spreading upward to the various antennas and dishes. There were patients as well, and they appeared to be busily working, administering to the awful, jellyfish-like animals.

"I . . . I don't understand," Deacon said. "What are they doing?"

Delilah found herself moving forward, drawn to the bizarre sight by some unknown magnetism. She needed to see what was happening.

She truly didn't understand their actions. The patients, their hands stained red with blood, were transporting the pieces of disassembled machinery that they had scavenged to the jellylike monsters and dropping them onto the gelatinous flesh—where they were promptly absorbed.

The creatures' bodies trembled and shook, changing colors as the bits of machinery became part of their bodies.

"The patients were taking the parts for them," Delilah said. She stood in the torrential rain, watching with curious eyes as the tentacles wrapped around the cell tower became thicker and more elaborate—and then gasped as smaller veinlike offshoots sprouted, coiling around even more of the tower.

"What are they doing?" Deacon asked again as he joined her to watch the nightmarish scene unfold.

"I don't know," she said, sure from the bottom of her soul that it wasn't anything good.

But what could they do?

She felt Deacon's hand grip her elbow.

"We need to go," he said. "Before we can't."

She nodded, knowing that he was right, and they both made their way toward the truck—where a rat was perched atop the hood, watching them with a silver right eye.

"Aw shit" was all Deacon said.

Delilah looked back to the cell tower. The patients had stopped what they were doing, now turning their own silvery eyes toward her.

"We've got to move," she said, and made a move toward the passenger door.

The rat scrabbled across the hood of the truck toward her. Deacon moved like a flash, grabbing the rat by the tail and pulling it from the hood. He then smashed the thing against the truck's metal bumper and tossed its limp body to the rooftop as he lunged for the driver's-side door.

They climbed into the car, slamming the doors in unison—wet, cold, and afraid.

Deacon turned over the engine, putting on the truck's wipers in the process, and gasped aloud at the sight. "May God forgive me," he said, stepping on the gas.

The truck's tires spun as it surged toward the patients. The men and woman did not move, attempting to grab at the vehicle as it sped at them. The sound of bodies being struck was sickening, and Delilah found herself closing her eyes with each consecutive impact.

Yet still the patients came. They did not stop, or slow their attacks—hurling their bodies at the vehicle as it drove toward the ramp that would take them out of the garage.

As they passed the cell tower, Sidney's eyes were snagged by the nightmarish sight of the strange, horrible creatures huddled about its base, their boneless limbs wrapped around every portion of the cell tower.

The question still tormented her: *What are they doing?*

Deacon suddenly slammed on the brakes.

"What?" Delilah shouted.

"I may not know what those things are . . . or what they're up to," he grumbled, putting the truck in reverse, "but I do know it's wrong."

He accelerated toward the base of the tower.

"And I'd hate myself for a good long time if I didn't at least try to do something to stop it."

Realizing what he was doing, Delilah braced herself for impact.

The truck plowed into the midst of the monsters, their fleshy, jelly-like bodies exploding as the metal of the bumper collided with them.

Deacon lurched back from the impact but still put the truck in drive, going forward before reversing again for another run at the monsters.

Delilah watched as the truck's back end connected with the writhing bodies, listening as the tires crushed them. The truck had been going so fast this time that it continued over the monsters and hit the tower's concrete base.

The tower vibrated with the impact—just before the fireworks began.

At first she thought it was something to do with the power source of the tower itself, a loose wire causing sparks to fly, but then she saw the strange flashes of electrical energy coming up from beneath the truck.

It was those things—the strange creatures—their bodies were somehow giving off bursts of electricity.

The tower crackled, the fleshy tentacles dropping to the floor.

"I think you did something," she said.

Deacon looked over to her. "Yeah, I think I did."

He put the car in drive again, the truck's back wheels spinning out on the flattened remains of the obscene life-forms before surging forward.

The patients seemed to be in disarray, whatever harm the truck had done to the creatures seemed to affect the behavior of the poor souls that were obviously under their control.

Deacon drove around the random patients, some just standing there, frozen in place, while others spun violently in a circle, arms flailing.

"What's wrong with them?" Delilah asked as they passed one patient who had dropped to the ground, rolling about as if having a seizure.

"I don't know," Deacon said. "Maybe I broke something when I backed into those things."

He said the word "things" as if it were poison, and maybe it was.

They drove on toward the exit, heading down a slight incline into the next level of the garage. Delilah turned around to see if they were being followed but just saw the random patient wandering about.

"I think we did it," she said, still turned in the seat. She watched while holding her breath.

"Don't say it," Deacon warned. He was driving very fast, his speed increasing as he crossed each of the levels, tires squealing as he made the turns onto the ramp that would eventually bring them down to the street level.

Delilah shut her mouth, feeling an anticipatory bubble growing inside her as she watched the painted signs informing drivers what level they were on go swiftly past.

LEVEL 4.

She wondered about the others and whether they had made it to their cars. She knew Phil's fate but had no idea about the rest, hoping for the best, but deep down believing the worst.

LEVEL 3.

The truck scraped along the side of a metal barrier in an explosion of sparks, and Delilah looked over to see Deacon's eyes wide and unblinking as he drove. She was going to warn him to slow down, but something told her that probably wouldn't be such a great idea.

LEVEL 2.

He was bound and determined to get them away from this place, and who was she to interfere?

There were bodies on the floor of the garage, larger in number as they got close to ground level. She didn't want to look, but her eyes found them, and she wondered who they were, wondered if she'd ever had any contact with them.

LEVEL 1.

She could actually see the exit and forced her eyes to focus entirely on that, even though she was tempted to look at the bodies that lay beside their cars, many of them torn to pieces by animal attack.

There were cars stopped sideways and crooked in the middle of the lanes. It appeared that some people had actually reached their cars, but that wasn't good enough to get them to safety. Deacon drove around them, not being at all careful, the bumper of his truck having little difficulty pushing the vehicles out of the way. She tried not to look but could see that there were indeed people in their cars, dead behind the steering wheels, and she wondered how they had died in the supposed safety of their vehicles.

Delilah was wondering this with a growing sense of dread as Deacon accelerated, the exit coming up fast.

We're gonna do this, she thought. They had escaped the hospital, made it out of the garage, and soon she would be home, holding her son and—

They were hit twice in rapid succession; first on her right, and then from Deacon's side.

At first she thought it was another vehicle, something dark and moving incredibly fast, but it wasn't a car at all. It was a living thing—no—it was lots of living things, combined together to make two powerful forces that sent the car careening first to one side and then over to the other, where it clipped the corner of the exit as they continued out into the pelting rain.

Deacon attempted to keep control but hit the top of the high curb just outside the garage, which caused the truck to tip onto two wheels as they continued down the rain-slick driveway, eventually flipping completely over onto its side as they slid another ten feet or more, hitting the cashier's booth before coming to a stop.

Delilah dangled sideways in her seat, pressed against her friend, who lay against his door.

"Deacon," she said groggily. She was dizzy from hitting her head on the side window and windshield as the truck had flipped.

Moving her arms and legs, she was grateful that nothing seemed broken, although she was certainly bruised and bleeding.

"Deacon," she said again, but the man remained silent. It was then that she noticed the blood on his part of the windshield. She tried to angle herself in such a way to check him out, noticing the gash in his forehead and the blood running down his face.

She was going to try to free him from the seat belt, and then herself, when she heard the sounds. At first she believed it to be the rain coming down, spattering upon their flipped-over vehicle.

But then she saw the first of the roaches, squeezing itself in through the foil of the truck's air vent, followed by another—then another.

And then another . . . and another . . . and another . . .

CHAPTER FIFTY-TWO

"What the hell is that supposed to mean?" Doc Martin asked, feeling her fear and frustration getting the better of her. "Beginning of the end?"

Isaac looked away, his eyes fixing upon the loathsome creatures attached to the cell tower.

"I'm talking to you," she prodded when he didn't answer. "Whoever you are . . . you're certainly not Isaac."

He looked at her then, and she felt a twist of revulsion in her stomach as she gazed into the silver-coated alien eyes.

"Isaac," he said carefully. "The correct . . . configuration . . . ," he began as he raised a hand to his ear.

"The correct configuration?" Doc Martin repeated. "Are you saying that his brain injuries made Isaac more . . . accessible?"

Isaac was silent for a moment, as if processing her words. "Accessible," he repeated. "Yes, Isaac is . . . accessible."

"So, why have you taken control of him?"

Isaac looked at her with that quirky, animal-like tilt of the head. "To tell . . . to explain . . . to interpret."

"So you're an interpreter? Is that what I should call you? Interpreter?"

"Interpreter," Isaac said slowly. "Yes."

"Okay then . . . Interpreter," Doc Martin began. If she was going to die, she might as well go out knowing what in the name of all that's holy was going on. "Why the business with the animals . . . why the attacks? Why all this violence and death?"

"The . . . beginning," Interpreter said.

"That again," Doc Martin said, rolling her eyes in exasperation. "But what is it all for?"

"To . . . take." The simple declaration said much, confirming everyone's suspicions as to why the alien species had come to the island.

"Then it *is* an invasion."

Interpreter looked around with his silver eyes. "Invasion," it repeated in that strange vibrating tone. "To take what is yours . . . and make it ours."

That statement was even more chilling, as was Interpreter's growing mastery of the spoken language.

"Is this how your kind does it?" Doc Martin asked. "Take control of the local wildlife and use it against the planet's inhabitants?"

"At first," Interpreter acknowledged.

"Yeah, well it's going to take a lot more than some bugs and squirrels to take this planet away from us," she said angrily.

Interpreter glanced at her with a strange, conflicted expression, before turning his attention back to the disgusting things that pulsated at the base of the cell tower. "Only the beginning," he said. "Only the beginning."

CHAPTER FIFTY-THREE

It was raining birds.

Crows, gulls, pigeons, sparrows and finches, and even some blue jays for color, all dropping out of the sky to smash their hollow-boned bodies against the windows of the hotel.

The children were screaming, but Sidney knew without a doubt that the birds were there for her. She was the target because she was getting closer, and although she didn't quite understand what that meant, she understood that *they* didn't care for it.

The glass was beginning to splinter and fall away with the onslaught. A crow managed to squeeze into the lobby and, as if confirming her suspicions, flew directly at her.

Instinctively Sidney grabbed a pillow from a nearby couch and whacked the bird as it spread its large black wings and reached for her with its hooked talons. It fell to the ground, fluttering its wings, momentarily stunned—long enough for her to stomp on its head with a sickening crunch.

"Screw you," she muttered.

She looked around and saw Cody, Rich, and Snowy herding the kids down a corridor toward the function rooms. Langridge and Sayid were frantically waving for the adults to follow.

None of them seemed to notice her, and, for their sake, she used the opportunity to head down another hallway, certain they would be better off without her. She passed the pool, the smell of chlorine strong, and continued on until she reached a fire door. She was just about to push it open into the storm when she sensed she was no longer alone.

Sidney quickly turned to see Snowy standing a few feet away, watching her with curious, blue eyes.

Shit.

The shepherd trotted toward her, tail wagging furiously.

"No," Sidney said, her expression firm and her hand outstretched.

Snowy immediately obeyed, sitting down, waiting.

Sidney looked at her, her beautiful friend, and felt her heart begin to break. It was like looking at the personification of everything she loved in her life. She remembered how upset she'd been with the idea of leaving Snowy behind when she left for college, but this was so much worse.

Because she had no idea if she was going to return. If she would ever see Snowy again.

She turned back to the door, and . . .

Snowy was there, by her side, ready to go out with her master.

"No," Sidney said, even though Snowy could not hear.

Sidney placed her hands around the dog's neck and forced her to sit.

"Listen to me," Sidney said, looking into the icy blue of her dog's eyes. "I have to go someplace, and you can't come, okay?"

The dog leaned forward, her tongue shooting out to lick Sidney's face.

And that was when Sidney lost it.

The tears were suddenly there, flowing down her face, and she grabbed the dog and pulled her close in a hug filled to overflowing with love.

"I've got to leave you, and everybody else. . . . It's for your own good, seriously," she said, speaking into Snowy's thick white fur. "This thing inside my head . . . it's bad, and it's getting worse, but I think I can use it somehow. . . ." Sidney sniffled, trying her damnedest to compose herself, but after the last day and a half it was hard to keep all the pent-up emotions inside.

She let Snowy pull back from her as she continued to explain.

"I think . . . I *know* that they're afraid of me, the invaders or whatever the hell you want to call them. I think that whatever happened to me in that cave was like nothing that ever happened before. I think my encounter with their monster . . . their transmitter . . . changed me into something that could be very dangerous to them . . . dangerous to their plans."

She grabbed Snowy's face and looked directly into her beautiful eyes for what just might be the last time.

"I'm going to go out there alone . . . I'm going to find the source of the problems inside my head, and I'm gonna try to stop it from doing whatever it is that it's going to try to do. Do you understand?"

Snowy whined a little, as if she did, which was good enough for Sidney.

"Okay, I've got to leave," she said to her. "So you be good, listen to Cody and Rich, and I'll try to be back to see you as quick as I can, okay?"

The tears wanted to flow again, and she managed to stifle the most pitiful of sobs.

"You be good," she told her best friend in the whole wide world. "And I'm gonna see what I can do about putting a stop to all this nonsense."

She made the hand gesture for Snowy to stay put, and the dog begrudgingly behaved, nervously moving from front paw to front paw.

And Sidney pushed open the fire door, causing an alarm to sound, swiftly closing it behind so that her best friend could not follow.

"Where's Snowy?" Cody asked, approaching Sayid and Langridge as they hustled into the room with the last of the hotel guests.

They looked around the room and then behind them down the corridor.

"Is she with Sidney?" Sayid asked.

Rich approached them. "What's going on?"

"Think we've lost Snowy and Sidney," Cody said.

And then they heard the steady barking of the dog and saw her as she appeared at the end of the corridor, ears and tail alert, watching them with eager eyes.

"There she is," Cody said, leaving the room and motioning for her to come.

The dog ignored him, turning and running in the direction she'd come from, before coming back, stomping her feet excitedly, and barking.

"Think she wants us to follow her," Rich said.

"And we still don't know where Sidney is," Sayid said.

They all started toward the dog, who darted away when she saw that they were following.

"All right, she definitely wants us to follow," Langridge said.

They were out in the lobby again and were surprised to see that the attack on the windows had stopped, leaving behind shattered glass stained scarlet with the blood of thousands of dive-bombing birds.

They rounded a corner and saw that Snowy was barking at a fire door at the end of the hallway, beyond the pool.

"I think Sidney has gone off on her own," Rich said.

"What makes you say that?" Langridge wanted to know.

"Look at her," Rich said, pointing out Snowy's behavior. "She only acts that way when Sidney isn't around. Sidney ditched her, and us."

"But why?" Cody asked. "Why would she even think of going out there on her own?"

"Maybe she wasn't doing the thinking," Langridge suggested.

"What the hell is that supposed to mean?" Cody asked.

"You've heard her," Langridge went on. "Talking about the presence inside her head."

"Yeah, but . . . ," Cody began.

"Maybe it's starting to influence her in such a way that she's unable to control it," Langridge went on.

"I guess it's possible," Sayid said.

"And that's all I'm suggesting," Langridge said.

"Okay," Rich said. "I'll bite. This thing—inside her head." He pointed to his skull. "It's taken her over. So where has she gone?"

Langridge and Sayid were silent.

"Do you think she's gone alien or something?" Cody suggested with a sarcastic laugh. "She's gone off to join the other side?"

"Elysium," Sayid suddenly said.

"Excuse me?" Langridge asked.

"Something that Sidney mentioned back in the airport hangar," he explained. "She said that she saw a sign that said 'Elysium.' Maybe that's where she's gone."

"Yeah, but where is that? What does it even mean?" Cody asked.

"It's a hospital." They turned to see Fred the security guard standing there. He had his gun out again. "Everything all right?" he then asked, noticing that they were all now staring at him.

"Elysium," Sayid said. "You said it's a hospital?"

Fred nodded. "Yeah, I actually used to work there a few years back. It's a hospital for traumatic brain injury patients."

Cody saw Sayid look at Langridge.

"Why do I suddenly have a bad feeling about this?" the woman asked.

"I have no idea what this means," Sayid said.

"I think what it means is that we should go there, and hopefully find Sidney," Cody said.

"And if not, maybe at least some answers," Langridge answered.

"So I guess we're going out there again," Rich said with a nod. "Great."

"We're going to need a map," Sayid said, looking toward Fred. "Directions to this Elysium."

Fred nodded. "I can do that—it isn't all that far from here."

"And we're going to need a car," Langridge said. "Something to protect us from the storm as well as the things prowling the streets."

She then looked at Fred too.

"What do you drive, Fred?"

CHAPTER **FIFTY-FOUR**

The roaches were pouring inside the truck as if somebody had turned on a faucet.

"Deacon!" Delilah yelled as loud as she was able. "Deacon, we really need to be getting out of this truck."

His head and nose were still bleeding, and she had to wonder if he might have a concussion. But she couldn't worry about that until they were out of the wreck and someplace safe.

With revulsion, she swiped at the cockroaches that crawled on her body, keeping herself from utterly freaking out as she focused on getting Deacon free from his belt.

The man moaned as she fumbled at his waist.

"Yeah, that's it," she said. "Wake up. You gotta wake up."

A roach was on the side of his face, and she lashed out, slapping it to paste, but also seriously connecting with him.

"Sorry, but I'm not," she said. "You need to wake up right this minute." She found the clip and released the seat belt.

Delilah looked to see if there was anything that might prevent him from being able to move, to escape the truck. Remembering all that she had learned about moving an unresponsive patient, she put her hands beneath his arms and attempted to pull him toward her.

Deacon started to moan, and she saw that his foot was caught, the driver's door having been pushed in during the crash, pinching his foot to the floor of the cab.

"Damn it," she cursed, reaching down to see if there was any way that she might maneuver the foot to free it. There wasn't.

Through the cracked, and spiderwebbed windshield she could see that not only was the ground being spattered relentlessly with rain, but it was also moving with life.

"Deacon," she said again all the more forcefully, and gave him a shake before wiping away the bugs that scurried up his body to his mouth. His eyes fluttered, and they remained open this time, and she actually believed that they just might have a chance.

"Deacon, your foot is caught." She tried again to pull his foot free but couldn't. "Can you move it at all?"

He seemed to understand what she was asking and started to move his body, but then cried out.

Delilah's heart was racing.

"You've got to try, Deacon," she urged. She was hearing things now, scratching sounds as something larger than bugs was moving around the truck.

"Stuck," he said, leaning his head against the side window.

"Well, get unstuck," she ordered, again attempting to go up into the area where his foot was trapped. She got a better look and saw that a section of the door had crimped entirely around his ankle.

"Can't," he managed.

"Don't say that," she said. "Let me see if we can get your boot off. . . . Do you think if the boot was off that—"

She felt his hand grab hold of her upper leg, and she looked at him.

"You've got to go," he said, his eyes sparkling with emotion.

"Yeah, we both do," she said, going back to trying to remove his boot.

"Delilah!" he screamed, but she refused to look. "You have to get away."

"I'm not leaving without you," she said. The top part of the boot was completely sandwiched in between metal. She couldn't get to the laces no matter how she tried.

"Then you're going to die," he said.

"No we're not," she said stubbornly, now trying to bend the metal apart, while ignoring the sounds of the torrential downpour, as well as the claws clicking upon the side of the truck.

His grip on her leg became stronger, and it hurt.

"Stop it," she cried, on the verge of collapse. She could feel herself beginning to crumble.

Is this where I'm going to die? a whispery voice asked inside her head.

"Get out now," Deacon said to her. She noticed how badly his face was covered in blood and that his eyes were dilated. A concussion—or something worse—for sure.

"I won't leave you," she said, her voice cracking. "I can't leave you."

"Then you will die, and your son will lose his mother . . . and your mother will lose a daughter."

It hit her like a physical blow, rearing up like a serpent, forcing her to confront the possible reality.

"I don't even know if they're still alive," she screamed, going back to his foot—that goddamned trapped foot.

"That's exactly right," Deacon said. "You don't know . . . and you need to find out."

She could see movement flowing past the shattered windshield, hear the claws scratching the metal as they tried to get in. The rats were outside the truck; there was no denying that.

Delilah froze, not knowing what to do, which is when, and why, Deacon decided for her.

"Get ready," he said to her, angling his body in such a way that he could lift his other leg. There were rats at the windshield, peering through the cracks with their awful silver eyes.

"What are you doing?" she asked, on the verge of panic. "Deacon?"

"Get ready," he said again, a little bit louder, kicking at the windshield, pushing the shattered safety glass outward.

"Deacon, oh no," she said, and started to cry. "Don't do it this way . . . don't do it!"

"Are you ready? I'm ready," he said, and kicked at the glass again. She could practically feel the animals collecting outside the window, waiting for their opportunity to stream in.

He glanced away from the windshield to her, and she saw a look there that she could only describe as acceptance.

"Are you ready?" he asked her again, and even though the tears streamed from her eyes and she wanted to scream, she nodded.

"Get home to your boy," he said. "Go on . . . now!"

Delilah unleashed a sob that came from the very bottom of her soul as she turned away from him and climbed up toward the passenger window. She could hear him grunt with exertion, and then he let loose a scream of anger and resignation as he kicked out the windshield, allowing the multitude of vermin to flow over him.

Delilah pulled herself through the window and tumbled to the ground. Immediately she jumped to her feet and peered back inside the truck, just as her friend was completely swarmed, any sign of the man quickly covered by glistening insect bodies, dark matted fur, and pink naked tails.

"Go . . . now!" Deacon screamed again through the covering of vermin, and she did what he asked of her—what he sacrificed so very much for.

But she wasn't alone. The rats and the bugs and other things that she could not identify came at her in a wave across the rain-soaked ground. She tried not to look, or to listen to Deacon's terrible screams, putting her entire focus on getting to her feet and running as fast as she was able to . . .

Where?

Her brain hadn't gotten that far as she managed to rise. The roaches and other biting insects had reached her first, flowing over the tops of her nurse shoes. Instinctively she cried out, swatting at her legs and feet, but that slowed her down long enough for the rats to turn *their* attention to her.

Delilah could only stare as the living carpet flowed across the ground toward her at a speed that she knew would be impossible to beat.

She had accepted her fate when the unexpected occurred.

A man in a heavy jumpsuit and respirator mask appeared. There was a canister on his back and a spray wand in his hand, and he stood in front of her, blocking her from the approaching wave of vermin as he began showering the attacking creatures with whatever was held inside that tank.

She couldn't believe her eyes, but there was an immediate reaction, the animals instantly repelled, their uniformed attack breaking up as the beasts attempted to escape the unknown substance sprayed upon them.

"Run," the man told her, his voice muffled by the plastic filter that covered his mouth.

She turned and did as she was told, but she had no idea where she was going. The rain continued to pour, soaking her through to the skin as she ran as fast as she could down the driveway, away from Elysium. At the end she turned to see the masked man now running after her.

"Go! Go! Go!" he said, waving his sprayer at her like a magic wand.

"Where?" she asked, looking around. She noticed movement from the opposite side of the street, packs of dogs and cats coming from different streets to merge together, to form one enormous pack. This was certain death, she thought as her eyes scanned the area for any place that might provide them with some cover. The man reached her; he too was looking around frantically.

"This way," he said from behind his mask, directing her to follow him down Cambridge Street.

But the new Elysium subway stop loomed before them, and although it was still under construction, Delilah realized it was where they would be safest the fastest.

"No! There," she said, already starting across the street from the end of the driveway.

The masked man was still headed in the opposite direction when he stopped.

"Here!" she said, pointing to the entrance. The glass front was yet to be exposed, large pieces of plywood nailed in place. There was also a makeshift wooden door used by the workers, instead of the actual door.

She saw a heavy padlock hanging from the door and felt her heart sink, but then noticed it was undone.

"It's locked," she heard the man's muffled voice yell as he came up behind her.

"No," she told him, grabbing the lock in hand, easily removing it from the latch and pulling the door open. She made it inside, the air choked with dampness and plaster dust.

The masked man quickly entered behind her, pulling the door closed. Standing there, she could see him looking around for something to close it more securely. There were some bungee cords in a plastic bucket, and he motioned for her to get them for him. She did what he asked, helping him to secure the barrier between them and what lurked just outside.

There was a half inch or so beneath the wooden door, and the bugs started their way in.

"Beneath the door," Delilah said, and looked for something to wedge into the cracks when the masked stranger began to use his spray gun and its toxic contents, spraying a thick line of the fluid under the door, stopping them.

"That should keep the bugs on the other side," the man said through his respirator, and in that second she recognized his voice.

He turned around to face, her, his shoulders sagging not only from the canister he wore upon his back, but from the weight of what he had experienced this day. She watched as he reached up to pull the mask away from his face, to breath in the damp air.

"I thought it was you," she said, an attempt at a smile making its way across her face.

Mason seemed to make an attempt as well.

"I tried to save him," she said then.

And suddenly the sadness washed over her in a scalding wave, and, for a brief moment, she allowed herself to cry.

CHAPTER FIFTY-FIVE

"What are you?" Doc Martin asked flat out. "Are you from another planet or . . ."

The thing controlling Isaac looked at her with his strange, reflective eyes, the aperture in the center opening and closing as he focused upon her.

"Another planet?" he repeated, his head slowly tilting to one side and then back again.

"You know, space," she said. "Out there beyond this world."

"Space," he said, tasting the word before slowly shaking his head from side to side. "Not space . . . not out there. The other side."

"The other side of what?"

Again he thought for a moment. "This."

She looked at him, attempting to figure out what he meant. "Are you talking about another dimension?"

In her younger years she'd been fascinated by the concepts of parallel worlds and alternate realities, reading science fiction, and smoking a bit of weed. She was surprised that she could still remember what she'd read.

"A world, or place, that exists alongside this one, but on another plane of existence?"

Interpreter actually smiled, an expression so chilling that she had to look away. "Yesssssss," he said, drawing out the last letter of the word like the hiss of a snake.

"So you're from another dimension, and you guys just broke into our reality?"

"Yesssssss," he answered again, his mouth becoming more adjusted to the pronunciations. "Break through to take . . . use world's . . . own resources . . . against . . ."

"Resources," Doc Martin said. "You're talking about the weather, and the animals."

"Yes . . . at first. And when you are surprised . . . and scared . . . and . . . distracted . . ."

A knot formed in the pit of her belly, something that was growing tighter and tighter with the passing seconds.

"And then what?" she asked, dreading the answer but needing to know.

"We use . . . more of your world's resources . . . against you."

"What resources?" she asked, feeling her mouth go completely dry as her throat started to constrict.

"Technology," the thing wearing Isaac's body said. He was looking up at the cell tower again.

"Technology will be your downfall."

CHAPTER **FIFTY-SIX**

She really didn't know where she was going, but somehow Sidney knew she was headed in the right direction.

Something inside her altered brain was drawing her close to . . .

What exactly?

Her stomach grew tight with the thought.

The streets were what she imagined hell must look like: buildings burning, cars abandoned, lifeless bodies strewn on the sidewalks.

And she could sense that she wasn't alone, that there were . . . things . . . just beyond her vision waiting for her. She jumped at every shadow or sound, no matter how faint, expecting to be attacked.

She passed a car that had run up onto the sidewalk, its female passenger, her body swollen with insect stings, hanging from the driver's seat onto the rain-swept street, as if she had been attempting to crawl to safety.

She hadn't made it.

Sidney found herself stopping, making up her mind in an instant. She was going to take the car. She looked down at the woman's body, then grabbed the waist of the woman's pants and hauled her from the vehicle, laying her gently on the street.

"I'm sorry about this," Sidney said to the corpse. The keys were in the ignition, and she hoped that the battery was still good. She sat down in the driver's seat and said a little prayer before turning the key. The engine started without any problem.

She was reaching out to close the car door when a nearby manhole cover exploded upward, crashing down on the hood of an abandoned car, nearly crushing it. And from the manhole, a living tentacle emerged—hundreds of life-forms coming together to form a single appendage of death.

She barely had the door shut before the tentacle slammed into the driver's side, rocking the car with the intensity of the impact. The life-form broke apart upon striking the car, insects, squirrels, and rats scrabbling across the surface of the car, attempting to find a way in.

Sidney slammed the car in reverse, tires squealing as she backed down the length of sidewalk. The windshield was covered with a writhing mass of insect life, and she put on the wipers to sweep away the obstructions so she could at least make an attempt to get away. Putting the car back in drive, she angled the ride to go into the street, avoiding the corpses lying about. She knew that they were dead but still couldn't bear the thought of running them over.

The street was like an obstacle course of cars and bodies. Sidney drove as quickly as she was able, paying attention to the weird sensation at the base of her brain. When she was traveling on course, it vibrated with an almost pleasurable sensation.

But when it looked as though she might be losing her way, the sharp, stabbing pain nearly brought tears to her eyes.

She was on course now, and getting the hang of driving the obstructed streets, when the car suddenly lurched, sputtered, and died.

"No!" she screamed, pulling on the steering wheel as the car coasted to a gradual stop. Her foot stomped on the gas, but nothing happened. Quickly she put the car in park, listening to the sounds of the storm above the accumulating animal life that had caught up to her, swarming upon the dead vehicle.

Sidney turned the key, praying for the engine to turn over.

Nothing.

She instantly knew what was happening, listening to the rattling and *ping*ing sounds from somewhere inside the car—more specifically, underneath the hood. The insects, and whatever else had managed to crawl up into the engine, had likely eaten away at the connections, shutting down the car's power source and causing the engine to fail.

The car was slowly becoming engulfed, the noises inside becoming more prominent. Louder. If they were under the hood, it wouldn't be long until they were inside with her. Fighting back panic, she looked for an escape route, but the vehicle was surrounded.

There was a good chance that she was about to die.

And that pissed her off more than she could have ever imagined. Sidney had often heard people talk about an anger so intense that they were seeing red—at that moment she knew exactly what they meant. Everything around her took on the scarlet hue of her fury.

I will not die like this! her thoughts cried.

Sidney was screaming as she pushed open the car door and dove from the car to the street. Instantly the rats and squirrels were on her, climbing her pants legs toward her face.

No! And suddenly that something inside her brain began to bend and twist.

The animals recoiled, jumping back from where she stood as the animals crawling on her body fell twitching to the street.

The animals reacted aggressively, climbing upon one another to form their single life-form again, rearing up and back like some huge tentacle-like limb preparing to swat her flat.

But Sidney wasn't having any of that, that newly awakened part of her brain reacting in a very similar fashion, reaching out to whatever was closest—seizing control.

Seeing with their eyes.

The dogs were suddenly there, and under her control, multiple breeds of all shapes and sizes running toward the serpent of vermin, throwing themselves at the swaying monstrosity before it could strike.

The rats and insects attacked their attackers, a maelstrom of snapping jaws, claws, and pincers.

Sidney stood there, feeling the thing inside her head flex, move, and pulsate as it never had done before. Whatever was inside her skull was growing.

Becoming stronger, writhing inside her brain.

Changing her into something more than she had been before.

The carnage went on for what seemed like hours, leaving the Boston street strewn with the bodies of dead animals that had been pitted against each other in a battle for supremacy.

A battle that Sidney believed she had won.

A gush of scalding blood poured from her nose down her face, and Sidney used her arm to wipe it away, surprised by the volume.

Fearing that she may be running out of time, she proceeded up the street, paying close attention to the odd sensation at the back of her skull as she headed toward her final destination.

CHAPTER FIFTY-SEVEN

Delilah allowed herself to mourn and cry for less than a minute before wiping the tears away.

"It's good to see you," she said, feeling stupid about the statement but truthful nonetheless.

"You too," he said, smiling sadly. "I didn't think that you . . . I didn't know . . ." Mason trailed off apologetically.

She could see the red and angry insect bites on his face, as well as deep, scabbing scratches. It was obvious that he'd survived an encounter.

"That's fine—we weren't sure if any of you had gotten out of the parking garage," she said. "Do you know if anybody else did?" She thought of Phil and what had happened to him.

Mason shook his head. "I don't know," he said. "We all split up, going our separate ways—running for our lives, really." His expression got very grim. "I almost didn't make it," he said. "If I hadn't managed to get to a staircase . . ." He pulled off his gloves to show his swollen and blood-encrusted hands.

Delilah almost gasped they looked so painful. "We'll have to clean those up," she began.

"Right," Mason agreed. "Just as soon as we manage to get out of here and find a ride. That's what I was looking for when I saw the flipped-over truck, and when I saw that there were people inside . . ." He held up the sprayer.

"What are you spraying?" Delilah asked.

"Found my way to a supply closet," Mason explained. "Had some heavy-duty insecticide that I thought might help me out."

"Good idea," she said.

"Yeah, I remember the state saying that we couldn't use this anymore because it was too strong, and that they were worried that it was gonna get into the water or something. It's pretty powerful stuff."

"The bugs don't seem to like it at all."

"Which is fine by me," Mason said.

There was loud scratching at the wooden door, and Sidney felt her blood begin to powerfully pulse.

"So what now?" she asked, starting to walk around the unfinished station. There was a customer service booth, a row of automated ticket machines, and, across the room, the escalator going down, as well as the staircase. There was a metal storage locker of some kind in the corner, probably belonging to the construction crew, and for a moment her heart leaped. Maybe there was something inside that could help them and . . .

And then she noticed the locked padlock, and she felt her spirits crash yet again to the bug-covered earth.

"We could make a run for it," Mason said. "I could open the door, spray like hell, and we could . . ."

"These stairs go down to the new station," Delilah said, turning her attention to something that might lead to a more positive outcome.

Mason turned from the door. "Yeah, I would imagine."

"New station stop, new tunnel," she then said, turning from the stairs to look at him. "We could use the tunnels to get to another stop where there might be some help, police maybe."

"But we don't know what's down there," Mason said worriedly. "In the tunnels."

"But we do know what's out there if we go out that door."

The custodian shrugged, obviously still not on board 100 percent with her idea.

She immediately started down the stairs. "You're coming, right?" she asked as she descended the incredibly steep stairway. "Of course you're coming. You've got a wife and little girl waiting for you at home."

It was the mention of his family that got him, and he started down behind her.

"Steep," he said, holding on to the railing as he went.

"They had to go extra deep due to the composition of the rock or something," she said, spewing some facts that she'd read online.

"Probably why it took them so long," he said.

The sound of a generator became much louder the closer they

got to the bottom, and she saw that there were bulbs strung up along the ceiling to provide the area with light.

She also saw two bodies.

"I was wonderin' if anybody was workin' today," Mason said.

They reached the bottom, keeping their distance from the badly ravaged corpses.

"So much for down here being safe," he said, eyes darting around, searching for danger.

"As safe as anyplace, I guess," she said, turning from the bodies to the corridor lined with scaffolding and sheets of plastic. It looked as though the two men had been applying plaster when they'd been attacked. The plastic moved strangely, like a chest moving up and down as someone breathed. She hesitated, wondering if it was safe.

What choice do we have? she finally decided, reaching out for the opening in the flapping sheaths of plastic and heading farther into the incomplete station.

"Wait up," Mason said from behind, slipping through to get in front of her. She gave him a look that questioned what he was doing, and he held up his nozzle.

"I'm the guy with the poison," he said.

"Good point," she said, allowing him to lead the way.

They were in an unfinished corridor leading down to where the station platform would be.

Delilah felt it before she saw anything. A strange tickling sensation at the base of her neck and an almost instantaneous headache. It felt as though her skull was expanding.

Mason stopped, the expression on his face suddenly pained. "Do you feel that?" he asked.

She nodded. "It's like the pressure in the air has changed or something."

They both started down the corridor again; the closer they got to the actual station platform the more careful they became. The strange pulsing sensation continued in her head, and she guessed in Mason's as well.

They reached the end and stood upon the new platform, looking down the four-foot drop to the shiny new rails. The platform was lit by a string of bulbs hung along the wall, the wiring feeding back to the generator at the bottom of the stairs.

"So which way?" Mason asked, peering over the edge, looking to the left and then the right. It was incredibly dark inside the new train tunnels.

She tried to see the subway map inside her head, imagining where the new tunnels might hook up with the already existing ones.

"I think we want to go that way," she said, pointing to the right, down into the inky blackness.

"What I wouldn't give for some lighting," Mason said cautiously.

Delilah considered this and had an idea.

She ran from the platform back down the corridor where they had come.

"Where are you going?" he asked her.

"I'll be right back," she said, reaching the dead bodies.

Standing over the corpses, she searched them for what might be there.

"What the hell? Change your mind?" Mason asked, coming up behind her.

"No," she said, deciding how she wanted to do this. "They might have something we can use." She squatted down and carefully turned one of the corpses over.

There were hundreds of dead roaches crushed beneath the man's body, and she could see that his face was incredibly swollen, with his eye bulging horribly and his mouth filled to overflowing with the bodies of the disgusting, shelled insects.

Clipped to the man's belt was what she was looking for, one of those small, high-powered flashlights.

"Aha!" she exclaimed.

Delilah reached down and removed it from the case that was attached to his belt, and clicked it on. The beam was bright, illuminating all the pockets of darkness in the lobby at the bottom of the stairs.

"That'll come in handy," Mason said.

She gently lowered the body to the floor and headed back down the brick corridor.

"So we're going to do this?" Mason asked.

Back at the platform she sat down on the floor, letting her legs dangle over the edge before dropping down to the ground alongside the tracks.

"I'm going to get home to my son and my mother," she said. "Nothing is too big of an obstacle." She looked at him, still standing up on the platform. "Are you coming, or am I doing this alone?"

Mason didn't look in the least bit happy but did as she had

done, lowering himself over the edge. Delilah helped him compensate for the awkwardness of the sprayer tank still on his back.

"Good?" she asked.

He took a deep breath and nodded, staring down the tunnel into the darkness that awaited them. She clicked on the flashlight and dispersed some of the shadows, but the beam of white only went so far before it was swallowed up by the inky black.

They started down the track, side by side, Delilah moving the beam along the ground, and then in front of them, searching for any signs of life. She felt her body practically vibrating with anticipation as the beam moved across the tunnel tracks; she was ready and waiting for . . .

The pain in her head was back, and more pronounced. She looked over to see Mason stumble from the path and lean against the tunnel wall.

"It's really bad," she said, fighting the urge to vomit.

He just grimaced and nodded.

They came to a dramatic curve in the tunnel, and just as they were about to go around—

The flash of white was so intense that she could feel it on her skin. Blinded, Delilah spun away from the light. The horrible throbbing in her skull became worse, and as she slowly opened her eyes again, she noticed that the pulsating of the light corresponded with the pounding in her head.

"What is this?" she asked aloud, looking over to see if Mason was all right. He had turned away as well, one of his hands now rubbing at his eyes.

"We . . . we should go back," he said, his voice filled with fear as he blinked repeatedly.

Instead, she found herself turning toward the light.

"Can't you feel that?" she asked. "Whatever it is, it's connected to the pain in our heads."

"We really should go," Mason said again, already moving back the way they had come.

But Delilah had no intention of going back. Cautiously she moved toward the bend in the tunnel. She could feel Mason watching her, waiting for her to join him, but she wasn't going to do it. She needed to know.

The terrible pain made her dizzy, and she had to move carefully or lose her balance. Delilah fell back against the wall, using it for support, moving along its rough plaster surface until she reached the bend. Squinting her eyes against further abuse, she slowly peered around the corner . . .

And felt her already damaged perceptions of reality slip away beneath her.

She didn't understand. Couldn't even begin to comprehend what it was that she was looking at.

In the open junction of the subway tunnel, where multiple sets of tracks intersected, Delilah caught sight of something totally unbelievable.

The longer she stared, the harder her brain worked to discern what exactly she was seeing, but there was no other way she could describe it.

There was a hole hanging in the air.

It reminded her a little of the whirlpool that formed in the sink or bathtub as the water went down, but this was far larger.

The pulsating light was coming from the center of the swirling hole, burps of some strange, almost waterlike substance reaching out from the center to eventually dissipate in the tunnel area beyond.

Delilah practically screamed as a hand dropped upon her shoulder. She looked over to see Mason standing there, a look of utter disbelief on his face.

"God" was all he could say as he gazed at the unimaginable.

The light emanating from the hole bathed the ground in an eerie incandescence, illuminating things that she hadn't noticed until then. At first she thought them a trick of the light, but then came to realize that they were real.

They reminded her of something, but it took a moment for her to find the comparison, and then it was there. Her first exposure to them had been in the Butterfly Garden at the Museum of Science. She had taken her son there a few months back on a lazy Sunday afternoon.

Cocoons. They reminded her of cocoons.

But these were large, about the size of a human body, and when they started to move . . . to writhe upon the ground . . .

"I think we should leave," Mason reminded her once again, sounding even more afraid than he had before.

And he might've had a point.

Delilah was considering turning around and heading in the opposite direction when the hole grew brighter, the swirling, fluid-like matter in its center spinning faster by the second.

And then there came a deafening roar, as if a fighter plane's engines had been ignited within the confines of the space. Mason winced, covering his ears, eyes wide and filled with terror.

Something crawled from the hole, something covered in tentacles and spines that drew itself from the center of the spinning maelstrom before plopping down boneless to the ground among the writhing cocoons.

The thing that arrived looked very much like the monster that she and Deacon had seen inside the Elysium shower room. Another one of the terrible things that maybe had been controlling the patients and the animals.

She heard a sound close by and looked over to see that Mason had covered his eyes, sliding down the wall of the tunnel, ready to curl himself into a trembling ball upon the ground.

As far as she was concerned that wasn't going to happen.

No matter how scared she was, it didn't change the fact that she wanted to get home to her family, that she wanted to stay alive. If she had to, she would most certainly try to continue to survive alone, but she wasn't about to leave Mason there without trying to convince him to follow.

She didn't want to make a sound, reaching down and placing her hand on his shoulder. He flinched, whimpering pathetically, and slowly raised his head.

We're going, she mouthed.

He continued to tremble, holding himself tighter. "We'll never get away," he said, shaking his head. "Those things . . . they'll get us . . . we'll never make it."

She felt her frustration begin to rise as she realized that at any moment they might be discovered. She had to make her move.

"Give me the spray," she said, reaching down to slip the canister from his back.

"What?" he began, looking at her with tear-filled eyes.

"I'm going to live," she told him. "You're giving up. And if you're giving up, I'm going to take the poison spray with me."

"I'm not giving up," he said pathetically. "There's just no use . . . can't you see? Can't you see what we're dealing with?"

She remembered how many times since that morning she'd thought that she was done for, that she was lost—that all was lost.

And here she still was.

"Yeah, I see," she said. "And I'm getting the hell out of here."

She gave the strap on the tank a good pull, and that seemed to be enough to convince Mason that she was serious. The custodian got to his feet, pulling himself together, as they both started back from where they'd come.

But the animals were there, silently waiting in the tunnel before them.

Delilah's heart skipped a beat at the sight: the dogs, cats, rats, and insects there, blocking their path, staring with their glistening silver right eyes.

And all seemed lost—again.

CHAPTER FIFTY-EIGHT

Sidney had a good half hour on them.

The Humvee threaded its way down the streets of Boston clogged with cars, trucks, and the dead.

"This thing rides like a tank," Cody said from the backseat, holding on as Langridge maneuvered the vehicle through the remnants of the ongoing apocalypse.

"Former combat transports really aren't built for comfort," she said from behind the wheel. "Never imagined I'd be driving one of these again, especially down the streets of Boston."

They had been met with the occasional attack: pockets of gulls, pigeons, and crows dropping down out of the stormy sky to pounce upon the blocky vehicle.

"But of course Dirty Harry drove a Humvee," Langridge said, making a sarcastic reference to the security guard back at the hotel.

Cody held on, watching through the windshield as Langridge drove up onto the curb near Government Center to get around a clump of cars that looked as though they'd collided before the drivers were attacked.

"There's the North End," Rich said, pointing out some cramped side streets that flowed up into what used to be a predominantly Italian-American neighborhood. "What I wouldn't give for a cannoli from Mike's Pastry right now."

"Maybe we'll stop on the way back," Cody responded sarcastically.

Sayid sat in the passenger seat, holding on to a piece of paper with the written directions like it was the most valuable thing in the world. Cody noticed that he stared at it almost the entire time, rarely looking up as they made their journey through the clogged streets. *Maybe he's had enough of the carnage,* Cody thought.

"We want to get back onto Cambridge Street," the doctor said, lifting his head and pointing.

Langridge did the best she could to maneuver the vehicle in the right direction through the graveyard of cars and trucks and bodies—and that was when they found it.

"What the hell happened here?" Rich said, sliding over in the backseat, much to Cody's annoyance.

It was a scene of bloodshed and violence unlike any they had already witnessed.

"It looks like the animals freakin' self-destructed or something," Rich commented in his understated way.

But Cody had to admit: He was right.

It was an entire area, close to a city block, that was littered with the corpses of every type of beast involved with the city attacks.

Snowy stuck her nose close to the window, sniffing the air, and began to whine.

Langridge moved the Humvee in closer for them to look, the disturbing sound of crunching bodies filling the cab as she did.

"What do you think, Doc?" she asked. "Anything we should be taking note of?"

Sayid was silent, his eyes darting about the carnage as the wind-shield wipers moved at a steady, rhythmic pace. "It looks as though they attacked each other," he said, pointing certain corpses out. A German shepherd with a smaller dog crushed in its jaws, multiple rats bloodily burrowed into the bodies of other rats, piles of dead birds of all kinds—all stricken dead in what looked to be some epic battle.

"So they're killing each other now?" Rich asked. "What sense does that make?"

Snowy was whining even louder now, a kind of sad howl that Rich had only heard when—

"Sidney," Cody said. "It's got something to do with her."

Sayid turned in his seat, considering what Cody had said, and then turned back.

Langridge was still looking at him in the rearview mirror, her eyes intense.

Rich laughed nervously. "Are you joking?" he asked. "How

could Sid . . . ?" His question trailed off as they all silently pondered the disturbing answer to the question.

They were still considering that, Snowy pacing back and forth on the seat, as Langridge got them back onto the main road, continuing their journey to Elysium.

CHAPTER FIFTY-NINE

Their instinct to survive caused them to run.

Delilah and Mason spun away from the animals that wished them harm and back toward something equally bad.

What was it that her grandmother used to say in these situations? Delilah's fevered brain thought, at the most inopportune of times.

Out of the frying pan and into the fire?

They both went down the tunnel, turning the corner to face the boneless monster and the swirling hole hanging in midair. Delilah tried to change course, to somehow go around, to find some means of escape, but Mason's sudden screams caused her to stop—to turn.

The cocoons had hatched.

It turned out that's exactly what they were—cocoons.

But instead of beautiful butterflies emerging, these were

monsters—pale-skinned things, human in basic design, but also sharing certain animal traits. Their faces were pointed, ratlike, their slime-covered bodies misshapen, and some even had vestigial tails.

They were nightmares. That was the best way that she could think of it. Nightmares that had captured her friend and were dragging him struggling and screaming toward the spine-covered monster that had been spit out of the whirlpool hanging in the air of the tunnel.

She saw an opportunity—brief and fleeting—to actually escape deeper into the tunnels—a split-second decision.

Either stay and try to help—or escape.

More monsters climbed from the cocoons, scrambling across the rocky ground toward her, obeying some unspoken command.

Maybe she would make it—ducking into shadows or hiding in one of the concave pockets built into the tunnel walls.

There was a chance—albeit slight. But she had to run.

Now.

They were almost on her, and she knew her time was up. Her loyalty had doomed her.

The monsters sprang upon her, driving her backward to the ground. She fought them the best she could, kicking and punching and clawing like some sort of animal herself, but they seemed impervious to her abuse.

Within seconds they had her, dragging her back toward Mason.

Back toward the throbbing, gelatinous life-form and the swirling hole in the air.

A passageway, she now believed, but from where she did not know. For all she knew, it could have been from hell.

CHAPTER SIXTY

Sidney's brain felt three sizes too big for her skull.

The pain was something the likes of which she'd never experienced before. Sure, she'd had headaches—the sinus ones being the worst—but nothing like this.

It felt as though her brain was continuing to swell, pushing against the sides of her skull, and would soon start to squeeze out through any holes available.

She imagined her eyeballs popping out and brain matter oozing hot and slimy down her cheeks.

But she couldn't dwell on the pain, because to do so might cause her to lose her life. Sidney was under constant attack. The closer she got to her destination, the more furious the attacks became.

Standing on Blossom Street, she flexed a swollen and bruised section of her brain, emitting something that caused a wave of rats to veer off, smashing their bodies into a nearby brick wall. For a brief moment she was inside their nasty minds, controlling them through the alien growth that the invaders had caused to develop inside the skulls of the animals.

But as soon as one attack was neutralized, there was another right behind it. Something did not want her to reach Elysium. Something wanted to stop her and was willing to throw just about anything at her to do it.

Crows, sparrows, and pigeons circled above her head, waiting for the perfect opportunity to strike, while a pack of dogs came at her from a nearby alleyway.

The pain was incredible, and it was taking everything she had to stay conscious. She knew that her nose was bleeding, feeling the warm trickling sensation as blood ran down from both nostrils.

First she handled the dogs, finding her way inside their altered brains and stopping them in their run. The birds were next, as she held the dogs in place. Her vision went double as she fought the urge to vomit, reaching up into the sky, into the brains of each and every bird that flew above her, ready to attack.

Sidney was amazed at what she was doing, holding on to the control of both groups of animals, but the wonder was quickly cancelled out by the excruciating agony inside her skull as the conflicting forces attempted to wrest control away from her.

Before she passed out, she directed the birds down to the ground, into the midst of the pack of dogs that she was still managing to hold in place. The birds dropped like missiles, striking the canines with such force that they shattered bones in some and killed others.

The rain was coming down even more heavily than before, a whitish-gray sheet of water obscuring her sight.

She stumbled down the street like a high school kid after her first six-pack, trying her hardest to walk straight, but somebody kept moving the sidewalk. Sidney didn't know how much longer she could keep this up; a voice inside her mind told her that there was only so much punishment the human body could take before . . .

The sidewalk rushed up to meet her knees. The impact was jarring, and Sidney's hands shot forward to stop herself from falling flat. It took her a moment to realize that she had fallen, that her body had stopped working properly and she was no longer upright.

Wave after wave of dizziness threatened to drag her forward, the ground acting as a kind of magnet pulling her to its hard surface.

"No!" she found herself screaming, the thunder seeming to mock her. Sidney fought the vertigo, squeezing her eyes closed as she attempted to stand. She could sense more attacks coming; birds, dogs, roaches, and rats—all being directed toward her. She guessed that the presence inside her brain could feel that she was weak, that what had been done to her was making it more and more difficult for her to go on.

But go on she did.

Sidney heard high-pitched screaming as she stood, not realizing that they were her own cries until she was upright, swaying upon legs that trembled as if thousands of volts of electricity were coursing through them. She had to concentrate to remain standing, defiantly waiting for the next wave of attack that she would hopefully be able to counter in some way.

She blinked her eyes and watched as her vision temporarily corrected, and she found herself looking at a sign. It was just like the one that she had seen in her strange vision, thick bronze letters on a gray, concrete background.

ELYSIUM HOSPITAL FOR BRAIN INJURY TREATMENT.

It took her a moment to realize that she was smiling, that despite all that the unseen force had thrown at her on her trek from the waterfront, she had made it—she had survived.

A newfound energy surged through her body, and she pushed herself toward the hospital. The driveway was littered with abandoned vehicles, doors open to reveal driverless front seats. She wondered about them as she passed, pelted by the heavy rainfall, turning her attention to the front entrance of the building.

And to the strange figures she saw standing there upon the steps. She noticed immediately how they were dressed, some in pajamas, others in hospital johnnies, and others completely naked. At once she knew that they were patients of the hospital, and she wondered what they were doing out here.

But suddenly she understood: The alien force had the ability to affect the brains of simpler life-forms—

Or those with damaged brain functions.

Sidney remembered Ronald Berthold back on Benediction and how the alien force had used the brain-injured man, and felt increasingly nauseous as she looked at the poor souls now under the invaders' control. Stopping mid-driveway, she stared at the entrance wondering how she could get into the building, past the waiting sentries, when it struck her.

The vision was like a physical blow, something that seemed to push itself up and out of her swollen brain for her to see.

She saw darkness and stone—a tunnel of some kind. Something hung in the air, a passage—a hole in time and space.

The vision confused her, and she tried to push it away, fearing that it might cause her brain to explode. But it was the last detail, the last piece of information that her swollen brain saw, that told her where she really wanted to go.

Tracks. Metal tracks on the rocky ground.

The vision cleared, and she found herself back in front of the hospital, patients now slowly descending the steps, knowing what she now knew.

Knowing that she was a danger to the ones that controlled them.

Sidney watched as the patients came toward her, and she reached out with her mind to garble their commands. The patients stopped, some tipping over and falling to the rain-swept ground. Temporarily safe, she looked around, realizing that it wasn't Elysium itself that was her destination, but something connected to it.

Something that appeared to be underground.

The incomplete subway station sat no more then ten yards away. She knew the minute her eyes touched it and that painfully terrible sensation electrified the base of her neck and spine that she had found what she was looking for.

Fearing that she could not keep this up for much longer, she walked toward the station, ready to face what was in store for her.

CHAPTER **SIXTY-ONE**

Is this it? Delilah wondered. *Is this how it's all going to end?*

The things from the cocoons had dragged her over to the jellyfish.

Jellyfish. If only. But that's what it looked like as it sat there, its body spreading out over the rocky floor, pulsating with tremulous life.

She could see what was going to happen to her, as it was already happening to Mason.

They had forced him to the ground, and these things—legs? tentacles?—had emerged from beneath the jellyfish. From the ends of these limbs a thick fluid was sprayed onto his struggling body, covering him up, cocooning him as he screamed.

And then he wasn't screaming anymore, his body completely rigid. Eyes bulging wide as his face was slowly covered up.

"Mason!" she screamed, fighting all the harder as they forced her to the ground. "Fight it, Mason! Whatever they're doing, fight it!"

Delilah's mind raced at what she'd seen emerge from the original cocoons. Was that to be her and Mason's fate? Were they to be cocooned, changed into monsters to serve the jellyfish?

If she wasn't so terrified, it would have been ridiculous.

Delilah fought with everything she had but knew that her strength was failing. There was only so much that she had to give, and exhaustion was most certainly setting in.

But it didn't mean that she was giving up.

As they forced her to the ground, she flailed and kicked. One of the tentacle limbs slithered snakelike out from beneath the fleshy skirt of the jellyfish, moving across the ground toward her to perform its disgusting function.

It got close to her and she kicked out, the heel of her shoe pinning the writhing limb to the ground. She actually managed to get one of her arms free and reached down to grab a handful of gravel and dirt. Delilah wasted no time in throwing this into the face of one of the creatures that was holding her arm. The thing recoiled, pulling its hands up to protect its face and eyes.

This gave her a chance . . . that one opportunity that she was hoping for. More tentacles were slithering toward her as she scrambled on the rocky ground to climb to her feet, lashing out at the animal things, pushing them backward into each other as she sprinted to escape.

Delilah didn't know where the strength had come from, only that she had it, and she needed to use it right away before it was gone. She was running as fast as she could, away from the creatures and down toward an offshoot tunnel that would hopefully bring her to another station where . . .

Something snagged her ankle, and she fell hard, chin whacking off the ground. It took a moment for the stars to clear, but Delilah wasn't about to give up. She attempted to crawl away, but the thick, muscular tentacle remained tightly wrapped around her leg. Struggling in its grasp, she screamed, digging her fingers and nails into the gravel as the limb dragged her back.

The animal people were waiting for her, their clawed hands reaching to take possession of her again. She was about to fight some more, to not give them the satisfaction of going quietly, when the wave struck them.

It was a living wave, made up of every type of horrible crawling thing that she could imagine. It struck with the force of a truck, throwing her from the grasp of the monstrous hybrids. She stared as the wave swarmed over them, biting, clawing animals ripping the creatures to pieces.

Delilah was able to pull her foot from the jellyfish's grasp and was terrified by the sight of an even larger wave of animals moving across the tunnel floor toward them like some sort of enormous snake.

She was going to run again, to head down toward the entrance to one of the other tunnels, when she saw her.

A woman, maybe a little younger than Delilah, standing defiantly, fists clenched at her side.

Who the hell was she, and why was she down there?

"Run!" Delilah screamed to the young woman. "Get out of here as fast as you can or . . ."

Even as she spoke, another serpent made up of roaches, rats, and even stray dogs and cats began to form.

"Run!" Delilah screamed again.

"I got this," she heard the young woman say.

And just as she said that, the first serpent of life lunged toward the newest, the two of them colliding in an explosion of vermin.

Delilah threw up her hands, shielding herself from the flying gore exploding from the impact between the two serpents. Wiping the thick spatter from her arms, she watched as the young woman approached the jellyfish, standing defiantly before the swirling portal in the air.

Not truly understanding why she did it, Delilah ran to her, grabbing her arm and trying to lead her away. "You don't want to be anywhere near that," she said.

The younger woman resisted, looking away from the whirlpool to look at her with wet and feverish eyes. Dark blood streamed from her nose, staining the front of her shirt.

"No, I do," she said, pulling her arm from Delilah's grasp. "You run . . . I can handle this."

Delilah was torn, but the thought of seeing her son pulled at her, and she found herself starting to back away.

The younger woman strode toward the jellyfish and swirling hole in the air. The animals were joining again, as well as the surviving things from the cocoons . . . all advancing on the bloody-faced woman as she stood there.

"Come on!" the young woman challenged them, just as she began to sway.

And collapsed to the ground.

CHAPTER SIXTY-TWO

Snowy had been anxious, whining and pacing, but now the German shepherd was going absolutely wild.

"What's wrong with her?" Langridge asked, fearing the worst, afraid that something might have happened to override the dog's deafness, which had acted as an obstacle to the alien forces.

"Don't have a clue," Cody said, trying to calm the white shepherd down. "Hey! Hey, Snowy girl, it's all right!"

Langridge watched Cody and Rich in the rearview, trying to get Snowy to calm down, but the dog wasn't paying any attention to them. She had started to whine and bark pathetically, moving from one side of the backseat to the other with zero concern that she was walking over Cody and Rich.

Dr. Sayid leaned over the front passenger seat for a closer look, and Langridge knew what he was doing. He was trying to look at the dog's right eye.

"Anything?" Langridge asked, one hand on the steering wheel as she continued down the street toward their destination while the other went down to the gun at her hip.

Just in case.

"No, she's fine," Sayid said. "Agitated as hell, but fine."

"I think I know why!" Rich then said, and pointed through the rain-spattered windshield.

Langridge didn't see it at first, paying more attention to the corpses and cars that clogged the street, but then she saw it. Saw the sign.

ELYSIUM HOSPITAL FOR BRAIN INJURY TREATMENT.

"I think she knows that Sidney is close by," Rich said, preparing himself as the wild shepherd bounded over to his side of the back-seat, attempting to look out the window. "I think she might be able to smell her or something."

Langridge thought that there might be something to that statement as she drove the Humvee closer to the hospital driveway. The dog was even wilder than she had been before, barking far more aggressively and even digging at the doors.

"Snowy, stop!" Cody commanded the animal, trying everything to make her listen, but nothing worked.

Langridge brought the vehicle to a stop, looking out through the wind- and rain-swept windows before turning in her seat to witness the dog's furious behavior.

"Let her go," Langridge said.

Cody looked stunned. "I'm not sure that would be . . ."

"Look at her," she said. "Let her go and we'll find Sidney . . . it's as simple as that."

Snowy was furious, clawing at the door on Cody's side, her whining reaching an ear-piercing level.

"Sidney is going to kill me for doing this," he said as he grabbed the door handle and opened it, just a crack.

"Tell her I was going to shoot you if you didn't," Langridge said as Snowy forced the door open wider and jumped out into the storm.

They watched her stand there, nose pressed firmly to the wet street as she went around the Humvee to the driveway of the hospital before suddenly turning around and bounding away.

"Where the hell is she going?" Langridge asked, watching through the temporary clear spots made by the wipers' passing.

Snowy bounded across the street toward a glass-and-wood structure that appeared to be still under construction.

"I think we know where she went," Langridge said, opening the car door into the pouring rain. The others followed cautiously, looking this way and that for signs of threat. Things seemed to be calm for the moment.

"Move!" Langridge yelled, her gun out as she motioned them over to where Snowy stood motionless in front of the wooden door into the station.

Sayid pulled on the door; it was locked from the other side.

"This seems . . . off," Rich said, looking around. "Where are all the animals?"

Langridge was working on the door, getting her fingers between the pieces of wood and yanking with all her might. "Maybe they're busy someplace else," she said, actually managing to break away a piece of the door big enough that she could get her hand through.

Snowy watched her intensely, waiting for the door to open so that she could go inside.

"Hang on to her," Langridge said, fiddling with the makeshift lock on the opposite side of the door. "Don't know what's waiting for us on the other side."

Cody leaned down, wrapping his arms around the dog's thick white neck.

Langridge fiddled a bit more, managing to unwind the piece of cord that had been put around the door to seal it, allowing it to swing open.

There were bulbs burning and the sound of a generator purring somewhere off in the distance.

They quickly went inside, looking around for signs of their friend while Rich used the piece of bungee cord to secure the door closed. Langridge spotted a heavy metal supply locker and headed toward it as Cody held tightly to Snowy's neck.

"Might be something we can use in here," she said, tugging on the padlock that held the metal doors closed.

Sayid found a plaster-covered hammer hidden behind the locker and brought it over, smashing at the padlock until it broke away, clattering to the rubber-tile floor. Langridge moved right in, opening the two metal doors to see what was inside.

"Excellent," she said, finding a wide array of tools, as well as some rags and two plastic containers of gasoline.

And then she saw the box.

"Boom," she said, leaning in and coming out with two examples of what the box contained.

"What's that supposed to mean?" Rich asked, coming to stand with Sayid.

"Just what I said," Langridge said, holding up the two pieces of dynamite. "Boom."

She shoved the two sticks into an old plastic shopping bag that she found inside the cabinet and helped herself to some of the cabinet's other contents, including wire and a detonator. "If we're going to look for Sidney, I suggest—"

Someone screamed far off in the distance, somewhere down the stairs and in the new station.

They all stopped.

But it was Cody who screamed next as Snowy actually bit him, escaping his clutches with a bark and growl and racing down the steps.

"She bit me!" the young man exclaimed, bringing his hand to his mouth.

"Break the skin?" Langridge asked.

Cody shook his head.

"Good," Langridge said, moving toward the stairs. "Help yourself to something that can be used as a weapon," she said, starting down the steps. "Might be more than Sidney lurking around down there."

CHAPTER SIXTY-THREE

Sidney awoke in her bed with a start, staring up at the ceiling, a feeling of dread making her heart hammer.

Throwing back the covers, she climbed from bed, nearly stepping on a sleeping Snowy, who looked up at her dreamily and wagged her tail.

"There's my girl," Sidney said, leaning forward to scratch behind the dog's pointed ears.

The uneasiness that she'd experienced when she'd first awakened was fading quickly, but the fact that she didn't know what it was all about still bothered her.

Had it been a reaction to a dream she'd had? Or maybe some sort of premonition?

The rich smell of brewing coffee took her from her ponderings, and she padded toward her door.

"C'mon, girl," she said, gesturing for Snowy to follow. "I'll get you some breakfast."

The dog rose happily, following her through the door and out into the hall, where the smell of coffee was even stronger, and something else that made her mouth water.

Bacon.

It had been ages since they'd had it, not since her father had his . . .

Her father was at the stove, using a fork to flip the bacon in the large frying pan.

"Hey, girly-girl," he said cheerily, tossing a smile over his shoulder. "Coffee's fresh and hot," he announced above the sound of sizzling meat. "Help yourself. Bacon should be done in a bit."

She stood watching the man that she loved with all her heart and soul, and felt that something wasn't right.

That something was very wrong.

Not quite being able to put her finger on it, she chalked it up to getting ready to leave for college soon and just how much she would miss the man when she was gone.

Yeah, that's it. What else could it be?

She poured herself a mug of coffee, and then went about getting Snowy her breakfast—all the while that something continued to nag at her, like an itch that she couldn't quite reach.

After putting Snowy's water bowl down on the place mat, and then her food bowl beside it, Sidney took her mug and moved toward the kitchen table. And that was when she noticed it.

The curtains across the sliding doors that led outside to the deck were closed.

"Why are the curtains closed?" she asked, making her way toward them.

"Kinda lousy out today . . . gray, ugly," her father said as he placed strips of the greasy bacon onto a plate lined with pieces of paper towel. "Hey," he then said, turning from the stove. "Before I forget, you got mail from your college."

He pointed to it on the kitchen table with the fork.

Sidney immediately felt that rush of excitement that she got when she thought of leaving Benediction and the new life she had ahead of her off the island.

"Wonder what it is?" she asked, forgetting the curtains as she went to investigate.

"Maybe it's a scholarship," Dad said, half turning as he cooked. She noticed the cigarette hanging from his mouth, and it caused a strange reaction that she couldn't quite place.

There was something very wrong about it.

An image forced its way into her mind that caused her to blink wildly. She saw her father lying in a hospital bed, and she knew he was close to death.

"You all right, kid?" he asked from the stove.

She pushed away the disturbing vision and looked at her father.

He was standing there, cigarette sticking from the corner of his mouth, a full plate of bacon in one hand.

"Yeah," she said, feeling the tug of the closed curtains again behind her. "I'm good."

"Can't wait to see what your college has to say," he said to her, coming over to place the plate of bacon down on the table. "Bet it's something amazing."

"That would be great," Sidney said, turning back to the curtains. "We need some light in here."

Snowy started to bark crazily, and Sidney looked over to see that one of Snowy's favorite tennis balls had become trapped beneath the wrought-iron planter, and she couldn't get it out.

Sidney walked toward the dog, and her predicament, when she stopped.

No, she thought, going back to, and reaching for, the curtains.

She pulled the first curtain aside and let loose a scream. There was a monster at the door.

The thing's body was pressed against the glass of the sliding doors, multiple eyes peering into the kitchen and slime-covered tentacles leaving dripping smears across the glass as it attempted to pull the doors apart.

As the nightmare tried to get in.

Sidney spun around to say something to her father, to tell him to get the phone and to call the police.

But he was right there, mere inches from her face, startling her.

She opened her mouth to speak, but the words were stopped short, trapped somewhere in her mouth by the hands that had suddenly wrapped about her throat.

By her father's hands, wrapped around her throat.

CHAPTER SIXTY-FOUR

Delilah went back to help the younger woman.

She couldn't help it; it was part of her nature, to help people whenever she possibly could.

Even at her own expense.

How often had she gone hungry at snack time during elementary school when a friend didn't have anything to eat? How often had she helped others pay their rent, barely having enough to cover the expenses of her own apartment?

It was just her nature and why she found herself running to where the blond-haired woman had fallen, as the rats and bugs and dogs and cats and people who looked like something out of her worst nightmare came crawling toward them.

At first she tried to shake her awake, to rouse her from her stupor, but the younger woman appeared to be out cold.

Not good, Delilah thought. Not good at all.

She bent down, putting her hands beneath the woman's arms and got her into an upright, sitting position. From there she managed to throw one of the young woman's arms over her shoulder and practically dragged her from the scene.

The jellyfish didn't appear in the least bit happy, swelling to twice its previous size. There actually seemed to be electricity, or something like it, crackling from the tips of these thick, hairlike spines that covered the entirety of its gross shape.

Delilah didn't want to stick around any longer than necessary to see what it all meant, and she half carried, half dragged the younger woman away as quickly as she was able.

Which wasn't that fast at all.

She heard the sounds of obvious pursuit behind her but didn't want to turn around—didn't want to see which particular nightmare was bearing down on her.

To look would slow her down, and she was going to do everything she could to get away.

She wished the younger woman would wake up . . . and then the two of them could start to run and maybe . . .

A clawed hand fell down hard upon her shoulder, black nails digging deep into her flesh as she was spun around.

The thing looked like a rat, its face long, one eye dark and beady, one covered in a shroud of silver, its teeth long, jagged, and eager to bite.

There were others coming to join it, to help it restrain her and the mysterious young woman. Delilah let her drop from her arms as gently as possible so that she could fight; she wasn't about to be taken by these things again. She lashed out, fists flying, legs kicking, but she knew she wouldn't last too long.

She knew that they would soon have her and the younger woman, and the fate of Mason—to be sealed inside a cocoon—likely awaited them.

Delilah fought like she'd never fought before, remembering all the brawls that she'd had in school and when she used to hang out on the streets before she actually started to think, and imagined a future for herself and her son.

A future that up until earlier this day had looked very, very promising.

But now . . .

They were coming for her in droves.

Something white moved in the twilight of the subway tunnel. It was moving very fast toward them. Delilah watched as it got closer and felt that terrible twinge of fear kick into high gear.

Even surrounded by jellyfish-like monsters, swarms of rats and bugs and people turned into bizarre, animal-like creatures . . .

The sight of a large dog still scared the hell out of her.

She didn't know what to think as the white-furred animal—it reminded her of some sort of animal ghost or something—ran furiously across the rocks and dirt toward them.

Is this how I'm to die? Delilah wondered. Would this be the thing that jumped upon her and ripped her throat out?

She knew that she wouldn't be able to outrun it and planted her feet as it came closer . . . and closer. . . .

Delilah braced herself for the impact that was sure to come.

The sound of struggle and savagery filled the tunnel, and her eyes snapped open to see the most amazing of sights. The big white dog was attacking the animal people, jaws biting and snapping savagely, moving from one to another, the damage its sharp teeth doing substantial.

She didn't understand it, but seeing another opportunity, reached down to help the younger woman up from the ground in yet another attempt to escape the tunnel.

Sensing movement, the white dog looked directly at her—its eyes an icy blue that froze her in place.

The dog came at her and she screamed. Delilah fell backward to the floor of the tunnel, arms raised to defend herself, but it barely paid her any mind, going to the unconscious young woman instead. The dog sniffed her furiously, crying and whining pitifully as it pawed at her and licked her face.

It didn't take a genius to see that the two were somehow connected.

The dog looked at Delilah again, the depth of feeling that she saw in those blue eyes unlike anything she'd ever seen in an animal's eyes before.

There was movement in front of them, and she and the dog both turned.

More of the animal people were coming, the ground thick with bugs.

The white dog took its position just in front of the still-unconscious young woman—its master—and lowered its head, the flesh pulling back from its yellowed, razor-sharp teeth.

And Delilah listened as it growled in defiance at the approaching horde.

CHAPTER SIXTY-FIVE

A silence that seemed to last for weeks passed between them.

Doc Martin tried to fit the strangeness—the outrageousness—of what she was learning into the basic design of the life she'd always known.

It didn't want to fit.

"So that's why *you're* here?" she asked with a certain grimness, watching the horrible things squatting around the cell tower pulsating with sickening life. "To tell us that we've already lost and should just quit without a fight."

Interpreter looked at her. It was getting harder and harder for her to see the sad young man that she'd come to know and like.

"Your kind . . . is different." He glanced at the throbbing instruments that were somehow part of their conquest and then back to Doc Martin before he said the oddest thing. "They have noticed."

"We're different all right; we're fighters—thinkers," she told him. "We may get knocked down a whole bunch of times, but some of us are always going to get up again." She smiled at her own words, believing every single one of them.

"One that has been . . . changed."

"We've all been changed by this shit," Doc Martin retorted bitterly.

"One that . . ." Interpreter searched for the word. "One that scares them."

And suddenly Doc Martin couldn't help but smile. "Sidney. Sidney scares you . . . scares them?"

His head moved from one side to the other.

"Sidney," he repeated, letting the name dance upon his tongue. "Sidney . . . Moore."

"That's her," Doc Martin said proudly, but at the same time feeling a tinge of unease. She'd always felt a certain amount of affection for the girl, imagining that it was something akin to how a mother feels for her daughter, even though she'd never had children.

"What happened . . . was a fluke," Interpreter explained. "Somehow this human woman . . . this Sidney Moore and the device became conjoined."

"Conjoined," Doc Martin repeated.

"The two became as one," Interpreter said. "On all the worlds that have fallen to us . . . nothing like that has ever occurred before."

"She's a threat to you then . . . to your plans."

Interpreter paused, again looking at the loathsome creatures around the base of the antenna. "She could ruin . . . everything."

Doc Martin's thoughts raced. Was this supposed representative of an alien race admitting to a weakness in their plans? Why would he be telling her that? Was it a trap to throw them off guard . . . to give them false hope?

She had to ask. "Why are you telling me this? Is this some sort of sick game your kind plays? Build up our hopes, and then— surprise, surprise—there isn't a chance at all."

Interpreter said nothing.

"Why are you telling me this?" Doc Martin nearly screamed her question.

Again Interpreter remained silent, and her frustration became like a lit match dropped into a bucket of gasoline. She stormed over to a pile of construction trash beside the maintenance shack, hefted a length of metal pipe. She caught movement beyond the cliff area, the living mass of controlled life slowly emerging from the underbrush. But it didn't stop her.

"You're not going to tell me your game?" she asked as she strode back toward the antenna. "Is that it? Let the inferior life-forms figure it out on their own?"

She loomed over the first of the jellyfish-like creatures at the base of the tower, its pale body puffing up and then deflating like a lung outside the body. Watching the expression on Isaac's face, she raised her pipe and drove it down into the creature's body. The thing screamed on some psychic level, and her head felt as though it was about to split, but that did not prevent her from bringing her makeshift spear up and down again on the second alien.

The wave surged out from the underbrush, a serpent of living things coming at her like a runaway freight train. Doc Martin stood above the next of the throbbing sacks of alien life, spear poised to fall as the serpent of living things reached her.

And stopped.

The serpent stopped, swaying before her.

An act that told her everything.

She brought the end of the pipe down into the gelatinous body of the third organism, and when she was done, the once pulsating bodies looked like deflated balloons days after a parade.

Her anger spent, and suddenly exhausted, Doc Martin leaned on her pipe. "So," she said, looking directly at Interpreter. "Are you going to help us defeat your kind?"

Interpreter just stared.

"Or am I reading this all wrong?"

CHAPTER SIXTY-SIX

It was all a dream . . . a nightmare.

But she knew that she could die there.

Her father's hands wrapped tightly around her throat.

She fought him, a part of her not wanting to hurt the man that she loved, but a realization dawned on her, triggering her will to survive.

That man was gone. Dead. And the forces that were now inside her mind attempting to kill her were responsible.

A surge of anger gave her what she needed.

Stepping closer to this dream version of her dad, Sidney pulled back her fist and drove it into the face of the imposter. She felt his fingers loosen, allowing her the opportunity to slip from his grasp.

"You're not who you're supposed to be," she said angrily, attacking the man. "That man is gone," she said. "That man is gone because of you!"

She punched his face again, and she felt the skin, and bone beneath, give way with a sickening crack. The nightmare version of her father tried to swat her away, but her anger was like a burning fire, driving her at the man, fists flailing.

Just the idea of this . . . thing . . . wearing her father's face and trying to hurt her? It made her mad enough to kill.

Her fists continued to land upon the figure's face, and she saw the damage that she was doing. The skin was breaking away like pieces of shattered plastic, revealing something wet and pulsating beneath.

Something that resembled the damp and clammy skin of one of the monsters that controlled the animals. Sidney drove the thing backward; it tripped over one of the kitchen chairs and fell to the floor. The body shattered like glass, the loathsome organism hidden inside shucking off its costume and crawling beneath the table to escape her fury.

"That's it," she sneered, fists still clenched. "You better run."

Sidney followed its course beneath the table, ready to pounce if the opportunity presented itself.

The monster slithered out from beneath the table, leaping up from the floor to attach itself to the sliding door, where the even larger organism waited.

She was rushing over to tear the filthy beast from the sliding door when the glass started to crack, sounding like multiple snaps of tiny whips.

And then it was over, the glass doors exploding inward in a flood of pale flesh and writhing tentacles. Sidney tried to get out of the way, to dive across the kitchen, but the reality of the room itself was crumbling away as well.

The kitchen was breaking apart, the pieces dissolving like smoke, only to reveal a world of total darkness beneath.

Total black.

At the corner of the room she paused, fearing the dark and what it might hold, only to be swept up from behind, the cold, clammy mass of the alien organism enveloping her body.

Swallowing her whole.

They had her.

They . . . the mysterious beings that were in the process of invading her world.

Sidney fought to break free but remained a prisoner of the flesh.

They were inside her mind—she could feel them rummaging around looking for something.

But what?

The pain made her cry out. They were far from gentle as they peeled back layers of her gray matter, poking roughly between the folds of her brain.

Something within her brain reacted.

Sidney felt it, a now-familiar sensation. Only this time it felt stronger.

It was like discovering a whole new muscle, and she flexed it.

And suddenly they were gone from her, receding back into the darkness.

Sidney could just about make out their presence, just beyond the veil of flesh and shadow. They seemed . . . bothered that she could look in their direction.

"I see you there," she said to them, finding that she was smiling with their discomfort.

The new muscle, she suddenly realized, *this* was what they had been interested in.

What scared them.

She flexed the new mental muscle, feeling it getting stronger each time she tried. "Is this what you're afraid of?"

She could actually feel their discomfort . . . their displeasure . . . their anger.

She could see their thoughts.

Sidney had been inside the minds of the invaders before—a jumbled mass of random thought and imagery.

But now it was different. Now she could truly see . . .

And understand.

They attempted to sever their hold on her, but Sidney held fast, seeing their plan.

The next phase was about to begin.

The realization of what she was seeing . . . hearing . . . distracted her enough that they managed to repel her, to drive her back.

Sidney tried to hold on, to take from them anything that might prove useful in humanity's struggle against the invaders, but they broke her grip—her psychic link—and sent her back.

Back to her flesh.

Back to the beginning of the next phase, and what could very well be the end of humanity.

CHAPTER SIXTY-SEVEN

The younger woman had started to convulse.

Delilah held on to her as her body quaked and bucked, blood dribbling down from her nostrils.

It would be so easy to just leave . . . to allow the white dog to continue to protect her as Delilah ran away as fast as she could.

She gazed down at the young woman's pale face and wiped the trickles of blood from beneath her nose.

She just couldn't do that. This woman had saved her somehow.

The dog was truly menacing in her protection, darting forward to savage anything that dared get within a certain radius of them—rats and even the human-shaped monsters.

But just beyond where the dog stalked back and forth like a jungle cat in its cage, Delilah could see a gathering of nightmares.

It won't be long now, she thought, watching the line of horrors forming before them.

And that was when she did the unthinkable.

Delilah gently laid the younger woman on the ground and stood beside the dog.

The shepherd glanced at her, and Delilah could have sworn something passed between them, something along the lines of *We're probably going to die in the next few minutes; might as well go down fighting side by side.*

The gathering of beasts and monstrosities continued to watch them.

"What are you waiting for?" Delilah mumbled beneath her breath as the dog barked her challenge. Delilah reached down and grabbed up a handful of loose rock and dirt, flinging it as hard as she could at them.

But still they waited.

For what?

The young woman on the ground behind Delilah began to cough, and Delilah turned to see her rolling onto her side, moaning as she fought to return to consciousness.

It was then that the monsters made their move.

Delilah was ready, throwing punches and kicking wildly as she and the dog were slowly driven back by the horrific flow of attack.

The explosion of fire up ahead of them was practically blinding in the poor lighting of the tunnel. Instinctively Delilah threw up her hands to shield her eyes. She could smell the heavy aroma of gasoline, the glow of the still-burning fire in the distance filtering between her fingers.

And then she heard the sound of gunfire.

In the part of the city where she'd grown up it wasn't an uncommon thing to hear gunshots, especially on a Friday or Saturday night, so there was no mistaking what she was hearing.

She lowered her hands as four figures entered the tunnel.

For a moment she thought she was saved.

For a moment.

The organism sensed the danger and began to vibrate with purpose, the quills upon its undulating mass extending to broadcast its newest message—its newest signal.

It had a purpose, and that purpose must be fulfilled.

Crackling sparks of bioelectricity leaped from the thick black hairs into the air.

Phase two was beginning.

Cody swung the sledgehammer into the side of a monster's head.

The thing went down to the ground in a twitching heap, and all he could do was stare. He was reminded of the animals that had been in the cave on Benediction, the things that had emerged from the cocoons.

This was so much worse. He was certain that at one time it had been human.

But there wasn't any time for horror, or fear or disgust; they were here for a reason—to find Sidney—and that's all that he would focus on.

The sledgehammer seemed to be increasing in weight; every time it was raised, every time that it smashed a skull or crushed a swarm of rats and cockroaches, it seemed to become heavier.

And he wasn't sure how much longer he could do this.

How much longer he could fight.

There was something happening in the tunnel, something that wasn't the least bit good.

Rich was reminded of what had happened on the island—in the caves of Benediction—he had been amazed and grateful that he had survived the night, and here he was again.

Fighting to survive against overwhelming odds, fighting for everything that mattered to him.

And as he swung the heavy metal plumber's wrench, keeping his attackers at bay, he saw in the eerie light of the burning gasoline that things were likely far worse than he cared to believe.

Not only was he fighting for his own survival and all that mattered personally to him . . .

He might have been fighting for the sake of the world.

Sayid was mesmerized by the sight of it.

The alien organism was huge, pulsating with a horrible, malignant life as it lay there surrounded by the translucent cocoonlike pods. He could see inside them, new life squirming with activity.

New life that would be used to usurp the old.

He couldn't allow this to happen. For the sake of his daughter, for the sake of the planet itself, he had to do everything to see it stopped.

But would it be enough?

He aimed his gun, firing his last shots into the pulsating mass of alien flesh.

He hoped to God it would be.

Langridge had gone into combat mode. It had been years since she'd fought in a war, and she'd assumed this way of thinking was behind her, but here it was again.

Practically saying *Did you miss me?* as the civilized part of her slipped quietly to the recesses of her consciousness, and a side fueled by survival and the hunger for violence took control.

This place . . . this tunnel was a place of absolute evil—she felt it in her bones. And it had to be cleaned out.

Cleansed of the bad.

Purified with fire, she thought as she poured more gasoline.

Before it was too late.

CHAPTER SIXTY-EIGHT

Sidney awoke to war.

The choking stink of fire and gasoline in her lungs.

She looked about, saw what was happening, but knew that the real danger had yet to happen. They were all dangling from the precipice by a fingernail.

About to fall to their dooms.

She found herself moving, the woman that she had saved in the tunnel watching her with an expression of shock. Snowy was there too—beautiful, lovely, loyal Snowy—she was barking at her, trying to get her attention, but she couldn't spare the moment. Not yet.

Sidney wanted to cry at the sight of her friends, covered with blood and gore, fighting for their lives.

Her friends. Her family. They had followed her. Come for her.

They did not see her there, too busy keeping themselves alive. Sidney planted her feet and reached out again to the newest muscle inside her brain, making it move and flex.

Taking control of the things that threatened her family.

The monsters stopped . . . the animals as well. It was as if time had frozen.

Wouldn't that have been a useful talent, especially right now, she thought, holding the minds of the multitude of creatures in place.

Especially now when . . .

Her friends saw her, calling out her name, but it was happening then . . . the thing that *they* were planning.

Sidney ignored their calls, turning and heading toward the shapeless organism nestled in the gravel. An organism that sensed her approach and, through an awful tickling sensation that she experienced at the base of her brain stem, informed her that there was nothing that she could do.

That her efforts were for naught.

That she was too late.

The alien creature's body had grown to twice its size, the quills upon it radiating some foul energy, some foul message from the tunnel out into the world.

She had a flash . . . a terrible bit of precognition where she saw other organisms, similar to this one, but hidden all over the planet, and each and every one of them was doing what it was supposed to do.

Performing the purpose that it was created for . . . that they were created for.

She felt it at once and knew that the organism was right: She was too late.

A terrible silence fell over the tunnel. It was as if the others could sense it as well . . . something awful had occurred.

And as if to mark the nightmarish occasion, music—multiple sing-song tunes and tones—echoed in the twilight of the subway tunnel.

Sidney turned her back to the sounds, at first not recognizing what they were, but then it dawned on her as she watched the actions of her friends.

The moment moved in some strange form of slow motion, the songs enticing them to reach into pockets to remove the devices that called for their attention.

Devices that had been silent since the beginning of the attacks.

Since the beginning of the invaders' plans.

But this was the next phase, Sidney knew, screaming as she ran toward them, as she watched those who had still managed to hang on to their cellular devices bring their precious phones up toward their faces.

"Don't answer that!" she screamed.

She had an idea what the screen of the device was telling them, who the call was from, and from the expressions on her friends' faces, she imagined that it was a loved one or a caller of some importance.

Langridge was who she reached first, swatting the illuminated smartphone from her hand, watching as it clattered to the ground, its face shattering with the impact.

She saw the fury in the woman's face—the fear, the gun in her hand slowly on the rise.

"It's part of their plan!" Sidney screamed, and saw that they were listening. Thank God, those who had phones were stopping before . . .

Rich stood perfectly rigid as he answered the call. Sidney actually saw a brief glimmer of joy on her best friend's face.

"Mom?" he said softly.

Before his mind was taken.

And his eyes clouded over and went to silver.

Sidney didn't even know she was screaming.

She found herself running to him, stumbling and nearly falling on her face to reach her friend whom she loved so much, even before what they'd experienced together over these last two days.

"Rich, no!" she was screaming—pleading with him as the tunnel area gradually returned to chaos.

The bugs and the rats and monsters were returning to the control of the organism, her hold upon them loosening in her turmoil.

Sidney fell against him, grabbing him by the front of his shirt as she looked into his eyes.

Those horrible silver eyes.

"Please, no," she said, and started to cry, everything starting to crumble. "This can't have happened . . . please."

And he looked at her then, those shiny orbs that once held the most mischievous of twinkles now showing something far more sinister.

Rich smiled at her, but there wasn't any Rich there anymore.

The blow came fast, a vicious slap that sent her flying to the ground . . . a ground covered with crawling life eager to steal hers away.

Sidney felt their teeth and their pincers as they threatened to tear away her flesh—to burrow deep inside her body and consume her precious organs. And there was a very sad part of her that almost wanted this to happen, to finally give up, to stop fighting, and to accept the weariness of it all.

She was so very tired, and so very sad.

It was Snowy's frantic barking that pulled her back.

Her dog was there, running toward the voracious swarm of life that threatened to take her, Snowy voicing her concern frantically as she ran around where Sidney lay, on the verge of giving up.

She could practically hear the message in Snowy's bark. *What the hell are you doing? Get up. You're not going to leave me. You're going to fight. Get up!*

And Snowy was right. That's exactly what she was going to do.

She was going to fight.

Sidney flexed the new muscle inside her brain, noticing that it was far less painful now to do so.

Instantly she was inside the minds of all the things that were trying to kill her—to kill her friends.

It was a struggle, but she moved them away.

Snowy came to her; even amid the insanity of the situation, the dog was there at her side showing her loyalty and love. Sidney took a moment to reach down to pet her girl, telling the dog with her eyes that she loved her with everything that she had, as she held the monsters at bay.

Which was why she was going to do what she was going to do.

———

Cody was terrified, not of the rats and bugs and monsters that threatened his life—he was terrified of losing her.

They had all been changed by this . . . experience, and Sidney Moore—the girl he had never stopped loving—had been changed most of all.

And as he watched her wade through the chaos, he wondered if she had changed so much, if there was a chance he could ever win her back.

Langridge knew that this was it, that this was their last stand. Something had happened, something involving some new sort of signal— something to do with their phones.

Deep in her gut she knew that things were now worse, that they were losing their struggle, losing the war.

And something drastic needed to be done.

Across the tunnel—across a sea of life determined to see them all dead—she watched the alien organism continue to move and writhe, and taunt her with its alien-ness.

You think that you've won, you ugly son of a bitch, she thought as she reached behind to her pocket. *You think you've beaten us.*

Removing the sticks of dynamite.

You haven't won shit.

The spike-tipped tentacle entered Dr. Sayid's shoulder, missing his heart by no more than six inches.

That's what you get, he thought in the throes of excruciating pain, *for shooting the alien organism.*

It was trying to pull him in, to draw him toward its soft, jellylike mass, to do with him God only knew what. Most likely consume him in some fashion, or maybe do something similar to what was being done to those still confined within the cocoons on the tunnel floor.

As the creature drew him in, his eyes fell upon the fleshy cocoons. He could see things moving around within, slowly coming awake—getting ready to be born.

More tentacles had emerged from beneath the fleshy skirt of the organism, slowly slithering across the ground toward his legs. Sayid tried to stop his progress, to plant his feet and fight against the pull, but the pain was too great, threatening to drag him down into unconsciousness. He wished that he hadn't fired all his bullets, disappointed that he hadn't saved one for himself, as the threat of being eaten became more of a reality with each passing second.

He'd just about given up all hope, praying that whatever he was about to go through would be quick, when she appeared.

Sayid had no idea who the woman was, grabbing hold of the tentacle just before his shoulder and using a jagged piece of rock to cut the fleshy appendage away as the alien organism screamed its fury.

"Help me," Delilah ordered the man she had just saved. His shoulder was bleeding, but it didn't look too bad.

He looked at her, sort of dazed, as she knelt down beside the cocoon that she'd seen Mason placed in. He eventually got the idea, bending down to help her peel away the fleshy covering.

"Thank you," the man said to her, pulling the flesh of the pod apart to reveal the sleeping form of her friend.

"Do you think he's dead?" Delilah asked the man.

He shoved his hands into the pod, near Mason's neck, searching for a pulse.

"He's alive," the man said. "Just unconscious."

And with those words, Mason's eye snapped open, and he gasped for air.

He looked at Delilah, his eyes wide in terror. She wished that she could tell him that it was all a dream, a terrible, terrible nightmare, but . . .

"It's all right," she told him, helping him to squirm free of the cocoon. "We're going to get you out of here . . . we're going to be safe."

And as she helped him to rise, her eyes locked with the stranger's—her gaze daring him to tell her otherwise.

One of her best friends was trying to kill her.

It made her want to cry to see Rich like this. He was completely engulfed in vermin, floating in a sea of rats, dogs, cats, and bugs of every conceivable variety.

It was like he was the pilot of some strange, living machine, his face sticking out from the center of a serpentine body composed entirely of living things.

A serpentine body that was trying to kill her.

It moved with incredible speed, diving down, attempting to engulf her in its amorphous mass, but she would not let it touch her.

Sidney flexed the muscle inside her skull, pushing the swarm away, attempting to disassemble the mass, to reduce it to its simplest parts. She knew that using the muscle was bad for her, even though it was getting easier with every use.

The blood from her nose was flowing again, warm and salty as it dribbled onto her lips and into her mouth. She was used to it by now, not even bothering to wipe the steady flow away.

There were more important things to concern herself with than her appearance.

The serpent with Rich's face towered above her, swaying menacingly as she again tried to take control. The alien organism within the tunnel was fighting back, blocking her attempts, making her strain in the use of her newfound abilities in an attempt to . . .

What?

She had no idea what the outcome might be. For all she knew her brain just might explode, and that would be that.

But it wasn't enough to stop her from trying to help her friend.

Rich fell upon her, arms flailing, fingers clawing as they searched for a way to hurt her. His hands closed around her throat, squeezing tighter by the second. Sidney flexed her mind, reaching inside Rich's head, searching for the alien presence controlling him.

It was there, like a spider in the center of some enormous web, and she tried everything that she could to stop it—to eject the presence and somehow shut down the growth of the organism inside her friend's head, but it would not leave.

The mass fought her with all it had, and her physical body began to die as she was strangled.

Sidney thought that she might be close, but it wasn't enough, and by the time she realized this . . .

Cody wanted to kill Rich for trying to hurt Sidney, but he knew the guy was no longer in his right mind. He didn't know what had actually happened but guessed that it had something to do with the signal from his phone.

He and Snowy had fought their way over, stomping, biting, punching, and smashing through wave after wave of creatures trying to stop them.

But they couldn't be stopped, not when Sidney was involved.

They loved her too much for that.

Cody had to stop himself from using the sledgehammer, instead grabbing Rich around the throat and pulling him off her. But Rich's hands remained tightly about her throat, and for a moment Cody feared that he might be too late, when . . .

Sidney realized that her physical body was dying. While she had been trying to destroy the alien presence in Rich's brain, the organism had been using Rich to kill her.

And it had almost succeeded.

Almost.

Sidney opened her bleary eyes, struggling for air. She saw that Cody and Snowy were there by her side, fighting to get Rich's hands from around her throat.

Rich bore down upon her, the shiny silver orbs inside his skull reminding her of two moons hanging in the night sky. As a last-ditch effort she pulled back her hand, made a fist, and drove it upward into her best friend's chin. She felt his jawbone slide, watched as his head snapped back, and felt his grip loosen ever so slightly upon her throat.

It was enough.

Enough for her to break free of his clutches, gasping for air as Cody dragged him backward to the bug-carpeted ground.

"Are you all right?" Cody asked, looking deeply into her eyes, the question encompassing far more than the present situation.

She never got the chance to answer him but was okay with that because she wasn't sure how she would have responded.

The tunnel became filled with the sound of thunder.

The awful sound was all encompassing, and all that she could think of was that it had happened—that she was too late, and this was the end of the world.

Sidney looked toward the source of the sound, seeing the alien organism in all its repulsive glory, and stared in awe at what was happening above it.

The air was moving, particles of dust and dirt floating there caught up in the cyclonic spin, moving faster and faster until the center of the vortex collapsed inward with a horrible sucking sound. It was getting larger.

A hole in the fabric of reality hanging in the air of the tunnel.

Sidney instantly knew what it was that she was looking at. A passage . . .

An opening to another world.

A passage from there . . . to here.

The bomb was almost done.

Langridge squatted down as the world seemed to explode around her, the opening in time and space growing in size.

Just another reason why it all had to be blown up.

She had all the ingredients she would need and a pretty good memory of stuff that she'd read on the Internet, as well as what she had seen over in Iraq with her troops. The improvised explosive was crude, but it should be more than enough to do some serious damage to the alien organism, as well as the opening in the air.

Langridge was just about done, wedging the two sticks of dynamite into the gas can, but not far enough in that they would become saturated, and attaching the detonation wires. She was going to have to move quick, carefully lifting the makeshift bomb from the ground and starting to carry it toward her target when . . .

Sidney was standing in front of her. The girl looked like hell, her face pale and filthy, her nose and chin crusted with blood.

"Is that a bomb?" Sidney asked her. "It looks like a bomb. Give it to me."

Langridge was taken aback by her demands. "I've got this," she said. "Help me get the others wrangled together and moving toward the exit before—"

"Give it to me," Sidney demanded, reaching down to take hold of the gas can's handle.

Langridge was about to argue when Sidney made her point.

"I'm dying," she said. "I can feel the thing inside my head

growing stronger and more powerful, but at the same time . . . it's killing me."

"You don't know that," Langridge said, attempting to pull the bomb away, but Sidney held fast.

"I do know that," she said. "Let me do this," she begged. "Get my friends out of here . . . get them to safety. The world is going to need to know everything that we've discovered if we're going to survive."

"Sidney, I . . ."

"The thing inside my head is angry . . . and it's trying to take control." She yanked hard then, and Langridge released the sloshing container to Sidney's control. "Let me do this . . . let me take it out before you have to put a bullet in my head."

Langridge was shocked by her words but also knew that there was truth in them.

"Save my friends, and save the world," Sidney said, turning abruptly away to walk toward the throbbing alien organism and the hole punched in the air. She stopped suddenly, turning back to her.

"How does this work?" Sidney asked, holding up the bomb for her to see.

"That button right there," Langridge said, making reference to the detonator taped to the side of the gas can. "Push it and . . ."

"Boom," Sidney said, a new trickle of blood running down her face from her nostril.

"Boom," Langridge agreed with a nod.

The organism knew she was coming, putting all its influence into driving her away. The animals came at her in a tidal wave of impending violence.

She faced it all, flexing the muscle in her head repeatedly, even though it hurt, even though the blood continued to pour from her nose.

The wave would pounce upon her but break apart, the animals and insects that comprised it no longer held together by one intelligence. The monsters came at her as well, those things twisted biologically by the alien organism.

They were stopped just as easily, turned against one another, allowing her to pass.

She was close to her destination and could feel a strange kind of pull from the swirling vortex in the air. She stopped and turned around to see if her friends were safe.

Langridge had indeed done what Sidney had asked, wrangling them all even though they protested. Snowy was the worst, her baby girl fighting Cody, even trying to bite him as she fought to get away and come to her side.

Sidney was turning away, her eyes filled with tears, when she was hit from the side. She had been distracted just enough not to have seen or heard them.

Rich had rejoined the serpent, bearing down on her as she struggled to regain control—to use her muscle to—

The serpent struck again, knocking her violently to the ground. The bomb dropped from her grip, clattering to the floor of the tunnel.

She was hurt, but still she continued to fight.

The serpent surged up into the air and directed its entire mass down upon her.

Sidney cried out, the intensity of her pain making it nearly impossible for her to concentrate, to use her ability. Lying on her back, and feeling something inside her grind, broken bones painfully rubbing together, she rolled onto her side, trying to crawl toward where the bomb had fallen.

The serpent drew near, its living mass swirling around her, lifting her up from the ground. Her body screamed as she was bitten and pinched and clawed in rapid succession.

Sidney looked into Rich's face, the eyes of something inhuman looking back at her. Although the pain was something unimaginable, she still tried to live—to fight—again reaching into Rich's skull to disrupt the alien's influence.

Rich cried out as she wrapped her mind around his, squeezing with all her might before—

The serpent went wild, lashing out and flinging her body away from its mass. Sidney flew through the air, landing in a broken heap before the organism.

The thing from another world throbbed and shook, knowing that this was the little thing that had caused it and its species so many problems.

This tired and broken little thing.

From the swirling vortex in the air she saw movement, something coming through from the other side, and she felt the horrible sensation of failure take hold of her.

Sidney knew she was broken, she could feel the pain both

physically and psychically, and she knew that there was nothing more that she could do—the enemy had won.

Or had it?

Footsteps close by caused her to look up just as the red gas canister and all its explosive trappings clattered to the ground in front of her.

Sidney saw Rich standing there, blood streaming from his nose as he swayed in the grip of what looked to be some great internal battle.

He looked down at her, one of his eyes still shrouded in a covering of silver, the other bloody yet clear of the alien influence.

"Sid," he said, his voice so weak from struggle. "Sorry," he managed to croak. "So, so sorry."

And she watched as he tumbled backward, his body convulsing upon the ground.

Without another thought, Sidney grabbed the canister and charged at the organism, her eyes on the sucking black hole swirling in the air, catching a glimpse of the alien world beyond before . . .

"Boom," Sidney said as she pushed the detonator, throwing herself at her enemies as the electrical charge detonated the dynamite.

And everything was lost to the sound of thunder.

CHAPTER **SIXTY-NINE**

The explosion drove them back, fiery and loud, bringing down large portions of the ceiling and tunnel walls with its fury.

Cody recovered quickly, a painful ringing inside his skull, all sounds muffled as if underwater.

Snowy had managed to break away from him, and she ran down the tunnel but could only get so far. A wall of rubble had come down to block her way.

Sadly he watched the dog pace in front of the barrier, barking pathetically as she stopped and attempted to dig her way through the rock and dirt.

Muffled voices could be heard somewhere behind him, and he turned to see both Langridge and Sayid, covered in blood and dust, the looks upon their faces showing complete and utter shock.

Surprised that they had managed to survive, he guessed.

He wished that they all had been as lucky, going to squat down before the fallen ceiling, comforting the anxious dog, lying to her that everything was going to be all right.

Delilah and Mason had gone in the opposite direction, heading down an alternate tunnel, which would bring them back toward a station closer to downtown Boston, she hoped.

The explosion had been loud, a shock wave rolling down the tunnel so powerfully, even where they were, that the force flung them both to the ground.

Mason was still in a state of shock, and Delilah helped him to stand, hurrying him along as the tunnel filled with black smoke and billowing dust. She turned a few times as they walked away, wondering about the others and doubting very much that they had made it.

She hoped that they had and said a little prayer for them, the first prayer that she had said in a very long time. She didn't think that it could hurt any, and who knew—if somebody was actually listening up there, perhaps it would even help.

Perhaps.

By the time they'd made it to the next station, they found it completely void of life. The corpses of hundreds of rats, insects, dogs, cats, and squirrels lay scattered about. It was as if they had just stopped where they had been standing, their power source cut off—whatever had been controlling them destroyed.

Mason was better now, at least able to walk on his own.

The power was still out as they climbed the steep escalator steps up to the surface and confronted an eerie calm. The storm had stopped as well.

"Is it over?" Mason asked almost dreamily, looking around the quiet Boston streets.

She did not answer his question, catching glimpses of movement from pockets of shadow, hoping that it was, but not really knowing.

They found a car with the keys in the ignition in the middle of Tremont Street and decided that they would borrow it.

They drove in silence up Tremont, navigating around the Common and then Park Square to Columbus Avenue, avoiding cars, trucks, and the bodies of people and animals that littered the already narrow streets.

The closer Delilah got to home the more nervous she became.

Maybe whatever happened at Elysium hadn't happened here, she thought, then said aloud.

"Maybe," Mason said.

They began to see people, alive, and for a moment Delilah felt like cheering. Others *had* survived. Suddenly she didn't feel quite so afraid or alone.

But then she realized that something was wrong with them, the way they seemed to be wandering, not seeming to be going anywhere, unaware of their surroundings.

"Must be shock," Mason suggested as they slowly passed a young woman in running clothes just standing at the corner, cell phone clutched in her hand.

Is there something wrong with her eyes? Delilah wondered fearfully, turning to look back, but they were already too far beyond her.

"Yeah, must be," Delilah agreed absently.

"Which number?" Mason asked, slowing the car down.

"Right there," she told him, pointing through the window. "Four twenty-five."

He brought the car to a stop and looked at her, fear in his eyes. "Are you going to be all right?"

She nodded quickly, opening the door. "You go home to your wife and baby," she said, climbing from the car onto the street. "Don't you worry about me—go."

She slammed the car door, shattering the eerie calm on the street.

Mason didn't even wave as he drove off, tires squealing as he took the corner way too fast.

Dead birds were strewn across the front steps of her building—crows. She felt as though someone was watching her and looked quickly around. She couldn't see anyone, but that didn't mean there was no one there.

She reached into her pocket for her keys, and her heart stopped. They were gone. She could have dropped them in hundreds of places.

She muttered about the basement as she turned and headed back down the stairs, careful not to step on the crows. She walked quickly around the building, down a side alley to a recessed stairway leading to an old wooden door that she knew wasn't the most secure, having used it to sneak in and out of the apartment in her wilder, earlier days.

Before she'd had her son, before she'd wisened up.

She remembered the trick with the door, pulling the knob toward her with all her might and slipping one of her fingers into the space near the lock to move the latch aside. The door opened toward her with a snap, and she ducked inside, being sure to close it behind her.

The cellar smelled of dampness and cat pee, and she moved between the crowded rows of odds and ends left behind by previous tenants.

Even in the darkness she found her way to the stairs and climbed them eagerly up to the first floor. She saw that some of the apartment doors were ajar and was almost tempted to check on those inside, but she pushed those thoughts aside, focusing instead on getting to her own apartment, to her mother and her son.

She didn't have a key, but that didn't matter; her mother had hidden a spare one at the top of the door jamb for an emergency, especially since her mom had locked herself out of the apartment one day while doing laundry.

Standing on tiptoes, she found the plastic case and slid it open to reveal the key. She plucked the key out, dropping the case into the pocket of her scrub pants as she slipped the key into the lock and opened the door.

Delilah rushed inside calling for her mother and son.

It took her a moment to realize that the power had returned, that the lights were on, but flickering, making the blood staining the walls and the front of the refrigerator shine wetly in the wavering light. She felt her heart seize as she looked at the dark stains, and then the signs of struggle in the kitchen.

"Mom!" Delilah called out. "Mom, where are you?"

She left the kitchen, moving into the small living room. That was where she found Tom and Jerry, both dead, their blood staining the beige carpet. On the floor nearby she found the bloody base of a table lamp and knew how the cats had died.

Her mother loved those cats, and she was gripped by a momentary sadness as to what it must have been like for her to have to kill them.

Her eyes then went to the door of her mother's bedroom, and she noticed that it was closed. She also noticed the deep claw marks that had been gouged in the flimsy wood of the door as the cats must have at some point tried to get in.

Cautiously she approached the door, leaning in close and listening. There was hissing on the other side, a sound like static from the television.

"Mom, it's okay," she said, gripping the knob and pushing the door, only to find it blocked. "Mom?" she called out, putting her shoulder to the door and sliding the dresser that had been moved behind it out of the way. "It's me. . . . Is Isaiah okay?"

She came around the dresser to find her mother and son standing with their backs to her, in front of the flat-screen TV showing only static.

"Mom?" she said, feeling something terrible begin to squirm inside her stomach. "Izzy, it's Mommy, why are you . . ."

And slowly they turned toward her.

And as she looked upon their faces, she saw it—her mother's and son's eyes covered in a wetly glistening shroud of silver.

And Delilah began to scream.

EPILOGUE

The pain was brief, followed by—nothing.

It was over. She was dead. Her story ended. There was nothing more to tell.

Or was there?

From nothing it came, the darkness all around her. It was like being in the deepest part of the ocean where the rays of the sun were unable to reach.

Something told her that she needed the light—those very rays— and she began her ascent. Climbing toward the surface.

Ascending toward the light.

Sidney Moore opened her eyes, gazing up at an unfamiliar ceiling. Eyes darting about, she saw the needle in her arm leading to the IV of clear fluid and realized she must be in a hospital.

Memories flooded her mind, painful flashes of where she had

been: the tunnels beneath the city and what had occurred there. She saw her final assault against the organism, remembering the swirling vortex hanging in the air and the bomb that she'd detonated.

Her heart beat crazily as she recalled the searing blast of heat . . .

And then nothing.

She pushed herself up in the bed, making sure that all her extremities were intact.

How is this possible? she wondered, seeing some cuts and bruises, but otherwise appearing to be fine.

There was a window across the room, and she threw her bare legs over the side of the bed and cautiously stood. There were some aches and pains, but she managed to stay on her feet as she grasped the IV pole and pushed it toward the window.

Her view was of a concrete courtyard, and beyond that a high stone-and-metal wall wrapped in barbwire.

A prison, she thought, beginning to panic.

There was movement beyond the wall, masses of people moving from side to side, looking as though they were waiting for something.

Waiting to come in?

The door swung open behind her, and Sidney turned as a man and a woman dressed in military fatigues entered the room. They smiled pleasantly at her.

"Are you feeling well, Ms. Moore?" the man asked.

"Where am I?" Sidney asked. "Why are there so many people outside that wall?"

The woman guided her back to bed and checked Sidney's vital signs.

"Something bad has happened to this country," the man continued as he strolled to the window and gazed outside. "To the world actually," he said, before turning his gaze to her. She noticed that his eyes were the nicest shade of blue. Funny the things one noticed when afraid.

"But we think you can help us, Ms. Moore," the military man said hopefully. "We think you can help us stop it."

The muscle twitched and then started to move inside her skull, reminding her of its presence.

Reminding her that it was still there.

"Tell me," she said. "Tell me what you need me to do."

THE END

ACKNOWLEDGMENTS

As always, love to my wife, LeeAnne, for all the help she provides. Love also to Kirby for his constant inspiration. With him in my life, I know the true face of evil.

Special thanks also to Michael Strother for getting the ball rolling, to Howard Morhaim for dotting all the i's and crossing all the t's, to Liesa Abrams for just being amazing, and thanks to Thomas Fitzgerald and Seamus, Dale Queenan and Allie, Barbara Simpson and Mugsy, Larry Johnson and Mel, Harrison (and Stephanie) Raciot and Chewy, Nicole Scopa, Frank Cho, Tom McWeeney, Mom Sniegoski, Pam Daley, Dave Kraus (You would have loved this one!), Kathy Kraus, and the beasts that walk like men down at Cole's Comics in Lynn, Massachusetts.

"Oh no, it wasn't the airplanes. It was Beauty killed the Beast."

ABOUT THE AUTHOR

Thomas E. Sniegoski is the author of more than two dozen novels for adults, teens, and children. His books for teens include *Legacy*, *Sleeper Code*, *Sleeper Agenda*, *Force Majeure*, and *Savage* as well as the series The Brimstone Network.

As a comic book writer, Sniegoski's work includes *Stupid, Stupid Rat-Tails*, a prequel miniseries to the international hit *Bone*. Sniegoski collaborated with *Bone* creator Jeff Smith on the project, making him the only writer Smith has ever asked to work on those characters.

Sniegoski was born and raised in Massachusetts, where he still lives with his wife, LeeAnne, and their French bulldog, Kirby. Visit him online at sniegoski.com.